Dangerous Ground

Forge Books by Larry Bond

• • •

Dangerous Ground

Larry Bond's First Team

Dangerous Ground

Larry Bond

A Tom Doherty Associates Book

New York

Bon

DANGEROUS GROUND

Copyright © 2005 by Larry Bond

This book is printed on acid-free paper.

Design by Jane Adele Regina

A Forge Book
Published by Tom Doherty Associates, LLC
175 Fifth Avenue
New York, NY 10010

www.tor.com

Forge® is a registered trademark of Tom Doherty Associates, LLC.

Library of Congress Cataloging-in-Publication Data

Bond, Larry.
    Dangerous ground / Larry Bond.—1st ed.
        p. cm.
    "A Tom Doherty Associates Book."
    ISBN 0-765-30788-X
    EAN 978-0765-30788-0
    1. Submarines (Ships)—Fiction. 2. Submarine captains—Fiction. 3. Americans—Russia—Fiction. 4. Nuclear fuels—Storage—Fiction. 5. Arctic regions—Fiction. I. Title.

PS3552.O59725D36 2005
813'.54—dc22

                                                                            2004062879

First Edition: May 2005

Printed in the United States of America

0 9 8 7 6 5 4 3 2 1

This book is dedicated to our executive officers: Lieutenant Commander Bob Bair, USN, Lieutenant Commander P. D. Quentin, USN, and Commander Michael J. Seiwald, USN (Ret.). Thank you for taking the time to teach us what it means to be a good naval officer. We learned a lot from your example.

In Memoriam

Captain Edward L. Beach, Jr., USN (Ret.)
submariner—writer—mentor

Acknowledgments

Special thanks to Lieutenant Commander Paul E. Ruud, USN (Ret.), for his insights on the layout, operations, and quirks of an early flight 688 class nuclear-powered attack submarine.

A heartfelt thanks also goes to our long-suffering wives, Jeanne and Katy, who put up with our constant discussions and late nights of typing. Without your love and support, we would have never been able to finish this book.

Author's Note

Chris Carlson and I have worked together on many different projects over the last twenty years. Chris is a former submariner, while I was surface navy. My naval experience was completely different from Chris's, and his submarining background was essential to the writing of this story. It wasn't the technical data. Anyone can find that. Submariners are a special breed of sailor, with their own attitudes, culture, and a really wicked sense of humor. Anyone who sails on a ship that deliberately sinks has to have a different outlook on life.

Chris's contribution was indispensable. He worked with me on every part of the book: characterization, technical details, plotting, and wrote many of the scenes. He vetted the text, edited, and kept me honest.

My name is on the cover, and I take responsibility for all errors and omissions, but this book wouldn't exist without Chris. Writing can be hard, and sharing the work with a friend improves the quality of the effort, as well as the final product. This book is as much Chris's as it is mine, and he deserves as much credit as I do for its success.

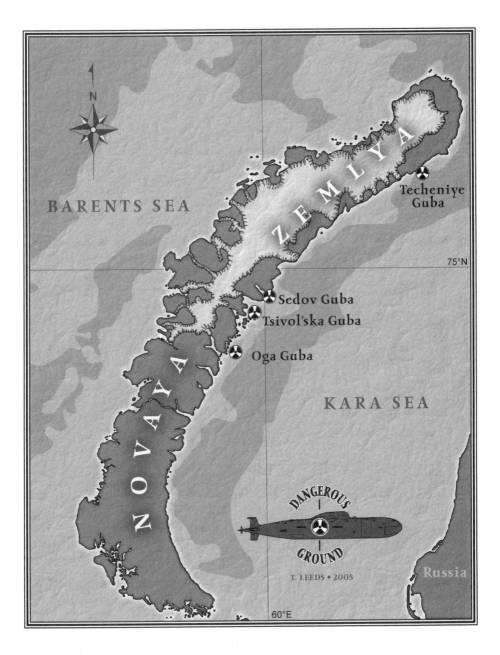

BARENTS SEA

ZEMLYA

NOVAYA

Techeniye
Guba

75°N

Sedov Guba

Tsivol'ska Guba

Oga Guba

KARA SEA

DANGEROUS

GROUND

T. LEEDS ✦ 2005

Russia

60°E

Prologue

January 1, 2003

●●●●●●●●●●●●●●●●●●●●●●●●●●●●●

Naval Air Station Lemoore
Near San Francisco, California

A Navy Hornet fighter sits at the end of Runway 32R, engines spooling up, pilot making final checks before takeoff. Receiving clearance from the tower, he releases the brakes and smoothly accelerates down the concrete surface.

Pressure on the seat behind him matches the HUD's numbers as his speed builds quickly. He approaches V_1, where he'll bring the nose up. Takeoff will be at V_2, just a few moments away.

The right main gear tire blows with a sound like a cannon shot. He feels the jar through his seat, then a slight tilt as the right wing drops a hair and the nose pulls to starboard. Already feeling time dilation, a corner of his mind sees the airspeed change on the HUD. It's dropping, and he realizes he'll never get it off the ground now.

He hesitates for half a beat. Can he somehow slow the plane safely? Yanking the throttle all the way back, he stomps on the left brake and pops the airbrakes, but it's a lost cause. The nose swings sharply to the right and with the engines off, he can now hear the screech of the right gear leg grinding against the concrete surface.

His training takes over and he slams his back hard against the seat and pulls the ejection handle. The canopy flies off and the seat follows, narrowly missed by the port wing, then the tail, as the plane cartwheels and explodes.

Crash crews reach the pilot moments after he's landed, his chute billowing out behind him. He's come down hard on one arm, and the sleeve of his flight suit is ripped, with white bone showing through the tear.

As they load the stretcher into the ambulance, he wakes up, calling over and over, "I'm sorry! I'm sorry!"

Navy Hospital Lemoore

Commander Albert Casey normally loved his job. He commanded squadron VFA-125, the "Roughriders," the best Hornet squadron on the West Coast, in his not-so-humble opinion.

Right now, though, he hated it. He'd been standing in front of the door to Jerry Mitchell's room for over five minutes, far exceeding the normal attention span of a fighter pilot. He'd come up with ten different ways to give Jerry the news, and they all sucked.

He didn't have to knock. The door was open, and he could hear two of Jerry's squadronmates inside visiting with him. As he turned the corner and stepped in, they saw him, and both immediately snapped to attention. They didn't have to do that in a hospital, but reflexes are hard to fight. The two pilots, clad in khakis and leather flight jackets, saw Casey's face and cleared out, with a few last encouragements to the patient.

Casey compared Jerry's appearance to the way he'd looked right after the accident. They'd cleaned him up and bandaged his injuries, including a nasty abrasion on one side of his face. Somewhere in there was a young man in his mid-twenties, with buzz-cut black hair and 20/10 blue eyes.

Mitchell's right arm was enveloped in a fat white cast, and the fingers protruding from one end were fire-engine red and swollen like sausages.

Casey wasn't sure that Jerry didn't try to come to attention lying in the bed, but obviously thought better of it as his body complained.

"Hello, Menace." Casey used Jerry's radio call sign. All pilots had them, and used them as casually as civilians used their first names. Every pilot had a different call sign, of course, picked for them or assigned when they arrived at the squadron. For a new pilot like Mitchell, the joke was whether he was more of a menace to the enemy or his own squadron, but everyone got ribbed, and he took it well.

"Good morning, sir." Commander Casey's call sign was "FEDEX," but lieutenants junior grade didn't use the CO's call sign unless they were in the air and actually talking to him on the radio.

Casey didn't bother asking if Jerry was in pain. "Have they still got you doped up?"

"Yes, sir," Mitchell replied. He held up a push button on the end of a cable. "Any time I get a twinge, I push this. Problem is, I start seeing strange things, then fall asleep."

"Sleep is what you need, kid. You've got some healing to do."

"I'd heal better outside, away from this hospital."

"You'd have to take the bed with you," Casey joked, then continued, screwing up his courage, "I just came from the flight surgeon. You seem to have taken ones from columns A, B, C, and D. Between the back, the arm, and other miscellaneous injuries, you're going to be here for another two weeks, at least, and then you can expect a few months of physical therapy."

Mitchell sighed. "I'd heard as much from the doctors."

"You've got to have at least one more operation on the arm, as well."

"I hadn't heard that," Mitchell's face was grim, but his tone matter-of-fact. "Whatever I have to do. So it's going to be a few months before I'm back on flight status? How much of the training cycle will I have to repeat? I was so close to finishing."

"The thing is, Jerry, like I said, I just talked to the flight surgeon. And the flight surgeon's boss, and a couple of orthopedic specialists. I can't read X-rays, but they all agreed that you can't come back to flight status."

"What?" Jerry's unbelieving question mixed pain and surprise.

"The break in your arm was close to the wrist, Jerry. And it was real messy. They won't be able to give you a full range of motion in your right wrist, and that means you won't be able to control the throttle properly."

"How can they tell that?" Mitchell demanded. "I haven't been in this bed for a week and now they're telling me I can't fly? Let's wait and get the cast off. Let me do some exercises." His tone was fierce, and he half-rose out of bed, which must have been agony with a sprained back.

"They've seen this before, Jerry, and if there was any hope, I'd keep you on the squadron rolls until you were old and gray. But there's no chance. None at all."

Casey leaded forward, his voice earnest. "This is worse than a raw deal, Jerry. You are a good pilot, and you might have been a great pilot. The Navy loses you, and you lose your career. It's taken you years of hard work to get this far, and if there was anything that could be done to keep you as a pilot, I'd be doing it right now.

"The accident board's already writing up the report, and confirms it was a blown tire—pure bad luck. It's definitely not your fault, and under other circumstances, I'd chew you out for trying to save the airplane, but I am convinced that hesitation did not affect your ejection. I've reviewed the tape, and you got out clean. Your landing and the broken arm was just more bad luck."

Jerry's world was turning upside down. What could he do? Pilots tend to be control freaks, depending on knowledge and skill to master any situation, but nobody could control this. And then Jerry realized that he couldn't even think of himself as a pilot anymore.

1 May She Ever Go to Sea

The Naval Submarine Base New London is located on the eastern shore of the Thames River in Groton, Connecticut. It has been there since the 1860s, although Jerry couldn't remember the exact date. More important, it had been a sub base since World War I. Nearly two dozen nuclear subs were based there, all of them attack boats, SSNs, with the exception of the deep-diving research sub NR-1.

Having been stationed at New London for the past two months while attending submarine school, Jerry knew all about the "Upper Base." He wasn't as well-versed as to where things were on the "Lower Base," though, and so he studied the base map until he'd memorized the layout of the squadron's piers. His knowledge of the nautical route in and out of the SUB-ASE was even more limited, and he had gone to the trouble of ordering his own copy of the harbor chart.

It hadn't been a long trip from Newport, Rhode Island, but he'd been nervous enough about his arrival to program extra time into his trip. He'd arrived back in Groton a day early, leaving as soon as Manta school had been completed, and had spent last night and part of this morning prepping his uniform and memorizing (again) everything he'd been able to find out about the boat. Her CO was Commander Lowell Hardy, the XO LCDR Robert Bair. The boat was commissioned in 1977 and was redesignated as an experimental submarine to test advanced submarine systems and sensors in 1989. She was one of six SSNs that made up Submarine Development Squadron (SUBDEVRON) Twelve. There were many more facts, mechanical and meaningless right now, in isolation, but they would soon be the foundation of his new life.

In spite of all his study, and although he'd attended sub school here, the New London base felt different, strange. He was coming back as a sub-mariner now, reporting to his first ship: USS *Memphis*, SSN 691.

Jerry looked around his apartment's living room one last time, making sure he had everything, and then shut and locked the door. He quickly glanced at his watch, checking the time. He'd allowed twenty minutes for the drive to the base, figuring the best time to arrive was 0900 (9:00 A.M.) The crew would be done with the bustle of Quarters, but he didn't want to appear tardy in reporting.

He checked his uniform again. The skipper would only get one first impression, and Jerry wanted it to be a good one. He carefully checked the driving directions to Lower Base (yet again) on the front seat and drove off.

He made the SUBASE's main gate right on schedule and was allowed to pass, after a brief security check. He turned onto Shark Boulevard and proceeded toward the Lower Base entrances, being very careful to mind the speed limit. Jerry had found out—the hard way, of course—that the SUBASE police had a thing for red sports cars that violated the speed limit by even two or three mph. Once he reached Dorado Road, he turned left and was waved through the Lower Base gate, having gotten his parking decal the day before. He even found a parking spot. Leaving his gear in the Porsche, he straightened his uniform one last time, and even remembered his orders. It was a good start.

Pier 32 was two blocks and two corners away, and he breasted the bitterly cold March wind, glad for the bridge coat he'd bought. It was a dark midnight blue, made of heavy wool, and long, reaching down to cover his legs, but most officers bought it for looks as much as for warmth. A shorter peacoat would be much more practical on a sub, where space was at a premium.

Memphis lay berthed on the north side of the pier. Only her name on the brow revealed the boat's identity. A low, weathered black shape on the water, most of her hull rose just a few feet above the wavelets that slapped against her rounded sides. Only a large rectangular structure aft broke up her smooth lines. The brow lay aft of the sail, leading to an open hatch in the deck. There was a small, battered gray wooden shack perched on the pier next to the brow, and Jerry could see an enlisted man inside. The petty officer, a second class, was speaking on the telephone.

Compared with a jet fighter or even a surface ship, the sub looked harmless. No visible weapons, not even all that big above the waterline. Most of her bulk, and all of her abilities, were hidden below the surface.

THE PETTY OFFICER of the Watch was keeping an alert lookout, and spotted Jerry as he turned the corner. He saw a short black-haired lieutenant junior grade in his mid-twenties. He looked slim, even in his bridge coat, and carried a manila envelope tucked under one arm.

It was clear he was headed for *Memphis*, and the petty officer summoned the duty officer, then stepped out of the shack to meet him.

Jerry stopped at the shack and returned the petty officer's salute, and in keeping with long-standing naval tradition, said, "Request permission to come aboard."

Commander, U.S. Fleet Forces Command Compound
Norfolk, Virginia

Commander Lowell Hardy sat nervously, waiting. A summons to see the big boss was to be expected. The Manta trials were over, *Memphis* was old, and Hardy's tour was nearly over. Hopefully, he was about to be congratulated on a job well-done. Or maybe not.

Memphis had been his first command, and he'd done his best with the old girl, and he'd turned in a good record. But it hadn't been perfect.

They called a captain the master of his ship, the last absolute monarch. Hardy was the master of 6,100 tons of complex, and in the case of *Memphis*, cranky machinery. He was the monarch of 135 rugged individualists whose chance of doing the right thing went down as its importance went up. Only his constant supervision had prevented some hapless teenage sailor from sending his career straight into the toilet.

And now his fate was in another's hands again. He was waiting for Rear Admiral Tom Masters, Commander Submarines Atlantic, to tell him what came next.

Memphis was scheduled for decommissioning, and preparations for that would take several months. There'd be the last trip to Bremerton, Washington, where she would actually be decommissioned, and the crew would split up, each with new orders. What would his read? Another boat immediately? That was the best he could hope for in his heart of hearts, but unlikely. Purgatory in a shore command for a year or two with the promise of another boat afterward? More probable, and by then there'd be a slightly better chance of him getting a newer . . .

"Commander, the admiral will see you now." The receptionist's summons surprised him, because as far as Hardy knew, there was still a herd of people in there with SUBLANT. He'd shown up early for his appointment and he'd seen them go in, but they hadn't come out yet. Still, if he was supposed to go in, he'd go. Bracing himself, he rapped twice on the dark wood door and opened it.

Hardy had been in the admiral's office before. It was spacious, filled with the obligatory flags, ball caps, plaques and a four-foot model of the admiral's first boat.

And people, lots of them. Hardy immediately recognized Rear Admiral Masters behind the desk and Captain Young, Commander SUBDEVRON Twelve and his immediate boss, to Masters' right. What surprised Hardy was seeing Vice Admiral William G. Barber, Director, Submarine Warfare Division, on the CNO's staff standing behind Masters. "What have I walked into?" Hardy asked himself.

Sitting in the only available chair was a tall, handsome woman in her late thirties or early forties, stylishly if severely dressed. A younger woman stood near her, and a young man in a gray suit stood to the left of the admiral. They all looked at him expectantly, and Hardy smelled a setup. Whatever was coming, he saw his next command spiraling down the drain.

Reflex took over. He came to attention, hat tucked under his arm, and announced, "Commander Hardy reporting, sir." Unnecessary, of course, but it broke the silence.

Admiral Masters nodded, "Good to see you, Hardy. I know what you expected to hear from me, but there's been a change in plans. We're not going to decommission *Memphis* just yet." The admiral motioned to his gray-suited guest. "This is Mr. Weyer Prescott. He's from President Huber's office."

"Deputy to Science Advisor Schaeffer," Prescott elaborated, as if that explained everything. Hardy noted the gray power suit, the expensive tie, and immediately typed him. There is a natural antipathy in the military services for political animals like Prescott, and from his expression, Hardy guessed the feeling was mutual.

"President Huber needs the Navy to help him with a special problem." Prescott intoned Huber's name as if he was invoking a deity, and in effect, he was. Any orders that came from the Commander-in-Chief went straight to the top of the U.S. Navy's to-do list. From Prescott's expression, Hardy guessed he either didn't think the Navy was up to the task or that the Navy would screw it up.

"As you all know, President Huber's recent mandate was based in large part on his support of environmental causes, and his concern for the damage to the environment . . ."

Actually, Hardy hadn't known that, or didn't care to know it. He'd voted for Coleman, for all the good it had done. He personally regarded Huber as a nitwit, although as the Commander-in-Chief, he'd faithfully execute any lawful orders the freshly inaugurated nitwit issued.

Prescott's speech was carefully worded, rehearsed, and Hardy suspected he loved the sound of his own voice. ". . . wants to be seen as an environmental champion, not only here at home but abroad as well."

"At the upcoming World Environmental Congress in São Paulo, Brazil, the President has decided to bring the Russians to task for their many ecological abuses, especially relating to nuclear waste disposal."

Good for Huber, thought Hardy. Maybe he's not a nitwit. The Soviets had been legendary for their disregard of even common-sense management of nuclear materials. The Russians had been only slightly better and had done little in the past fifteen years to deal with the messes left by their predecessors.

"The Russian government has ignored repeated calls to deal with the crisis, in spite of evidence provided by international organizations." Get to the point, man, Hardy thought.

"The U.S. Navy has long operated subs near the Soviet and Russian coasts to gather intelligence on its potential enemy. Well, we now want the Navy to enter those same waters to collect *environmental* intelligence." Prescott smiled broadly, and Hardy knew just who had come up with that buzzword.

Prescott looked over at Vice Admiral Barber, who nodded to Rear Admiral Masters. "Captain Hardy, you will prepare *Memphis* for deployment, and as soon as you are ready for sea, proceed to the Russian coast off the eastern side of Novaya Zemlaya. Using the Manta and other special equipment that will be provided, make a detailed environmental survey of the seabed there." Masters sounded like he'd also rehearsed his speech, but it was couched in the language of the service and didn't grate as badly as the civilian's platitudes. Then Hardy realized what the orders meant.

Prescott smiled, an almost predatory expression. "The samples and photographs of what we expect you to obtain will give President Huber the ammunition he needs at the conference. He will be able to reveal the true extent of Russian environmental abuse and secure his position as the leader of the environmental cause worldwide."

Hardy didn't reply immediately. His first response, which he fought back, was to say that *Memphis* wasn't ready for a mission. They'd already started to defer maintenance in anticipation of the boat's decommissioning. Several rather important items of equipment needed either a thorough refit or outright replacement. As the testing platform for the Manta prototype, they'd been involved in a lot of short, intense cruises, with lots of inport time to keep the old girl running. But telling the admiral that *Memphis* wasn't ready would be professional suicide. Besides, Masters had to know the state of his boat. Hardy was required to send in regular reports on his material condition, and nobody could ever accuse him of gundecking a report.

Hardy searched for something intelligent to ask. "How specialized is this equipment, sir? How long will I have to train my crew in its use?" Months, he hoped.

"The equipment consists of two remotely-operated vehicles, their support equipment, and an environmental test lab." The seated woman stood as she addressed Hardy. Her tone and manner were coldly formal.

"This is Doctor Joanna Patterson, Captain." The admiral hurriedly introduced her. "She's from the President's Science Advisory Board and a specialist on nuclear waste disposal." Standing, Dr. Patterson was almost as tall as Hardy's six feet, with a pale complexion, ash-blonde hair, and blue eyes.

Hardy started to step forward and offer his hand, but she made no move to respond, and he quickly stopped himself. "You'll be the one training my crew?" he asked.

Masters explained, "Dr. Patterson will oversee the installation, yes.

She's also in overall charge of the mission." The admiral had an odd expression, and Hardy suddenly had a hollow feeling in his stomach.

"As in mission commander?" Hardy asked carefully.

"Both Dr. Patterson and Dr. Davis will accompany *Memphis* on this mission," Masters explained.

The other woman, who'd stood beside and behind Patterson's chair, stepped forward and offered her hand. "I'm Emily Davis, sir. I'm with Draper Labs." Davis was a shorter woman, especially standing next to Patterson, with straight black hair and round glasses. She was dressed practically, if not stylishly. She seemed uncomfortable and glanced at Patterson nervously, as if looking for permission to speak.

"Dr. Davis will operate the ROVs and Dr. Patterson will analyze the results." Masters explained. "There's no way to teach your crew what they need to know in the time available."

"In any amount of time," added Patterson caustically, and Hardy's feelings of unease sharpened into intense dislike. Professional suicide be damned.

"Sir, I'm sure you've recalled Navy policy regarding women and especially civilians . . ."

Prescott interrupted Hardy smoothly, his tone reassuring. "We've already discussed this matter with the Secretary of the Navy, the CNO, and the Joint Chiefs. Navy policy has been waived before when necessary, and in view of the special needs of this mission . . . Well, I'm sure arrangements can be made."

Waived, hell. Overridden is more like it, Hardy thought. And what arrangements? Where in hell am I going to put two females on my boat?

"And Dr. Patterson is more than just a mission specialist, Captain. She is the President's personal representative, and as you correctly recognized, mission commander." Prescott's tone was harder.

It started to sink in. A civilian woman with some sort of political scientific agenda would look over his shoulder while he took *Memphis*, due for decommissioning, into Russian waters so they could count barrels of nuclear waste. And she would decide what kind of a job he'd done. And she had the ear of the President. This was insane. There were things worse than purgatory.

"Sir, my only qualified Manta operator's already been detached, along with some of my crew. He's left the Navy." Hardy tried not to sound like a kid looking for an excuse to skip class, although that's what he felt like.

"That's already been taken care of, Captain. We checked into your personnel status several weeks ago when we started putting this mission together. You've got a new arrival who's just finished the Manta operator course at the Naval Underwater Warfare Center."

"New arrival?" asked Hardy, knowing he sounded dense. Since *Memphis* was slated for decommissioning, they weren't supposed to be getting any new personnel.

"A special case, Captain, but one that fits well with your needs," Masters answered. "According to our information, and your record, *Memphis* is more than capable of handling this assignment."

"Yes, sir, she is," answered Hardy, straightening. He knew when to shut up and salute. "When will the equipment arrive?"

"The two ladies will arrive in New London in a few days," replied Masters. "Captain Young will give your boat priority in any matter relating to this mission." He handed Hardy a thick manila envelope covered with classification markings. "This is for the trip back. It should tell you everything you need to know."

Hardy took a step back, came to attention, and said, "Thank you, sir." He turned to face Patterson and Davis. "I'll see you in a few days, then, ladies. By the way, you may want to pack your bathing suits. After all, this will be a Bluenose run."

The puzzled look on their faces gave him some pleasure, and taking that small victory, Hardy left.

USS *Memphis,* SSN 691
SUBASE, New London

The ship's duty officer emerged from the hatch as Jerry returned the watchstander's salute. He was an ensign and saluted as Jerry explained: "I'm Jerry Mitchell. I've been assigned to *Memphis*." The confused officer accepted the manila envelope from Jerry and examined the enclosed orders. As duty officer, he wouldn't allow anyone aboard who didn't have explicit business there.

The ensign's reply was friendly, if puzzled. "Are you part of the decomm crew, then?"

Jerry was now puzzled. "What decomm? All I know is, I'm supposed to report to *Memphis*. I just finished Manta school at NUWC."

"And we've got the Manta prototype. I'm Tom Holtzmann, by the way. Reactor Officer. XO's aboard, but the Captain's off the boat, due back tonight." Holtzmann had a square, friendly face, with dark hair and eyes. He was a little taller than Jerry, but Mitchell was used to that.

"Captain Hardy?" asked Jerry.

"You've heard of him, then?" asked Holtzmann. There was a dark edge to the question, but Jerry didn't want to follow that up right now.

"No, just checking to see if I'd gotten the right gouge," replied Jerry. "I've still got my gear in the car, but I'll go below and report in, if that's okay."

"Right. I'll have the petty officer take you forward. This is ET2 Anderson, by the way, one of my guys." He turned to the petty officer. "Please take Mr. Mitchell forward to the XO's stateroom."

"Aye, aye, sir." He turned briefly to Mitchell. "Follow me, please."

Anderson dropped smoothly through the hatch, and Jerry followed, slower and with much more care. Submarines were designed to have as few holes in their pressure hulls as possible, and this was one of the biggest, a twenty-five-inch circular opening that looked like the door to a bank vault, if banks put their vaults in the floor.

Technically, it was the Forward Escape Trunk. Everything that the sub needed, except for torpedoes, had to fit through that hatch. Food, repair parts, tools, and appliances all came through that two-foot hole or they didn't go in at all.

Two vertical ladders brought him down to the middle level of the forward compartment, one of the three decks in the sub. Although he'd been aboard other subs during his training, he still wasn't used to the jumble of green- and gray-painted metal shapes, which only grudgingly allowed humans to pass between them. Everywhere he looked, Jerry saw machinery, cables, and pipes, all systematically labeled. Part of his job would be to learn every inch of them.

He spotted Anderson's receding form, headed forward, and hurried to follow, removing his cap and bulky bridge coat. Instinctively, he pulled in his elbows and crouched slightly, in spite of his short stature. He passed the crew's mess, the galley, and sickbay. Climbing a short ladder, Jerry found himself in the control room. If the reactor was her heart, the control room was *Memphis'* brain.

Immediately forward of the control room, right in the bow, were the CO's and XO's staterooms, both on the port side of the passageway. The only thing forward of them was a room full of switchboards and beyond that the sub's massive bow sonar sphere, outside the pressure hull but inside a streamlined fairing. The sonar shack, both the eyes and ears of this underwater animal, was on the right side of the passageway.

The XO's stateroom had an honest-to-God door with a small sign that read "Executive Officer." The petty officer knocked twice, lightly, and waited for a muffled "Come" before turning the knob. Anderson then backed up, giving Jerry room in the narrow passageway to go through the door.

The Executive Officer was Lieutenant Commander Robert Bair, at least according to *Memphis'* web page. There was no photo, but Jerry saw a man in khakis with gold oak leaves on his shirt collar. He didn't look very old, but his hair was almost completely white, and the front of his uniform bulged just a little. He was seated at the fold-down desk in his stateroom, which was covered with neat bundles of folders and paperwork. Jerry noticed three baskets fastened to the right side of the desk, labeled LOAD, SHOOT, and CHECK FIRE.

Automatically, Jerry straightened to attention and offered the envelope he'd been carrying. "Lieutenant (j.g.) Jerry Mitchell, reporting, sir." He didn't salute, since naval officers don't salute uncovered.

Bair took the envelope without immediately responding and examined the address on the outside before reading the enclosed orders. He sighed tiredly, and gave Mitchell a small smile. "Well, mister, these orders are correct, and you're supposed to be here, but I can't imagine why. Our captain's in Norfolk getting orders to decommission this boat. Can you explain what you're supposed to be doing here?"

Then Bair's eyes spotted the golden wings on Jerry's uniform coat. "And why in hell did they send us an aviator?"

"Not an aviator anymore, sir. I medicaled out of the training program." Jerry held up his right hand. The sleeve slid back far enough to show a road map of scars over his wrist and lower arm.

"Well, those wings have no place on this boat. You can wear your diver's pin, but leave the wings off while you're here." The XO's preemptory order disappointed Jerry. He'd worked a long time to get those wings, and technically, they were part of his uniform. But the XO was right. They really didn't matter here.

"I see you've even been to Manta school," Bair remarked.

"Yes, sir. That's when they told me I was coming to *Memphis*, when I received orders to the school."

"Well, I wish they'd told us at the same time," muttered the XO sourly. "Look, Captain Hardy's due back later today. Just go ahead and get your paperwork started, and we'll sort out what to do with you later."

He handed the orders back to Jerry. "Take these down to the yeoman. He'll get you checked in." He pointed to a stairway just across from his stateroom, at the end of the passageway. "Just use that ladder."

"Aye, aye, sir." Jerry turned to leave, but the XO called after him.

"Lieutenant Mitchell, one more thing." He smiled again, the same tired smile he'd given Jerry earlier. "Welcome aboard."

YEOMAN FIRST CLASS Glover, a slim, dark-haired man with an incredibly neat office, seemed unsurprised by Mitchell's appearance. He greeted Jerry with a broad smile and handshake. "Welcome aboard, sir. I've started your checklist," he remarked, neatly taking the orders from Jerry's hand.

"I've also asked the messenger of the watch to meet you topside. He'll help you get your gear aboard. I've put you in Mr. Adelman's bunk. He was our Manta specialist, but he left last week."

A little nonplussed by Glover's brisk efficiency, Jerry retraced his steps to the forward escape hatch and met a young seaman, so young Jerry wasn't sure he was old enough to drive, much less enlist in the Navy. His sandy blond hair stuck out from under a "dixie cup" sailor's hat. He stiffened and saluted when he saw Jerry climb out of the hatch. "Seaman Gunther, sir." Jerry returned the salute, then offered his hand, which seemed to surprise the enlisted man.

"Glad to know you, Gunther." He motioned to the pier. "My car's in a lot a couple of blocks from here."

Gunther nodded and buttoned up his peacoat, following Jerry down the brow, saluting the flag and the duty officer as they stepped off onto the pier. They trudged in silence, the wind at their backs hurrying them along.

Gunther whistled at the red '02 Porsche when he first saw it, then whistled again when he realized that it was Jerry's car. "That's a sweet car, sir." Gunther remarked as Jerry opened the trunk.

"Thanks, Gunther, and before you ask, I bought it used," Mitchell answered. He handed the sailor a suitcase, then picked up his briefcase and garment bag.

Gunther noticed a set of golden wings on the briefcase and a FLY HIGH sticker on the Porsche's rear bumper. "Are you an aviator, sir?"

Jerry answered honestly, if incompletely. "I was, for a while, but I had some medical problems and they let me transfer to submarines."

During the mercifully short walk back, Gunther pelted Jerry with questions about the aircraft he'd flown, especially how fast they could fly. Jerry had occasionally flown past Mach 1, but disappointed the sailor when he insisted he'd never come close to Mach 2.

As they approached *Memphis* again, Gunther exclaimed, "I remember now! You were on the news a while back. They had a video of your crash and then they wanted to kick you out of the Navy. . . ."

Mitchell nodded. "That was me. I convinced them to let me stay."

"Cool. That was an amazing crash, sir." Gunther was even more animated now as he helped pass the bags through the hatch and manhandle them forward to the officers' berthing area. He was reluctant to leave Jerry, even as the officer started to unpack, but remembered he had other duties and left after one last question about the ejection seat.

The rest of the morning passed quickly as Jerry filled out forms, received his dosimeter or "TLD" (regulation on all nuclear subs) and tried to find his way around. He met or passed by most of the ship's 130-odd crew in the crowded passageways. He'd left his wings off when he'd changed into his khaki work uniform, which left his shirt uncomfortably bare. Eventually, he'd pin on his gold dolphins, a qualification process as difficult and as lengthy as getting his wings.

The wardroom was directly aft of the officers' berthing, starboard side, and already crowded with officers when he stepped in a few minutes after twelve. Some stood at places around the small table, but most were milling around. Jerry had hurriedly met most of the officers during the morning, but now he took the time for proper introductions. Two of the department heads, Lieutenant Commander Jeff Ho, the ship's Engineer, and Lieutenant Cal Richards, the Weapons Officer, were the senior officers present. Tom Holtz-mann, the Reactor Officer, and Ensign Jim Porter, the Electrical Officer, were both division officers under Ho, a big Hawaiian, certainly too big to be comfortable in a sub's confined environment. One other officer, Lenny Berg, in charge of the radiomen and a lieutenant (junior grade) like Jerry, was present for the first seating.

They were still finishing introductions when another officer entered. He introduced himself to Jerry as Bill Washburn, the Supply Officer, then turned to Ho, the senior officer in the room. "The XO says to save him a place, but start without him." He frowned a little. "He just got a call from the CO."

Ho nodded, then replied, "Good enough. Seats please, gentlemen."

Lunch was stuffed pork chops and a fresh salad. They hadn't been lying about the food aboard subs.

"How far along in your training were you when you had your accident?" Cal Richards came straight to the point. Jerry guessed Gunther's news had spread fast.

"I was in my final cycle," Jerry answered quietly. "I already had orders to a squadron at Oceana. A few more weeks."

"After how long? A year and a half of training? That's rough." Tom Holtzmann's comment was sympathetic, but reminded Jerry of all the time he'd lost. And he'd never fly again.

"What made you decide to transfer to submarines?" Washburn asked.

An honest question, but one that Jerry had answered a hundred times since the accident, and continued to ask himself. He gave the stock answer, practiced and repeated until it emerged almost automatically.

"They were going to medical me out of the service, but I liked the Navy and wanted to be a part of it. My hand didn't keep me from normal duties, so I signed up for subs."

"But it wasn't your first choice," prompted Richards.

"No sir. I'd picked aviation, and done well at it. I've always liked air-planes, really anything that goes fast, and being outside as well . . ."

That prompted a round of hearty laughter from every man in the ward-room. When it died down, Richards commented, still chuckling, "You may want to reexamine your career choice before it's too late."

Jerry had no reply, but Ho said. "I remember seeing that crash, and you ejecting, and I followed the story after you got out of the hospital. There was a senator, a relative, who helped you stay in."

"That's right. My mom's brother is Senator Thorvald, from Nebraska. Without him I'd be out on the street."

"Nice to have friends in high places," Richards commented. There was an undercurrent to the remark that worried Jerry. Richards wasn't smiling.

The XO came in and dropped into a seat at the head of the table. "Good afternoon, gentlemen." The other officers all greeted Bair quietly, who seemed tired, almost worn out. The mess attendant poured coffee and made sure the dishes were within his reach.

Bair started to fill his plate and announced, "I've just gotten the news from the Captain. There's been a slight change in plans." He paused to take a bite and chewed, enjoying everyone's anticipation. "The decomm's been delayed. We're going to make another run north, as far north as we've ever gone."

Bair stopped talking and took another bite, but the silence continued for a few more beats as the officers absorbed the news. Jerry felt some relief. At least his first cruise wouldn't be to a scrapyard.

Finally Washburn, the Supply Officer, asked, "How long have we got to get ready, sir?

The XO's answer was vague. "A few weeks, but I don't have the schedule yet. The Captain says this will be a 'special' run, and he'll brief the crew tomorrow morning, but until then we're to begin preparations for sea." Jerry watched their faces. Some of them hurried to finish their meals. "A few weeks" wasn't much time to turn around a sub and prepare it for a hazardous deployment.

He turned to face Jerry, "And it turns out Mr. Mitchell and the Manta will play a critical role. I'd like you to stay after lunch, Jerry. The rest of you pass the word. Start putting your lists together."

Several of the officers muttered, "Aye, aye, sir," and the wardroom quickly cleared, except for Bair, Jerry, and the mess steward, who started to clean up for the second sitting, then saw the XO's face and disappeared.

"Is there anything about this mission that you've forgotten to tell me?"

Jerry, surprised and confused, quickly answered, "No, sir!"

"Captain Hardy indicated you'd been hand-picked for this assignment."

"Nobody told me if they did."

Bair didn't look convinced. "Look, mister, your story is all over the ship. It's nice to see a man fighting to stay in the Navy, but people with pull aren't going to impress anyone on this boat." He leaned forward in his chair, spearing Mitchell with his eyes. "Did you use your pull to get aboard *Memphis*? Did this 'special mission' sound exciting?"

"No, sir, absolutely not! I was supposed to go to another boat, USS *Hartford*, until my orders were changed to add Manta school. That was just a few weeks ago, and I swear I don't have a clue about why I was assigned here."

The XO didn't look happy, but didn't press Jerry further. "All right, mister. Finish getting squared away. The Captain will be back aboard this evening, and he wants to talk to me about you," he said, pointing at Mitchell. "I suspect that he'll also want a word with you himself."

"Aye, aye, sir." Jerry got out and took the few steps forward to his stateroom. He shared the space with Lieutenant (j.g.) Berg, the Communications Officer, and Lieutenant Washburn, but right now he had the place to himself. He finished unpacking, organizing his clothes and books in a space that made a closet look roomy.

His right arm was sore, and he absentmindedly picked up a hand exerciser and began squeezing it. It still hurt, maybe a little more than usual, but the action gave him the illusion of doing something constructive.

The pain was okay, according to the docs, even a year and a half after the crash. He smiled. At least it didn't hurt as much as it did a year and a half ago.

"A COMPOUND FRACTURE of the radius and ulna." They didn't even need X-rays to diagnose it. And it wasn't a clean break, either. It had finally taken three operations and three months before they were done with him. And from now on, he'd always know when it was going to rain.

The Navy always taped air operations, in case of accidents, and they'd released the video of Jerry's crash. It showed his Hornet smoothly accelerating down the runway, jet exhausts filled with blue flame, then a small puff of white appeared by the right wheel. That was the only sign of trouble, but the jet suddenly veered off to the right. The canopy flew off a fraction of a second after the puff, followed by the pilot's seat (That's me, thought Jerry) on a pillar of flame and smoke. The chute popped, but didn't deploy fully before Jerry was slammed onto the concrete surface. It had even made the news.

He'd seen it a dozen times and could look at it now without feeling the pain of the landing—and of failure. Loss of an airplane, loss of a career. The Board had cleared him completely, and he almost believed them.

Between operations, he'd stayed at the squadron, his career on medical hold. He'd hated it, hanging around pilots and airplanes but unable to fly. Commander Casey had given him a boatload of collateral duties to keep him busy, but it hadn't taken Jerry's mind off the accident. And then the Navy had started.

It was a fair offer. It wasn't Jerry's fault he wasn't able to fly anymore, so they gave him a choice. He could transfer to the surface fleet or accept an honorable discharge.

Jerry couldn't abide the idea of a discharge. He'd joined the Navy because he liked what it stood for and what it did. He'd always liked speed, and a challenge, since he'd been old enough to walk. First stunts on skateboards, then motorbikes, and skydiving. His girlfriends had called him an "adrenaline junkie," usually right before they dumped him, but it wasn't the danger he loved so much as the rush from succeeding at some difficult task. He was an A student for the same reason.

Now the Navy wanted to take away his latest success, when it was in his hands. Except one of his hands didn't work so well anymore. But he was all right for surface ships, said the detailer. He could still have a naval career. The medical restriction only applied to aviation.

What about subs? Jerry had asked. The detailer had said that yes, he was certainly fit for duty on subs, but the submariners had their own training pipeline, and he was too far along in his training to start. . . .

But Jerry's mind had suddenly fixed on subs as his goal. If he couldn't fly, he'd serve in subs instead. He'd need a waiver, the detailer had said, as if that decided the issue.

A "waiver" was Navyspeak for permission to break a rule. The Navy would grant waivers to selected individuals on a case-by-case basis. He'd seen guys too old for flying get waivers because they'd had previous service experience. He'd seen guys with family problems get waivers allowing them to take extra time in the training program. The Navy wrote the rules, and the Navy could break them, too. When it wanted to. Usually, it didn't want to.

Commander Casey knew Jerry well enough to understand what drove him, and he believed that Jerry would be ". . . an asset to the service. But I'll have to tell you, kid, that the Navy spends just as much training a submariner as it does an aviator."

"Why does that matter?"

"They've spent as much time and money on you as they want to. It didn't play out, and that's nobody's fault, but now they want to get some work out of you in return for your paycheck. Or stop the paychecks and give you a discharge," he said sourly. Casey didn't think much of that idea, either.

"But I can make the grade," Jerry insisted. "Six months at Nuclear Power School, then six months at prototype. I can do it."

"Jerry, you could be a brain surgeon if you wanted to," replied Casey, but then he paused, glancing at his scars. "Well, maybe not that. But this isn't about whether you're capable." He sighed. "It's about 'the road not traveled.' You made your choice when you joined the Fleet. It's too late to go back and start over."

"I'm not too old," Jerry countered.

"Yes, you're within the age limit, but every time the Navy spends money training a new officer, it takes a risk. He can do well in training, but still make a poor officer. If he's no good, or even if he's good but decides he doesn't like the Navy, and leaves after his first term of service, the Navy loses its investment. If you trained to be a submariner, it would double their financial risk, as well as eating up another year and a half of your first four years. You'd barely have a year left before you could leave the service."

"But I don't want to leave! I'll extend. They can start my four years from when I begin sub school."

The commander had run out of arguments, but he couldn't just give Jerry an order. "Jerry, I've seen how you apply yourself to any task. This situation's no different. You have to choose a new path. Apply yourself to making that choice with the same effort you applied to flying an airplane."

It was good advice, but Jerry hadn't used it the way Casey had meant it. The next morning Jerry had laid a request for a waiver allowing him to transfer to submarines on the skipper's desk. Casey had shaken his head, but passed it up the chain. He'd even "strongly recommended" approval, knowing that it wouldn't make any difference. Jerry had to run with this. Once it had run its course, Jerry could get on with the rest of his life.

Jerry did run with it. He argued and wheedled his way up the chain of command. In between physical therapy sessions, he read every Navy personnel manual he could borrow. He hunted down anyone on the base who had been a submariner, or who had known a submariner, looking for information, angles to play, maybe even a new connection.

He'd also called Uncle Jim, or Senator James G. Thorvald, Republican senator from Nebraska. His mother's oldest brother, they still saw him at family gatherings. He'd been delighted to hear from Jerry. His mother had been keeping the senator informed after the accident, but it was still good to hear his voice. Jerry had felt strange asking his uncle for help, but he needed every friend he could get.

"I think it's great that you want to stay in the Navy, Jerry. It's foolish for the Navy to get rid of someone as capable as you, who wants to serve. Didn't this get some media play? Can you send me a copy of any news stories? That'll help a lot. Makes it personal."

Uncle Jim had called "a few friends on the Hill." His timing had been perfect, because Jerry's request had just reached the Chief of Naval Personnel. Jerry had been ordered out to Washington, D.C. to explain to the U.S. Navy exactly why Ensign Jeremy N. Mitchell should get a special break.

Casey had flown Jerry out personally in a two-seat Hornet. It was one last flight for Jerry, and the only support he could give his former pupil. He'd also accompanied Jerry to his 0900 appointment with the admiral.

They'd skipped the green tablecloth, but it still felt a lot like a court-martial. Three captains, two admirals, Jerry, and his skipper, all seated at a long table. The brass looked irritated, and impatient.

"Mr. Mitchell, you're asking a lot of the Navy."

"I understand that, sir, but I also want to give a lot to the Navy."

"You could do that by serving in surface ships, without the Navy losing anywhere near as much money."

"I'd do a better job serving in subs, and I'd be more likely to stay in beyond my obligated service." He knew there was a threat buried in that statement, but it was also the truth. If they sent him to the surface fleet, he'd be gone at the end of his required four years.

"Even if we agreed to extend your obligation, there would have to be other conditions." The admiral had a sour look, and it took a moment for Jerry to realize they'd already decided. Well, shoot, they could paint him red and use him for a harbor buoy it they wanted to.

"First, we are going to extend your obligated service. Second, we want to make sure that if you do enter the submarine program, you'll make a good officer. The normal requirement for passing any Navy school is a grade of two point five, the lower quarter of those that make it. In your case, you will have to be in the upper quarter of your nuke school, prototype, and sub school classes. If you fail to excel, you will be reassigned according to the needs of the Navy."

Jerry nodded. He could do it. He had to, or he'd be counting blankets in Adak for years.

"Finally, there's the issue of your seniority. You'll be promoted to lieutenant (j.g.) while you're in prototype, and you'll be halfway to lieutenant by the time you arrive at your first ship. That three-year delay has to be made up or it will plague you throughout the rest of your career."

The admiral continued, "We're going to shorten your first tour as a division officer so that you can get your career track back in line with your contemporaries. You'll have to qualify on submarines quickly, though—within a year."

Jerry bit back his immediate reply. He considered offering the harbor buoy option as an alternative. "Qualifying in submarines," earning the coveted gold dolphins of a nuclear submarine officer, was an important, maybe the most important part of being a division officer.

An officer reporting to a boat was required to learn its systems—not just in a general way, but every pipe and valve, what they did, and what to do if they didn't work. Reactors and propulsion, high-pressure air, low-pressure air, electrical, hydraulics—all had to be studied until you could march through the ship blindfolded, correctly naming any item you encountered. On an officer's first boat, working hard, it normally took over a year to qualify.

Failing to qualify in submarines was reason for separation from the submarine service. Jerry naturally rose to a challenge, but this would be rough.

"Of course, sir, I'll do my best."

"I'm sure you will do well," replied the admiral, and Jerry knew he was lying. The brass might have their arms twisted into giving him subs, but they'd be damned if they had to let him stay there.

And now Jerry was willing to bet that his assignment to *Memphis* was supposed to be the final nail in his coffin. An older boat, a hurried-up deployment, and he's the man with the critical skills?

First Impressions

March 15, 2005

●●●●●●●●●●●●●●●●●●●●●●●

USS *Memphis,* SSN 691
SUBASE, New London

Jerry met the rest of the wardroom at dinner that evening, essentially all twelve officers except for Hardy. Most had families in the area and would normally have gone home at the end of the working day, but Bair's announcement had changed everyone's plans. To a man, they were working late, furiously compiling their lists of things that had to be ordered or done to prepare the boat for one more patrol.

Their conversation centered on preparations for the as-yet-undefined mission. Even without the details, many of the routine items could be done, and Jerry was impressed with the energy behind their efforts. Washburn, the Supply Officer, was moving heaven and earth to get stores and parts delivered, and the engineers had already started tearing down some auxiliary pumps that needed repair. Lieutenant Commander Ho and Lieutenant Millunzi, the Main Propulsion Assistant, gave Bair an extremely detailed report on exactly why the pumps needed the work done, and what steps they'd taken to make sure it could be done without interfering with the rest of the ship's preparations.

Bair quizzed each officer in turn, and those who didn't have answers made careful notes. Jerry kept a low profile, wishing he could help, and knowing that sooner rather than later he would be helping—just not how. The XO's deadline for everyone's answers was Hardy's arrival back on board, a mere two or three hours away.

Only after all possible ship's business had been discussed was there any personal conversation. Jerry fielded a few more questions about his background, but that was old news. The new schedule, and its effect on the crew's lives, raised other issues. None of the officers had been able to tell their wives anything more than they were working late, but each of them had a life that had suddenly been put on cosmic hold. Not only would the patrol mean leaving their families again, it would delay the sub's decommissioning.

Decommissioning meant leaving *Memphis* for another duty station. It meant houses sold and bought, kids changing schools, and new jobs elsewhere in the Navy. Nobody had called their detailers yet, there hadn't been time, but all planned to do so as soon as they knew anything at all.

Each time a service member changes assignments, he works with a "detailer." This personnel officer balances the officer's or sailor's desires, for instance, assignment to Hawaii, with the Navy's needs, for instance, an open billet in Alaska. Since most tours of duty are of a fixed length, officers start working with their detailers as much as a year ahead of time, and the process can take months to resolve. It's not as complicated for enlisted personnel, but it still takes time.

Part clerk, part accountant, and part used-car salesman, the detailer searches for billets opening up at the appropriate time, matching them against an officer's skills and the Navy's requirements for "career growth." This means that if an officer is presently in an engineering post, he should go to an operations or weapons posting next, not another engineering slot. If he's at sea, he'll probably get a shore posting. Guys on shore duty try to go back to sea.

The Navy, in spite of its size, may have only three or two or possibly just one open billet that matches the officer's skills, career needs, and timing. Hopefully it's something the officer likes. Should an officer need training to help them with a new assignment, then that has to be arranged first. Of course, school schedules and class sizes may not match the rest of the schedule, and this requires even more finagling. And let's not talk about what failing a school would do to the detailer's plans or the person's career.

Finally, after all the pieces have been carefully fitted together, the service member will use the time remaining, hopefully a month or two, to househunt, probably in an unfamiliar location, find new schools for his kids and possibly even a new job for his spouse. It is not uncommon, however, for all these significant responsibilities to be unceremoniously dumped on the spouse while the Navy member immediately reports to his next assignment. The needs of the Navy, at times, can be hard on a Navy family.

And right now, 135 carefully prepared plans had just been thrown up into the air, and only the Almighty knew where they would land. The single officers and sailors had less to worry about—only where they'd be working for the next few years.

Again, Jerry just kept quiet and listened. Some were fatalistic, and some were bitter about this latest turn in their fortunes. Harry O'Connell, the Navigator, was scheduled for PXO school, "Prospective Executive Officer School." He had been promoted to Lieutenant Commander just two years earlier, and he was on the list to get an Executive Officer's billet on another attack boat. The problem was timing. If he didn't leave *Memphis* in time, he'd miss the start of the course. More important, it could get him bumped from his billet. "Hardy's worked my tail off here, and it's time for me to move on. It's going to be a major pain in the ass if I can't make the start of that course." He said the last part with a tone that implied that the problems he foresaw might not be exclusively his own.

After dinner, Jerry retreated to his three-man stateroom again, with Lenny Berg following him in. Jerry, with little to do, curled up on his bunk and pretended to read a paperback while Berg worked at the desk. There wasn't much space in their stateroom, even with just two bodies occupying it. Berg in the chair took up half the available floor space.

The room ("space" in Navy talk) was only slightly longer than the length of the cramped bunks and just a few feet wide. The bulkhead opposite the door held the three-man bunks, lockers occupied the left side of the room, and the right side was filled with two side-by-side desks, each with a fold-down work surface and a small closet. In the right corner was a small sink and mirror. A fluorescent fixture half-hid among a jumble of pipes and cables on the "overhead" (more Navy talk for ceiling). Most of the surfaces were painted a very distasteful pale green.

Berg had an angular face and an almost Roman nose under an untidy short mop of brown hair. He pushed the paperwork to one side, then turned his chair to face Jerry's bunk, the lowest of the three. "So, Jerry, what do you think?"

"I don't know what to think about first," evaded Jerry. Then, more honestly, he answered, "I think this boat's just been stood on one end and shaken."

Berg nodded. "Things are really confused. Even when we get more information, it still means a total turnaround in our schedule, both here on the boat and our next assignments. And nobody in the Navy likes uncertainty or confusion. When we decommission, I'm supposed to go to another boat, a boomer in Bremerton. I don't have a family to worry about, so if I end up going to a different boat, that's okay, I'm flexible." He sighed. "Just so long as it's off this one."

"You're not happy here?" Jerry asked.

"I've been here one year, seven months, and five days, and I'm definitely ready to move on."

"LCDR O'Connell said the same thing."

Berg replied, "We'd all say that, no matter how long we've been aboard." He seemed to hesitate, then continued, lowering his voice almost to a whisper. "Look, you'll form your own opinion of the Captain, but here are a few thoughts to stuff in your seabag." He started ticking off items on his fingers.

"One. This is a tight ship, and things run smoothly, because that's what the Captain likes. If it doesn't run smoothly, the Captain lets us know about it—big time.

"Two. The Captain knows his stuff. He's very good, but he's a detail freak and a micro-micro manager. Which means he also knows your stuff, and expects you to be a detail freak, too. If he asks you a question, you'd better damn well know the answer.

"Three. Every man on this boat has been looking forward to getting out from under him. This patrol, whatever it is, will delay that, as well as upsetting everyone's orders."

Jerry felt his future grow more uncertain with each passing moment. "So the Captain's a hard master."

"The hardest," Berg confirmed, still in a low voice. "We could shoot him, but they hang you for that." The pixie-like grin on Lenny's face made it clear that he was joking, of course. But it was forced humor, one born out of frustration and fatigue. "The only way to get away from him is to have orders off the boat."

Jerry lay in his bunk, pondering this new information, while Berg finished checking his clipboard and shook his head. "I'm definitely staying on board tonight," he announced. "I'll see you later, shipmate. Try and get a decent night's sleep. It may be the last time for quite a while." With that, Berg collected his paperwork and left.

Bair was hard at work in his stateroom when the topside watch buzzed him. "Mr. B, sir, the Captain's coming down the pier."

Grabbing his ball cap and clipboard, he headed for the forward escape hatch and managed to make it topside just as Commander Hardy stepped off the brow onto *Memphis*. Bair saluted. "Good evening, Captain."

Hardy returned the salute, but in reply, simply asked, "Where do we stand?"

Bair filled him in on the ship's preparations, following as Hardy proceeded briskly down the hatch, then forward to his stateroom. Crewmen stepped into doorways or flattened themselves against the bulkhead as the pair passed.

In a much-rehearsed brief, Bair filled in his captain on the status of each department. Supply department had already scheduled with Group Two for provisions and fuel oil. Spare part request chits were to be submitted by the other departments by the end of the week. Weapons department had requested SUBASE technical assistance to help them track down the problem they were having with the number four sonar command and display console, and surprisingly it had already been approved. Torpedoes still needed to be requested and a date set to load them. Navigation department was pretty much ready to go. All they needed to finish up were some calibrations to the ring-laser gyro and the mini-SINS. Engineering department had big problems with the number one lube oil pump and the number two auxiliary seawater pump. Both needed bearing replacements and had to be stripped down. There was more, a lot more, but Bair had hit all the high points. Hardy quizzed him heavily, especially about engineering. *Memphis* was old and needed an overhaul, but she was at the end of her service life and the Navy had decided it was cheaper to decommission her. Now they had to make her ready for one more cruise.

They reached Hardy's stateroom as the XO finished. As the final item of his brief, Bair offered the Captain Jerry Mitchell's personnel file. "He came aboard at oh nine hundred this morning."

"Yes, you told me all that this afternoon," Hardy answered impatiently. "The aviator with 'pull.' Where did you assign him?"

"Well, sir, I'd recommend Mr. Adelman's billet. We need a torpedo officer and . . ."

"But you haven't done it yet?" Hardy interrupted. His tone was more than critical.

"Not without your approval, sir." Bair carefully kept this tone neutral.

"All right, then. Do it," Hardy ordered. He sounded slightly mollified.

Careful to keep his tone neutral, the XO asked, "Sir, can you tell me anything more about the mission?"

Hardy's face darkened, and Bair thought he was about to lash out, but instead the Captain started unpacking his briefcase, almost attacking its contents. "Yes, there is. I can tell you that this mission is the misguided product of poor leadership and political expediency." He yanked a bundle of papers out and stuffed them in a drawer. "That it's a waste of our time and a risk to our careers." He slammed the case closed and shoved it into a corner.

"And I can tell you that if this mission succeeds, it will be a miracle," he declared, suddenly turning to face his XO, "but if it fails, it will not be our fault. Is that clear, Commander?"

"Absolutely, sir," replied Bair in his firmest, most positive voice.

Hardy handed Bair a thick folder. "Here's what they gave me in Norfolk. Read it, then report back to me with any problems you have right away."

"Aye, aye, sir." Bair looked at Jerry's personnel folder. "What about Mitchell?" he asked.

"Give me ten minutes, then send him up here."

"Aye, aye, sir."

JERRY HAD MANAGED to locate a ship's information book and was leafing though the pages when the phone rang.

"The Captain wants to see you," Bair's voice informed him, and Jerry jumped up, nervousness drenching him. He suddenly wished Lenny Berg hadn't given him a heads-up about the Captain, and also wished he'd thought ahead. The Captain's cabin was only a dozen steps away and one ladder up, so there was no time to delay. His first impression of Jerry would have to include a rumpled shirt and a five o'clock shadow.

Jerry hurried to the ladder, then climbed up and took the few steps forward to the Captain's cabin. He knocked and waited to hear "Come" before turning the knob and stepping in.

Captain Hardy sat at his desk, still in his blues but with his uniform jacket hung on a nearby hook. Feeling underdressed in his khakis, Mitchell announced, "Reporting as ordered, sir."

Hardy didn't reply immediately, but studied his newest junior officer carefully. All Jerry could do was meet his gaze without challenging him. Hardy was bigger than Mitchell, in his mid-forties, with salt-and-pepper black hair. His face was lined, and Mitchell saw them converge into a scowl.

"Mr. Mitchell, you're going to be my new Torpedo Officer." Hardy made the statement flatly, without any tone, but his expression said he wasn't happy with the situation.

"Aye, aye, sir. I'll do my best."

"I'll expect more than that, mister," the Captain told him. "You're a key man on this patrol, and your performance will have a direct effect on the success of the mission, the careers of the men aboard, and possibly on their survival."

"Yes, sir. May I ask what the mission is?"

"You may not," Hardy replied tersely. "It's not my job to explain things to division officers. The crew, of which you are now a member, will be briefed at Quarters tomorrow morning." He paused for a moment, as if finished, but then continued.

"I *will* explain this to you, Mr. Mitchell." The Captain leaned forward in his chair a little. "You've used political pull to jump from one set of rails to another and I don't like it. You couldn't make it here on your own or you wouldn't have needed pull to get here. You think you're a special case, and I don't like special cases."

He pointed at the personnel file. "And frankly, I don't care what kind of grades you got in the nuclear pipeline or sub school. I've seen plenty of theory men fall flat on their faces when they actually had to perform in the real world, so whatever you may think of your skills, at this point they count for zero."

Then Hardy corrected himself. "No, they don't count for zero. They're unknown, and I don't like unknowns, either."

Jerry had stood stock-still through Hardy's lecture, searching for a reply. He wanted to answer Hardy, to explain, but couldn't think of anything that didn't sound either silly or disrespectful.

Finally, after a few moments of silence, Hardy glanced at the folder again. "And this says you're supposed to qualify in subs in less than a year." He looked sharply at Mitchell. "Was this some sort of deal your patron got for you? Some sort of softball qualification process?"

"Sir, I didn't ask for anything special . . ." Jerry protested.

"But you got it, all the same," Hardy interrupted. "I happen to agree with this requirement. You need to pull your weight, and you can't do that unless you know this boat. But I won't give you a free ride. No shortcuts."

Jerry ventured a hopefully safe, "Yes, sir."

"You will spend every free moment learning this boat and filling in the signatures in your qualification book. If I see you reading anything on this boat, it damn well better have a piping diagram in it. . . . Clear?"

"Yes, sir."

"And this will in no way excuse you from your regular duties, which you will exercise perfectly. Any screw-ups by you will affect the success of this upcoming patrol. And if your error causes us to fail, I'll make sure the Navy knows exactly whose fault it was. Are we clear?"

"Yes, sir." Jerry, who'd been standing at attention the entire time, tried to straighten even further.

"Now get out."

Jerry quickly backed out of the CO's stateroom. He made his way back to his stateroom and leaned against the bunks. He was drained, emotionally and physically, but sleep seemed impossible. He shed his uniform, climbed into his coffin-sized bunk, and pulled the privacy curtain shut. As he worked to relax his body, his mind spun with fearful possibilities. Reason told him it couldn't be as bad as it seemed, but the day's events didn't give him much hope. He finally fell asleep arguing with himself.

 A New Day

"Reveille, reveille, up all bunks. All hands turn to and commence ship's work. Quarters to be held on the pier at oh eight hundred," squawked the ship's main announcing system, or 1MC. Jerry slowly, groggily, fumbled for his watch and checked the time: 0630. It was earlier than Jerry would have liked, particularly given the hard time he'd had in falling asleep, but he was awake now. Pulling the curtain on his bunk back, Jerry started crawling out on to the deck when the shadow of two feet magically appeared on the floor in front of him. Jerry recoiled back as Lenny Berg hit the deck with a dull *thump*. Berg straightened up from his landing, stretched, and turned on the lights. He looked down for his flip-flops and saw Jerry's face poking out of his bunk with a surprised expression on it. Berg quickly figured out what had almost happened and made room for Jerry to get out of his bunk.

"Good morning, Jerry. Sorry about just jumping out of my rack, I, ah, forgot you were down here," Berg said apologetically. "I trust I didn't startle you too much with my graceful rollout."

"That's okay, Lenny. I prefer a good dose of adrenaline to coffee in the morning. It gets the blood flowing so much more quickly," replied Jerry with as much humor as sarcasm.

"Even Navy coffee? I find that hard to believe."

Jerry could only grin at Berg's humor. As if on cue, Berg cleared his throat. "Ahem. So, how was your interview with the Captain?"

"I guess the best way to describe it would be as unexpected."

"Yeah, that sounds about right. He said I was useless ballast until I finished my quals. The Captain is not one to mince words, even unpleasant ones. But Jerry, the secret to surviving on *Memphis* is to not let it bother you." Berg then moved closer to Jerry and slapped him on the back. Lowering his voice a little, he advised, "I know that's easier said than done, but you won't make it if you take everything the Captain says personally."

Jerry nodded his understanding and gathered his shaving kit and towel. He was looking forward to a hot shower and a chance to collect his thoughts. As he was starting to leave the stateroom, Berg called to him.

"Oh, Jerry, remember to take a submarine shower. The XO likes to shut the hot water off on those who dare to take a Hollywood, even in port." The humor in his voice bespoke of personal experience and Jerry thanked him for his words of wisdom as he set off for the officer's head.

Like everything else in *Memphis*, the officer's head was small. There was a single shower off to the right with a sink next to it. The remaining space held one commode and a urinal. All this for a dozen guys. Things were going to get quite cozy indeed, Jerry thought.

He turned on the water and waited for it to warm up. Once the water had reached an acceptable temperature, he went in and quickly got thoroughly wet. He then closed a valve at the base of the showerhead, shutting off the flow of water, lathered up his washcloth, and scrubbed himself down. Jerry opened the valve after he was finished scrubbing and rinsed himself off. He then repeated the same procedure for washing his hair.

While Jerry basically understood the need to conserve water on a submarine, a long hot shower where the water poured on his body for fifteen minutes sounded really good right now, and in port, with the sub's water supply hooked up to the pier, *Memphis* had an unlimited supply. Jerry regarded the XO's prohibition against "Hollywood showers" as a minor injustice, but avoiding the XO's ire was much more important than comfort. Before Jerry left the shower stall, he grabbed the squeegee hanging on the soap dish and removed all the excess water from the shower's steel walls. This was done in order to prevent mildew from forming on the walls and making the head more unpleasant.

After shaving, Jerry headed back to his stateroom to get dressed. Ten minutes had gone by. Berg was already gone by the time Jerry got back; he was probably in the wardroom getting breakfast. Jerry's other roommate, Lieutenant Washburn, had gone home for the night and was likely already aboard. Jerry put his gear away in one of the wall lockers and made up his bunk before proceeding to the wardroom.

The cramped wardroom was filled. At most, it could seat ten, and all the chairs, save the Captain's, were occupied, so Jerry had to wait for someone to finish before he could sit down. The mess steward, bustling around with serving dishes and dirty plates, offered Jerry a cup of coffee. He gladly accepted the coffee and stood quietly, as out of the way as best he could and studied his new shipmates.

All were in khaki working uniforms, sitting silently, reading their morning message traffic as they hurriedly ate. Berg was demolishing a plate of scrambled eggs and hash browns, but most settled for cereal or a fresh sticky bun with their coffee.

It was quiet, too quiet. The only words spoken were the occasional comments or questions when someone discussed ship's business with another officer. It was completely unlike a squadron mess. This wardroom was tense, cold, and uncomfortable.

As he studied his fellow officers, he also studied the wardroom, which didn't take long, considering its size. It was about the size of a small bedroom, with most of the space taken up by the ten-foot by three-foot table, roughly in the middle. The décor was Navy standard, with fake wood paneling wallpaper on all the walls and drawers and blue vinyl covers on the chairs, table, and the couch at the forward end of the room. Except for a picture of *Memphis'* launching and some plaques from other U.S. Navy commands and various foreign navies, there were no decorations. The wardroom's spartan look only reinforced the isolation, the lack of camaraderie that Jerry felt.

Besides being the place where all officers on board had their meals, the wardroom table also functioned as a workspace for pre-deployment briefs, drill critiques, tactical reviews, and as a place to relax. Here the officers could watch a movie or play some games to help unwind a little. In an emergency, the wardroom could also be turned into an operating room. At that thought, Jerry's right arm started to ache and he decided that perhaps it wasn't such a good idea to think about the wardroom's auxiliary medical function.

He spotted a bulletin board on the forward bulkhead and edged over to it, dodging the mess steward on the way. Several sheets of paper had been tacked over a layer of older notices and newspaper clippings. The new sheets were printouts from an internet news service, and Jerry started to read the one closest to him. Under the brightly colored banner, the headline read NAVY JET CRASHES IN CALIFORNIA. He started to read the piece, assuming it was a report from this morning, and felt déjà vu when he saw that it was an F/A-18, then more so when he read it was at Naval Air Station Lemoore. When he saw that the cause was a flat tire, he felt positively creeped out, but the pilot, Lieutenant (j.g.) Jerry Mitchell, was recovering from his injuries. . . .

His eyes flashed back to the headline and then to the date: JANUARY 2, 2003. He looked at the second sheet. It was dated a few months later and was titled AVIATOR FIGHTS TO STAY. It described Jerry's aviation background, his political connections, and his attempts to transfer to the submarine service. In the section describing Jerry's aviation training, his call sign, "Menace," was mentioned, and someone had marked the word with a yellow highlighter.

The call sign, so appropriate for an aviator, sounded silly and trivial now. He fought the urge to rip the pages off the board, then another impulse to turn and scan the room, as if he could detect the individual who put them up just by looking. He finally turned around, reluctantly, feeling even more isolated, singled out. He knew someone, maybe all of them, was watching him, waiting for a reaction, but did his best to deny them the pleasure.

"Mr. Mitchell, sir? You can sit down now. What would you like for breakfast?"

JERRY SETTLED FOR some cereal and fruit, then tried to listen and learn. There was no message traffic for him, of course, but he kept an ear cocked to anything Cal Richards, his new boss, had to say. Richards didn't acknowledge his presence at breakfast, and spoke little, instead writing furiously on a clipboard. After a minute or two, Richards began to flip through the pages on his clipboard, and his face seemed to turn white before Jerry's eyes.

"Mr. Weyer, when did SUBASE say they were sending over the team to help you troubleshoot the sonar display console?"

"They said it would be sometime this afternoon, sir," responded Lieutenant (j.g.) Tim Weyer, *Memphis'* Sonar Officer. "They have to completely redo their schedule to fit us in and the Repair Officer said he wouldn't know the time until this morning."

"Well, if you haven't noticed, Mr. Weyer, *it is morning* and I need that time so I can finish my morning report for the Captain. So why don't you get your butt in gear and find out!" snapped Richards.

"Yes, sir," replied Weyer tersely as he quickly rose from his chair, threw his napkin on the table, and left the wardroom.

Surprised by the sudden exchange between his department head and a fellow division officer, Jerry hunkered down and concentrated on finishing his breakfast, desperately trying not to meet Richards' cold stare.

"As for you, Mr. Mitchell," said Richards sternly. "You have five minutes to finish, and then you are to meet me in the torpedo room. I assume you can find your way there?"

"Yes, sir, of course, sir," Jerry answered.

Without responding, Cal Richards collected the small pile of paperwork he was working on and walked out of the wardroom. After Richards had gone, Jerry let out a deep sigh and pushed the bowl with some fruit left in it away from him. Putting the napkin on the table, he stood up and started making his way to the door.

"Excuse me sir. Are you finished?" asked the mess steward.

"Yes, yes, I am. Thank you." And with that, Jerry returned to his stateroom to get his cover, jacket, and notebook. Checking his watch, he had three minutes to get to the torpedo room, Jerry walked quickly back toward the main passageway. As he walked, Jerry couldn't help but be reminded just how much space was at a premium on a submarine. The passageway couldn't be more than two feet wide and two people going opposite directions would have to turn sideways just to get past each other. On a submarine, outside of your rack, there was no such thing as "personal space." After reaching the wardroom, Jerry turned the corner and exited the opening in the bulkhead that separated officers' country from the rest of the boat and walked across to the ladder that went down to the torpedo room in the forward compartment lower level.

Jerry had only been to this part of *Memphis* once before, so it took him a few seconds to orient himself. The heavy traffic was also momentarily confusing, as sailors were going back and forth between a berthing area on the starboard side and a head by the base of the ladder on the port side. One of the sailors shook his head, smiling, and pointed to a door at the forward end of the passageway. Jerry nodded and headed into the torpedo room, carefully closing the door behind him. Entering "his spaces," Jerry saw Lieutenant Richards talking to a chief petty officer and two first class petty officers. As he approached the foursome, he only heard the last part of Richards' instructions. ". . . and I want a list of all the necessary repair parts on my desk by 1700. If there is nothing else, I suggest you get started and remember we'll be forming up for Quarters in about twenty minutes."

As the two petty officers left, Lieutenant Richards brought over the chief. Correction, Jerry thought as they got closer, a senior chief. Jerry was immediately encouraged, having a man with such a wealth of experience as the leading chief would be very beneficial to Jerry to help run the division and for his own education. Jerry paused to think that this might be one of the first rays of hope since he had come to *Memphis*. He was immediately snapped out of his musings when Richards addressed him.

"Well, I see you made it," Jerry couldn't help but notice the biting sarcasm in Richards' voice. "Mr. Mitchell, this is Senior Chief Torpedoman's Mate Foster. Senior Chief Foster, this is Lieutenant (j.g.) Mitchell. He is Mr. Adelman's relief."

"Pleased to meet you, Senior Chief," said Jerry as he extended his hand. Foster looked confused by what Richards had just said, and it took him a moment to recover and to shake Jerry's hand. "Sir," was all Foster said. Jerry sensed that something wasn't quite right, but he didn't have time to think it about as Richards kept on going.

"There will be time for you two to begin turnover later today, Senior Chief, but right now I need to talk to Mr. Mitchell before Quarters. Make sure that everyone in the division is topside and on time."

"Aye, aye sir," replied Foster, who now was staring intently at Jerry. "I'll have the men up promptly at 0745." Foster then left the torpedo room through the same door that Jerry had used, only the senior chief slammed the door shut on his way out. Jerry didn't understand why the senior chief would do such a thing, but before he could ask Richards what was wrong, his department head lashed into him.

"All right, let me make myself perfectly clear, Mr. Mitchell. You will become intimately familiar with every piece of equipment in this room. You'll ensure that all maintenance is done properly and on time and that your maintenance records will be flawlessly maintained. Don't bring me any problem that you haven't already thought of a solution. And don't bring me sloppy or incorrect paperwork. I expect you to perform all of your duties impeccably and that includes your qualifications. Any questions?"

Jerry was stunned by the way Richards dressed him down. He hadn't done anything yet, but apparently that was the problem. The duties that Richards described were the norm for a new officer on board his first ship, but the venom with which Richards had delivered them was totally inappropriate. Jerry felt angry for the first time since his arrival. The fighter pilot aggression that had served him so well during his flight training bubbled to the surface, and he straightened himself and looked Richards straight in the eye.

"No, sir. I clearly understand *exactly* what you expect from me."

Cal Richards noticeably balked when Jerry stood his ground. And with a far more civil tone he said, "Very well, then, Mr. Mitchell. Carry on." Richards then turned around and left the torpedo room.

Leaning up against the centerline torpedo stowage rack, Jerry tried to make sense out of the last ten minutes. What was it about him that Richards viewed as threatening? Surely it wasn't him personally, Richards had only met him yesterday. But something was obviously bugging his department head, the look on Richards' face, his treatment of Tim Weyer in the wardroom, his boisterousness. It was as if Richards had to intimidate or frighten others to have them do what he wanted done. Then it clicked; Richards was faking it, trying to act as if he had everything under control when in fact he was barely hanging on; it was all a façade.

Jerry had seen this before down at the training squadron. It was the sign of a man running scared. Cal Richards was afraid, but afraid of what or whom? Immediately after he had asked himself that question, Jerry intuitively knew the answer: Lieutenant Richards lived in dreadful fear of Captain Hardy.

Just as Jerry was making some progress in understanding his situation, the 1MC announced "All hands not on watch lay topside for Quarters." Jerry quickly made his way up to forward compartment middle level and then waited for his turn to climb up the forward escape trunk. Emerging from *Memphis*, Jerry found the weather to be sunny and milder than yesterday. In fact, it was quite pleasant by comparison. Still a bit nippy, but nothing a Midwestern boy couldn't handle. Jerry then made his way to the gangplank, saluted the colors, and walked down on to the pier in search of his division. He soon found Senior Chief Foster with a group of ten sailors forming up in the second row of three. Jerry walked over and stood next to Foster, but the senior chief did not acknowledge his presence. The wind seemed colder than Jerry had first thought.

The XO was carefully watching the forward escape trunk, and as soon as Hardy emerged from the hatch, Bair shouted, "Attention on deck!" The crew, standing at ease, instantly became three neat, motionless lines, drawn up on the pier. The only sounds left were the cold breeze and the waves as they slapped against the pier and the submarine's hull. Every man's attention was on Hardy. Now they would get some answers.

"All right, listen up." Hardy's tone matched his expression—both were stern, almost angry. "The CNO has given us one more patrol to do, one that will be more difficult than the last few we've done. We'll be getting underway on May 13th, about sixty days from now. I can't tell you our destination or what our mission is until we're underway, but I can tell you that we will have guests aboard." That started a chorus of whispers in the ranks, but that stopped as the Captain continued.

"This boat not only has to be made ready for patrol, but all the preparations made for the decommissioning have to be turned around. And there are a lot of deficiencies that have to be corrected." This earned the crew a hard glare from Hardy.

"Anyone who was scheduled to transfer off *Memphis* will have their orders deferred until we finish this patrol. All leaves are canceled, and until this boat is completely ready for sea, the crew will go to port and starboard duty sections."

That raised a real murmur, almost a groan. "Port and starboard" meant that half the crew would stay aboard after the working day was finished. On Navy subs in port, part of the crew always stayed aboard each night to deal with emergencies and monitor the reactor, which was never left unattended, but those tasks didn't take half the crew.

"Understand, this patrol is not my idea, but come mid-May, we will get underway and this boat will be ready in all respects for its mission. Executive Officer, take charge and carry out the plan of the day."

The XO called out as Hardy quickly walked up the gangplank and disappeared below. "All right, people, we have a lot of work to do and not much time to do it in, so let's get moving. There will be a department head meeting immediately after lunch. Dismissed!"

JERRY LOOKED OVER at Foster, who seemed preoccupied with the news. Several of the torpedo gang approached the senior chief, ready to protest or ask him questions, but Jerry spoke up. "Senior Chief Foster, I'd like to meet the division."

Foster's reaction was surprising. In a hurried voice, he replied, "Of course, sir. Torpedo gang and FTs, this is Lieutenant (j.g)"—he paused, glancing at Jerry's nametag—"Mitchell. He's the new Torpedo and FT Division Officer."

Some of the men near Jerry offered him a quick greeting, while the others moved in closer, surrounding Jerry and Senior Chief Foster. Jerry started to speak. "I've got a few things I want to say. . . ."

Foster interrupted. "Sir, I don't think we've got time for that right now. I've got to get these men to work."

Nonplussed, Jerry nodded. "All right, Senior Chief." Disappointed, he tried to look at each of the men now under his command, to memorize their names and faces. "I'll talk to you all at another time." He added, "Carry on," unnecessarily, as Foster had already started leading the division back aboard.

Jerry hung back as the crew slowly filed on to *Memphis*. He'd been all primed for "the talk," his first speech to the men under his command. They'd drummed it into him at the Academy that this was his best, maybe his only chance to make a good first impression, to tell the men what he expected of them, and to start building his own personal command style. All junior officers entertained grandiose hopes of inspiring their men, but would usually settle for not looking like an idiot.

And Foster had taken that opportunity away by interrupting him, and in general, treating him as irrelevant. Jerry had backed down, automatically avoiding a confrontation with his leading chief in front of the division, but on reflection, he realized that might not have been the best choice.

As Jerry walked back on to the sub, he tried to put himself in Foster's place. The senior chief had been the acting division officer and had expected to fulfill that role until *Memphis* was decommissioned. Now he'd have to step down. It was part of the service's tradition, but still, it had to grate, at least a little.

And what kind of a man was Foster? Jerry hadn't had time to study any of the men's service records, but he resolved to do it as soon as he could.

Back aboard, Jerry headed for the torpedo room. It was time to get started in his new job. He found Senior Chief Foster already at work, filling out what appeared to be a new duty schedule. One of the torpedoman's mates, a second class named Greer, was leaving and nodded politely to his new division officer.

Foster looked up wordlessly as Jerry maneuvered into the cramped corner in the forward and starboard side of the torpedo room that functioned as the division's administrative office.

"Well, Senior Chief, let's get started on the turnover. What do you recommend we should do first?" Normally, when a new officer arrived, his predecessor would "turn over" materials like paperwork and keys that the new officer would need to do his job. There were classified pubs to inventory, maintenance records to review, and a host of other administrative issues.

"I don't think I can do anything with you right now, sir." Foster's tone was hurried again, almost dismissive. "The Weapons Officer wants the new duty section done in half an hour, and then I've got to supervise a test of the fire-control circuit." He paused, and looked almost kindly at Jerry. "I'd ask you to do the duty section, but you don't know any of the men yet."

Jerry tried to be positive. "You sound overloaded, Senior. You're wearing too many hats, and I'm supposed to be wearing one of them. The quicker you turn over the division officer responsibilities to me, the sooner you'll be able to slow down."

"Nobody slows down on *Memphis*, sir," Foster responded coldly. "This job has to be done properly, and I can't take the time to teach you how right now." He paused, as if thinking, and said, "Perhaps you should get the service records for the TMs and FTs and review them, sir. I'll try and make some time this afternoon to start the turnover." Foster said it the way a grown-up might promise to play ball with a small child.

Reluctantly, Jerry agreed and headed for the ship's office. Yeoman Glover quickly retrieved an armful of dark brown folders from the filing cabinets, and after signing a form, Jerry took them back to his stateroom. Berg and Washburn were elsewhere, so he had what little space there was to himself, but he felt useless. Studying records wasn't going to help get *Memphis* ready.

An hour and a half later, his head full of names and facts, Jerry threw the pile of folders down in frustration on his bunk. This wasn't the way it was supposed to work. There'd be time to look over this stuff later. He'd learn more about his division by working with the men, not by hiding in his stateroom.

Senior Chief Foster was doing his level best to keep Jerry from taking over as division officer. Jerry could see that now, although he wasn't quite sure what to do about it. It wasn't logical. This certainly wasn't the way it was supposed to work.

It was universally acknowledged that chief petty officers actually ran the Navy. The chiefs largely tolerated officers because they were willing to do paperwork. Like a shop foreman and a factory manager, each had important tasks.

Junior officers, fresh out of school and new to everything, needed a lot of guidance. It was no accident that the Navy teamed up a green division officer with a much more experienced chief. On the books, the officer had the authority, but only a fool would act without listening to what his chief had to say.

The division officer had to interpret the orders that came down from his department head and to get his division what it needed, whether it was repair parts, nominations for a school, or annual personnel ratings. If the division officer was good, he could resolve the inevitable conflicts between orders from above and reality impinging from below. Even the mediocre ones did their best to screen their men from the bovine byproducts that often accompanied guidance from above.

The chief was usually the best technical man in the division. He knew his equipment, his troops, and what they were able to do. That knowledge took at least ten years to acquire, and many chief petty officers served more than twenty.

So why was Foster refusing to even deal with Jerry? Confused and in need of some guidance, Mitchell left his stateroom and took a few steps forward to Lieutenant Richards' stateroom. The Weapons Officer was inside, searching through a stack of papers. He looked up when Jerry knocked on the doorjamb. "Yes?"

"Sir, I'd like to talk to you about Senior Chief Foster."

"What about him?"

Jerry wished he'd thought this though a little bit more, but plunged ahead anyway. "He seems reluctant to turn over his division officer duties to me, and I was wondering if you . . ."

"What?" Richards' tone was unbelieving, as if he couldn't understand what Mitchell had told him.

"I went to see Foster about turning over the division as you instructed, and he said he was too busy, that we'd have to do it later. Sir, he's deliberately stalling."

Richards absorbed Jerry's statement and sat motionless for a few moments.

"And why do you need me?" Richards asked curtly. Jerry started to reply, but as he opened his mouth to speak, the lieutenant cut him off.

"No, wait, I don't want to know," the weapons boss told him. "Mister, I've got twenty urgent things to do right now. And one of them is not holding your hand while you deal with your senior chief!"

"Yessir," Jerry replied quickly.

"If you've got a problem with your leading chief, work it out. I suspect the problem may not be with the Senior Chief, either. I've known Foster a lot longer than I've known you, and he's good. In fact, he's very good at his job. We still don't know about you."

Richards dismissed him. "Now, go make yourself useful. I'm still waiting for that new duty schedule from the Senior Chief, and I want a list of all repair parts the Torpedo and FT division needs on my desk by 1700."

"Aye, aye, sir."

JERRY HALF-FLED RICHARDS' stateroom, thinking, Stupid, Jerry, just plain stupid! Originally, he intended to go back to his cabin and think, but decided instead to go looking for Foster. He ran into the senior chief by the galley, heading forward with some papers in his hand.

"Senior Chief, is that the new duty schedule for the division?"

"Yes, sir." Foster moved as if to pass him and head forward, but Jerry held out his hand. "I'd like to see it, please."

Foster seemed reluctant to hand it over, almost as if it held secret information. "The WEPS wanted to see it right away, sir."

"Don't you think the division officer should see it first?"

Sensing defeat, Foster wordlessly handed it over. Jerry studied the unfamiliar form for a minute. To his credit, Jerry recognized most of the names from his recent study of the personnel records. It wasn't terribly complex. Half the division would remain on board each night. Jerry noted that the senior man after Foster, TM1 Moran, also had the two most inexperienced men: TM3 Lee and TMSN Jobin.

Jerry handed the paper back to Foster. "Thanks, Senior Chief." He kept his tone casual and stepped out of the way so that Foster could head forward.

After Foster disappeared, Jerry headed for the torpedo room, to familiarize himself with the spaces if he couldn't do anything else. As its name implies, the room was designed to store and fire torpedoes and cruise missiles. There was little space for humans to walk around and work in, but to Foster's credit everything was well organized and properly stowed. The only things out of place were a coffee cup and a beat-up paperback book on the starboard torpedo storage rack.

Jerry was opening cabinets when Senior Chief Foster returned. The look on his face made Jerry start to feel like a burglar, but then he remembered that this space was his responsibility.

"Is the WEPS happy with the duty roster?" Again, Jerry kept his tone casual, matter-of-fact.

"Yes, sir." Foster replied.

"You said you were going to test the fire-control circuits next."

"Yes, sir, I have to supervise a test of the fire-control circuit interface with the port tube nest." Foster sounded like he was in a hurry, but Jerry refused to be rushed.

"Do you have the PMS card for the check, Senior Chief?"

Foster went over to a card index and removed a stiff 8 x 10 card. Filled

with text and symbols, it was titled FIRE CONTROL CIRCUIT CHECK OF THE
MK67 TORPEDO TUBE SYSTEM.

Jerry had studied the Planned Maintenance System (PMS) at the Academy and at submarine school. It was the Navy's way of standardizing the routine maintenance work on all the equipment aboard a ship. Before it was installed on any ship, a team of engineers studied each new piece of equipment. How often did a component need to be cleaned or lubricated? When did it need to be checked or replaced? Once the bright boys had listed what checks needed to be done and when, they'd figure out what skills were needed, what tools and materials should be used, and even how long it should take.

All that information, in excruciating detail, was printed on the card Jerry held in his hand. It was a weekly check that required the following tools, and the following personnel. . . .

"Senior Chief, you said you were going to supervise the test. According to this card, a first class should be able to perform the check."

Foster replied, "Well, yes, but I want to make sure . . ."

"Is there a problem with Moran? Does he have the skills?" Jerry wasn't demanding, but he was insistent.

"Yes, sir. Absolutely," the senior chief answered firmly.

"Then you don't need to be there. We have to start the turnover. You know it, and I know it, so let's begin. I want to see the division's spaces."

Foster glared at Jerry, "Certainly, Mr. Mitchell, as you wish. Let's start over here with the starboard tube nest."

It was hardly the best tour Jerry had ever had, but he had to concede one thing: Foster knew his stuff and he knew it cold. As they walked around the room, Foster kept pointing to pipes, valves, and other mechanical components, spitting out facts and specifications at a rapid rate. So rapid, in fact, that Jerry couldn't keep up. He had had some basic instruction on the Mk67 torpedo tubes in submarine school, but everything there had been on paper. Now Jerry was trying to merge some of his basic knowledge with chunks of metal that were all clustered on top of each other and interwoven with piping and electrical cables.

The four torpedo tubes were nearly identical. Broken out into two nests or groups, tubes one and three were on the starboard side and had been modified for ROV testing back in the late-1990s. Tubes two and four were on the port side and were standard 688-class torpedo tubes. As with every U.S. Navy attack submarine built since the early 1960s, the torpedo tubes were moved aft from their traditional position in the bow, and on 688-class submarines, angled out at seven degrees. This arrangement was necessary because the fifteen-foot bow sonar sphere prevented bow-mounted tubes. Each tube nest had its own ram ejection pump located beneath the torpedo tubes. These pumps used high-pressure air to drive a slug of water into a tube, which would forcefully eject a 3,700-pound Mk48 ADCAP torpedo from the sub.

In the middle of the torpedo room, directly between the two tube nests, was the Mk19 weapons launching console. From this position, a torpedo-man's mate could operate all of the four tubes' various functions. Everything from opening the breech door, flooding a tube, even firing one could be done from this console. Foster pointed out, of course, that all the automatic functions on the console had a manual backup and his torpedomen could work these in their sleep.

Behind the torpedo tubes, in the middle of the room, were the three two-leveled torpedo stowage racks where up to twenty-two weapons could be stored. Normally, a 688-class boat would leave two slots, or "stows" vacant, so that torpedoes could be removed from the tubes for maintenance. With four weapons in the tubes, a 688 would usually go to sea with a mix of twenty-four torpedoes and Tomahawk cruise missiles. *Memphis*, however, was not a normal 688. The Manta control station, located at the port, aft end of the centerline stowage rack, reduced the number of weapons that could be stored by four.

Integral to the outboard torpedo stowage racks was the reloading equipment. Loading trays on the inboard side of the two racks were designed to pivot, so that they could align themselves with the canted tubes. Hydraulic rams would then push the weapons into the tubes. Moving weapons on the racks, or indexing weapons, was also done with a complex system of hydraulically driven gears and linkages. Again, if necessary, loading could be done manually with a block and tackle and lots of manpower.

Jerry knew Foster was intentionally moving at warp speed, either to show how much he knew about *Memphis'* main armament and how little Jerry knew, or to get the tour of the spaces over and done with as soon as possible. Probably both, Jerry thought. Still, he asked his senior chief numerous questions that required Foster to slow down to answer. Most of the questions Jerry asked were honest inquiries for clarification of something that Foster had said or for additional explanation of a system's function. For some of his questions, however, Jerry already knew the answer and he wanted to compare it to what Foster would tell him.

After a couple of hours, Jerry allowed his first tour of the torpedo room to come to an end. TM1 Moran and two of the more junior torpedomen were well into their PMS check on tubes two and four. Undoubtedly, Foster would want to look in on them; something Jerry wholeheartedly approved of. Impressed by Foster's knowledge, Jerry was sincerely appreciative for the tour, even if it was given begrudgingly.

"Thank you for the tour, Senior Chief. It would seem that I have an awful lot to learn about the systems that are in this room. I trust you won't mind if I ask you some more questions from time to time."

"You're most welcome, sir," responded Foster with some sarcasm. "Sir, I would like to go and look in on the maintenance check. Petty Officer Moran has the two most junior torpedomen working with him and I'd like to see how *they* are doing." The emphasis on the junior TMs hopefully would free him from this overly inquisitive officer.

"Certainly, Senior, carry on." Jerry made sure his voice was neutral and polite. Despite Foster's less than friendly behavior over the last few hours, Jerry knew that he had to work with this man if he was to have a smooth-running division. And he needed that if he was to obtain his ultimate goal: his gold dolphins and a career in submarines.

Just as Senior Chief Foster was preparing to leave, Lieutenant Richards popped out from behind the starboard tube nest and made his way down to Jerry and Foster.

"There you are, Mr. Mitchell. I see you and the Senior Chief have begun your turnover."

"Yes, sir," replied Jerry. "Senior Chief Foster has just finished giving me a tour of the torpedo room and it is clear that I have much to learn."

"Well, that's a start, at least," said Richards as he tossed some folded papers into Jerry's hands. "I need a new watch schedule for your division ASAP, the other one is now OBE."

"Sir, I don't understand. I'm sure Senior Chief Foster's watch schedule was correct for a port and starboard duty section." Jerry wasn't entirely certain of this, but defending his leading chief was the right thing to do.

"I said it was OBE, Mr. Mitchell, not incorrect. The XO and the COB have convinced the Captain that a Port and Starboard watch rotation isn't necessary and would likely have a negative impact on the crew's performance when we finally get underway. So we are now going to a three-section duty rotation."

Foster let out a short whistle and said, "Leave it to Mr. B and Master Chief Reynolds to tag-team the Captain, again!"

"Regardless of how it happened, Senior Chief, I still need a new watch bill for your division and I want it by 1700 today," snapped Richards.

"Understood, sir," replied Jerry, who then turned to Foster. "Senior Chief, I'll take the first stab at the new three-section duty schedule while you handle the repair parts list and are looking in on the PM work. I'll bring the schedule by for your review before I turn it in to the WEPS."

"Yes, sir, if you insist, sir," said Foster coldly.

"Yes, Senior Chief, I do insist. I need to start pulling my weight on this boat and I can begin by doing this. Oh, and Senior Chief, please pass on the news to the rest of the division. I'm sure they'll appreciate it."

Foster merely nodded and walked over to where Moran and company were performing the maintenance check.

"I expect your schedule to be correct, Mr. Mitchell," warned Richards.

"Of course, sir. You've made that very clear. Now, if you will excuse me, sir." And with that, Jerry headed back to his stateroom to begin his first assignment.

As Jerry was hustling back to his stateroom, he nearly collided with Lenny Berg as he and Washburn were leaving.

"That's the second time in one day that I almost collided with you, Jerry!" exclaimed Berg, who feigned a fainting spell. "You, sir, are a menace to navigation."

Jerry was also surprised by the near miss and while he heard Berg's little quip, for some reason he homed in on the word "menace," his former call sign. Jerry's face must have been a looking glass to his heart as Berg quickly dropped his goofy smile and said, "Hey, Jerry, lighten up. It was only a joke. Hey, the Chop and I were just going to lunch. Care to join us? I know this neat little place down the passageway that serves great fried chicken."

"Uh, no thanks, Lenny. I'm really not all that hungry and I have to redo the watch bill for the WEPS, so I guess I'll pass."

"Oh, Jerry, bad move, dude! You don't want to insult the Chop here. You'll find puree of peas at your next meal. It's naasty."

"Knock it off, Lenny," said Washburn. "If the man has work to do and he wants to skip a meal, I will in no way be insulted. However, if I hear any more about the smashed peas I served with the fish and chips from you again, it will become a self-fulfilling prophecy!"

"Okay, okay! Some people just can't handle honest criticism. See ya later, Jerry."

Jerry entered his stateroom and retrieved the service jackets he had left on his bunk. He started to review them again with a new sense of purpose, as he had to identify who had the proper qualifications and compare the records to the original watch bill that Senior Chief Foster had put together. The process took longer than Jerry had thought it would, a lot longer. But at 1600, he had what he believed was a good draft watch bill. With an hour left before his deadline, Jerry returned the service jackets to YN1 Glover and he went in search of Senior Chief Foster.

When Jerry reached the torpedo room, Foster was nowhere to be found. Jerry looked around the room and saw one of the TMs cleaning up over by the port tube nest. As Jerry approached, the sailor stood up and Jerry recognized him as the second class he had seen earlier.

"Excuse me, Petty Officer Greer, do you know where I can find the senior chief?"

"No, sir, I haven't seen him for about half an hour. He left after putting the repairs parts list together and filling out the electronic two-kilos," replied Greer. The "two-kilo" is the standard Navy requisition form that has to be filled out for every spare part in the supply system. The fact that Foster had already done them was encouraging.

"Thank you, Petty Officer Greer. Maybe he's in the chiefs' quarters."

"You're welcome, sir. And if I see Senior Chief Foster, I'll let him know you are looking for him."

Jerry proceeded back toward the chiefs' quarters, or Goat Locker, which was immediately outboard of the ship's office in Forward compartment middle level. He was seasoned enough to know that a junior officer did not just barge into the Goat Locker; one knocked on the door and waited for permission to enter. Only the CO had the right to walk in without knocking, although a smart one did not, out of respect for his chiefs.

The door opened and a huge man poked his upper body through the clearly inadequate opening. The nametag said REYNOLDS and his collar devices had the anchor and two stars of a master chief. This man is the Chief of the Boat, Jerry thought. The Chief of the Boat, or COB, is the senior enlisted man on the submarine and the direct representative of the crew to the CO and XO.

"Yes, Lieutenant, what can I do for you?" asked Reynolds in a voice that was as deep and impressive as his size.

Jerry momentarily hesitated, as all he could think of was the line from the original *Star Wars* movie: "Let the wookie win!" Quickly recovering his composure, Jerry replied, "Excuse me, Master Chief, I'm Lieutenant (j.g.) Mitchell, the new Torpedo Officer. I'm looking for Senior Chief Foster. Is he here?"

"Senior Chief Foster, aye, wait one," boomed the COB. Turning toward the interior of the chiefs' quarters, he called, "Has anyone seen Foster?"

A voice from inside responded, "I saw him and Bearden heading to the torpedo shop on base about fifteen minutes ago."

The COB turned around and said, "Did you get that, Mr. Mitchell?"

Jerry nodded and asked, "Did they say when they would be back?"

Again, the COB relayed the question. No one knew when they were to return. Now Jerry would have to take his draft watch bill to the WEPS without the most senior man in the division being able to review it and correct any mistakes he had made. As Jerry's frustration grew, he was certain that the timing of this trip to the SUBASE torpedo shop wasn't just a coincidence.

"Thank you, Master Chief. I'll just finish up without him."

"I prefer 'COB,' Mr. Mitchell, and welcome aboard." Reynolds then extended his massive hand. Jerry gladly accepted the COB's offer and as they shook hands, Jerry noticed that in addition to the silver dolphins on the COB's chest, he also wore the helmet with sea horses pin of a master diver.

Jerry started heading toward the WEPS' stateroom, then thought the better of it and went back to the torpedo room. Since Foster was unavailable, he would at least have TM1 Moran give it a quick look over. Arriving in the torpedo room, Jerry found Moran talking to the rest of the division about a problem they had discovered during the maintenance check that morning. As Jerry came up to the group, he didn't immediately interrupt as Moran was going over the procedures that would have to be used to troubleshoot the problem. However, Jerry couldn't help but notice that time was growing short and he raised his hand and made a slashing movement across his throat. Moran nodded his head in acknowledgement of Jerry's order and sent the other TMs off to do some more cleaning before knocking off for the day. He reminded all of them to come back and see him before hitting the beach as the watch bill hadn't been finalized yet.

"Yes, sir, you wanted to see me?" said Moran as he walked over to Jerry.

"Petty Officer Moran, I'd like you to take a few minutes and review this draft watch bill before I turn it in to the WEPS."

"Sir, Senior Chief Foster typically reviews these," replied Moran nervously.

"I understand that, Petty Officer Moran, but the Senior Chief isn't on the boat right now and I have to turn this in soon. You're the senior petty officer aboard right now, and I need a pair of experienced eyes to look it over." Jerry smiled as he emphasized the last part, hoping to reduce the tension that he felt growing.

"Yes, sir, of course." Moran took the paper from Jerry's hand examined at the draft watch bill. Every now and then, Moran would look up at Jerry, clearly uncomfortable with the task. Jerry tried not to let on that he knew just how jittery Moran was; embarrassing him wouldn't help the situation. Just what I need, Jerry thought, another scared rabbit. Moran soon finished and handed the paper back to his division officer.

"It looks good to me, sir. The only change I'd recommend is that you switch Seaman Jobin to my watch section. I'm his 'sea daddy,' his mentor, and I've been working with him now for the past two months. I'd like to keep him with me if you don't mind."

"Not at all, Petty Officer Moran. Thank you for informing me. I'll make the change and turn in the watch bill. I'll let you know as soon as the WEPS approves it." Jerry left the torpedo room feeling good about his watch bill, a trivial assignment in the grand scheme of things, but it had passed muster with a senior petty officer and he would be turning it in on time. Returning to his stateroom, Jerry quickly made the change and then took the final version to the WEPS with five minutes to spare.

Richards took the paper without saying anything. As he started reading it, his face became crimson. Then he slammed the watch bill on his desktop and yelled, "What kind of bullshit are you trying to give me, Mitchell!"

"Excuse me, sir?" Jerry replied in a confused tone.

"This watch bill is all hosed up! You have Jobin and Davidson in the same watch section. Jobin isn't qualified to do anything yet and Davidson will be gone for three weeks. This leaves only two qualified people in the first section."

"I wasn't aware that Davidson was going to be gone," said Jerry as his temper started rising. "He was on the Senior Chief's port and starboard watch bill and I assumed he would be available. And as for Seaman Jobin, TM1 Moran specifically requested that I put Jobin in his watch section."

Jerry's response seemed to irritate Richards even more as he rose from his chair and started speaking through clinched teeth. "Mr. Mitchell, FT2 Davidson has a quota to an advanced maintenance course for the CCS Mk 2 fire-control system. Once it was announced that we were going to a three-section duty rotation, Senior Chief Foster asked me to let Davidson go to the course as originally planned. If you would bother to talk to your leading chief, you would know what the hell is going on in your division."

Jerry had to fight hard to keep from blowing up on his department head. Senior Chief Foster had intentionally withheld information he needed to know, and on top of that, had left the boat so that he couldn't be ordered to ensure that the watch bill was correct. Jerry sensed that arguing with Cal Richards about the senior chief's malicious attempts at sabotage would be a lost cause and would only make things worse. Instead, Jerry took a number of slow, deep breaths and pulled the watch bill from Richards' desk.

"Sir, given this new information, all we need to do is move Petty Officer Larsen from the third section to the first and each section now has three qualified watch standers."

Richards seemed to be mollified by Jerry's calm reply and he sat back down. "Very well, Mr. Mitchell. I accept your recommendation."

Jerry turned to leave, but Richards called him back. "Where is your re-pair parts list, mister? Senior Chief Foster said he had finished it and the two-kilos over an hour ago."

"I don't know where the list is, sir. Senior Chief Foster never gave it to me," said Jerry in a non-confrontational, matter-of-fact tone. "But I'll go find the list and get it to you ASAP." The puzzled look on Richards' face told Jerry that perhaps he was starting to get through to the WEPS. Jerry certainly hoped so. Richards said nothing. He simply returned to his mountain of paperwork while Jerry quickly returned to his stateroom. Once there, Jerry picked up the boat's internal telephone and called down to the torpedo room.

"Torpedo room," responded the other person on the line. Jerry didn't recognize the voice.

"This is Mr. Mitchell. Is TM1 Moran there?"

"Yes sir. Wait one."

After a brief pause, Jerry heard a familiar voice: "Moran here. What can I do for you, sir?"

"Petty Officer Moran, the WEPS has approved the watch bill with minor modifications. You, Jobin, Willis, and Larsen have the duty, the rest may knock off work and go home for the night after they check out with you."

"Thank you, sir. I'll pass the word to the division. Anything else?"

"Yes, just one question," said Jerry. "Do you know if Senior Chief Foster and Petty Officer Bearden have returned to the boat yet?"

"I haven't seen the Senior Chief, but FT1 Bearden is here now. Would you like to speak to him?" replied Moran.

"Yes, please."

After another brief pause, the lead fire-control technician was on the line, "Bearden, sir."

"Petty Officer Bearden, do you know where Senior Chief Foster is? I need to get the repair part list he was working on into the WEPS."

There was absolute silence on the other end. Then, somewhat hesitantly, Bearden answered, "Sir, I believe the Senior Chief went home for the day."

"Really? Well, that wasn't very wise now, was it?" responded Jerry in a cynical tone. He wasn't at all surprised that Foster had not returned. "Petty Officer Bearden, do you know where he normally keeps the division's laptop?"

"Certainly, sir. Senior Chief Foster usually keeps it in his locker under his bunk in the chiefs' quarters."

"Thank you, I'll take care of the matter. Have a good evening." And with that Jerry hung up the phone and headed back to the chiefs' quarters. As Jerry went by the wardroom, he could see that dinner was being served and he realized that he was a bit hungry himself. The COB answered the door again and Jerry apologized profusely for interrupting the chiefs' meal. He explained that he needed the division's laptop to answer the WEPS' requirement and that it was very likely in Senior Chief Foster's bunk locker. The COB disappeared for a few minutes and then returned with the laptop in hand. Jerry thanked the COB and hurried back to his stateroom.

Fortunately, Foster hadn't buried the files in some folder that was deeply nested in another. Jerry took a quick look at the list. He didn't have the time or expertise to know if it was complete and printed out a copy on paper and saved the files to two diskettes. Jerry took one of the diskettes and the paper copy and laid it on top of the WEPS' desk and proceeded to the wardroom to get something to eat. Since he had arrived very late, Jerry ate, alone, at the second sitting.

Exhausted, Jerry went back to his stateroom and literally fell into his rack. He tried to read some more out of the ship's information book, but he was mentally and physically spent and he just couldn't concentrate. Realizing that this was a waste of time, Jerry got ready for bed, crawled back in, and closed the curtain on his rack. After getting comfortable, Jerry thought back on the terrible day he had had. And for the second night in a row he found himself asking the same nagging question: Had he done the right thing in asking for subs?

JERRY REMEMBERED THE last hurdle he had to clear before the Navy would grant his request. It was an interview with the Director of Naval Reactors. Before that meeting, Jerry and his squadron commander had visited "Uncle Jim" Thorvald in his office. The senator would not, of course, attend the meeting, but wanted to wish Jerry well. And Jerry wanted to thank the senator for his efforts.

Jerry had never been in Washington, D.C. before, or the Russell Senate Office Building, or a senator's office. Starting with the seal of the Great State of Nebraska on the door, it was filled with symbols of the state, as well as a fair amount of Cornhuskers memorabilia.

They went into the senator's inner office, and he welcomed the two officers warmly. "Jerry, Commander Casey, please come in. Take a seat." An aide materialized with juice and rolls, appropriate for the early hour. Jerry sat nervously on the leather couch.

The balding, thin, almost scrawny senator regarded his nephew fondly, but also appraisingly. "I've spent some political coin to get you a second chance with the Navy, Jerry. Assuming you pass the Naval Reactors inquisition, are the taxpayers going to get their money back?" Although he smiled and joked a little, Jerry knew the senator was serious.

"You know I'll do my best, Senator . . . Uncle Jim."

"But is that enough, Jerry? We all knew you'd be a good pilot. You're the type, and it's all you've ever wanted. I can remember you saying it when you were six, and it never changed. Now, suddenly, it's subs. You know the Navy will make it hard for you. Can you do it?"

Jerry nodded. "Remember when I taught myself Japanese so I could watch all those anime films undubbed? How about when I built that hang glider?"

"You mean the scaring us to death part?" Thorvald asked, smiling.

Jerry laughed, remembering. "No, I mean the part where I met all the FAA safety requirements—and Mom's. Built it, and paid for it, all by myself, when I was seventeen."

"Maybe you should have built a minisub," the senator responded, half-jokingly.

"And I've been scuba diving since my senior year in high school."

Torvald held up his hands in surrender. "All right, Jerry, I remember."

His voice became firmer. "And I believe you can do anything that's physically possible."

So was this physically possible? Jerry felt like the entire crew of *Memphis* considered him to be either a lightweight or a political hack. He fell asleep wondering if he could win against odds of 134 to 1.

 Fitting In

The next morning Jerry felt less like an impostor at Quarters. He belonged there, even if Foster didn't want him. And while Jerry might not like it, he at least knew where he stood.

And knowing, he could plan. Before Quarters started, Jerry told the senior chief that he would to speak to the division before they were dismissed. He'd felt foolish rehearsing it ahead of time, but it was clear that unless he took the right tone, Foster would roll right over him.

After Jerry went over the plan of the day and read a few announcements, he gave "the speech." It wasn't the one he'd planned to give the day before, but that may have been for the good. This one was better tuned to *Memphis* and the division.

He mentioned his background, giving a little more detail than may have been generally known. He admitted this was his first leadership opportunity and made it clear that he depended on their skills, especially those of Senior Chief Foster. The finish was the most important part.

"My only policy change is that from now on, everyone in the division should check in with their supervisor before leaving the ship, just as Senior Chief Foster will check in with me." That earned him a few curious looks, because that was supposed to be the policy, but Jerry was looking at Senior Chief Foster as he said it. There'd be less chance for a repeat of yesterday.

He'd planned to continue the turnover with Senior Chief Foster, but the 1MC loudspeaker announced, "Lieutenant Mitchell, lay topside." The senior chief gave a small smile as Jerry left.

He stopped to grab his coat and cover, which slowed him down enough to earn another summons from the loudspeaker. He emerged from the forward escape trunk to find the XO waiting for him, along with two women.

"This is Dr. Patterson and Dr. Davis. They'll be . . . er, supervising the installation of some special mission equipment for the patrol." Jerry noticed that Bair's correction earned him a scathing look from Dr. Patterson, the older of the two women. She looked to be in her early forties, while Davis seemed to be in her late twenties. Neither looked happy, although Davis just looked uncomfortable. Patterson scowled as if she disapproved of *Memphis* and everyone around her. Jerry wondered how a Navy tech rep functioned with an attitude like that.

"Ladies, this is Lieutenant (j.g.) Mitchell. He's the Torpedo Division Officer and the Manta operator." He turned to Jerry. "Show them to the wardroom. The Captain will be joining us there shortly."

"Aye, aye, sir." He offered his hand to the ladies and Davis shook it, while Patterson hung back and frowned. "Pleased to meet you both. This way, please." Recalling his own first time aboard just a few days ago, Jerry followed the two women down the hatch.

As they moved through the narrow passageways, Jerry watched the visitors dodge corners and equipment that encroached into the passageway. Davis looked more at ease, wide-eyed with curiosity, and obviously interested in everything. While she was peeking into the ship's sickbay, which also held the three-inch countermeasure launchers, she almost missed the turn into the wardroom, but caught up in time. Jerry could see she was full of questions and wondered if he knew enough to answer them.

When they reached the wardroom Jerry took their coats while the mess steward organized coffee and pastries. Nobody could ever accuse *Memphis* of being a poor host.

"What kind of special equipment will we be receiving?" Jerry asked curiously.

Davis started to speak, but Patterson stopped her. "I'm not sure I can tell you that," Patterson replied. "It's classified."

Jerry felt a little hurt. Security on a submarine was usually tight, and everyone had clearances. Not like they would be able to hide something in such close quarters anyway. Still, if she didn't think he was cleared to know, so be it.

Captain Hardy came into the wardroom, and Jerry snapped to attention. Bair and Richards followed him, and Richards asked for coffee for all of them.

Mitchell started to excuse himself and leave, but Bair said, "You need to be here, Mr. Mitchell. Have a seat."

Captain Hardy looked at Jerry and said, "These two ladies are technical reps from Draper Labs. They'll oversee the installation of a pair of remote operating vehicles (ROVs) and their handling gear in the torpedo room. The equipment will be installed in the starboard tube nest before we leave on patrol. Your people will, of course, assist with the work. Is that clear?"

Jerry felt a little vindicated. So he did have a "need to know." He glanced over at Patterson, who was frowning.

As Jerry answered, "Yes, sir," his brain processed the implications of losing the starboard tubes. "So we will have only two operational tubes for the upcoming patrol?"

"That is exactly what it means," Hardy replied. He didn't look happy with either Jerry's question or the situation.

The Captain continued. "Dr. Davis is here to survey the torpedo room before the actual installation. There is also some special analytical equipment that Dr. Patterson will be in charge of, but that will be installed elsewhere on the boat."

Jerry asked, "What will the equipment be used for?"

Both Hardy and Patterson started to answer, but Hardy paused, letting the woman speak. "That is classified—for the moment, at least."

After she stopped, Hardy amplified her comment. "Its presence on this boat is classified. If you draw any conclusions or speculate about the use of the ROVs, keep it to yourself, and tell your men the same thing. You are not to discuss the presence or function of any of the equipment, except as necessary for installation and testing."

"Aye, aye, sir."

"Stop any work on the starboard tube nest and have your people stand by to assist Dr. Davis this afternoon with the survey. That is all."

Jerry left and headed down one deck to the torpedo room. Senior Chief Foster was there, along with several sailors from torpedo division. "Senior Chief, there's been a change in plans. What's scheduled for this afternoon?"

"Moran and I and some of the others have to work on the weapons launching console, we're getting some incorrect signals from the fire-control system."

"Well, as of now, that's off. There's a visitor aboard that we have to . . ."

"I'm sorry, sir, but I don't think we can do that. Mr. Richards was pretty clear about getting this problem fixed."

Mitchell felt his anger building. Foster's resistance to even a simple order was unbelievable. "Senior Chief, this takes priority. I just came from a meeting with the CO, XO, and the WEPS." Working on keeping calm, he repeated, "Plans have changed."

"They didn't tell me about it." Foster remarked.

That did it. Mitchell looked at the other torpedo gang sailors and said, "Give us a minute, please."

The others left, quickly. Senior Chief Foster watched them go with a small smile, as if he knew what was coming and enjoyed the idea.

"Senior Chief, I want to know what your problem is."

"Sir, I don't understand what you mean." Jerry felt his irritation grow and fought to control it. Foster had donned an "innocent" expression so classic that under other circumstances it might have made Jerry laugh. Now it only emphasized how much Foster was playing with him.

"I want it perfectly clear that I am . . ." Jerry stopped himself, and took a breath. Asserting his authority was pointless. Not only was the senior chief already ignoring his rank, he seemed to take pleasure in frustrating him. And what was he supposed to do? Take him up to captain's mast? Right.

Jerry could see Foster watching him as he thought, studying him.

Jerry started again. "Senior Chief, if you don't want to talk about this, that's your choice, but I'm just trying to get the job done. If you don't like me, I think I can live with that. But whether you like it or not, I am the Torpedo Officer and if I give you an order, I expect you to follow it."

Foster's face became a mask. "Yes, sir."

Mitchell pressed his point. "As the division officer, it's my job to deal with the WEPS. If I say something needs to be done, you do not have to check with Mr. Richards. I will have already done that."

"If you say so, sir." Foster pronounced the last word as if it left a bad taste in his mouth.

"All right, then. Stop any maintenance on the starboard tube nest and have the division ready this afternoon to assist with a pre-installation survey. This is for some special equipment that we'll be loading later for the patrol. We probably won't need everyone, but it will be easier to have the men return to their work if they aren't necessary than to try and bring them in at the last minute. Any questions?" Mitchell saw a flash of curiosity pass over Foster's face, but he knew the man would not give Jerry the satisfaction of asking for more information. Foster just shook his head.

"Very well, then, Senior Chief, carry on." Jerry left, with bridges burning behind him. He was unhappy, almost despairing, about his confrontation with Foster. He'd hoped to resolve whatever conflict there was, but instead had formalized it. On the other hand, Foster now knew where Jerry stood.

He headed back to the wardroom, intending to get more information from Richards or the two women about what was going to be done. He found the lieutenant in the passageway, but didn't get a chance to ask about the ROV. Instead, the WEPS called him into his stateroom.

"How is your qualification program coming, mister?"

Mentally, Jerry shifted gears, hesitating for a moment before answering. He knew Richards would want to hear something positive. "I've been studying the ship's data book."

"Really? Good for you." Richards' cold tone did not match the praise. "Have you talked to the qualifications officer yet?"

"No, sir. I don't know who that is."

"It's me, and it's time you got busy." Richards turned in his chair, reached into a drawer, and pulled out a fat notebook. "Here's your qualification book. Frankly, I don't see how you can do this, but it won't be my fault if you fail. Figuring for the time you're going to be aboard and the amount of material you've got to cover"—he pulled out a sheet of paper—"I've made up a schedule." He handed it to Jerry, shaking his head as he did. "The clock is ticking, Mr. Mitchell. Good luck." Richards almost sounded like he meant it.

Jerry dumped the notebook in his stateroom and went looking for Davis. He found her in the wardroom, sitting alone with her coffee, looking bored.

"Dr. Davis?"

"Please call me Emily."

"And I'm Jerry," he said automatically. "I was hoping I could get some more information about the gear and what's going to happen in my torpedo room, if that's not classified." He grinned, and Davis smiled back.

"Well, could we start the survey now? I've been trying to work from drawings, and I'm having some trouble visualizing where everything needs to go. And, if you haven't already noticed, I've never been aboard a submarine before."

Jerry shook his head, "I'm sorry, Dr., . . . I mean Emily, but my men won't be ready until this afternoon."

Jerry could tell by the look on Davis' face that she was disappointed. Sighing, Jerry smiled and suggested, "We could go down and have a quick look around. We'll just have to keep out of the way of my men while they work."

Davis' face quickly transformed from gloomy to beaming. "Oh! That would be great! Thank you."

"We're just one deck up. It's almost directly below us." Jerry then looked around for Dr. Patterson.

"Will your partner want to come with us?"

Davis' expression at his use of the word "partner" made him realize that Patterson must be the boss.

"No." Davis shook her head sharply. "She's working with the Captain and the Executive Officer."

"Then let's go for a quick tour."

Jerry led Davis out of the wardroom and toward the ladder by the crew's berthing. Jerry belatedly hoped that the crew had been informed that there were female visitors on board, otherwise this could get interesting. Entering into the torpedo room, Jerry and Davis found it buzzing with activity. A number of the TMs and FTs were huddled around the launching console and several of the access panels were open. TM1 Moran looked up from the panel and saw Jerry and Dr. Davis in the back of the room. Grabbing a rag, he walked over to his division officer and the visitor.

"Mr. Mitchell, I thought the survey was this afternoon," Moran seemed nervous and surprised by Jerry's arrival with Davis.

"Not to worry, Petty Officer Moran, I haven't changed anything. I'm just letting Dr. Davis have a quick look around." Moran visibly relaxed after Jerry had replied.

"Dr. Emily Davis, this is Torpedoman's Mate First Class Moran. Petty Officer Moran, Dr. Davis."

"Pleased to meet you," said Davis as she extended her hand.

"You'll excuse me if I don't shake your hand, ma'am. Mine are covered in grease. I've been doing some maintenance on the port tubes and this stuff doesn't come off very easily."

"Have you tried gasoline? I've always found that it works pretty well in removing marine grease," suggested Davis.

Moran stared at her with amusement.

"What? What's wrong with what I said? It does work!" replied Davis defensively.

Moran looked at Jerry, who motioned to him, as if to tell him to explain. "I'm sure it does work, ma'am," said Moran. "But you can't bring gasoline onto a sub. There's nowhere for the vapors to go. They would collect and become toxic, in addition to being very flammable."

Davis suddenly became wide-eyed and momentarily covered her mouth in embarrassment, "That was stupid of me! I guess I'm too used to working in a well-ventilated lab."

"That's okay, ma'am. Most people don't realize that we can't use a lot of things on board a submarine for safety reasons. Take deodorant, for example. We can't use aerosols on board because the propellants are bad for our atmosphere, so we all use stick deodorant," said Moran.

"Thank you, Mr. Moran. I'll try to remember that in the future."

"Your welcome, and ma'am, its 'Petty Officer Moran' or 'TM1.' That's a mister," stated Moran as he pointed at Jerry.

When Davis looked at Jerry with confusion, he said, "Never mind, I'll explain later." Turning back toward Moran, Jerry said, "We'll try to keep out of your way, Petty Officer Moran. By the way, where's the Senior Chief?"

"He went back to the chiefs' quarters, sir. He, umm, said he had to unload a bunch of paperwork. He should be back soon," replied Moran, again with some apprehension.

"Thanks, TM1. We won't keep you any longer." Moran nodded and returned to his work.

"All right, what did I do wrong this time?" asked Davis with a note of frustration.

"Hmmm? Oh nothing. However, the title 'mister' is usually reserved for addressing officers junior to you in rank. While it's not inappropriate for a civilian to address an enlisted man as 'mister,' it's not customary aboard ship and some enlisted don't like to be addressed that way. Shall we proceed with the tour?"

Jerry escorted Davis over to the starboard tube nest and began to discuss the features of the Mk67 torpedo tubes on *Memphis* while Davis listened with rapt attention. Jerry was beginning to enjoy himself, feeling more confident about his abilities, and it didn't hurt that this young woman seemed to hang on every word he said.

But after about twenty minutes, Jerry's confidence began to waver as he started to run out of things to say, and as Davis' questions became increasingly more technical. Jerry loathed the idea of calling Moran over to help, particularly since he and the other TMs were still troubleshooting the launching console.

As if on cue, Senior Chief Foster appeared by the port tube nest. He looked over and saw the two of them by the starboard tubes; this earned Jerry a deep scowl. Jerry ignored the senior chief's displeasure and motioned for him to come over.

"Excellent timing, Senior Chief, I'm afraid that I've exhausted my limited knowledge of the torpedo tubes, and Dr. Davis here is full of questions. Dr. Davis, this is Senior Chief Foster, my division's leading chief. Senior Chief, Dr. Davis."

As Foster shook Davis' hand, he looked straight at Jerry and said, "Sir, I thought you said the survey was this afternoon. I've gone to a lot of trouble to get people freed up for that and . . ."

"Whoa, Senior. I haven't changed a thing, so stand down," replied Jerry tersely. "Dr. Davis was curious and asked for a quick look around before the survey this afternoon, and seeing as she is a guest on board our boat, I saw no reason not to grant her request. We've made every effort to stay clear of the men. And now that you are here, you can help reduce the good doctor's curiosity."

Foster looked pained and embarrassed. Jerry sensed that his mild chastisement of the senior chief in front of a visitor had just blown up the abutments to the bridges he had torched earlier. Oh well, thought Jerry, he's a big boy. He'll just have to get over it. For his part, Foster merely nodded stiffly and then turned to address Davis. "What do you want to know, ma'am?"

"In talking with Mr. Mitchell, I gather that your torpedoes are about 19 feet in length, but what I need to know is how long is the tube itself?"

"First off, ma'am, with the torpedo mount dispenser attached, the length of a Mk48 Mod 6 is twenty feet six inches. The length of the tube itself is twenty-two feet two inches."

Davis jotted down the figure and looked relieved. "Whew, that leaves three inches to spare. They said my babies would fit, but I didn't think it would be this tight."

"Your 'babies' ma'am?" asked a perplexed Foster.

"Yes, they are part of the special equipment we'll load on your submarine in a few weeks. I'm not at liberty to say much more right now," responded Davis nervously.

"Excuse me, Dr. Davis," said Jerry. "But I think you can tell him at least as much as I've been told. I've only been on *Memphis* for a couple of days now, and Senior Chief Foster and the others will do most of the work installing your equipment. I believe that puts him in the 'need to know' category. Wouldn't you agree, Senior?"

Foster was momentarily taken aback by Jerry's remark and could only utter a halfhearted, "Yes, sir."

Sighing, Davis quickly looked around and said, "All right, I guess you have a point. We'll be loading two ROVs and their support equipment for the upcoming mission. The ROVs are modified Near Term Mine Reconnaissance System vehicles. I had to lengthen them slightly to accommodate some of the modifications and I was concerned that they wouldn't fit. The survey this afternoon is to go over our space requirements and to work out any possible issues with the loading and installation."

"I see," said Foster only slightly less confused. "Will we be able to look over the technical documentation for these ROVs? I'm assuming we'll also be maintaining as well as operating the vehicles."

"That's right, Senior Chief," replied Davis with some caution. "But I can't let any of you see the documentation until just before we leave. It would reveal the purpose of the mission and, for now, that is only to be known by myself, Dr. Patterson, your Captain and your Executive Officer."

Foster was obviously dying of curiosity. He looked at Jerry with an annoyed and questioning expression, but all Jerry could do was shrug his shoulders and shake his head no. "Very well, ma'am. Do you have any other questions?"

"Yes, I do, several, as a matter of fact." Her expression brightened. "Is it possible to open the outer doors on both the starboard tubes at the same time? I believe you have an interlock that normally prevents this from happening, but can it be overridden?"

Foster explained that the nesting interlock used mechanical linkages and that it could be disabled by removing a padlock at one of the connection points. The Weapons Officer held the key, but it required the Captain's permission, since it was a safety feature.

Davis nodded and fired the next question, which Foster answered succinctly and quickly. The questions kept coming, well beyond any reasonable definition of "several." And once again, Jerry was impressed with Foster's knowledge. It seemed like there was nothing this man didn't know about the torpedo tubes or the supporting systems. Still, after about forty minutes Jerry noticed that Foster was becoming annoyed with Dr. Davis' unending stream of questions. Before matters could get out of hand, Jerry inserted himself to draw the interrogation to a close.

"Excuse me Dr. Davis, I hate to interrupt, but the Senior Chief still has a few hundred things to do before the formal survey, and it's almost lunchtime. I suggest we save the rest of your questions for this afternoon."

"But I only have a few more!" exclaimed Davis. "Really, I'm serious. It will take just a little longer."

"Later, Dr. Davis, please," replied Jerry in a firm tone as he gently started turning her back toward the ladder. Reluctantly, Emily began moving—slowly. As they were just about to leave the torpedo room she suddenly spun around and faced Jerry. She looked like a kid who had just lost a prized possession. "The Manta! I forgot all about my questions on the Manta! Do we have time for those now?" Jerry could only roll his eyes. Then, with a very a deliberate motion, he pointed his finger toward the door.

"Okay, okay. I understand. Later," said Davis with more than a hint of disappointment, but she also smiled at Jerry's expression. Jerry softly chuckled as they headed up the ladder to forward compartment middle level. He had known a number of bookish engineer types at the Academy, but this was the first time he had met a young woman who could match them. She was just as passionate and intense about underwater vehicles as he had been about his beloved F-18s. That suited him just fine. She cared deeply about her work and would likely move heaven and earth to make sure everything worked perfectly. This reassured Jerry, since the crew of *Memphis* would have to use her ROVs to do something, somewhere—something that obviously meant a lot to the CNO and his staff. No, *Memphis* could certainly do worse than to work with the likes of Dr. Emily Davis.

By the time Jerry had finished this train of thought, he and Davis walked into the wardroom—and into a full blast from Patterson.

"Emily! Where the hell have you been? We need to leave *now*, if we are going to get ready for the survey this afternoon."

"I'm . . . I'm sorry Dr. Patterson. Lieutenant Mitchell was giving me a quick tour of the torpedo room. I thought it would help speed things up to get some of my questions out of the way." Jerry noticed that Davis looked very uncomfortable and embarrassed by Patterson's unexpected hostility. For that matter, no one in the wardroom looked at all comfortable with Dr. Patterson. Even Captain Hardy, whose face was crimson, suffered in silence, even though he looked like he was going to erupt at any moment.

"Fine, fine, Emily, get your coat and let's go," replied Patterson in a patronizing tone. As Patterson and Davis collected their coats and other belongings, the mess steward emerged from the pantry with a set of plates. He set them down on the table and walked up to Hardy and asked, "Excuse me, sir. Will our guests be staying for lunch?"

Before Hardy could say a word, Patterson looked menacingly at the mess steward and said, "I'm not spending any more time on this rust bucket than I absolutely have to." She then turned toward Jerry and pointed a finger at him. "You! Show me how to get off this piece of junk."

Jerry quickly looked at Bair, who stiffly nodded his head in the direction of the door. Jerry then motioned to the door and said, "This way, Dr. Patterson." In her haste to leave the wardroom, she pushed Jerry out of the way and stomped down the passageway toward the forward escape trunk.

As Davis passed by Captain Hardy, she uttered a barely audible "Thank you" and proceeded out into the passageway. Jerry followed the two women toward the escape trunk, but Patterson seemed to remember the way. By the time he was topside, Patterson was already storming off the boat, with Davis running behind to catch up. He shrugged and went below.

When Jerry returned to the wardroom, he found it incredibly quiet and even tenser than before. Hardy ate little and said not a word, although it was obvious that something really bad had happened. Bair's expression matched Hardy's. Lunch was eaten in absolute silence, and only after Hardy had left did any of the other officers even dare to ask the XO about what had happened.

Bair pushed himself away from the table, rose, and said, "Gentlemen, believe me, you don't want to know. And even if for some insane reason you did, I couldn't tell you. All I can say is this mission will be closest thing to hell that I have ever seen in this man's Navy."

As Bair left, the remaining officers looked at each other with astonishment and dread. A sense of despair seemed to descend on all in the wardroom. Jerry was also confused by what the XO had said and couldn't understand what had brought him so far down. Lenny Berg saw the questioning look on Jerry's face and tried to explain.

"Jerry, the XO has always been one of the few bright lights on this boat. He is the man who has served directly under Hardy for almost two years and he has been our BS filter from day one. Believe me, he's taken a lot of hits for this crew. If being this Captain's personal whipping boy isn't hell, then I do not want to find out what hell is really like."

The other officers murmured their assent and slowly filed out of the room. Jerry stayed behind, trying to comprehend the enormity of what Berg had said. The normally jovial Lenny Berg had been cast into the pit of depression by the XO's three sentences. And while Jerry didn't understand the exact ramifications of those words, he knew that things on board *Memphis* had taken a turn for the worse.

Jerry looked up at the clock and realized that he only had about an hour and a half before the ladies returned for the survey. Remembering the thick qualification book and schedule he received from Richards, Jerry decided to go to his stateroom and see just how much work he faced in his quest for the gold dolphins.

As he entered his stateroom, Jerry saw a stack of documents and three-ring binders over a foot tall sitting on his desk. In awe, Jerry investigated the mountain of paper. After looking at a few pages, it soon became apparent that these were the division's records. Maintenance logs, calibration logs, training and readiness records, various inventories, and more, a lot more. Jerry remembered Moran's comment about the senior chief "unloading" some paperwork. Well, thought Jerry, I guess Senior Chief Foster has officially turned over the division. He looked around his cramped stateroom. Now where the hell am I going to put all this stuff?

Jerry spent the next hour segregating and organizing the division's records. He skimmed each packet of paper and placed it in one of four piles—maintenance, personnel, training, or supply—on his bunk. He vowed to look at everything in more detail later, but right now he just wanted to get a handle on his job as a division officer. As daunting as the huge pile looked at first, from what Jerry could tell, the senior chief seemed to have run a pretty tight division. Once again, Jerry was impressed with the man's abilities. If only we could get along, he thought ruefully.

Looking down by his pillow, Jerry saw his qual book. He picked it up and saw that it was well over an inch thick. He began to wonder if he could finish in time. Flipping through the book, Jerry noticed all the signatures he needed to obtain before he would be awarded his dolphins. There were watches to stand under instruction, tens of system checkouts and practical exercises to perform, and dozens of standard operating and emergency procedures to memorize. Setting it aside, Jerry picked up the schedule that Richards had recommended and started looking at what he should be doing first. The list was oppressively long and the pace demanding.

The more Jerry looked at his qualification requirements, the more apprehensive he became. He then lifted his eyes over the schedule to the four mounds of paper on his bunk and tried to figure out how he was going to juggle his qualification needs with his responsibilities as a division officer.

Then it dawned on him that as the Manta operator, he was probably going to be in the torpedo room manning the UUV control console for a lot of the time once they got on station. As the fear of failure started growing, Jerry recalled the aura of pessimism in the wardroom over lunch and that fear started to give way to panic. "Whoa," Jerry said to himself. "Don't try to swallow an elephant whole. Take this one bite at a time."

It was almost time for the good doctors to return, and the thought of dealing with Patterson again was not particularly a pleasant one. However, this time Jerry wanted to be topside to greet them. Besides, a little fresh air sounded really good right now. Before he grabbed his coat and ball cap, Jerry took out a pen and wrote his name on the cover of the qual book. This is now my book, he thought, and I'll finish it one signature at a time. He then placed the book on his bunk and headed for the forward escape trunk.

It was windy topside, but the wind was from the south, so it wasn't bitingly cold. The sun occasionally shone through the streaks of gray clouds. All in all, not a bad March afternoon. Jerry took a few deep breaths, relishing the outside air. There was a momentary flash down at the end of the pier and Jerry saw Dr. Patterson getting out of a car. Emily appeared a few seconds later. Jerry allowed himself a smug moment. Those 20/10 fighter pilot eyes of his were still working to spec. Patterson was now past the pier guard and was moving quickly toward the brow. Emily, with her shorter gait, was struggling to keep up. As Patterson approached, Jerry could swear he heard her stomping on the concrete pier. Okaaay, Jerry thought, she is still pissed off from this morning. This should make for a lovely afternoon—NOT.

"Good afternoon Dr. Patterson, Emily. I trust you had a good lunch," said Jerry as he pointed to a number of breadcrumbs on Davis' coat.

"Oh yes," replied Davis as she brushed the crumbs off. "We had grinders at a very nice restaurant called Spiros."

"Yes, I'm familiar with it. It's a popular haunt for submariners."

"So I noticed," interrupted Patterson. "Can we skip the unnecessary pleasantries and get this survey over and done? Now, take us to the torpedo room, Lieutenant."

Patterson's rude remark caused something inside Jerry to pop.

Jerry walked up and looked Patterson straight in the eye and said, "Dr. Patterson, might I make a slight suggestion? Since it's obvious that this morning's meeting with the Captain and the XO didn't go very well, exercising a little common courtesy might make this afternoon's evolution less painful."

Patterson stared at Jerry in utter amazement. Recovering quickly, she gave Jerry a "Who are *you* to question me, little man?" look, then said, "I don't have to, Mr. Mitchell, because I work for the President." And with that, she tried to push Jerry back so she could get to the hatch. But he was ready for her this time, and he held his ground.

"Interesting," responded Jerry. "So do we." He then stepped away from the hatch and motioned for Patterson to proceed. She did so in silence.

The survey in the torpedo room began with a strict warning from Hardy that anything heard during the meeting was not to be discussed with anyone outside of the present group. Furthermore, any speculations about the nature of the mission were to be kept strictly to oneself. The Captain spelled out in detail exactly how the restrictions were to be applied, assuming nothing. It was so detailed that Jerry began to get a little insulted. This wasn't the first security briefing he'd ever attended. He watched the torpedo gang for a similar reaction, but they endured it in patient silence.

Finishing with another stern warning about the penalties facing anyone who disclosed classified information, Hardy then turned over the meeting to the XO, who introduced Dr. Patterson and Dr. Davis. Patterson reemphasized the Captain's admonition for strict security and explained that the orders for this mission came from the President himself. This drew a low murmur from the TMs and FTs, which the XO quickly silenced.

Emily Davis then took over and started telling Jerry and his men what they needed to do to prepare *Memphis* for the patrol. They would be loading two ROVs and their support equipment. Everything was loaded on pallets sized to fit through the weapons shipping hatch, the same one used to load torpedoes.

"The ROVs are modified Near Term Mine Reconnaissance System (NMRS) vehicles," she explained. "They were used as early mine clearance vehicles, but we've adapted them for this mission.

"The changes include a different sensor package and a thrust vector axial pump jet for precision navigation. Each vehicle has its own cradle, which is compatible with the torpedo storage rack's tie-down arrangements. All of the launching and recovery operations, and most of the maintenance work, will be done using Navy-approved NMRS procedures." Jerry made a quick note to himself to make sure that they obtained a full set of manuals from SUBASE.

Davis continued. "The support equipment will be fitted on seven pallets. There will also be a retrieval arm assembly placed into tube number one to help properly position the ROV so that it can be recovered."

Turning toward Hardy, Davis said, "This will require disabling the starboard tubes nesting interlock," the safety device she'd asked Foster about that morning. Both Hardy and Richards nodded their understanding.

"Finally, two much smaller instrumentation kits will be installed in the engine room." This last statement generated some questioning looks from virtually everyone present, but no further explanation was forthcoming.

Davis then asked if anyone had previous NMRS experience. No one, not even Foster, raised his hand. She went on to explain that just about everything concerning NMRS vehicle operations was done in the best of Polish traditions. After the laughter died down, Davis went on to explain that a NMRS ROV is loaded into a torpedo tube backward and upside down. When it deploys, the vehicle pulls itself out of the tube and then swings about, righting itself. This will also affect how a ROV is loaded on board, as the orientation of the vehicle will be backward from how torpedoes are loaded.

With the end of the formal presentation by Davis, questions from both sides flew across the room. LTJG Frank Lopez, *Memphis'* Damage Control Assistant and the ship's diving officer, needed the weights of all the equipment for his initial dive compensation calculations. Foster wanted to know what type of batteries the ROVs used and how they were to be recharged. Davis asked about storage space for her equipment. The give-and-take continued for an hour. At this point, Jerry asked a crucial question, one that had been neglected throughout the technical discussions.

"Dr. Davis, none of my people have any experience on the ROV. How much time will we have to train?"

Davis hesitated, glanced at Patterson, and said, "Due to security constraints, Mr. Mitchell, the ROVs and their equipment will only be loaded the day before you depart. Furthermore, there is only time and consumables available for four training launches and recoveries—essentially, two for each ROV as a final system check before performing mission-related work."

Jerry was dumbstruck by Davis' reply—and he wasn't the only one. Everyone from *Memphis'* crew, except the Captain and the XO, was just as dumbfounded. Shaking his head vigorously, Jerry said, "Only two checkout runs each? Dr. Davis, that is completely inadequate. There is no way we can become proficient with these vehicles in only four test runs."

Before Davis could respond, Patterson spoke up, "I understand your concerns Lieutenant Mitchell, but there is nothing that can be done. We have a very tight window for this mission. I've discussed this at length with SUBLANT and the CNO's staff, and they have assured me that this crew can fulfill all mission objectives with minimal training."

Jerry looked to Richards for support, but his department head only looked at the deck. The Captain and XO were also both silent, but it was clear from the look on their faces that they weren't happy with this at all.

Then it dawned on Jerry that this was probably what caused this morning's blowout. Both Hardy and Bair had likely argued vehemently that more training was needed and Patterson simply pulled a "collar check" on them, stating that the submarine admirals had "said" it could be done. Both also understood that the lack of training could very well doom this mission to failure and end both their careers. Hell indeed, thought Jerry, remembering the XO's words from lunch.

"All right, people, if there are no more questions, let me sum up what needs to be done," said Bair. "By my count, Dr. Davis will need nine torpedo stows for the two ROVs and the seven supporting pallets, correct?"

"Yes, sir," responded Foster.

"Very well. Mr. Mitchell, you will coordinate with SUBASE to get us everything we need on the NMRS ROVs. If you have to say anything to justify the request, the cover story is that we are going to AUTEC, the acoustic test range in the Bahamas with a NMRS vehicle in July, and we'll need the documentation. You'll also have to get the starboard tubes ready to support ROV operations. I want you to stay on top of this. I don't want to have any surprises. Mr. Richards, you will put in a request for ten torpedoes with SUBASE. And Mr. Lopez, you need to get the weight information for the compensation calculations from Dr. Davis. Did I miss anything?"

No one spoke.

"All right, then, gentlemen, we've got work to do." Bair then turned to Patterson and Davis and asked, "Will you ladies be joining us for dinner?"

"No, Commander. Emily and I must return to Washington this evening. We also have work to do," replied Patterson.

"Understood. Mr. Mitchell, please escort our guests off the boat. Goodbye, Dr. Patterson, Dr. Davis."

Jerry acknowledged the order and took the women back to the wardroom to retrieve their gear. Once topside, Patterson quickly walked onto the pier and headed toward the car. Davis held back, handed Jerry a business card, and said, "If you need any additional information, I'll do what I can to help."

Jerry pocketed the card. "Emily, you know that we don't have sufficient training time for this mission. Is whatever we are about to do so damned critical that we can't take the time to do it right?"

"I'm sorry, Jerry, but it's not my decision. For what it's worth, I raised the same concerns and got the same reply." She lowered her voice a little. "All I can say is that the timing's very tight."

"Okay," said Jerry with a sigh.

"I'll see you in about a month, then. When it's time to load my babies on your sub."

"Until then," said Jerry, bowing slightly. Smiling, Davis walked down the gangplank to the pier. Jerry watched her walk all the way down to the car before he went down below.

Dinner was less severe than lunch. Although the crew of the *Memphis* had a hard task ahead of them, they could at least get started. Even Berg had regained some of his sense of humor and cracked a few jokes during the meal. Jerry actually saw the XO laugh for the first time, although he still looked stressed. The Captain had left the boat for the evening, which might have contributed to the more relaxed atmosphere.

Jerry worked late sorting the division's unfamiliar paperwork and finding places to put it.

With the passageway lights rigged for red and the 1MC loudspeaker stilled, the boat settled in for the night. Jerry thought about sleep. Then he remembered Richards' schedule and his own qualification process. He'd shoved his qualification book onto the bookrack to make room for the paperwork he'd just managed to put away. His rack looked terribly inviting, but instead of turning in, he grabbed the ship's data and qualification books and headed for the wardroom.

He spread out his books on the table, got a cup of not-too-stale coffee and a few cookies from the pantry, and settled in. The setting, as well as the subject matter, reminded him of being on the old USS *Sam Rayburn*, SSBN 635, berthed at Charleston, South Carolina. Formerly a ballistic missile submarine, or SSBN, she had been converted into a moored training ship, or MTS. The old girl was now a floating prototype, where students from Nuclear Power School went and put their theoretical knowledge to work running a real reactor. Sans missile tubes and heavily modified for her training role, the MTS 635 prototype trainer had a nuclear reactor and a complete submarine engineering plant bolted to South Carolina. Everything worked, except that no matter how much steam the plant made, they never went anywhere. Many nuclear submarine officers went through that school, the last step in their nuclear power training.

And Jerry had loved it. He knew exactly what to do, how to study, how to pace himself, how not to be intimidated by what seemed like an overwhelming task. He'd learned to fly that way as well, and he could learn this boat too. It took energy, a steady stream of effort over a long time. It came from his desire to succeed—and his desire to prove the admirals wrong. And it was something he could do. Foster might hate him, the other officers might think he was a lightweight, but this he could do without interference. He wasn't sure about the rest of his job, but this would be all right.

Jerry was in the process of drawing the boat's trim system in his notebook when the wardroom door opened and Bair walked in. Seeing Jerry at the table studying, the XO approached and said, "Good evening, Mr. Mitchell. Mind if I join you?"

"No, sir, not at all."

Bair pulled up a chair next to Jerry and sort of fell into it. The paperwork he had been carrying hit the table with a dull *thump*. He looked dog-tired.

"I couldn't help but overhear the Captain's welcome the other day," said Bair with a touch of sarcasm. "But I haven't been much better myself. It's clear from the mission orders and our meetings today with Patterson that you aren't to blame for this extra patrol, and I apologize for accusing you of arranging it just to prove yourself."

"Uh, thank you, sir" was all that Jerry could muster in reply.

"Your record is quite good, for an aviator," teased Bair. More seriously, he added, "But *Memphis* isn't a fighter. She's an old, worn-out submarine, and she gets cranky from time to time." The XO then leaned forward a little and pointed at the dolphins on his shirt. "To earn these, you need to not only understand her individual systems, but you need to learn about her mood swings as well. And the only way you can do that is to throw yourself into learning absolutely everything about her."

Jerry was surprised to hear Bair speak in such a reverent tone as he talked about *Memphis*. This boat meant something to him. While it seemed a little weird, Jerry knew that he had to have a similar relationship with this "cranky" old sub if he was to make the grade.

"Now, the Navy and the Captain are demanding a very aggressive qualification schedule from you," Bair continued. "And I agree. You need to catch up with your peers if you are going to make a career in submarines. I also agree that there can be no special dispensation. You must earn your dolphins," the XO placed extra emphasis on the word "earn."

"However, one of my responsibilities is to make sure that junior officers assigned to this boat are properly trained. And in that regard, I will do everything I can to see that you have the opportunity to complete your qualifications. The rest is up to you, Jerry."

For the first time since coming on board, Jerry actually felt welcomed, and sensed that the XO was sincere in his offer. "Sir, I appreciate your advice and I will work my tail off to not disappoint you."

"The only one who will be truly disappointed, Jerry, should you fail, is you," said Bair. "However, Mr. Mitchell, judging by your past performance as a fighter pilot and the dogged pursuit of your transfer to submarines, I have a feeling that it won't happen." The XO stifled a yawn and looked at his watch. "It's getting late. Jerry, why don't you hit the rack and get some sleep? You can start off fresh on your qualifications in the morning."

"Aye, aye, sir! And thank you, XO," Jerry said. "Good night, sir."

"Good night, Jerry." And with that the XO stuck the load of paperwork under his arm and headed toward his stateroom.

Jerry made his way back to his stateroom and leaned against the bunks. He didn't realize just how tired he really was, until he started undressing. As Jerry settled into bed, he paused to reflect on the events of the day and was confident that tomorrow would be better. Yes, tomorrow would see him start the process of becoming a dolphin-wearing submariner. And with that pleasant thought, Jerry fell asleep.

5 First Underway

April 18, 2005

●●●●●●●●●●●●●●●●●●●●●●

SUBASE, New London

Jerry climbed out of the bridge access trunk into the cockpit atop *Memphis'* sail. He was greeted by dazzling sunlight and it took his eyes a minute to adjust to the brightness. It was a glorious spring day, not a cloud in the sky, warm, and with a moderate breeze. It was a perfect day to go to sea. And Jerry was excited. Excited and nervous, because the XO had suggested to the Navigator that Jerry conn the boat out as Junior Officer of the Deck. Being the senior watch officer, as well as the ship's Navigator, Lieutenant Commander

Harry O'Connell assigned officers to their watch stations and oversaw their qualifications and "professional development." Training junior officers in the fine art of shiphandling definitely fell into both categories, and he completely concurred with the XO's suggestion. Even though the scheduled departure was still a couple of hours away, Jerry already had a good case of the butterflies. Smiling, he fondly remembered that the last time he felt this way was just before his first training flight in an F-18.

Looking out over the sail, Jerry could see members of the crew working to finish the preparations for going to sea. Some were loading the last of the provisions, removing the lifelines, and disconnecting the shore power cables. While everyone was busy, Jerry knew that most of the work was done. Thinking back, Jerry wondered where the past month and a half had gone. It seemed to have passed by him in a blink of an eye. On the other hand, there were moments when he felt as if he were in suspended animation.

He had made excellent progress on his qualifications, having completed most of the system checkouts and a number of the procedural ones as well. But that progress had come at a price: Jerry didn't have a life outside of *Memphis*. While his shipmates got off as often as they could, Jerry stayed aboard almost every night studying for the next signature in his qual book. After about five straight days, the XO would track him down and order him to go home.

Jerry remembered the first time the XO threw him off the boat. He came into the wardroom after Jerry had remained onboard for the entire first week. Grabbing the ship's data book that Jerry was trying to study, the XO slammed it shut as hard as he could. The loud thud made Jerry jump, the effect enhanced considerably by his semiconscious state. The XO then sat down, looked Jerry straight in the eye, and said, "Mr. Mitchell, go home."

"Sir?" Jerry stammered as his eyes tried to focus. "I, uh, can't. XO. I really need to study for my ventilation system checkout."

"I don't recall giving you a choice in the matter, mister," replied Bair sternly. Then, in a less severe tone, he said, "Jerry, your dedication is commendable and you've made a good start on your quals. But after many days of very long hours and very little sleep, your brain WILL turn into tomato paste and you WILL be worthless." Bair covered the closed book with his hand. "I've been peeking in on you over the past hour and you have been staring at the same page the whole time. I bet you don't even know what ventilation lineup you were looking at."

Jerry smiled weakly and looked down at the closed book in front of him. "No bet, sir."

"All right, then. I want you to go home, take a long hot shower, and then get some sleep in a bed that is larger than a coffin. You'll feel a lot better and you'll be more alert in the morning."

Of course, the XO was right—again. Even though Jerry felt like he had to be working virtually every hour of every day, it just wasn't practical. Jerry then came to the realization that the race he was running was a marathon, not the hundred-yard dash. He had to learn to pace himself if he was going to complete all that he had set out to do. Once Jerry had accepted that idea, it was a little easier to take some personal time off, but every now and then he still needed a gentle reminder from the XO to hit the beach. Jerry also realized an unexpected benefit from Bair's nagging. Some of the other officers and chiefs noticed the considerable effort that Jerry applied to all his duties, including his qualifications, and that the XO often had to tell him to get off the boat.

Word also started to get around from those who gave Jerry his checkouts that he came prepared and usually did very well. Hard work and competence is a winning combination in the submarine force and it often earns respect. It took some time, but the chill in the wardroom toward him started to thaw. And while things were still strained between him and Cal Richards, at least the WEPS wasn't quite so cutting with the sarcasm now. Unfortunately, the same could not be said of Senior Chief Foster.

If anything, Foster had become harder to deal with. When they were alone, Foster was borderline insubordinate and only a little more civilized when they were in the company of others. Jerry just couldn't figure out what was wrong between them.

He tried hard to iron things out, but Jerry's attempts at reconciling their problems only made things worse. Jerry found that he could work with Foster only by being extremely specific in his orders and following up to make sure that Foster hadn't left him hanging with the job half-done. It took a lot of energy, attention, and time he didn't have.

It wasn't the best way of doing business, and Jerry certainly wasn't happy with the situation, but he'd have to make it work for now. Thinking about the dysfunctional relationship with his leading chief only made Jerry tense, and he took a couple of deep breaths to ease his stress. As he let out a big sigh, a voice from below broke his moment of silent reflection.

"Excuse me, sir," said the voice. "We need to rig the bridge for the surface transit and it's going to be tight with you up here. Would you mind going below until we're finished? It should only take about twenty minutes."

Jerry looked down as a petty officer emerged from the shadows of the bridge access trunk. There were hints of another man below, along with the sounds of gear being hauled up. Jerry watched as the sailor climbed up into the cockpit, squinting hard as he emerged into the sunlight.

"Bright enough for you, Petty Officer Stewart?" asked Jerry.

"Certainly is, sir," said Stewart as he stood there blinking. "Please disregard the dull *klunks*, sir. It's only my pupils slamming shut."

Jerry grinned and maneuvered out of the way as a Plexiglas windscreen appeared from below. Stewart grabbed the screen and set it down on the top of the sail behind him. The cockpit was nothing more than a small opening, four feet by three feet, in the forward part of the sail. Normally, it would be cramped with just three men in the cockpit, but trying to install all the gear with that many people would be very difficult indeed.

"I'll get out of your way, Petty Officer Stewart. Enjoy the nice weather," said Jerry.

"Thank you, sir. Hey, Jack, hold on a second, Mr. Mitchell is coming down."

Jerry ducked under the sail and worked his way around the other sailor, who he could barely see in the dim light. When he got to the top of the bridge access trunk itself, Jerry yelled, "Down ladder." After making sure no one was below him, he climbed down the ladder into control. Once down, he reported to the duty petty officer that he was no longer on the bridge. The sailor acknowledged the report and wiped Jerry's grease-penciled name off the status board.

With that taken care of, Jerry headed toward the torpedo room for one final inspection. After that, he would meet with the Navigator and the scheduled Officer of the Deck, Lieutenant Millunzi, to go over the boat's departure route one more time. As Jerry descended the ladder to forward compartment lower level, the 1MC crackled to life, "There are men working in the sail. Do not raise or lower any mast or antenna. Do not rotate, radiate, or energize any electronic equipment while men are working in the sail."

Glancing at his watch, Jerry marked the time and toyed with the idea of testing Stewart's estimated time to rig the bridge. Anything to get back topside and get underway, eh? Jerry thought. There was no doubt in his mind that he was eager to go to sea. It had been nearly four years since his last Midshipman cruise and that had been on a large-deck amphibious assault ship. His total time underway on a submarine could be measured in hours, single digits at that, and the thought of being at sea for three whole days sounded absolutely wonderful. Jerry recalled hinting at this during Quarters that morning and how most of the division laughed at his naïveté.

"Worst case of Newbeeitis I've seen in all my years on subs," joked Bearden.

"Seems to be resistant to treatment too," added TM2 Tom Boyd. "You'd think Fast Cruise would have cured him!" This comment brought more laughter, as the counterintuitive three-day, in-port drill period had been grueling and anything but fun.

"Can the levity. We still have work to do before we get underway, so turn to," barked a scowling Foster.

Jerry remembered the tension that descended immediately on the group and that only TM1 Moran had walked away before Jerry dismissed his division. The glare from Foster was intense, and only hinted at his anger. Jerry ignored it. The senior chief seemed to be angry a lot lately, probably because Foster sensed that Jerry was slowly gaining the trust of his men, and for some reason this threatened him. Work began in the torpedo room in near silence.

Making his way back to the torpedo room, Jerry saw that the atmosphere had improved and that his guys were just finishing up the odds and ends. A number of the TMs and FTs were standing around talking and appeared to have relaxed some. Jerry nodded as they acknowledged his presence and walked over to the Manta control station and looked over the results of the system diagnostics he had started after Quarters. Everything looked good and he powered down the console.

The NUWC reps had worked on the prototype the week before, stripped the vehicle to parade rest, and performed every maintenance procedure known to mankind. After replacing the main and auxiliary batteries and a number of circuit cards, the Manta was issued a clean bill of health. Just as Jerry was pulling the Naugahyde cover over the control console, Richards walked into the room and quickly approached him. The WEPS seemed to be more harried than usual.

"Mr. Mitchell, what is the status of your division?" demanded Richards. Jerry was momentarily confused, as he had already given the WEPS his report earlier. Once again, Cal Richards had his sweat pumps in high speed and anything but a repeat of his earlier report would only add to the WEPS' consternation.

"Sir, the torpedo room and fire-control system are ready for sea. Repairs to the Mk19 weapons launching console have been completed. We have five Mk48 Mod 5 torpedoes on board; one is loaded in tube two and the remaining four are secured in the port storage racks. Tube one has the NMRS retrieval arm installed and is not capable of firing weapons. The Manta prototype has been cleared for at-sea operations and *two* runs of the daily diagnostics have been completed satisfactorily."

"Very well," responded Richards with a calmer voice. "Has the OOD's status board been updated?"

"Yes, sir. Senior Chief Foster is doing that as we speak," answered Jerry confidently.

"Good. Now move along or you'll be late for the last pre-underway brief with the NAV and MPA."

"Aye, aye, sir," replied Jerry with eagerness.

The brief was short, to the point, and very professional. The Navigator went over all the points where course changes were needed to keep *Memphis* in the center of the channel and all the associated turn bearings and landmarks.

He also reviewed the procedures for getting underway. Lieutenant Al Millunzi listened carefully as he studied the projected track on the New London harbor chart and asked questions about which tug they'd have, who was the pilot, and what was the updated weather forecast for the Long Island and Block Island sounds.

As the Main Propulsion Assistant (MPA), Millunzi was responsible for the boat's main mechanical systems. Tom Holtzmann's reactor made the steam, but it was Millunzi's systems that put it to work. Driving not only the main propulsion turbines that turned the screw, but also the ship's service turbine generators that provided electricity. He was also the next most senior officer in the Engineering Department, after the Engineer himself, and was completely qualified to stand in for him if necessary. Millunzi also had the reputation on the waterfront as being one of the best shiphandlers in the squadron. Hence his pairing with the very inexperienced Jerry Mitchell.

In his late twenties, Millunzi had a big, square face and a nose that could have belonged to Julius Caesar. He had a frame that matched and had to carefully work to fit his way through the many narrow hatches and passageways on *Memphis*. Although Jerry knew where he stood with many of the ship's officers, for good or ill, he hadn't had to deal with Millunzi much during his month and a half aboard. Their respective responsibilities kept them pretty much apart. Fortunately, the MPA was all business, but he wasn't taking any chances.

"Jerry, before you give any order, I want you to tell me what you want to do and what you're going to say. If I agree, I'll say so, and you can go ahead. If I've got a problem, and there's time, I'll give you a chance to rethink your plan. If there isn't, I'll take the conn and sort things out. I will also ask you questions during our run to the dive point. And they won't be academic. Is this all clear?"

"Yes, sir," Jerry answered. In a way, Jerry felt a little relieved. Millunzi wasn't going to let him make any big mistakes. And Millunzi wouldn't take over unless Jerry was really messing up; in which case Jerry wanted the MPA to take over. But that wasn't going to happen, Jerry thought. Not on his watch.

After the brief, both O'Connell and Millunzi quizzed Jerry on the conning orders he would have to give to get *Memphis* away from the pier, down the Thames River, and out to the Atlantic Ocean. Jerry answered the questions correctly, but he was not always confident of his response. Despite this, the Navigator seemed satisfied that Jerry had a reasonable idea of what to do and how to do it.

"All right, Mr. Mitchell, report to the bridge in fifteen minutes," said O'Connell looking at his watch. "I want an on-time departure at 1100."

"Aye, aye, sir," responded Jerry. But just as he was about to head down to his stateroom, Captain Hardy came bounding up the ladder screaming at Lieutenant Commander Ho, *Memphis'* Engineer.

"What the hell are you doing down there, Engineer? Why did the pump fail this time?"

"Captain, the motor controller blew about ten minutes ago when we tried to pump the sanitary tanks in preparation for our departure. It will take several hours to make the repairs," responded Ho nervously.

"If you haven't noticed, Engineer, we don't have several hours! The squadron commander will be here any moment now," exclaimed Hardy shaking his head in disbelief. Getting a hold of himself Hardy asked, "How full are the sanitary tanks?"

"Sir, sanitary tanks number one and number two are about fifty percent, and sanitary tank number three is about twenty-five percent."

"Very well, have the duty officer get the drydock connections removed and we'll blow the tanks once we are at sea."

"Yes, sir, and we'll begin working on the sewer discharge pump immediately," replied Ho.

"That would be very wise, Engineer," responded Hardy sarcastically. "I also want the maintenance logs for that pump, here, in my stateroom, within the hour. I want to know the idiot who performed the last preventative maintenance check and missed such an obvious problem." With that, Hardy slammed the stateroom door shut in his Engineer's face. Ho backed away, his face still a little pale, combed his hand through his hair, and trudged down the ladder to forward compartment middle level.

Jerry watched as the tired-looking man disappeared from view. He wasn't surprised at the CO's tirade; he'd seen far too many of those over the past weeks. Millunzi walked up behind Jerry and said in a low voice, "I would not want to be Frank Lopez right now. That's his gear and the Captain will be all over his butt on account of this latest incident. Not that the Captain will bother to remember that we've had nothing but trouble from that particular pump for almost two years now and that our requests for a replacement have been repeatedly denied." The MPA then looked at Jerry and said, "The shit pump has had a bad habit of eating motor controllers. Now, get a move on and I'll see you up on the bridge."

Reaching his stateroom, Jerry found Lenny Berg putting his jacket on. A life jacket and safety harness were on the deck by his feet. "Ahh, our intrepid JOOD arrives to mentally prepare for his first underway. Need any Maalox?"

"Ha, ha, very funny, Lenny. I happen to feel just fine, thank you." A little lie, Jerry thought, because he was a tad nervous and could feel it in his stomach.

Berg was about to fire another round of witticisms when the squawking of the 1MC interrupted their exchange, "COMSUBDEVRON TWELVE, arriving."

"Well, well, the commodore is finally here. I bet the Captain is having a snit fit over something right now, even as his boss is crossing the gangway," said Berg seriously.

"Yeah, well, he just chewed out the Engineer over the sewer discharge pump. The motor controller was fried."

"Hmmm, not like *that* hasn't happened before." Then, in a more light-hearted way, Berg remarked, "Maybe the pump just wants a new job, and frying motor controllers is its way of expressing its frustration. I mean, moving human waste around isn't all that glamorous, you know."

Jerry laughed as he put on his jacket and ball cap. He then started digging through his desk, looking for his sunglasses. Finding them, he put them in his pocket and turned to face Berg.

"Lenny, is the Captain always this nervous when getting underway?"

Berg laughed. But the laughter was forced mixture of amusement and irony. "It's because of Captain Young. As long as the squadron commander is on board, everything has to be perfect."

Berg picked up the life jacket and harness and then looked at Jerry with a smile and said, "Correction, more than perfect."

Jerry nodded, understanding his friend's observation, and asked. "This is Hardy's first boat, isn't it? Is he all that eager to get promoted?"

"I don't really know, Jerry," Berg answered. "But I don't think it's all about ambition. Remember, he is a triple A personality control freak."

"Hey, Lenny," Jerry called out to his friend as he was leaving. "You be careful out on deck. I really don't want to get signed off on the man overboard drill today."

"Yes, sir! Oh Wise and Benevolent Junior Officer of the Deck, sir," mocked Berg as he bowed and doffed his cap. "Just don't go and pull any five-gee turns while you're up there and we'll be fine."

Jerry rolled his eyes at Berg's last comment and followed him out of the stateroom. As Jerry entered control, he saw the XO getting ready to set the maneuvering watch. A bit early, given the schedule in the plan of the day, but not unexpected, given Hardy's nervous state. Looking up from the navigation plotting tables, Bair saw Jerry over by the duty petty officer reporting in. As Jerry made his way to the ladder, the XO called over, "Mr. Mitchell, good luck on your first underway." Winking, he added, "Just keep her between the buoys and you'll do fine."

"Aye, sir, I'll do my best," Jerry replied as he gave his XO an informal salute. Lifting his head to the bridge access trunk, Jerry yelled, "Up ladder," and started climbing.

The bridge was prepared for sea with an assortment of electronic gadgets installed in the cockpit. The portable "bridge suitcase" with the communications gear and navigation instruments had been installed and tested.

Since anything left on the bridge would be exposed to extreme water pressure when the boat submerged, the instruments used to conn *Memphis* were built into a removable case that could be quickly detached when the boat was ready to submerge. Next to the suitcase were an electronic chart plotter and a GPS receiver. A satchel bag lashed to the side contained paper charts, a flashlight, and a bullhorn. The Plexiglas windscreen had been secured in front of the cockpit, along with a grease pencil on a string. Behind Jerry was the "flying bridge," an area atop the sail where an installed steel frame allowed additional people to stand safely while the ship made its surface transit.

Jerry checked the pier. The boat was divorced from shore power and the sanitary and potable water connections had also been removed. A small crane was working its way down the pier; it would be needed to lift the gangplank off the sub's hull. Down on the deck, Jerry could see the line handlers mustering with the COB and Lenny Berg. Undoubtedly, the COB was reminding everyone about the proper safety precautions when handling the bulky mooring lines.

He looked at his pocket checklist to make sure he had gone over everything he would have to do to get the sub underway. He was thankful he had spent some extra time studying, even though he had fallen asleep the night before while reviewing Dutton's *Naval Shiphandling*. But not all knowledge can be gained through an intensive book study effort. Theoretically, he knew what to do. Now it was time to put that theory into practice.

Noises from below told Jerry that others were coming up. Within a few seconds, a familiar voice spoke, "Permission to come up to the bridge."

"Granted," replied Jerry.

Petty Officer Stewart climbed into the cockpit with a pair of binoculars and a sound-powered phone headset. "Here you go, sir," said Stewart as he handed the binoculars to Jerry. Jerry took them and thanked Stewart, who was busily putting on the sound-powered phones. Soon thereafter, Lieutenant Millunzi climbed up the ladder and joined Jerry in the cockpit. Millunzi had barely straightened up when he began bombarding Jerry with questions on the status of the bridge equipment and the topside area below. Jerry answered them quickly and concisely. Satisfied, Millunzi turned to Jerry and said, "Jerry, this is the one time that I will give you free advice. After this I charge a can of soda for every problem you want me to help you with." The smirky grin on Millunzi's face told Jerry that the MPA was quite serious.

"In that case, sir, what is your favorite liquid refreshment? Because I'm going to need a couple of six-packs to get me through our upcoming deployment."

"Dr Pepper, of course. And you'd better make it three."

Both men chuckled a bit and Jerry started feeling a little less tense. He didn't realize just how anxious he was as he waited for things to get started.

"The secret of being a good shiphandler, Jerry, is to be able to manage inertia and momentum," said Millunzi in a more sober tone. "You are used to driving a fighter that doesn't weigh a lot but goes really fast. *Memphis* weighs several thousand tons and moves at a snail's pace, by comparison." He then pointed aft and asked, "What do you see back there, Jerry?"

Jerry faced aft and after a moment turned back toward the MPA, looking confused. "I don't understand, sir."

Millunzi pointed toward *Memphis'* stern and said. "What do you see?"

Jerry looked again. "The rudder, sir?"

"Exactly!" shouted Millunzi happily. "Half of the rudder, your control surface, is out of the water flapping in the breeze, where it doesn't do a damn thing for you. She's great underwater, but on the surface and at slow speed, *Memphis* is a pig. She won't respond quickly to rudder orders, so you have to think way ahead if you are going to effectively maneuver her. That's the deceptive part of conning a sub on the surface: They move slow enough so that you think you have plenty of time to get out of trouble. In fact, if you don't react in time, which means early, inertia will take over and ruin your entire day."

"Mr. Millunzi, sir," interrupted Stewart. "The XO reports that the maneuvering watch is set and that the Captain, the Commodore, and the pilot will be up shortly."

"Very well," responded Millunzi. Picking up the microphone and handing it to Jerry, he added, "Okay, Jerry, time to take the conn. You know what needs to be said. Just take a deep breath and let the maneuvering party know who is giving the rudder orders."

Reaching for the mike, Jerry actually felt his hand shake a little. "Attention in the maneuvering party. This is Lieutenant (j.g.) Mitchell; I have the conn. Lieutenant Millunzi retains the deck."

One by one, the various positions acknowledged the announcement.

"Helm aye."

"Nav aye."

"Radio aye."

"Contact coordinator aye."

"Maneuvering aye."

"See? That wasn't so hard. Ahh, here is our friendly tug to assist us," said Millunzi.

Jerry looked up and saw a small red and black tug, with a great big yellow capital T on its black stack, maneuvering into position on *Memphis'* port quarter. The handheld radio crackled to life and Millunzi exchanged a communications check and greetings with the master of the tug *Paul A. Wronowski*—or "*Tug Paul*" for short. Once *Memphis* was firmly secured to *Tug Paul*, Millunzi grabbed the bullhorn and shouted, "On deck, single up all lines!" The linehandlers quickly moved to reduce the number of lines between *Memphis'* cleats and the pier's bollards from two to one.

Millunzi was getting ready to say something when Hardy, climbing up the ladder, interrupted him. "Captain to the bridge."

Both junior officers crammed themselves to one side to make room for Hardy, the commodore, and the pilot to come up from the bridge access trunk. After the three of them were situated on the flying bridge, Hardy asked, "Mr. Millunzi, are we ready?"

"Just finishing the final arrangements topside, sir." He nodded to Jerry. "I was instructing Mr. Mitchell on some of the trickier parts of conning a submarine on the surface."

"Hmpf," replied Hardy, turning to face Jerry. "Mr. Mitchell, I agreed with the XO's recommendation that we make you the conning officer for the maneuvering watch, in spite of the fact that you have only been a member of my crew for a short period of time. This is a required assignment for all junior officers and you need the experience. I wish your first time underway was under different circumstances, but there are no easy underways on my boat."

Jerry could only nod. "Yes, sir, I'll do my best."

"What's the hand signal for a tug to make half speed?"

"Point with your index finger in the direction you want the tug to push, either ahead or astern."

It was the correct answer, but Hardy only frowned. "Will you be using hand signals today?"

"No, sir. With *Tug Paul*'s bridge facing aft, it would be better to use the handheld radio to reduce the chance of a misunderstanding."

Again, Jerry gave the correct answer. Hardy looked unimpressed. "Very well, make your report."

Jerry looked at Millunzi, who nodded slightly, and then began the long and detailed report on the status of *Memphis'* preparation for getting underway. This formal, almost ritualistic, approach ensured that the Captain and the Officer of the Deck were both working with the same information. And while a good CO probably already knew everything his OOD was reporting, double checks were never wasted.

Completing his report, Jerry requested permission to get underway. Hardy took a quick look around, and once satisfied that his JOOD had made an accurate report, said, "Permission granted."

Picking up the radio, Jerry called over to the tug, "*Tug Paul*, this is U.S. Navy submarine, stand by for tug orders."

"Roger," squawked the radio.

"On deck," Jerry yelled through the bullhorn. "Take in all lines!" The line handlers below started pulling frantically on the mooring lines to get them all on board as quickly as possible. As the last line came over, Jerry pulled the lever for the ship's horn and let loose a prolonged blast. This told everyone in the harbor that a boat was getting underway. At the same time, Stewart hoisted a large U.S. flag on a pole behind the flying bridge.

"*Tug Paul*, back one third," Jerry commanded. As the diesel engines on the tug roared to life, *Memphis* began to slowly pull away from the pier. Jerry watched as the distance between them increased. Turing toward Millunzi, Jerry asked, "Enough?"

"Wait. Give it a few more seconds," replied Millunzi. "Okay, now."

"*Tug Paul*, all stop." Picking up the mike, Jerry issued his first conning order. "Helm, bridge, back one third, left full rudder."

"Bridge, helm, maneuvering answers back one third, my rudder is left full with no ordered course."

"Very well, helm."

Jerry immediately looked aft to make sure the rudder had been turned in the correct direction, but with so many people on the bridge he had a hard time seeing the rudder. When it took him a little too long to do this, Millunzi prompted him, "Don't forget the tug, Jerry. You need her horsepower to get us out properly."

Fumbling for the radio, Jerry ordered the tug ahead one third. As *Memphis* moved slowly into the Thames River, Millunzi leaned over and said, "Watch the stern and make sure it swings to port. A submarine with stern way on is very unpredictable. It's easier with a tug, but you still need to keep a close eye on it. There! Do you see it? The stern is starting to swing."

Jerry didn't see it at first, but after a moment, he also spotted the slight swing to the left. Millunzi is very good at this, thought Jerry. As the sub continued its slow arc into the river, Jerry watched the compass repeater on the suitcase and digital map display. Once *Memphis* came within thirty degrees of the channel course, Millunzi whispered, "Let inertia work for you now." Jerry ordered the rudder amidships and all stop. He then ordered *Tug Paul* to answer all stop, and then to take in all lines. Jerry politely thanked the tug master over the radio for his services.

Once the tug was clear, *Memphis* was free to begin moving downriver. Jerry felt the deck begin to vibrate as *Memphis*' screw bit into the river. It felt a little like his fighter at full military power, but once the sub's backward motion was countered, and she started moving forward, the vibrations subsided.

As they left the area of the sub base, Jerry Mitchell, an aviator by first choice, was now finally on his way to becoming a submariner. The sounds and smells of the river and especially the sights of the historic Thames filled his senses. The well-settled, cluttered shoreline testified to how long men and ships had been here. As they passed the Submarine Museum, Jerry saw the *Nautilus* moored to her quay. A little over fifty years ago, he thought, she would have taken this same route out to sea. *Memphis* passed under the I-95 and railroad bridges within two minutes of the planned time. The initial part of Jerry's underway had gone remarkably smoothly. The Navigator would be pleased.

As they came up on the Electric Boat construction yard, the boat for the pilot pulled alongside and he bid farewell to the Captain and expressed his best wishes for a successful sea trial.

But before he went below, the pilot slapped Jerry on the back and said, "That was a very reasonable underway, Lieutenant. You made a few minor mistakes here and there, of which I'm sure Mr. Millunzi here will tell you all about in fine detail. However, for a first time out you did well. Good luck on the rest of your qualifications." A few minutes later, with the pilot gone, the topside rigged for dive, and the last man down, Jerry increased speed to eight knots.

After another fifteen minutes, *Memphis* passed New London Ledge Light, the square redbricked lighthouse that marked the mouth of the Thames River. As Jerry ordered the speed increased to ahead standard, about twelve knots, the commodore climbed down from the flying bridge. "Excuse me, gentlemen, but I'm going below." Turning toward Jerry, Captain Young said, "Mr. Mitchell, my compliments on a fine first underway. Keep up the good work."

"Thank you, sir," replied Jerry.

The commodore then looked up at Hardy, "Captain, I suggest we meet in your stateroom to go over the drill schedule for the next two days. Say, in fifteen minutes?"

Hardy looked pained by the commodore's "suggestion," but acknowledged the order with a perfunctory "Aye, aye, sir."

For the next ten minutes, all that could be heard on the bridge was the wind and waves flowing past the submarine's hull. Visibly disgusted that he had to leave the bridge, Hardy climbed down into the cockpit and addressed Millunzi. "MPA, strike down and stow the flying bridge and then get us to the dive point as quickly as you can. If you need me, I'll be in my stateroom."

Millunzi acknowledged the Captain's order and had Stewart relay the order to control for two sailors to come up and disassemble the flying bridge. As Hardy was about to go below, he turned toward Jerry and said, "Don't let the commodore's comment go to your head, Mitchell. By my standards, your performance was adequate. Nothing more."

"Yes, sir," replied Jerry, more surprised than hurt. As soon as Hardy had disappeared into the bridge access trunk, Millunzi shook his head and issued a short snicker.

"Away the morale suppression team," cried Millunzi. "The floggings will continue until morale improves."

Both Jerry and Stewart laughed softly at the MPA's sarcastic comment, and a lot of the tension Jerry had felt seemed to wash away. He was also relieved that the senior officers had departed the bridge. Now he could freely ask Millunzi for an honest critique of his performance.

As if he were reading Jerry's mind, Millunzi said, "We'll go over the mistakes the pilot mentioned once we get out of the channel. Then we can open her up and have some real fun."

"Sounds good to me, sir," Jerry replied. "For the record, how many did I make?"

"Five minor ones, that's all. And despite the Captain's views, you done good for your first time out."

Five! Thought Jerry. He was having a hard time thinking of more than three. Still, he was pleased with Millunzi's compliment. The two sailors summoned to the bridge now arrived. They immediately began to take the flying bridge down, handing sections of piping that made up the frame to Stewart, who passed them below. Millunzi urged them to work quickly, but not to skip on safety.

"What's the rush, sir?" asked Jerry.

Millunzi pointed to two buoy symbols on the map display and then to a pair of red and green flashing buoys a couple of miles in the distance. "Those are buoys two and three. They mark the mouth of the channel. Once we pass them, we can rev this puppy up to flank speed. Provided these turkeys get their act together and get the flying bridge taken apart." Millunzi grinned while jerking his thumb in the general direction of the two sailors up on the sail.

"In the meantime, Jerry, we need to crank up the RCPs soon."

"Yes, sir!" Jerry looked back and saw that the last of the frame was just about detached from the sail. Reaching down, Jerry picked up the mike and said, "Maneuvering, bridge, shift reactor coolant pumps to fast speed."

"Shift reactor coolant pumps to fast speed, bridge, maneuvering aye."

A few moments later the suitcase speaker blared, "Bridge, maneuvering, reactor coolant pumps are in fast speed."

"Maneuvering, bridge aye."

The buoys were clearly visible and they would soon be passing them. The two sailors reported that they were done and the flying bridge had been stowed for sea. Millunzi acknowledged their report and the two went below. A few minutes later the suitcase speaker blared again, "Bridge, Navigator, two hundred yards to the turn point. New course, one six five."

"Navigator, bridge aye," replied Jerry.

"Okay, Jerry, this is a small course change, so what are you going to do?"

"Just order the helmsman to use ten degrees left rudder and steady on the new course," answered Jerry confidently.

"Correct."

"Bridge, Navigator, mark the turn!"

"Helm, bridge, left ten degrees rudder, steady course one six five."

"Left ten degrees rudder, steady course one six zero, bridge, helm aye."

As *Memphis* started turning, Jerry could feel the difference that eight knots of speed made in her response. She quickly came up on her new course and settled in for the long run through the Long Island and Block Island sounds out to the Atlantic Ocean.

"All right, Jerry, let's pick up the pace, shall we?" said Millunzi with a gleam in his eye.

"Aye, aye, sir." Keying the mike again, Jerry spoke, "Helm, bridge, all ahead flank!"

"All ahead flank, bridge, helm aye. Sir, maneuvering answers all ahead flank."

"Very well, helm."

As *Memphis* began to surge ahead, the bow wave grew larger and larger until it was crashing against the base of the sail. The roar of the water as it flowed over the hull was deafening. Jerry felt as if he was at the base of Niagara Falls as tons of water came crashing down. The deck trembled as the main propulsion turbines slammed 35,000 shaft horsepower into the screw, which chewed up the water like a blender. *Memphis'* wake was frothy and huge and could be seen for miles in the bright sunlight. Salt spray was thrown high into the air as the bow plowed through the slight rolling waves. And even with the protection of the Plexiglas windscreen, Jerry and the others were still occasionally hit in the face with cold seawater.

Jerry looked over at Al Millunzi and saw that he had removed his ball cap, his black hair streaming in the stiff wind. Meeting Jerry's gaze, Millunzi leaned over and yelled, "I defy you to find a better mode of transportation than this!"

"Honestly, sir, I don't think I can!" Jerry yelled back—and he meant every word. True, flying at supersonic speeds, yanking and banking, was a surefire way to get an incredible rush. But what he was feeling now was even stronger. In fact, he probably had so much adrenaline running in his system right now that it was making his stomach a little bit queasy. As the wind and spray whipped by his face, Jerry was finally able to let go of his precious F-18E Super Hornet. His heart and soul now belonged to another: *Memphis*.

For the next hour, Jerry reveled in his new love. Millunzi quizzed Jerry on various situations they might encounter and pointed out the major landmarks as they sped past them. Of particular interest was Race Rock, the wave-lashed lighthouse on a bunch of rocks at the westernmost tip of Fishers Island. This lighthouse marked the northern end of the passage known as "The Race," the boundary between Long Island Sound and Block Island Sound.

Traffic was very light, with only a single contact, a long black barge pushed by a tug. It was coming up from the south and appeared to be heading straight for the entrance to the New London harbor channel. It was several miles distant and drawing away, designated "Master Two" by the Contact Coordinator. Since it was held both visually and on radar, it wasn't a navigation hazard.

Finally *Memphis* passed between Block Island and Montauk Point on Long Island and entered the Atlantic Ocean proper. As soon as they cleared Long Island, the seas became rougher and the boat started to pitch and roll a little.

"We are now out of the lee of Long Island, so we are no longer being protected from the wind. This means the ride will be rougher for the rest of our run to the dive point," commented Millunzi.

Now *Memphis* was heading for the open sea. Instead of land on both sides of them or filling one side of the horizon, it was just a small dark line behind them, growing thinner with each minute. The broad horizon was as novel to Jerry as everything else, but it was unchanging. Within a few minutes, he'd worked out a routine of checking the compass, the radar repeater, the map display, then scanning the horizon with his binoculars. There was no other surface traffic in sight.

"How much longer?" asked Jerry.

"About three hours until we're past the hundred-fathom curve. About here." Millunzi tapped the map display.

As Jerry looked down at the instruments, the bow rose a little more steeply than before and fell back to the sea with a noticeable drop. Jerry automatically tightened his grip on the edge of the cockpit and shifted his weight.

Millunzi grinned. "Nothing like this in a fighter, is there?"

"No, we usually flew well above any turbulence," Jerry answered, "or we were yanking and banking and—" Jerry's stomach suddenly flipped—or felt like it did. Puzzled, he straightened and tried to continue. "If we did hit turbulence, it was really more like a bumpy road than this pitching or rolling movement." He had to force the last word out, because as his mind was drawn to the motion, a wave of weakness and nausea passed through him.

"Jerry, what's wrong? You're white as a sheet!" Millunzi sounded puzzled and concerned.

Jerry swallowed hard, fighting reflexively to control his rebellious insides. As he struggled, *Memphis* pitched forward and lurched to the right. His stomach surged upward, and only by a supreme effort did he force its contents back down.

This was impossible. He'd flown all kinds of maneuvers in jet fighters. He couldn't . . ."

Hot flashes and cold chills ran across his skin. The nausea was overwhelming. His stomach made another attempt to empty itself, and he flung himself to the side of the cockpit and leaned out as far as he could. It wasn't a conscious decision to throw up, just an automatic reaction to avoid making a mess in the cockpit.

Millunzi and Stewart watched in amazement as Jerry threw up violently, or more correctly, threw out and then back as the wind caught the vile substance and pulled it aft, spreading it along the sail. It was pure luck that he'd chosen the leeward and not the windward side.

As he threw up, Jerry hoped that once his stomach had emptied itself, the nausea would pass. But just as soon as the first spasm stopped, another began. The gut-churning misery continued for several minutes, until his cramping stomach muscles were too exhausted to contract.

Jerry turned back, leaning weakly on the edge, and wiped his mouth with a handkerchief.

Both Millunzi and Stewart looked at him and burst into laughter. "Look at him. He's actually green!" the enlisted man exclaimed.

"I'm sorry," Millunzi apologized, but still laughing. "It was your expression."

Too near death to respond, Jerry struggled with this new affliction. The novelty and surprise of his seasickness were gone, but the weakness and nausea remained. Could he function? He had to, but all he wanted to do was lie down somewhere. Or throw himself over the side. He really didn't care.

Jerry didn't know which was worse: the terrible fact that he was seasick or the embarrassment of throwing up. He didn't have long to reflect on his dilemma as his stomach lurched again and Jerry had to lean over the edge. In tears from his laughter, Millunzi tried to show some sympathy for his pathetically green JOOD.

"Ahh God, Jerry, *sniff*, I'm truly sorry that you're sick. Really I am!" said Millunzi apologetically. "But I haven't seen someone emergency blow his cookies like that for a long time, and while you probably won't believe this, it is rather humorous."

Jerry could only moan a response, but his glare made it clear that he was not amused.

Petty Officer Stewart bent down and took something from a sailor below. Rising, he handed Millunzi a can and a small bag.

"Sir, this is from the Doc. He says make sure Mr. Mitchell takes the pills first."

"Thank you, Petty Officer Stewart. Okay, Jerry, get your sorry green butt over here. The corpsman has sent up some stuff to help relieve your suffering."

Jerry took the Dramamine tablets and washed them down with sips of

Sprite. He then slowly nibbled on some saltine crackers and gradually began to feel somewhat human again. Millunzi watched him for a while and then asked, "Jerry, do you feel up to finishing up the watch or do you want to go below?"

"I finish what I start, sir," rasped Jerry. "So unless you specifically order me below, I'll stick it out."

"That's the spirit, lad. We'll make a real submariner out of you yet—even if it kills you!"

Jerry could only manage a feeble smile in response to Millunzi's remark. But he appreciated the sentiment behind it just the same. The boat rolled again and Jerry's stomach felt like it had been turned upside down.

"Uugghh, I can't believe I'm this seasick!" complained Jerry. "I never had any problems when I flew. I mean, I was never airsick!"

"Like I told you earlier: two very different platforms," said Millunzi as he chomped down on a Slim Jim. Jerry quickly turned away and kept munching his saltines.

For the next two hours, Jerry fought his queasiness and tried hard to concentrate on his duties. And while the medication reduced the effects of his seasickness, it certainly didn't get rid of them. Still, he managed to stand the rest of the watch without making a complete fool of himself. Next time, he thought, I'll get some of those patches that prevent this sort of thing from happening. Mercifully, the nearly six-hour-long surface transit finally drew to a close.

At 1711, control reported that the latest sounding was 115 fathoms, or 690 feet, and that it was almost time to dive the boat. Since Jerry and Millunzi would have to rig the bridge for dive, which would cause them to lose their ability to safely drive the sub, Lenny Berg assumed the deck and the conn down in control.

"Let's hop to it," announced Millunzi. "Petty Officer Stewart, you get the sound-powered phones and the colors while Mr. Mitchell and I get the suitcase and the other electronics."

Stewart acknowledged the order and pulled the sound-powered phones from the jack and screwed the cap over the external connection. Millunzi showed Jerry how the other equipment was removed and the external connections made watertight. Finally, the windscreen and flagpole were unbolted and handed down. Once everything had been removed, Millunzi and Jerry raised the clamshells and locked them into place. These two doors faired the cockpit area into the rest of the sail, presenting a smooth, streamlined surface to the water as it flowed over the sail. By doing this, a significant source of flow noise—like the tone that is made by blowing across an empty Coke bottle—was eliminated.

Jerry and Millunzi then climbed down the ladder, with Millunzi shutting and securing the upper and lower bridge access trunk hatches. After that,

Millunzi reported, "Chief of the Watch, the bridge is rigged for dive, last man down, hatch secure." The Chief of the Watch then reported to Berg that the ship was rigged for dive, that is, all conditions had now been met to allow the submarine to safely submerge.

Millunzi stepped up on to the periscope stand, talked briefly with Berg, and reassumed the watch as Officer of the Deck. Jerry waited until the two were done and then tried to join Millunzi. But before he could a second step, Lenny pulled him aside and said, "Al says you've done your job for today. He wants you to sit at POS 1 and carefully watch what goes on as he submerges the ship." When Jerry tried to resist, Berg grabbed him more firmly by the arm and pulled him over to the first fire-control position.

"Trust me on this, Jerry, Al is doing this for your own good. If the Captain saw you wobbling up there as the conning officer with Captain Young on board, he'd give live birth to a litter of warthogs and then sic them on you! Now sit down."

Jerry looked up to Millunzi, who drew his right hand rapidly across his throat, meaning stop it, and then forcefully pointed for him to stay put. Recognizing an order when he saw one, Jerry nodded and sat down. No sooner had he done so, Captain Hardy marched into the control room and demanded to know the ship's status.

"OOD, report," bellowed Hardy.

Calmly, Millunzi began the lengthy report on the ship's condition. He provided Hardy with the current course and speed, information on any contacts held, navigation system status, depth of water beneath the keel, and finally, that the ship was rigged for dive. He then took a breath and requested permission to submerge the ship. Hardy paused briefly to check the compass repeater and speed indication on the ship's control panel. Satisfied with the report, he faced Millunzi and said, "Very well, OOD. Submerge the ship to one five zero feet."

"Submerge the ship to one five zero feet, aye, sir. Diving Officer, submerge the ship to one five zero feet."

As Jerry listened to the exchange and acknowledgment of orders, he realized that the same thing had just been said four times by three different people. To an outsider, this whole idea of repeating the same thing over and over again would seem absurd. However, the principle of repeating back orders was adopted by the Navy to help forge a solid communication chain so that the right people took the right actions at the right time. It wasn't foolproof, but it did considerably reduce the number of errors that were made.

"Dive! Dive!" announced the Diving Officer over the 1MC. Then, reaching for the diving alarm, he pushed the lever twice. *WREEEEEE, WREEEEEE* reverberated throughout the ship, closely followed by a second announcement, "Dive! Dive!"

Jerry then watched as the Diving Officer, Chief of the Watch, and the planesmen worked together to slowly drive *Memphis* underwater. Millunzi manned the periscope and kept providing the foursome with important feedback information on how things were going outside. It took several minutes, but Millunzi finally reported, "Scope's under, lowering number one scope."

Once *Memphis* was below one hundred feet, Millunzi called Berg over and said, "Get Jerry to his rack. He puked himself silly on the bridge and he's dog-tired. Doc Noonan said to give some more Sprite and saltines if he's hungry, but above all Doc said he needs rest."

"Aye, aye, Your OODness," responded Berg.

Jerry stood up, ready to protest, but then realized that he really did feel weak. All the adrenaline had worn off, and all that remained was the fatigue. Berg helped him up and started for the ladder to middle level when Jerry stopped, turned toward Millunzi and said, "Thanks for the sage advice, sir."

"You're welcome, Mr. Mitchell. But that will cost you a can," grinned Millunzi.

"Dr Pepper, right? You'll have it as soon as we get back, sir."

"Very good. Oh . . . and Jerry, when it's appropriate, you can call me Al." With that, Millunzi went back to the business of settling *Memphis* into her natural element.

"All right, green one, come with me," nagged Berg. "You've had a rough day and the doctor's orders must be obeyed. It's off to your rack for a few hours of blissful slumber so that you'll be well-rested and ready to face that vile creature, the drill monitor."

Jerry didn't remember even making it to his stateroom before he fell asleep.

6 Sea Trials and Errors

April 20, 2005

Atlantic Ocean

"FIRE IN THE GALLEY! CASUALTY ASSISTANCE TEAM LAY TO THE GALLEY! ALL HANDS DON EABS!" screeched the 1MC. Immediately after the announcement shattered the evening's silence, the ship's general alarm sounded. BONG, BONG, BONG, followed again by "FIRE IN THE GALLEY! CASUALTY ASSISTANCE TEAM LAY TO THE GALLEY! ALL HANDS DON EABS!"

"The man is a sadist!" whined Berg loudly as he tumbled out of his rack. As Jerry, Berg, and Washburn struggled into their poopy suits, Berg continued his lament with: "I might as well not even take the damn thing off at the rate we're going."

Reaching into one of the lockers, Jerry pulled out three bags with the Emergency Air Breathing system masks and handed Washburn and Berg one each.

"Come on, Lenny, get a move on. You're the CAT phone talker. The XO's going to be pissed as hell if you don't get to the galley pronto," warned Washburn.

"I know, I know. I'm going as fast as I can," replied Berg as he pulled the EAB mask over his face and tightened the straps. Plugging the hose connection into the one hundred pound air manifold, he took a couple of deep breaths, disconnected the hose and quickly moved out of the stateroom. Washburn followed Berg out as they both headed for the scene of the casualty. For the first time in the last two days, Jerry didn't have to go rushing off immediately, so he had a little more time to get ready before making his way to the wardroom. Normally, he would go to the torpedo room or the crew's mess during a casualty. But since the "fire" was in the galley across from the crew's mess, he would only be getting in the way of the casualty assistance team if he tried to go to either location. As the offgoing OOD, Berg was, by procedure, the designated sound-powered phone talker, so he had a reason to be at the scene. So too did Washburn who, as the Supply Officer, was responsible for the galley. Jerry's job was to stay out of the way and muster in the wardroom, where he would sit quietly breathing dry, metallic-tasting air. How exciting, he thought. Grabbing his qual notes, Jerry took a deep breath, unplugged his EAB, and walked quickly to the wardroom.

In the wardroom, Jerry found Tom Holtzmann already on the sound-powered phones passing reports to and from control. The Navigator was sitting next to him, listening to what was going on. Maneuvering over to the couch, Jerry plugged himself back into the air system and started breathing again. Sitting down, he began going over his notes on casualty procedures and tried to follow the drill through its stages.

"THE CAUSE OF THE FIRE IN THE GALLEY IS A FIRE IN THE DEEP-FAT FRYER," shouted Holtzmann loudly and slowly through his mask. Even so, he was barely understandable. Talking through an EAB mask is like trying to talk with your hand over your mouth. With every word muffled, any extraneous noise made verbal communication difficult at best. And with six guys breathing like Darth Vader, it was hard to hear what was going on.

"THE FIRE IS OUT," reported Holtzmann. "PREPARING TO EMERGENCY VENTILATE THE FORWARD COMPARTMENT WITH THE DIESEL."

Jerry sat back, closed his eyes, and tried to visualize what was going on in control. The small up angle indicated that the boat was already coming up to periscope depth. From the compass repeater on the bulkhead, Jerry saw that *Memphis* was turning slowly to the left. This would be the baffle-clearing maneuver, checking the area immediately behind the submarine where the hull arrays couldn't hear, to make sure there were no contacts behind them as they came shallow. After verifying the baffles were clear, the OOD would raise the periscope to visually check that the area was free of any close contacts. Sometimes it was difficult to hear even a large merchant ship on sonar if its bow was pointed right at the sub. The worst were Very Large Crude Carriers, or supertankers. They were amazingly quiet bow-on and had fully-loaded drafts of up to seventy-five feet. *Memphis* would be nothing more than a speed bump to one of those behemoths if she came up in front of one.

Once the OOD announced, "No close contacts," the Chief of the Watch would be ordered to raise the snorkel mast and test the head valve at the top of the mast. This verified that the head valve would close automatically when it got wet and would prevent seawater from rushing down into the boat and make things much worse. After opening the induction and diesel exhaust valves and clearing the lines of seawater, the emergency diesel could be started.

While the OOD and the rest of the ship's control party got *Memphis* positioned to snorkel, watchstanders in the various spaces would be placing dampers and vent valves in the correct position for the diesel to suck the air and smoke from the affected compartment and discharge it overboard. Fresh air would then be sucked down through the induction valves and replace the toxic atmosphere. After about thirty minutes, the air in the forward compartment would be breathable again. No sooner had Jerry finished his mental walk-through of the procedure when he heard "COMMENCE SNORKELING" over the 1MC. About a minute later, he could feel the vibration of the diesel running. The slight rolling of the boat told him that the sea state was pretty mild. Jerry allowed himself a small smile of satisfaction as he realized that he was becoming more confident of his ability to read the feel of the boat and his knowledge of emergency procedures.

"Secure snorkeling. Recirculate," spoke a clear voice over the 1MC a few minutes later. "Secure from drill. Drill monitors muster in the wardroom for the critique."

Jerry removed his EAB, unplugged it, gathered his notes, and headed back to his stateroom. He'd seen a number of these drill critiques and none were pretty. The Captain never seemed to be satisfied with the crew's performance and he would use these critique sessions to berate the officers and senior enlisted involved. Nobody left one of these meetings happy, so Jerry decided to clear datum before the Commodore and the Captain arrived.

Twenty minutes later, Berg and Washburn stumbled backed into the stateroom. Both were chortling and having a hard time restraining their glee. This was a very unusual outcome from a *Memphis* drill critique. The perplexed look on Jerry's face only made the two laugh some more.

"Oh man, Jerry, you missed a good one," said Berg with his usual pixie-like grin. "The Captain didn't even wait for the critique before he started chewing out the Chop here for having incompetent people in the galley. He was *sooooo* pissed off, I thought that he was going to lift a relief right then and there."

"Forgive my ignorance, Lenny, but why would this be funny?" replied a very confused Jerry. "It sounds like Bill here got his butt reamed in a major league way."

Berg was about to respond, when he stopped, waved flamboyantly at Washburn, and said, "Bill, this is your coup. Please enlighten Mr. Jerry here on the outcome of said ass-chewing."

"Thank you, Your Officerness," replied Washburn with an equally exaggerated hand gesture. "You see, while the Captain was busy winding himself into the overhead and yelling at me about how poorly trained my people were, the Commodore stepped out of galley behind him and just stood there listening. When the Captain demanded an explanation for the abysmal performance of my people, what pitiful excuse did I have for my MS2 not activating the fire-suppression system installed in the deep-fat fryer's exhaust hood, the Commodore butted in and said, 'Because I told him he was dead.' Oh Lord!" sputtered Washburn as both he and Berg struggled valiantly not to break out in loud laughter. "The look on CO's face was absolutely priceless!"

Jerry gasped and winced, "Ouch! Talk about being hoisted on one's own petard." The thought of Hardy being publicly embarrassed by his boss was both appalling and delightful. Given Hardy's predilection for public criticism, the concept of him getting a little dose of his own medicine from the Commodore was very satisfying. And yet, it flew in the face of everything Jerry had been taught at the Academy, and at the squadron, on the basic principles of leadership. Praise in public, correct in private was supposed to be a good officer's modus operandi. He hadn't seen too much of that on *Memphis*.

Still chuckling, Berg kicked off his shoes and climbed into his rack. "I don't know about you guys, but after thirteen drills in the last day and a half, I'm pooped."

"Hang in there, Lenny, my sources tell me there is only one drill left," said Washburn.

"And how would *you* know this?" asked Berg sarcastically.

"Do not underestimate the power of hot coffee and fresh chocolate chip cookies, young Jedi," Washburn replied. "The squadron staff has received both in large quantities, which gave my guys a number of opportunities to peek over their shoulder. According to their schedule, there is only one more drill after the interviews."

"Ah yes, caffeine and sugar, the Dark Side, are they," rasped Berg in his best Yoda-like voice. "Do you have any idea what the drill will be, Bill?"

"I think it is either a fire in the torpedo room or another approach and attack scenario."

"Oh boy, Jerry! Another one for you, you lucky dog," exclaimed Berg. "By the way, have you recovered from that dreadful Otto fuel spill drill they ran yesterday?"

"Yeah, I think so," said Jerry as he plopped back into his chair. "I just don't understand how we could have screwed up that casualty drill so badly. It's not like we haven't done similar drills before. We just seemed to always be running behind the power curve in responding to the casualty."

This was a bald-faced lie. Jerry was convinced that Senior Chief Foster had deliberately interfered with the division's response to the drill. According to TM3 Lee, the torpedo room watchstander, and one of the drill monitors, Foster appeared to have intentionally distracted Lee as the squadron staff member came into the room and dumped liquid orange Jell-O on the deck by the port storage rack. The Jell-O simulated a spill of Otto fuel, the monopropellant used by Mk48 ADCAP torpedoes.

While Otto fuel in and of itself is chemically hazardous, it is much worse if it catches fire. Because the fuel and oxygen are mixed together in a thick syrup-like fluid, an Otto fuel fire is extremely difficult to extinguish. If a hot fire was allowed to develop in close proximity to warshot torpedoes, it would likely lead to a catastrophic explosion and the loss of the sub. That kind of accident had destroyed the Russian guided-missile submarine *Kursk*.

Furthermore, the fumes from an Otto fuel fire are extremely toxic. So, even if the torpedo warheads didn't cook off, a lot of people would still get hurt or killed from the poisonous fumes. Hence, timely response to an Otto fuel spill is absolutely critical. By keeping the watchstander's attention away from his duties, Foster made sure that there was a significant delay in discovering the problem and getting the word out.

Then, during the actual casualty response, the drill schedule had Foster designated as the sound-powered phone talker for the casualty assistance team. As the man-in-charge at the scene, Jerry recalled all the problems he had communicating with control on the status of the cleanup. On several occasions, he had to repeat his report, two or even three times, before Foster would relay them to the OOD. By delaying the flow of information, the ship's crew took longer than it should have to respond to the simulated problem and their grade suffered because of it. The chewing out Jerry and his division received from Hardy was very unpleasant and humiliating. Foster's wicked grin only made it worse.

"Helloooo! Earth to Jerry, come in, please!" shouted Berg.

"Huh? Oh—sorry, Lenny. I was just going over the Otto fuel spill in my head again. I guess I'm still trying to figure out what went wrong."

"What's to figure out, you had bad comms with control and that will always screw you during a graded drill. Senior Chief Foster should have known better, but even the best of us have off days. So stop with the self-recriminations and get over it. You'll do better next time."

Jerry became a little angry at Berg's cavalier response. It was clear he had no idea that Foster had almost certainly sabotaged the drill, and it would be hard to do better next time if Foster continued to interfere. As Jerry considered correcting Berg's ignorance, Bair stuck his head into the room.

"Good afternoon, gentlemen. I gather you are enjoying yourselves, given all this laughter."

"No, sir, XO," said Berg soberly. "We're just a little punchy after so many drills, and I guess we got a little silly."

"I see. Well, get unsilly, as the inspection interviews will begin shortly. The Commodore has decided to only talk to the younger JOs. That means you and Jerry here. The Chop has been excused."

"Aye, aye, sir," replied Berg.

"They'll call you when it's your turn," said Bair. "Oh—and one more thing. Try to be confident when you answer his questions. Nothing is worse than appearing to be uncertain of your answer, and regardless of whether you're right or wrong, the interview can only go downhill from there. If you are uncertain, stick to the first one. At least be wrong with conviction. Understood?"

"Yes, sir," replied Jerry and Berg in unison.

No sooner had the Executive Officer departed than the Dialex in the stateroom rang. Washburn answered the phone, listened for a moment, and said, "Yes, sir, I'll let him know you're waiting for him." Hanging up, Washburn pointed at Berg and motioned toward the passageway. "Your turn, Lenny. The Spanish Inquisition awaits your presence in the wardroom."

Sighing, Berg once again crawled out of his rack and put on his shoes. "I *really* didn't want to take a short nap anyway," he said as he tied the laces. Berg then stood up, straightened his poopy suit, and marched out of the stateroom, executing a sharp square turn at the passageway. As he departed, Jerry and Washburn heard him utter in an English accent, "Alas, poor Leonard. I knew him well."

Jerry and Washburn looked at each other as their roommate left, both wondering whether Lenny Berg was slightly insane. Washburn then shrugged his shoulders and said, "Actors. You gotta love 'em."

As the Supply Officer settled into his rack, Jerry sincerely asked, "Bill, how did a theater major ever get into the nuclear power pipeline in the first place?"

"Only God and Naval Reactors know, Jerry," responded Washburn as he reached for the novel he had been reading. "Either Lenny is a really good actor or the Navy was really that desperate. Still, it's good to have the guy on board."

"Absolutely," replied Jerry as he sat down and opened his qual book to the diving officer section. He had just started reviewing some of the casualty procedures when Jerry heard a muffled snore. Looking over his shoulder, he saw that Washburn had fallen asleep before he had even finished a single page of the book. I know how you feel, thought Jerry. Stifling a yawn, he returned to his studies.

Jerry must have dozed off as well, for he found himself being lightly shaken by Berg who whispered, "Your turn, old boy." Jerry rose, stretched and headed for the wardroom. He knocked on the door and then entered. Captain Young was the only other person in the room.

"Reporting as ordered, sir," said Jerry while standing at attention.

"At ease, Mr. Mitchell. Please sit down," replied Young. Jerry quickly moved over to a chair and seated himself across from the commodore. "In my discussions with your XO," Young continued, "he tells me he is very pleased with the progress you've made on your qualifications thus far. He also says your pace to date is one of the fastest he's seen. I don't know whether you realize it or not, but that is high praise from Bob Bair. Especially since he qualified under me in record time on *Batfish* back in the midnineties."

"I've been fortunate, sir. The XO has been very supportive of my efforts and the Captain has given me numerous opportunities to get my drill requirements completed." Jerry winced internally and hoped that didn't sound too much like a backhanded compliment.

"I'm sure he has," replied Young matter-of-factly. "Still, you had to do the work necessary to capitalize on those opportunities and that is what has impressed your XO." Leaning back in his chair, Young opened a folder in front of him and examined its contents for a moment.

He then looked up at Jerry and said, "In reviewing your record, Lieutenant, I have to admit that I'm pleasantly surprised myself. I'll be frank with you. I was opposed to your transfer from aviation to submarines. I didn't like how you went about using family political ties to force the issue. But your performance to date has met or exceeded all the requirements placed on you. You graduated in the top twenty-five percent of your class at Nuclear Power School. You were the first officer to qualify as Engineering Officer of the Watch on your crew at prototype, as well as graduating third in your class overall. And you finished fourth in your class at the Officer's Basic course at Submarine School. I can't help but draw the conclusion that you are trying to prove a few flag officers wrong."

Jerry was getting more uncomfortable as Captain Young went on. He had been expecting questions on system specifications and procedures, not an overall evaluation of his past performance coupled with a statement that could be interpreted as an accusation, even if it was an accurate one.

"Sir, I made a promise to do my utmost if they approved my transfer. I'm just trying to hold up my end of the bargain."

"Relax, Lieutenant. I'm not accusing you of anything. Part of that deal you made required that your progress be reported up the chain at each phase. Since you've been assigned to my squadron, you're my responsibility now. I just thought you'd want to know the gist of my report."

"My apologies, sir. I guess I misunderstood what you meant by proving senior officers wrong," replied Jerry sheepishly. "And I do appreciate your comments, sir."

"Well, I suppose I better ask you at least one question before we move on to the next topic. I can't let you out of here with just a pep talk, now, can I?"

"Sir?" responded Jerry, curious as to what the commodore meant by the "next topic."

"How many EAB connections are there on this ship?"

Initially startled by the Commodore's question, Jerry quickly recovered and answered, "Approximately eight hundred sixty, sir."

"Really. Are you sure of that, mister?" demanded Young.

"Yes, sir. Absolutely, sir," replied Jerry.

"Very well, then. How do you justify that number?"

"There are one hundred sixty-nine EAB manifolds on this boat, and each manifold has four connections. That makes for a total of six hundred seventy-six connections in the EAB system itself. However, assuming a normal complement of one hundred thirty men and a one hundred and forty percent load out of EAB masks, and each mask has a connection on it, that gives another one hundred and eighty-two. This brings the grand total to eight hundred fifty-eight connections, sir."

"Am I to understand that you've personally counted each and every EAB mask?" pressed Young.

"No, sir. I looked up the EAB loadout in the ship's data book and then asked the DCA what *Memphis* had on his last inventory. He said he didn't remember the exact number, but he was very confident we had at least that many masks on board, he thought we might even have a few extra as well. I never verified the actual number, hence my answer of approximately eight hundred sixty."

Jerry felt strangely calm after his little dissertation to the commodore, who simply sat there and looked at him. Silently, Jerry thanked Chief Gilson for being so thorough during his damage control checkout. While a long and painful ordeal, with numerous lookups that Jerry had to answer afterward, he now knew his DC equipment cold and that little extra detail on the EAB connections had just come in very handy.

A slight smile broke out on Young's face as he said, "I would have been happy with the number of connections on the manifolds, but you are quite correct, Mr. Mitchell. Well done." Young opened the folder again and quickly wrote a few notes down. Probably something along the lines of "Mr. Mitchell is a smart-ass," thought Jerry.

"Umm, sir, you mentioned another topic?" asked Jerry, trying to move the interview to a rapid conclusion.

"Yes, yes, I did," replied Young as he closed the folder. "We have one more drill to run, a battle stations torpedo drill, and I'm going to need your help in conducting the exercise. How much time do you need to prepare the Manta for launch?"

"About thirty minutes, sir. May I ask what you want me to do?"

"I want you to pilot the Manta as a hostile submarine in a mock attack against *Memphis*," answered Young.

Jerry felt a cold sweat forming on his forehead. "Y-you, you want me to fight against the Captain and the rest of my crew?"

"Not exactly, Lieutenant. One of my staff will tell you what to do. I just need you to guide the Manta accordingly."

I am royally screwed, thought Jerry. Hardy won't bother with the commodore's little distinction if *Memphis* does badly during the drill—the CO would place the fault squarely on him and would chew on his butt all the way back to New London. And with a staff rider looking over his shoulder the whole time, Jerry couldn't intentionally make it easier for his crew. Frantically, Jerry tried to think of a way out of this dilemma.

"Sir, I must inform you that I've never flown the prototype off of *Memphis*. I have lots of simulator time and some hours with the smaller prototype at Newport, but none with the UUV we are carrying right now."

"Yes, I was aware of that," responded Young. "All the more reason to conduct this exercise, wouldn't you agree?"

Jerry desperately wanted to say, "Hell no, sir!" but he couldn't say that to the man who was sending a progress report on him to those reluctant flag officers. Besides, his Navy training had drilled into him that there was only one correct answer.

"Yes, sir. When do you want to launch?" Jerry tried to sound more confident than he felt. And right now he felt like a trapped animal, with nowhere to go.

"Excellent!" exclaimed Young jubilantly. "Report to the torpedo room in fifteen minutes. Lieutenant Commander Monroe will meet you there. And Mr. Mitchell, not a word to any other member of your crew."

"Aye, aye, sir," said Jerry as he stood up and left the wardroom.

Once he was out in the passageway, Jerry leaned up against the bulk-head and tried to reduce the knot he felt in his gut. He really wanted to talk to Lenny. He needed Berg's unique insight to help him with this one, but he was under explicit orders not to speak to anyone about the drill. Fearing that his resolve wouldn't hold up if he returned to his stateroom, Jerry headed aft toward the torpedo room.

Breaking out into almost a jog, Jerry reached the torpedo room quickly and immediately sought out the duty watchstander. He found TM2 Boyd at the weapons launching console, making his quarterly hour log entries.

"Good afternoon, sir," said Boyd, greeting his division officer. "Is there something I can do for you?"

"Yes, Petty Officer Boyd, I have a question. Who would man the Manta launch stations during this watch?"

"The offgoing torpedo room and fire-control watchstanders would normally do that. That would be Greer and Davidson. Do you want me to find them, sir?"

"Yes, please. I need them here in ten minutes," replied Jerry somewhat nervously.

"Anything wrong, sir?" inquired Boyd. "You don't look so good."

"I'll be all right, but thanks for asking. Just ask the Chief of the Watch to get them here ASAP."

"Aye, aye, sir," nodded Boyd, who picked up the sound-powered phone handset and called control.

Jerry went back to the Manta control area, lifted up the Naugahyde cover, and powered up the control console. After the initial system diagnostics were completed, Jerry started a full system check. As expected, the ten-minute automatic test showed no problems. Jerry logged the time of the check and the results and then waited for Lieutenant Commander Monroe to show up.

Soon thereafter, Greer and Davidson appeared over by the starboard tube nest. Jerry called and waved for them to come back to the control console, informed them of the impending launch, and then told them to be ready to assume their stations.

Both were curious as to what was going to happen and asked some legitimate questions. Jerry responded that he wasn't at liberty to discuss it, but that all would be clear soon. This only made the two even more curious, and they peppered him with even more questions. Jerry was about to order the two of them to shut up when he saw a squadron staffer walk into the torpedo room. Motioning for Greer and Davidson to hush, Jerry pointed to the lieutenant commander who was approaching them.

"Good afternoon, Mr. Mitchell. I'm Lieutenant Commander Andy Monroe. Are you ready to launch the Manta?"

Doesn't waste any time, does he? Jerry thought. Well, I can deal with that. "Yes, sir. We're ready, any time you want. My team is assembled and I've already performed the preflight maintenance check." Jerry then pointed to the two petty officers and said, "This is TM2 Greer and FT2 Davidson. They will be assisting me during the launch and recovery."

"Very good," said Monroe as he shook their hands. "I'll inform the commodore that we are ready to begin." Picking up the phone, Monroe called control. While Monroe was busy talking to the commodore, Jerry sent Greer aft to the engine room to monitor the mechanical indications of the launch process and to use the manual overrides if a problem arose. Davidson sat down next to Jerry and would assist him at the control console and be Jerry's communications link with Greer. Jerry put on his own communications headset, a high-tech version of the bulky sound-powered phone set, and waited for control to come on the line.

"Man Manta launch stations," squawked the 1MC. Soon thereafter, Jerry heard the Chief of the Watch announce on the sound-powered phones, "All stations, control, control on the line."

"Control, U-bay. U-bay on the line," responded Jerry.

"U-bay?" asked Monroe with a puzzled look on his face.

"We had to call it something, sir," said Jerry defensively. "And we couldn't use Manta control or UUV control; that would be too confusing. So we called it U-bay, you know like e-bay, only it means UUV bay."

"Yeah, right. Whatever," said Monroe, who didn't looked impressed. "How long before the nav system is aligned and ready to go?"

"It's ready now, sir," replied Jerry. "The Manta uses a strapdown ring-laser gyro for the inertial navigation system."

"Very well. Proceed with the launch."

"Aye, aye, sir."

Jerry reached over and picked up a small yellow binder with all the Manta procedures in it. He opened the laminated pages to the launch section. Using a grease pencil, Jerry and Davidson went down the procedure one step and a time and marked off each step as it was accomplished.

"Control, U-bay. Request ship's speed be reduced to four knots," said Jerry.

"Request ship's speed be reduced to four knots. Control aye."

Knowing that it would take a little while for *Memphis* to drop to the launch speed, Jerry continued with the checklist.

"Retracting battery umbilical cable," announced Jerry as he pushed the button on the touch screen. The display paused for a moment and then indicated that the cable had been detached from the Manta and stowed in the docking structure.

"Engine room upper level reports the umbilical has been retracted and stowed," stated Davidson.

"Very well. Flooding docking skirt and equalizing to sea pressure," said Jerry as he activated several of the onscreen controls. A few moments later, Davidson reported, "Engine room upper level reports the docking skirt flooded and equalized to sea pressure."

Jerry acknowledged the report and looked over his shoulder toward Monroe, "Sir, where do you want the Manta to go after launch?"

"Have the Manta assume station five hundred yards off the starboard quarter after launch. However, during the exercise, you'll pilot the vehicle directly. Understood?"

"Yes, sir. I understand completely," Jerry replied. Davidson looked at his division officer with a puzzled expression. It was unusual for someone to manually pilot the Manta; its whole design was predicated on operating largely without continuous human guidance. Jerry saw the questioning look on Davidson's face and motioned for him to stay on the checklist.

"U-bay, control. Ship's speed is now four knots," said the Chief of the Watch.

"Very well, control." Jerry leaned over and looked at the checklist Davidson was holding and saw that there was only one step left. "Control, U-bay. Request permission to launch the Manta."

"Request permission to launch the Manta. Control aye." Jerry waited only a few moments before the Chief of the Watch passed on the Captain's approval, "U-bay, control. Permission granted to launch the Manta."

"Very well, control." Jerry detached the docking latches and then pushed the LAUNCH button. The rest of the launching sequence was done automatically by the Manta's programming.

"Engine room upper level reports the docking latches have detached and the Manta has lifted off the docking skirt," said Davidson.

Jerry nodded as the telemetry update from the Manta through the acoustic modem was coming in strong. He watched closely as the UUV's position on the display moved away from *Memphis*. Everything seemed to be working fine and after a minute, the Manta had assumed its position on *Memphis'* starboard quarter. Turning to LCDR Monroe, Jerry reported, "Sir, Manta on station and ready to maneuver."

"Very well," replied Monroe. Taking his clipboard, Monroe recorded *Memphis'* course and speed on a miniature maneuvering board-plotting sheet. He then drew a couple of lines, pulled out a pocket ruler and measured something. Satisfied with his results, Monroe looked at Jerry and said, "Mr. Mitchell, I want you to send the Manta five thousand yards dead astern of *Memphis*. I trust the acoustic modem will allow that?"

"Yes, sir, easily. Depending on the acoustic conditions, we could have three times that range."

"Excellent. Once the Manta reaches that position, turn it around and match *Memphis'* course and speed. I'll give you the next leg at that time."

"Aye, aye, sir," replied Jerry as he typed in the new position and the necessary course and speed. The Manta peeled off to the right and headed directly away from *Memphis* at ten knots. He also noticed that the boat had started to increase speed again and was at six knots. Probably going back to a normal one-third bell, or about seven knots, thought Jerry. Doing some quick math in his head, Jerry figured out about how long it would take for the Manta to reach the end of the first leg. "Commander Monroe, it will take a little less than ten minutes for the Manta to reach the designated location."

"Thank you, Mr. Mitchell" was all Jerry received in response. The next nine minutes passed by in silence as Jerry watched the navigation screen on the control console display.

"Sir, the Manta is five thousand yards astern on course zero four zero degrees, speed seven knots," reported Jerry.

"Very well," responded Monroe. "Mr. Mitchell, the second leg is another five thousand yards perpendicular to the present course. Have the Manta steer course one three zero degrees at ten knots. And while you are at it, how long till the Manta reaches the end of the second leg?"

With perpendicular courses, thought Jerry, only the Manta's speed mattered. Again, after a little mental gymnastics, he came up with the answer. "Fifteen minutes, sir."

"Correct. And that's when we get to the good part."

"Sir, may I ask what we are supposed to be doing during this drill?" asked an unbearably curious Davidson. "I don't have a clue as to what is going on."

"Certainly, Petty Officer Davidson. You and Lieutenant Mitchell here are the faithful crew of my Russian nuclear-powered attack submarine. Mr. Mitchell is my helmsman and you are my sonar shack. Together we are going to make a mock attack on *Memphis*, using the Manta."

"Well, this should be quick," said Davidson sarcastically. "With a TB-29 towed array, *Memphis* will make short work of us. The Manta ain't that quiet."

"Do not lose heart, comrade," answered Monroe in a dreadful Russian accent. "Saint Nicholas—or is it Saint Andrew? Oh well, whomever it is, he will protect us and Mother Russia from those imperialists."

"Huh, sir? I don't get it."

"Okay, let me be a little more clear. The commodore has already ordered your captain to stow both the TB-16 and TB-29 tails. Because you guys are going into really shallow water on your next run, you won't be able to use the towed arrays. So the commodore wants to see how the crew performs against a quiet target with hull arrays only."

"No shit, sir?" exclaimed Davidson, now considerably more interested. "Er, excuse me. You mean we get to hose over the old man, er, I mean the Captain? Kewl!"

"That's the spirit," replied Monroe more pleasantly.

Jerry just sat there and contemplated what was about to become his worst nightmare. Without the towed arrays, the Manta at slow speed would be a very difficult target to detect. This meant there was a good chance that LCDR Monroe would be able to take on Captain Hardy and win. The prospect filled Jerry with dread.

"Comrades, if I can have your attention please," said Monroe as he tapped Jerry's shoulder, bringing him out of his trancelike state. "The battle plan is as follows: We've intentionally sent the Manta down the hull array's baffles so the sonar girls wouldn't be able to cheat while we positioned the vehicle for the exercise. So now they only know that the Manta will come at them from abaft the beam. That's still a lot of territory to keep under observation, which helps to make the exercise more realistic. We've also muddied the water a little more by taking a long time before things get interesting. It's going to be an hour before *Memphis'* sonar shack will even get a whiff of the Manta. This should help reduce the 'alerted operator syndrome,' since the sonar operators will have had time for the adrenaline to wear off."

The more Jerry listened, the more he had to admire Monroe's plan. It was brilliant, devious, and would certainly stress the sonar shack's operators to no end. Jerry wondered if Monroe would spot the operator's a few decibels in reduced performance due to increased system self-noise. Hardy would almost certainly be in the shack yelling at the sonar supervisor to find him his target. Jerry watched Davidson as he became more excited as the plan was explained to him. The very idea of beating the Captain at his own game was an incredibly motivating concept for the young torpedoman's mate.

"Now, after we gain contact," Monroe continued, "I want you to drive the Manta right across *Memphis'* stern and generate a closest point of approach, a CPA. We probably won't detect her at long range, so this maneuver should allow us to generate a good fire-control solution. I want you to travel about one thousand yards past the CPA and then turn in the direction of the target and match the target's course and speed based on the solution. Since the target will be ahead of us and will be going in the same general direction, there is almost no chance of a collision with this maneuver. Do you think you can do that?"

Jerry thought for a moment and said, "Let me see if I have this straight, sir. You want me to cross astern of the target like this—" Jerry used his hands to show the relative positions of the Manta and *Memphis*—"go one thousand yards, then turn toward *Memphis* and match her course and speed. I then maintain that relative position so that we stay at about a constant range from the target, right?

"Precisely, Mr. Mitchell!" said Monroe enthusiastically. "You now have a fair understanding of Russian submarine target motion analysis tactics."

"Thank you, sir. But to be honest, I've heard about it before. What you've described is also a basic fighter maneuver called 'lag pursuit.' And I know how to execute that maneuver," responded Jerry confidently.

"Very good!" replied Monroe. "Ahhh, I see that the Manta is just about at the start position. Let's have some fun now, shall we?"

Jerry looked at the navigation display and saw that the Manta had less than one hundred yards to go. Jerry punched the manual control button and tested the joystick. The controls seemed to be sluggish. Remember, be light on the stick, Jerry thought to himself. With the Manta that far away, it would take about five seconds for the maneuvering commands to reach the vehicle and another five seconds before he would be able to see any results on his displays. After verifying that everything seemed to be operating normally, Jerry reported. "Sir, the test of the Manta's manual controls has been completed satisfactorily. Oh, and while I don't disagree with anything you've said about the low probability of a collision, Just to be safe, I'd like to start the Manta off with a one-hundred-foot depth separation."

"A prudent suggestion, Mr. Mitchell. Very well, make your depth three five zero feet and come left to course zero four zero."

"Make my depth three five zero feet and come left to course zero four zero, aye, sir."

As Jerry executed the maneuver, Davidson called up the sonar displays and adjusted the brightness and contrast. The use of color made these displays easier to use than the old green screens that the sonar techs were using. And even though detection was largely automated with the Manta sonar systems, Davidson really wanted to find *Memphis* before the sonar techs found the Manta.

"Easy there, Petty Officer Davidson," said Monroe jokingly. "Don't burn a hole in the flat screen by staring so hard! We've got a little ways to go before we even have a chance of picking up *Memphis*."

"Yes, sir. Do you think we really have a chance?"

Monroe nodded vigorously and replied, "Absolutely! All right, Mr. Mitchell, it's time we looked like a Russian SSN. Slow to eight knots."

Jerry dropped the Manta's speed by two knots and settled in for the potentially long wait. He snickered to himself as he remembered his submarine tactics instructor's description of antisubmarine warfare, or ASW, and what it really meant was Awfully Slow Warfare. "You must be patient when you go hunting submarines," his instructor said. "Impatience can get you killed." But as the minutes passed, Jerry noticed that Davidson was losing interest in the sonar displays. For almost forty minutes, they refused to provide any indication of *Memphis'* presence. Monroe's delaying tactics were probably having an equally unpleasant effect in the sonar shack two decks up as well.

About an hour and five minutes into the drill, Davidson was startled by something on the display. He leaned forward and stared intently for a few moments and almost shouted, "Mr. Monroe, I think I have a contact!"

"Bearing?" barked Monroe.

"Contact bears zero one zero with a moderate right bearing rate," answered Davidson quickly.

"Very well. Mr. Mitchell, come left to zero one zero."

"Come left to zero one zero, aye," replied Jerry. Moments later, "Sir, steady on course zero one zero."

Suddenly the 1MC blared, "MAN BATTLE STATIONS TORPEDO!" *BONG, BONG, BONG.* "MAN BATTLE STATIONS TORPEDO!"

"Well, well, I do believe they managed to pick up our scent. Look alive now, lads, for the game is afoot!"

Monroe moved over closer to Davidson and looked at the sonar display. After a few minutes, Monroe said, "Yes indeed, a very nice two to three degree per minute right bearing rate. There is no hint of cavitation on the narrowband display either. I would definitely say we have found our adversary. Mr. Mitchell, come right to," Monroe paused momentarily as he took one more glance at the primary detection display, "come right to zero four zero."

"Coming right to zero four zero, aye, sir," acknowledged Jerry. He could feel his heart rate speeding up as the hunt began.

"Sir! Possible target zig," reported Davidson.

Monroe nearly fell off his stool as he quickly leaned over to look at the display. "Good call, Davidson. She's either turned toward us or increased speed." After another thirty seconds of watching, Monroe exclaimed, "Look at that bearing rate! It has shot through the roof! And still no cavitation. She's close, and she had to have turned toward us. Mr. Mitchell, stand by to come hard left on my mark!"

"Yes, sir!" said Jerry. All three men were now totally engrossed in the engagement that was unfolding before them.

Monroe monitored the sonar display carefully and slowly raised his left hand, poised to signal his order. "Contact has just past through CPA, aaaand mark! Hard left rudder! Mr. Mitchell, steady on course three four zero, increase speed to twelve knots, and execute your lag pursuit maneuver!"

"Coming hard left to three four zero, increasing speed to twelve knots, and beginning lag pursuit!" replied Jerry excitedly. Gently pushing the joystick over, Jerry pulled the Manta through a tight turn and crossed behind *Memphis*. A couple of minutes later, Jerry executed a hard right turn and brought the Manta close to *Memphis'* estimated course. According to the target motion analysis algorithm, they had passed *Memphis* about two thousand yards astern and they were now on her port quarter.

"Perfect, Mr. Mitchell! Now keep us on her tail," encouraged Monroe.

"Aye, aye, sir! We are in the sweet spot and I intend to take up permanent residence."

Monroe and Davidson watched as Jerry matched *Memphis* maneuver for maneuver for the next six minutes. Keeping a close eye on the target's estimated course and speed, Jerry adroitly adjusted the Manta's course and speed so that it maintained its relative position with respect to *Memphis*. Captain Hardy must be beside himself with frustration, thought Jerry. With the Manta still in his baffles, there was nothing the Captain could do. He couldn't hear the Manta and—more important—he couldn't simulate a torpedo shot on it. Jerry was in control of the situation, and Jerry knew that Hardy knew it as well. But all of a sudden, the small smile on Jerry's face was replaced with a frown. *Memphis* had not executed a maneuver in over three minutes. Something was up.

"Mr. Monroe, sir, the Captain is up to something. He hasn't maneuvered at all in the three plus minutes and I think he's going to break, and break hard, soon."

"Concur. Which way do you think he'll go?" Monroe asked.

"He'll go to the left. All of his past maneuvers, as small as they were, have been to the right. He's going to go to the left in a major league way, I just know it!" exclaimed Jerry. "And when he does, I'll go hard right, cross behind again, and settle in on the starboard side of the baffles."

"Won't that be risky? Our TMA solution is a little old," questioned Davidson.

"Not really," responded Jerry. "I've kept our relative position pretty constant, so the solution is still accurate and we haven't closed the target all that much. That's the whole point behind the lag pursuit maneuver. Furthermore, as soon as we see him commit to a left turn—and we will if he breaks hard—we start turning to the right and with our superior maneuverability we'll finish our maneuver before he does."

"Do we still have depth separation?" asked Monroe.

"I don't know, sir. That's hard to estimate. I think *Memphis* is a little deeper, but I can't say how much."

Monroe sat down and thought for a moment. He looked at his own notes and then the TMA solution. A smile slowly grew on his face. "If he turns left, Mr. Mitchell, execute a hard right turn!"

"Aye, aye, sir," said Jerry. The three of them then sat there, glued to the sonar display, awaiting the first clue that *Memphis* was starting her turn. They didn't have long to wait.

Within thirty seconds of Monroe's decision, *Memphis* executed the hard left turn that Jerry had predicted. With almost lightning reflexes, Jerry simultaneously drove the Manta into a hard right turn and then eased off before they emerged from the starboard baffles. By the time Jerry finished fine-tuning, the Manta occupied the exact same position on *Memphis'* starboard quarter.

"Sweeet," muttered Davidson.

"Nicely done, Mr. Mitchell," praised Monroe. "Now, before they can figure out what just happened, increase speed to fifteen knots. Davidson, prepare to go active."

"Increase speed to fifteen knots, aye, sir," replied Jerry.

With the added speed, the Manta broke from the starboard baffles. Waiting just a few seconds to let the maneuver's effect sink in. Monroe ordered Davidson to go active on the bow array with four sharp pulses; meaning simply, "bang, you're dead."

"*Touché, mon capitaine,*" said Monroe triumphantly as he slapped both Jerry and Davidson on the back.

A couple of minutes later, the 1MC announced, "Secure from battle stations. Secure from drill. Drill monitors muster in the wardroom for the critique."

"Mr. Mitchell, you and your team recover the Manta and then join us in the wardroom," ordered Monroe. "And a very well done to both of you."

As Monroe headed forward, Davidson turned toward Jerry and said, "That was awesome, sir! You really handled the Manta well."

"Thanks, Petty Officer Davidson. The funny thing is, the Manta felt a lot like an airplane. And I just fell back on my aviation training."

"Well, sir, Mr. Adelman was never that good, and this was your first time with the real deal. Maybe that's why the Navy sent you here for this mission. They knew you had the proper skills."

Jerry laughed and responded sarcastically to Davidson's naïveté, "Somehow TM2, I don't think I can attribute that kind of forethought to the senior leadership of the U.S. Navy. Now, let's get the Manta back on board."

As Davidson contacted Greer to begin the recovery procedure, Jerry looked up and noticed for the first time that all of the torpedoman's mates were looking at him and Davidson. A few nodded their approval; Foster clearly made his feelings known by his glare. Jerry chose to ignore his senior chief's disapproval and turned the Manta procedure book to the recovery section.

Ten minutes later, with the Manta firmly secured in its dock, Jerry headed forward toward the wardroom. With any luck, the critique would be almost over. Hardy was bound to be in a foul mood after Monroe's lopsided victory over *Memphis'* fire-control party. Turning the corner around the bulkhead that separated officers' country from the rest of the boat, Jerry heard a loud and angry voice coming from the wardroom. He couldn't make out all the words, but the voice was very familiar. The Captain was obviously beside himself with anger over this drill and he was making his displeasure known to one and all. Stopping by the door to the wardroom, Jerry took a deep breath and went in.

"It's about time you showed up Mitchell. We've been waiting for you," growled Hardy.

Inwardly Jerry groaned. Now he would have to endure the Captain's wrath as each embarrassing moment was gone over in detail. Since there was nothing Jerry could do about it, might as well get it over with. "Sorry, sir, we were recovering the Manta and I wish to report that the vehicle is now secured."

"Very well," grumbled Hardy.

"Let's continue with the critique, please," remarked Young rather testily. "As you were saying, Mr. Monroe."

Lieutenant Commander Monroe looked down at his notepad and picked up where he had let off. He described the maneuvers used during the exercise and how they were based on classic Russian SSN tactics. He then made several complimentary statements on Jerry's ability to grasp the essence of the tactics and to employ them. Monroe even went so far as to say that Jerry's previous aviation experience proved to be extremely valuable in this instance. Jerry watched as Hardy seemed to turn more and more crimson as the squadron staffer praised one of his officers. When they reached the point in drill when *Memphis* turned hard left, Bair piped up and asked, "Why did you turn hard right as we turned left? I don't quite understand the rationale behind that action."

Monroe motioned for Jerry to answer his XO. "Well, sir, we could have easily turned with *Memphis*, but in doing so we would have ended up in a disadvantaged position where you would have been able to shoot us. By turning right and crossing astern for the second time, we retained the position of advantage. We knew about where you were and that you were in our weapons envelope. But we were not in yours. When I saw the hard left break, I recognized the situation as being similar to what aviators call a 'flat scissors' and I maneuvered accordingly."

"Are you saying you beat the crap out of us by using dogfighting tactics, mister?" demanded Bair.

"Uh, yes, yes, sir. I guess that is what I'm saying."

Bair sat back in his chair and shook his head. "No wonder we couldn't figure out what they were doing. We were expecting them to behave like submariners and planned our attack based on this assumption. But instead, they acted more like fighter pilots. And in this case, they actually had one."

"Yes, XO, I agree!" Hardy said angrily. "And that is exactly why I object to this whole drill. How can we be expected to fight a small, highly maneuverable vehicle with traditional tactics and weapons?"

"Your point is well taken, Captain," replied Young icily. "But the last time I heard, the CNO is encouraging *exactly* this kind of out-of-the-box thinking!" Rising, Young positioned himself so that everyone could hear him. "What we learned today from this exercise was not what we had intended. Instead of ending up with a traditional sub-on-sub encounter that would just test your fire-control party's skills, we found that a highly maneuverable vehicle with a well-trained operator unexpectedly dominated the scenario. And I submit to you, Captain, that this result is of far greater interest to my staff and me than what we did expect."

"Since other nations will undoubtedly follow our lead in developing combat UUVs, this exercise has given us some insight into the problems we'll face in developing future tactics and systems to address the threat. Now, if you will excuse us, Captain, we'll sit down and determine your final grade for these sea trials. In the meantime, please set a course for home."

As the members of *Memphis'* crew filed out of the wardroom, Jerry received a number of slaps on the back and some words of congratulations—all out of the Captain's earshot, of course. Even the XO, who had been in charge of the fire control party he and Monroe had so thoroughly bested, winked his approval.

But even more surprising to Jerry was the fact that Hardy was amazingly civil on the trip back to New London. Undoubtedly, the excellent grade *Memphis* received from the Commodore had done much to salve the Captain's wounds. But Jerry hoped that maybe the Captain was starting to see that he was worth having on board. Of greater importance to Jerry, though, was his realization that he could be a good sub driver. And for the first time since he started down his new career path, Jerry saw light at the end of the tunnel.

7 Unwelcome Guests

May 12, 2005

●●●●●●●●●●●●●●●●●●●●●●

SUBASE, New London

"Reveille, reveille, up all bunks. All hands turn to and commence ship's work. Quarters to be held on the pier at 0800," droned the 1MC mercilessly. Jerry groaned quietly and muttered, "But I just closed my eyes a minute ago." Unfortunately, his watch confirmed that he had actually been asleep for four hours. Jerry was still dog-tired and he really wanted to sleep. The rustlings and *thumps* told him that his roommates were up and getting dressed.

"C'mon, Jerry, rise and shine," said Berg as he lightly kicked Jerry in the rear.

"Just five more minutes, Mom," whimpered Jerry.

"Sorry, dear, but you don't want to miss the school bus," replied Berg as he kicked Jerry again.

"You're a cruel man, Lenny. You're only kicking me because you can," said Jerry as he slowly slithered out of his rack.

"How true," responded Berg in a deadpan manner. Then, a little more lightheartedly, "There are some advantages to having the top bunk."

As Jerry shaved and got dressed, he tried to get his disorganized mental house in order. Today was May 12, and it was going to be another busy day. Dr. Davis and Dr. Patterson would be arriving this morning with the ROVs and Lord knows whatever else *Memphis* would need for the patrol. Ever since they had returned from sea trials, preparations had reached a breakneck pace all over the boat. Hardy had told them, back in March, that they only had two months to get ready for a lengthy deployment. That had seemed an incredibly short time then. Now, with the reality of tomorrow's departure date looming like an oncoming express train, everyone was flailing to finish up. Some were more successful than others. Washburn was waiting for critical supplies, and Millunzi's engineers were still working on cranky machinery. Lenny Berg couldn't receive the new crypto codes for the upcoming cruise until his COMSEC procedures had been reviewed, and the inspector was behind schedule—by five days. Lenny spent a lot of time on the phone.

As the crew mustered for Quarters, Jerry's division stood in its normal place on the pier. The weather was kind, a beautiful spring morning, with only an occasional breeze moving the cool morning air. Jerry tried to enjoy it, but weeks of furious activity made it hard for him to stand still. Where the hell is Hardy? he thought. It was already ten minutes past eight o'clock.

Bair kept watching the forward escape trunk, and as Hardy emerged, the XO called, "Attention on deck!" The ship's company snapped into immobility, then waited as the Captain crossed the brow, walked to where the XO waited in front of the assembled crew, then returned Bair's salute.

Bair stepped to one side, and Hardy stood for a moment, looking up and down the line of sailors. Along with the rest of them, Jerry waited as patiently as he could. Rumor had it Hardy would give them more details about the mission, and beyond normal curiosity, Jerry would like to know just what he was going to be doing for the next few months.

It might also put to rest some of the rumors flying around the boat. "Guess the mission" had become *Memphis'* most popular game. The special equipment was rumored to be a new weapon, a new propulsion system, or remote controls that would turn the sub into a giant UUV. Their destination was Greenland, South Africa, or possibly Havana harbor in Cuba. To their credit, Jerry's division had been as silent as stones. Foster would have dealt harshly with any leak—and the division knew it.

Hardy seemed reluctant to start, or at least, in no hurry to speak. Jerry noticed Bair to one side, fidgeting. The Captain's expression was grimmer than usual.

"Our orders send us far north," Hardy finally announced. Jerry knew that meant north of the Arctic Circle, into Russia's backyard. "We will be gone for several months, which should be no surprise to anyone here. Due to security concerns, I won't be able to tell you exactly where and exactly what we'll be doing until after we're under way."

"You all know that we will be loading some special equipment today. The civilian tech reps who install it will also be accompanying us." That started a low buzz of conversation. "That's right. The two ladies, Dr. Patterson and Dr. Davis, will ride the boat on this next patrol."

Jerry tried to absorb the news. Women on the sub? Although females routinely served on surface ships and on aircraft, they'd never been part of any submarine's crew. Space was too tight. There was no privacy. No wonder the President's name kept coming up. He was the only one with the clout to overrule Navy policy.

And *those* two women? Emily Davis was all right; he could deal with her, but Dr. "I work for the President" Patterson? Jerry's heart sank to his shoes. She hated the Navy. Why was she going along? Not willingly, Jerry assumed. Had the President ordered her to go? Mitchell was suddenly glad he'd voted for the other guy.

Hardy's voice hardened as he continued. "I want it thoroughly understood that our two guests will be treated not only as ladies, but as senior officers while they are aboard. Any disrespect or any attempt at fraternization will make the offender wish he'd never been born." He paused for a moment and added a theatrical glare that included the entire ship's company.

Adopting a more matter-of-fact tone, he explained, "The ladies will berth in the XO's cabin and eat in the wardroom. The ship will be rigged for female visitors throughout the entire deployment. I don't want to see one piece of inappropriate literature out in the open. The speech and decorum of the entire crew, including the officers, will also be under the closest scrutiny during this patrol."

Thanks for that ringing vote of confidence, Jerry mused. From the sour expressions on the faces of some of the crew, they felt the same way, either about having women aboard the sub, about Patterson, or about the CO's lack of trust. Jerry wondered how many of the other sailors were just better at hiding their feelings.

Hardy left and the XO dismissed the crew from Quarters. Jerry immediately hurried down to the torpedo room, to make sure it was ready for the special equipment's arrival. It had been last night, when he made his rounds, but double-checking never hurt.

His division had just finished loading torpedoes yesterday. The torpedo room looked incomplete with only eight weapons stowed instead of twenty-two, but the empty racks would be filled today with the ROVs and support gear and who knew what else.

The torpedo division, under Foster's direction, had already started to set up the loading tray and rig the downhauls. Most of the loading gear had to be stowed after loading the torpedoes yesterday, especially since some of the parts were deck plates from in front of the Captain's stateroom and by the crew berthing. The Captain and the crew would have missed those sections last night.

Looking up from between the torpedo tubes, Jerry saw that the plates from the two decks above had already been removed. The loading tray itself was being hoisted out the weapons shipping hatch and guide rails from the torpedo room deck were being put in place. Once done, there would be a complete path from the hatch to the centerline stowage rack in the torpedo room. Everything seemed to be moving along just fine. The only things missing now were the equipment and the tech reps. Unfortunately for Jerry and his division, they stayed missing for several hours.

It was well past lunch before the women and their gear arrived. Both Hardy and Foster were seething over the delay, not that Jerry wasn't irritated as well. In the age of cellular phones and wireless capable PDA's, it was absolutely incomprehensible that they hadn't heard from them. Finally the 1MC called, "Mr. Mitchell, lay topside." Jerry hurried to the forward escape hatch and got up on deck in time to see a semi-tractor truck with a canvas-covered flatbed trailer rumble to a stop on the pier. A base security car was in front, and a van labeled CHARLES STARK DRAPER LABORATORY completed the convoy. Patterson and Davis got out of the van and started to pull their luggage from the back.

Jerry told the topside watchstander, "Pass the word to the Captain that they've arrived and ask Senior Chief Foster to come topside."

Hurrying onto the pier, Jerry greeted the two women as they stepped away from the van, but only Dr. Davis returned his "hello." Patterson simply announced, "There are my bags," as she passed Jerry and strode toward the brow.

Jerry smiled cynically as he turned back to Davis and asked, "What kept you? You guys are over three hours late."

"Sorry about that. The traffic out of Boston was hideous."

"You should've called to let us know that you were going to be delayed," teased Jerry. "It would have been the polite thing to do."

"You're right, of course. But simple courtesy is not high on Dr. Patterson's list of things to do today."

"So I've noticed. She seems to be in her normal foul mood."

Davis didn't respond to Jerry's little quip, but simply looked down at the ground, slightly biting her lower lip. Jerry gathered that the trip down from Boston was more unpleasant then she cared to talk about. Motioning toward the brow, he said, "Come on, Emily, I'll have someone get your personal gear on board." The two of them headed toward the submarine.

As Dr. Patterson approached the brow, the messenger of the watch, Seaman Gunther, came to attention and saluted her.

"What the hell is this all about?" she demanded.

"Captain Hardy said that you should be treated as senior officers while you're aboard, ma'am."

Patterson still looked puzzled. "Senior?" she asked.

Jerry came over. "Commander and above. Lieutenant commander and below are 'junior officers,'" he explained.

"Oh." Patterson looked momentarily pleased at her sudden change in status, but then scowled. "What's wrong with you people? Don't you know how to relate to someone who doesn't have stripes on their arm somewhere?"

Jerry quickly replied, "I'm sure the Captain was . . ."

"I'll take this up with the Captain myself," Patterson interrupted, almost huffing. She headed below.

Jerry turned to Gunther. "It's okay. You don't have to salute Dr. Patterson or Dr. Davis. They can't return your salute anyway."

Gunther, a little confused and embarrassed, nodded. "Yessir."

"Please make sure that the ladies' bags are taken to the XO's cabin."

Glad for something constructive to do, Gunther nodded and took off.

Senior Chief Foster suddenly emerged from the forward escape hatch. The sour expression he carried made Jerry think that he'd met Patterson going down while he went up.

Jerry asked, "Are we ready to load?"

"Yes, sir." Foster seemed irritated by the question, but Jerry ignored it. Foster was always irritated by his questions.

While Jerry reviewed the inventory and signed for the equipment, Emily Davis supervised as Foster and his men unloaded the truck. The procedure was similar to the one used for loading torpedoes, and the cargo was handled just as delicately. Although it couldn't explode, if any of the equipment was damaged, the mission, whatever it was, might be delayed or even aborted.

After removing the canvas, each pallet had four lifting lines and two guidelines attached and was swung over by crane onto the loading tray. Dr. Davis monitored the loading evolution closely, like a mother hen fussing over her chicks, and made sure they were handled gently. The pallets were all wrapped in dark gray plastic and carried no markings except for a large number made of silver tape. The numbers matched a list Davis had, and she referred to it to make sure the pallets were brought aboard in the correct order.

Number Three happened to be first, and Davis hurried across to the sub's deck, matching the pallet's progress as it was swung over. The weapons loading hatch was located on the bow, in front of sail. Unlike the two escape hatches aft of the sail, this hatch was angled and matched up with the holes in the decks below. It allowed a torpedo or missile, twenty-one inches in diameter, to be brought aboard and loaded, tail first, into the torpedo room.

Once placed on the loading tray, the downhaul lines were attached, and the crane on the pier lifted the tray to the proper angle. Then the heavy pallet was slowly lowered down inside the hull.

Yesterday, during torpedo loading, Foster and the division had averaged about thirty minutes per weapon. It took almost an hour and a half just to get the first equipment pallet stowed, mostly because of Davis' constant checking and her entreaties to move slowly and carefully. The second pallet was going a little faster, but Jerry predicted they would be at it well past dinnertime.

Dr. Patterson did nothing to speed the process. She showed up as the second pallet was being lifted across to the sub, and when she saw the pallet swinging in the air, shouted, "Stop!"

Senior Chief Foster, directing the crane, held both arms up, his hands balled into fists. The crane operator immediately halted, and everyone froze in their places, quickly, almost frantically, searching for a problem. "What's wrong?" someone asked.

Patterson ignored the question and turned to the nearest sailor, TM1 Moran. He was holding one of the lines that steadied the pallet while it was swung over. "How can you let that pallet swing about like that? Are those cables strong enough to hold the pallet when you let it swing all over the place?" she demanded.

Moran looked at her in puzzlement, then turned toward the Senior Chief, pleading in his expression. Both Foster and Jerry hurried over, while Patterson continued ranting. "Why isn't the pallet properly supported?"

Foster overheard the last question and quickly asked, "What's wrong with the rig, ma'am?"

"It's only suspended by a single cable! What if it breaks?" she demanded. "When we loaded the pallets on the trailer, we used a crane with two cables!"

"Ma'am, that cable's rated for five tons, and the pallet weighs less than two tons."

She wasn't satisfied. "How do you know that one cable won't break? When was it last inspected?"

"The crane is inspected monthly by SUBASE and I checked it myself this morning, ma'am."

"And what do you know about cables?" she retorted contemptuously. She turned to toward the topside watch, a short distance away, and called, "Tell the Captain to come up here now. I need to see him immediately!"

She wasn't facing Jerry, which was good, because his face must have mirrored his surprise. Who did this woman think she was? Only the Captain's "senior officer" admonition prevented Jerry from countermanding her order. Nobody "tells" the Captain anything. You may inform him of certain facts, but you don't tell him what to do—especially Captain Hardy.

Jerry also watched Foster, struggling to control his anger. "Dr. Patterson," Foster began slowly. "This is the exact same crane and rig we used to bring ten torpedoes aboard yesterday, and they weigh thirty-seven hundred pounds each. I've been in subs for . . ."

"Yes, but these pallets are worth millions of dollars each!"

Jerry almost burst out laughing. Mark 48 torpedoes cost about one and a half million each. Submarine sailors and officers handle costly high-tech equipment every day. Hell, they lived inside one of the most complex and expensive machines ever built.

Captain Hardy appeared at the escape trunk, almost running as he climbed onto the deck and crossed the brow. He hurriedly returned the topside watch's salute as he strode toward the group. Emily Davis followed closely behind.

Patterson was careful to get in the first word. "These men are not handling the equipment pallets carefully enough. It's unsafe," she announced with a tone of authority.

"Mr. Mitchell?" Hardy's question was obvious as he returned Jerry's salute.

"The rig is the same one . . ." Jerry started.

Patterson interrupted again. "Look at the crane! They only have a single cable supporting the pallet! My God," she realized, "it's still in the air. Get it down!" she ordered. "Now!" She looked at the Captain.

So did everyone else. Hardy nodded. "Bring it down," he repeated and walked to one side, allowing the torpedo gang to gently bring it down to the pier. Patterson, Davis, Jerry, and Foster followed, formed a small group away from the others.

"Dr. Patterson," Hardy began. "I'm sure the rig is correct."

"I'm not interested in your opinion," she countered. "Make it safe or these pallets are not going aboard." Her tone was absolute.

Hardy looked at her, then the torpedo gang. There was a strange twinkle in his eye. "Fine then. We'll stop loading. I'm sure we can find a mobile crane with your desired overcapacity in a few days."

"A few days!" screamed Patterson. "We're supposed to leave tomorrow! This delay is absolutely unacceptable!"

"Excuse me, Captain," interrupted Davis. "Could I have a word with Dr. Patterson, please?"

Hardy nodded and Davis and Patterson stepped away from the three *Memphis* crewmembers.

"Emily, what is the meaning of this?" asked Patterson once they were out of earshot. "We have a huge problem here and these clowns aren't capable of solving it."

"Dr. Patterson, I went over the crane's latest inspection results with Lieutenant Mitchell and Senior Chief Foster before we started, and they are within specifications. I then gave them *my* permission to start loading. If there is a problem, it's not their fault."

"I see," responded Patterson coolly. Then, in a less tense tone, she asked, "Is that crane safe enough to load your equipment?"

"Absolutely," replied Davis. Without another word, Patterson and Davis rejoined Captain Hardy and his two subordinates.

"Dr. Davis has informed me that this crane is acceptable," declared Patterson. "But I insist that your people exercise better control of the pallets as they are transferred. Don't let them swing around so much."

"As you wish," responded Hardy. Then, looking at Jerry, he said, "Mr. Mitchell, double the number of guidelines and slow the crane down to keep the pallet's swing to a minimum." He looked at Patterson, who still looked unhappy. "And don't lift the pallet any higher than you have to when you swing it across," he said, sighing. He looked back again at Patterson, who nodded, still frowning. He walked away quickly.

Patterson also left, leaving Jerry, Foster, Davis, and the others all looking at each other. As little as Jerry knew, he thought the rig had worked fine yesterday. Foster, shaking his head, started barking orders to rig the extra guidelines. They had lost thirty minutes from Patterson's tiff, but finally resumed bringing the pallets aboard "safely."

Jerry overheard Seaman Jobin and TM3 Lee talking as they lashed the extra guidelines to the pallet. Troylor Jobin was a Virginia boy and his Southern drawl wrapped around his words like a blanket. "Did you see the way Hardy hopped when she hollered?"

"He certainly didn't fight her very hard," Lee agreed.

"All this extra work and time wasted, just on her say-so," Jobin grumbled. "And we've got to put up with that witch for the whole patrol?" He sounded incredulous.

Lee remarked. "I don't think she's just a tech rep."

Jobin nodded agreement. "Bearden says she bragged how she worked for the President. Ah'm thinking she's calling all the shots."

Moran walked over, and pretended to check the lashings. "Stow it. Here comes Broomhilda," he stage-whispered.

Jerry looked over to see Patterson climbing onto the deck. She didn't bother crossing over to the pier, but seemed to be checking to see if the torpedo gang was following Hardy's recent orders. When she saw the pallet being rigged with the extra lines, she went back below.

Once she was safely gone, Jobin laughed. "Broomhilda. I like it."

Hardy, Bair, Richards, and Patterson continued to check on the division's progress during the day. Jerry took to keeping one eye on the forward escape trunk, or when he was below, on the door to the torpedo room. As soon as Patterson or one of the senior officers approached, he'd intercept them and deliver a quick, cheerful report on how smoothly things were going. The tactic worked about half the time.

Jerry spent the rest of his time dealing with the paperwork and answering Davis' questions. He also tried to keep track of Foster. While Jerry believed that the Senior Chief would not sabotage the loading operation or the equipment, he wouldn't pass up a chance to make Jerry look foolish or create a mistake that could be blamed on the officer.

One of the documents Jerry was working with was the Weapon Stowage Record Book. It tallied, by type and serial number, what torpedoes or missiles were stowed where in the torpedo room. He was using it for the mission equipment as well. Jerry had added two of the equipment pallets to the record, but when he went to make an entry for the third, he couldn't find the book. It was a black three-ring binder and was clearly labeled. He'd parked it on top of the centerline torpedo storage rack, a reasonably flat spot in the middle of the compartment.

He looked around, thinking that it might have been knocked onto the deck, but there was so little deck space in the torpedo room that someone, most likely Jerry, would have tripped over it immediately. He was about to ask for a general search when he stopped himself. He didn't want to interrupt the loading to look for the record book, and he was sure he'd left it right on top of the console.

Jerry then remembered Foster standing near the aft end of the compartment, away from the loading activity, for several minutes. The senior chief was gone right now. On an impulse, Jerry walked aft and noticed several shadowed crevices among the torpedo racks and other equipment. The third one he checked held the missing notebook.

Jerry had barely retrieved it and begun making his next entry when Foster returned, along with Hardy. Jerry wondered what excuse Foster had used to get the Captain there. A progress report? A question? As he watched Foster, Jerry might have imagined a momentary flash of surprise on the Senior Chief's face.

Jerry reported their progress to Hardy, who quickly lost interest when he saw that there weren't any problems. The Senior Chief's face became a stoic mask. Jerry's small feeling of triumph was mixed with disappointment at having to waste mental energy on bull like this.

Despite the delays and constant "supervision" by Hardy or Patterson, the torpedomen managed to find their rhythm and the pallets started to come across in a regular fashion. As the support pallets, essentially crates full of supplies, came aboard, they were stowed in spaces normally reserved for torpedoes on the upper centerline rack. Finally the control and display pallet, filled with computers, displays, and power supplies needed to control the ROVs, was lowered into the torpedo room and stored near the Manta control console. The ROVs themselves were placed in the starboard stowage racks along with the winch and maintenance pallets, although putting them in place did not mean they were "installed." Boxes of cabling and miscellaneous equipment filled corners of the torpedo room. Davis assured Jerry and Foster that the clutter would be gone once everything was hooked up.

Although they'd started at 1330, it was nearly 2000 (eight in the evening) by the time the torpedo division finished bringing the last pallet aboard. By that time, Davis had methodically checked the support pallets and had started on the retrieval winch. Leads had to be run to power the winch, the controls had to be hooked up, and everything had to be tested until it was rock-solid reliable. There were no Radio Shacks where they were going.

Even after the last of the pallets were aboard, the division had a lot of work to do. All the loading gear had to be struck below and stowed. The torpedo loading tray had to be turned back into deck plates, and the weapons shipping hatch closed and inspected. Jerry's division performed a dozen tasks carefully, using checklists, all under Foster's careful eye.

They'd broken for dinner, with Lieutenant Washburn, the Supply Officer, checking with Jerry when his men would be able to stop and eat. It was well after the normal mealtime, but Washburn had kept the mess cooks standing by until the torpedo gang could be fed. He'd laid on a good meal for the crew's last night in port, with roast chicken and mashed potatoes and two kinds of pie for dessert. Jerry was starving by the time they all sat down, and even Emily Davis was ready to stop for a decent meal.

For convenience, they all ate together in the crew's mess, with Jerry and Davis seated at their own table and the rest of the torpedo division filling two others. Foster sat at the head of the enlisted group.

The men ate quietly, so quietly that Jerry noticed the silence. No grumbling, but no joking either. Jerry was tired and was sure his men were as well, but he wasn't so exhausted he couldn't talk. Emily kept up her customary stream of questions, about the boat, the living and eating arrangements for the enlisted men, what the food would be like after they'd been at sea for a month.

Jerry couldn't answer all of her questions completely, so Emily moved over to the enlisted table and asked to join them. The conversation picked up, and with a feminine audience, the torpedomen shared some of their stories about "life on a boat."

After dinner, they headed back to the torpedo room. It took two more hours for the torpedomen to finish their tasks, and they were almost as quiet as they were at dinner. In other circumstances, Jerry would have taken the Senior Chief aside and asked him what was wrong, but that wouldn't work with Foster.

So instead, Jerry listened and watched, and practiced making himself as invisible as circumstances allowed. As the torpedomen became involved in their tasks, Jerry eventually heard TM2 Boyd and TM3 Lee talking as they worked on a cable connection from the control pallet to a switch box for tube one. Boyd complimented Davis. "She's a pretty good tech. And she's got a good attitude." Jerry recalled that Boyd had been answering a lot of Emily's questions about life aboard a sub.

"She's okay, but that other one!" Lee shuddered. "I just re-upped so I could get a boat on the West Coast. Right now I wish I'd just gotten out."

"You and the rest of this division," Boyd agreed. "If everyone shows up for Quarters tomorrow morning, it'll be a miracle."

Underway

The shutting of a locker door brought Jerry to consciousness a few minutes before his alarm went off. It was just before six, with Quarters an hour away, but from the sounds in the passageway, half the crew must already be up. Jerry took a deep breath and stretched as much as the confines of his rack would allow. He could smell the enticing scents of breakfast from the wardroom next door, and that ended any further thoughts of lounging in his bunk. Getting up, Jerry dressed. Both Washburn and Berg were already gone and likely in the wardroom. Remembering that there were now ladies aboard, Jerry made sure he was respectable before stepping into the passageway.

The wardroom was crowded, with most of the junior officers either eating breakfast, or waiting their turn to sit down. Sitting on the couch was Emily Davis. Even in a beige-colored shirt and Dockers, Emily stood out among the khaki-clad officers. Dr. Patterson was nowhere in sight.

"Good morning, Emily. Is our boss sleeping in?" Jerry asked her, half-joking. Both of them knew he wasn't asking about Hardy.

"Dr. Patterson said she wasn't getting up until it stopped being so crowded," Davis replied seriously.

Almost everyone, including Jerry, laughed and Tom Holzmann immediately remarked, "That won't be for quite a while." Lenny Berg then asked, "Is that a promise?"

The laughter died suddenly and Jerry turned to see Patterson at the door, scowling at Berg. Silently, she moved toward the coffeepot as several officers scrambled out of her path. She poured a cup, added two sugars, and left, leaving an uncomfortable silence behind.

Berg looked at Jerry and shrugged. "What can she do, send me to sea?"

Lenny's quip failed to revive the wardroom's atmosphere and they ate silently, the mood clinging to the wardroom as officers ate their breakfast, left, and others took their place at the table. Jerry was glad to finish and headed for the torpedo room. The unfamiliar equipment they installed last night seemed to be in order, but Jerry couldn't shake his discomfort.

It wasn't the technology. As a pilot, Jerry had lived with complex equipment, had depended on it for his life. It was one characteristic that aviators and submariners had in common. Both trusted machines because they thoroughly understood them—how they worked, what their limits were, and exactly what to do if any of a hundred things went wrong. That kind of competence didn't come without long hours of drills, study, and more drills. It took time to obtain that level of competence—time that they didn't have.

Tomorrow, on a politician's say-so, they would get one chance with each ROV, and if they didn't work, that was it: the patrol would be scrubbed, and possibly, Jerry's new career along with it. He wasn't foolish enough to believe in third chances. Jerry knew he should care more about the mission than his career, but he still didn't have a clue what they were going to do with all this stuff.

QUARTERS ON THE pier were mostly for show. Families were allowed to watch and the crew was given a few minutes for good-byes before the maneuvering watch was set. Jerry watched from the bridge, already at his station, as fathers and husbands hugged, waved, and promised their wives and children things they couldn't control. The single guys, like Jerry, had fewer connections. He'd remembered to send a letter to his sister Clarice in Minnesota, asking her to make sure Mom didn't worry too much. The cold drizzle that started to fall mirrored the somber mood of the families and crew.

Jerry felt eager to get underway, in spite of all the obstacles he faced. Now he'd finally get the chance to prove himself. And when they returned, it would be resolved, one way or another.

He spotted Emily Davis on deck as she stumbled on a fitting and almost fell into the water. The contrast between her and Patterson was never more apparent. Davis was down among the men, asking questions and finding out everything she could. She was interested in what they did and how they did it, which came across to the crew as a professional compliment. The last time he'd seen Patterson, she'd been in the wardroom, typing on her laptop, doing her best to shut out everything and everybody.

By 0730, all stations were manned, the tug was secured alongside, and Jerry gave the order to single up all lines. The wind helped this time, setting *Memphis* off the pier, and Jerry almost felt at home as he conned the sub away from the base.

JERRY WAS KEPT busy throughout the surface transit, but even with a patch, Jerry's unhappy stomach constantly threatened to betray him. It took almost three hours to reach the gap between Block Island and Montauk Point and another three before they could submerge.

The diving alarm was a welcome sound. He could feel the boat's side-to-side motion fade as their depth increased. It also got him off the exposed bridge, which was cold and wet. Although he'd only been aboard a relatively short time, the sounds and sensations of *Memphis* submerging were familiar now. This was where she was supposed to be.

He'd just changed into dry clothes and stepped into the passageway when he saw Emily Davis leaving the wardroom. She looked nervous and tense, clearly upset.

"Emily, are you all right?"

She noticed Jerry and nodded hesitantly. "I'm fine. I'm just being foolish."

Jerry's face must have shown his confusion. "It's the first time I've ever been aboard a submerged submarine," she explained. She looked around, then stepped back into the wardroom, motioning for Jerry to follow. As soon as he stepped in, she closed the door. Jerry was suddenly—and acutely—conscious of the CO's orders against "fraternization" and how little slack Hardy would give if he were found alone with Emily.

"I feel like an idiot," Emily confessed. Her tone was measured, almost controlled, but she was visibly shaking. "I'm an engineer, and I know what pressure this boat can stand, but as soon as we submerged, I could sense all the water above us, tons of it. Hundreds of feet of it." She paused as fear flashed on her face. "How deep are we right now?"

"Two hundred and fifty feet." Jerry answered, pointing to the depth gauge on the bulkhead. He tried to keep his voice calm and steady, but knowing the exact number only increased her distress. Emily was on the verge of panicking. Great, thought Jerry, just great. She's claustrophobic. "Don't you work with submarines all the time?"

"Yes, but I specialized in ROVs. And being a woman, as well as a junior employee at the lab, I was never picked for any of the at sea trials. I've only been to sea once before and that was on the research ship *Knorr* back in '98." She paused, then almost started crying. "And I had no idea I'd feel like this! It never crossed my mind that I'd be so afraid! I should know better."

"You do know better, Emily, but this isn't a rational thing. It's pure emotion."

"So what do I do about it?" At this point, with her anxiety out in the open, facing her new fear, she was trembling and pale.

"I don't know," he said honestly. He was too new to submarines himself to have ever dealt with anything like this. Besides, the Navy's psychological screening process weeded out any applicants for subs who showed even the slightest signs of claustrophobia. "Does Dr. Patterson know?"

"No!" She shook her head violently.

Ill-equipped to handle the situation, Jerry tried to think of whom he should hand over this delicate problem to. There weren't too many sympathetic ears on this boat. In the end, Jerry went with his training. "Would you like to talk to the XO?"

"All right," said Emily. The idea seemed to calm her a bit, and Jerry realized that talking about her fear might be the best therapy.

"Okay, then, why don't you go to your stateroom and I'll go find the XO and ask him to come and see you," replied Jerry. Emily nodded and wiped her eyes with her shirtsleeve.

Hoping nobody was watching, the two ducked out of the wardroom and Jerry headed to control in search of the XO. He found him near the plotting tables talking to one of the quartermasters. Jerry waited until Bair had finished his conversation before approaching. "Sir, Dr. Davis would like to talk to you."

Bair nodded and said, "Fine. Where is she?" he asked, looking around.

"In your, I mean her, stateroom."

"And why is she there instead of here?" Bair asked.

"She needs to speak to you privately," Jerry answered softy.

"This can't be good." Bair observed and left, heading forward to his old stateroom. Relieved, Jerry felt absolutely no guilt about passing the buck to the XO.

It was a late lunch, scheduled after *Memphis* had submerged. Apparently, Jerry wasn't the only one aboard with a queasy stomach. He ate in the second sitting, which was fine with him. Not only did it give him a few more minutes for his appetite to return, but he could also pick out a good spot for the mission brief. All the junior officers ate quickly, so that the mess stewards could clean up by 1500. That's when the Captain and Patterson had promised to finally brief the crew on their destination and what they would do when they got there.

The chiefs started showing up before the JOs had even finished eating, and by 1500, the tiny wardroom was jammed with all the officers not on watch and most of the chiefs.

Hardy entered, followed by the two ladies, and everyone did their best in the cramped space to come to attention. The Captain let them stand for a moment, then said, "Seats." Emily Davis looked nervous, but that could have been for several reasons. Neither Hardy nor Patterson looked pleased.

The XO spread out a nautical chart and taped it to the bulkhead. A thick, dark black line stood out against the light blue and gray contours. It showed their track from New London, past Newfoundland, through the Denmark Strait between Iceland and Greenland, then past Jan Mayen Island and Spitsbergen, and finally across the Barents Sea. It almost touched Novaya Zemlaya, a barren finger of land that reached up from the far northern coast of Russia. The Barents Sea lay on its western side, the smaller Kara Sea to the east. Novaya Zemlaya was part of the Russian Federation.

Hardy let everyone study the chart for a few moments, then stood.

"At the direction of the President, this boat has been assigned a special mission." He pointed to the chart. "This is our route for the next twelve days. We will approach the eastern coast of Novaya Zemlaya, survey several environmentally sensitive sites, collect water and sediment samples, as well as other information, then return."

Jerry heard a buzz of conversation, with the word "environmental" repeated several times, always with a questioning tone. Mitchell was more puzzled at the general reaction than Hardy's announcement. He guessed this was not a typical mission.

"Dr. Patterson will now explain exactly what we're going to do." Hardy motioned to Patterson, who was sitting to his right. She stood up quickly and glanced at a pad of paper.

"President Huber has been a champion of the environment since his days as governor of Arizona. Even before that, as a state senator, he had led the drive for the cleanup of the San Sebastian waste site, as well as . . ."

Jerry fought the urge to tune her out completely. There was always the chance she might say something useful.

Patterson droned on for another five minutes about Huber's environmental consciousness, managing to work in how essential her expertise had been to the President during the election, and now as part of the President's Science Advisory Board. "It's vital that the President do well with this issue. The environmental vote is one of his core constituencies. It's never too early to start thinking about the next election."

Maybe she thought the silence in the room was polite attentiveness. Jerry, proudly apolitical, was repelled by the entire concept. A patrol to further a president's reelection chances?

She handed a second chart to Davis, who taped it up over the first one. A detailed chart of the Novaya Zemlaya's east coast, it was marked TOP SECRET, and was covered with angular shapes, crosshatched in several colors.

"These are locations that we know have been used by the Soviets—and now the Russians—as dumps for everything from toxic waste to fueled nuclear reactors. Red marks radioactive waste, orange is machinery, yellow toxic material, and purple is unknown. We are going to collect photographs and samples from these sites, enough evidence to convince any objective observer that the waste is leaking into the environment on a massive scale. They've denied it, of course."

She looked out at the officers and chiefs, as if expecting an answer—or at least agreement. For the first time since she'd come aboard, Patterson was smiling, her manner animated. It was clear to Jerry that she cared deeply about this, although he wasn't sure if it was the environment or the President's political agenda.

"In two months, at the World Environmental Congress in São Paulo,

Brazil, the President will confront the Russian delegation with the evidence we collect. He'll discredit them and gain stature with every country there. And then there's the domestic audience. This has the potential to add at least ten points to his approval rating."

She said the last sentence with so much enthusiasm Jerry almost laughed. She obviously expected her audience to react to this happy possibility. When they didn't, she stood silently for a moment, then seemed to shrug it off.

She turned to Hardy. "I want to talk about the ship's speed. Your 'transit speed' is fifteen knots." She consulted her notes to make sure she used the proper term.

Looking at the list, she asked, "Who is Lieutenant Commander Ho?"

The Engineer raised his hand. "Yes, ma'am?"

"As soon as we're done with the ROV trials this afternoon, change our speed to twenty-five knots." She saw surprise in the Engineer's face and paused. "This sub can move at least twenty-five knots, can't it? I looked up your speed. We can reach our destination in about half the time."

Hardy spoke up. "Standard transit speed is fifteen knots, because at higher speeds, we become more detectable. . . ."

"By whom?" Patterson asked. "We're not at war."

"The Russians will still try to detect us, and the higher speed will also put a strain on the engineering plant," he explained.

"Oh, so this thing really is a nuclear-powered junk pile." She smiled, almost triumphant.

Hardy bristled. "We were scheduled for decommissioning until they slapped us with this junket. We didn't ask for this mission."

"Look, your job is simple," she countered. "Just drive Dr. Davis and myself north and we'll do all the work."

She handed out papers to the Captain and XO. "See, I've already set up a survey plan." She taped one copy of the plan to the bulkhead. It was the same chart of the waste sites, marked with a route between the areas.

Bair stood to study the map, and Hardy turned in his seat to look at Lieutenant Commander O'Connell, the Navigator. "Did you help her with this?" Hardy's tone and expression were both stern, almost angry. He didn't like surprises.

O'Connell quickly shook his head. "No, sir. I've never seen this."

Hardy said, "Ma'am, our charts of that area are poor. Normally the Navigator develops a track and the XO and I approve it."

The XO, who had been studying the track, chimed in. "Sir, she's got us moving through some pretty shallow water." Hardy quickly stood up and examined Patterson's track.

Patterson refused to budge. "This plan will work. It's perfectly all right."

Hardy, studying the chart, said, "No, ma'am, it's not. You've just drawn lines connecting these different sites. We pass too close to some known wrecks, over an explosive dumping area, through very shallow water, and in some of these locations it's almost impossible to get out of if we're detected. The Navigator will review your plan. He will make sure to show you any changes and get your approval," he offered.

Patterson agreed reluctantly. "As long as it doesn't add a lot of time to the mission. We have to be back with the samples by the end of June. The São Paulo congress starts on July 8. If we're too late, then the whole mission will be wasted."

"I won't risk the ship's machinery breaking down in the middle of the Atlantic or running aground on the Russian coast for some political boondoggle."

"You'll do whatever's required to accomplish the mission. Those are the President's orders." Her tone was preemptory. Jerry certainly didn't like Captain Hardy, but he resented her speaking to his captain that way.

Hardy, angry and defensive, started to reply, then stopped himself, fighting for control. Jerry watched emotions play over his face, and then the Captain sighed. "We'll get back by the end of June."

Patterson smiled, almost triumphantly, but she tried to make it just a pleasant expression. She picked up her pad and studied it, trying to get the brief back to business. "I just have one more question. How can I send and receive e-mail while I'm aboard? I'm sure there are already several urgent messages waiting for me."

Hardy, for once surprised, didn't answer immediately, and Bair spoke up. "Ma'am, we can receive the Fleet broadcast three times a day. Any messages to you will be added to that. The crew receives personal messages the same way."

"No, no," she countered. "I asked about this before I left. They said that all Navy ships can send and receive e-mail these days."

"Navy surface ships, yes, through a commercial satellite system. We can't transmit while submerged, and even when we come up for the Fleet broadcasts, we usually only receive. Transmitting any radio signal is like waving a big 'We're over here' sign. Our mission orders specifically cite security as having a high priority."

Patterson became alarmed. "But that means I'll be out of touch for weeks. You don't understand. I work for the President. I deal with crises every day. If I can't communicate, . . ." she paused, as she tried to imagine being incommunicado for months. Finally she faced Hardy and said, "This is simply unacceptable. You have to let me read my e-mail," she announced.

Hardy had trouble hiding his enjoyment. "I'm sorry, Doctor. It's impossible."

"It's entirely possible. I'm the mission commander and I need to stay in close touch with my office and with the President."

His expression hardened. "And I'm the captain of this vessel. I will not do anything that so grossly compromises our security. And the mission, I might add."

"You're a glorified bus driver who needs to remember who's in charge!"

"And you need a lesson on the chain of command," Hardy stormed. He started to say something else, then stopped himself again and quickly left the wardroom.

Patterson, also fuming, followed.

A few moments later, Jerry heard the door to the Captain's cabin slam shut, and after a pause, open, and slam again. Considering that Hardy's stateroom was one deck up, Jerry wondered if it was still on its hinges.

Bair, finding himself suddenly in charge of the briefing, looked at the charts for a minute, then turned to the assembled officers and chiefs. "The briefing's over. I'm sure everyone has duties elsewhere," he said firmly.

The wardroom quickly emptied. Jerry grabbed his qualification book and headed aft—and almost got caught in the crush of everyone else with the same idea. A small part of Jerry wanted to be a fly on the wall in the Captain's stateroom, but most of him wanted to be as far away from forward compartment upper level as possible. Nothing good would come of the Captain's fight with Patterson and Jerry wanted to be long gone when they came out.

And at that moment, Jerry really wanted to be somewhere else, far away from *Memphis*. They'd just started out on the mission and already they seemed headed for disaster. With Hardy and Patterson at each other's throats over who was in charge, it seemed unlikely that the rest of the crew would be able to function properly. The thought of an antagonistic command element combined with the unfamiliar equipment, gave Jerry little hope for success. Searching for distraction, he fortified his resolve with a cup of hot cocoa from the galley and marched off to the engine room to delve into the mysteries of the lube oil system.

Dinner that night in the wardroom was silent, tense, and uncomfortable. While Patterson wasn't at the first sitting, Hardy was, and it was obvious to everyone that he was still in a foul mood. Jerry noticed that Emily was still a little pale and ate sparingly. Whether this was due to her claustrophobia or embarrassment over Patterson's behavior, he didn't know. Regardless, she retired to her stateroom immediately after dinner. Jerry did likewise, but he spent most of the evening preparing for his next checkout and turned in late. Sleep came surprisingly easily.

Early the next morning the mood on board had improved somewhat. At least some of the junior officers talked with each other during breakfast. But if Patterson or Hardy entered the wardroom, all conversation immediately ceased and everyone stared intently at their meal, careful to avoid direct eye contact with either of them. Neither seemed to care that their ongoing feud was adversely affecting everyone else on board.

And Jerry's musings made him lose track of the time. He had to get up to control for his first watch as Diving Officer under instruction. Jerry wolfed down a sticky bun and some cereal, grabbed his qual book, and literally ran up to control. For the next six hours, Jerry started applying some of the basic concepts necessary to keep *Memphis* at its ordered depth with a balanced trim. Lenny Berg was the OOD on the 0600 to 1200 watch and he passed on a few tricks as well.

Before they went to the wardroom for lunch, both Jerry and Lenny went to the stateroom to grab their notebooks. There would be little time after lunch before Davis would give her presentation on the capabilities of the ROVs and go over the launch and retrieval procedures. Rustling around his disorganized desk, Lenny looked over his shoulder at Jerry and asked, "So, who do you think is going to win round two? Yesterday was a bit of a draw."

Sighing, Jerry replied, "I'm entertaining the fleeting hope that both will act like civilized human beings this afternoon."

"Ha! Little chance of that, I'm afraid," chortled Berg. "But, as much as I hate to admit it, the Captain has every right to be pissed off. Patterson is way out of line."

"She certainly knows all the right buttons to push, doesn't she?"

"Well, since they are both control freaks, it doesn't take a Sherlock Holmes to see that they have the same buttons," stated Lenny firmly. "Ah, there's my notebook. What say we go and enjoy a quiet lunch at Chez *Memphis* before this afternoon's festivities."

Lunch was indeed quiet, with only four at second sitting. Jerry, Lenny, Al Millunzi, and Jim Porter had all just come off watch and they enjoyed their temporary isolation from the rest of the boat. During the meal, they talked, joked, and generally enjoyed each other's company. For a brief moment, Jerry saw the wardroom atmosphere he appreciated so much during his days at the squadron. He was glad to see that the camaraderie he missed wasn't completely dead on *Memphis*, just buried under the oppressive cloud cast by Hardy's command style.

Just as the dishes were being cleared away, Emily Davis walked in with her laptop. The four officers rose to greet her and then helped her hook up the computer to the flat panel display on the forward bulkhead. The mood remained pleasant and the banter lighthearted. It included the predictable joke by Berg on how many engineers did it take to screw in a light bulb. No sooner had the groans died down when Patterson burst into the wardroom.

The change in the room was palpable. Instantly everyone, including Emily, became tense and silent. Everywhere she went, Jerry thought, her sour, cold disposition dragged everyone down. Jerry found himself deeply resenting Patterson's influence.

After briefly conferring with Emily about the afternoon's presentation, Patterson poured a cup of coffee and sat down at the wardroom table. The room was now so quiet that her sipping could easily be heard. Ten minutes later, the wardroom was full to capacity, but it remained just as quiet. Hardy finally entered and motioned for those that had them to take their seats. He didn't even look at Patterson.

"Dr. Davis is going to brief us on the capabilities of the ROVs. Since very few of us have NMRS experience, I expect you all to give her your undivided attention. In an hour and a half, we'll slow down and give each ROV a shakedown test. We'll resume our transit north once the tests have been completed," declared Hardy. "These ROVs are crucial to the success of our mission and I expect a flawless performance from everyone involved. Dr. Davis, the floor is yours."

"Thank you, sir," replied Emily nervously. "As the Captain has already mentioned, the Draper Environmental Survey ROVs are based on Near Term Mine Reconnaissance System vehicles. However, they have been heavily modified to collect environmental data from undersea sites that are suspected to contain radiological contamination."

Emily was fidgety, tense, and definitely uncomfortable giving the briefing as she moved through the introductory material very quickly. As hard as he tried, Jerry just couldn't keep up with all the new information as Emily flew from one slide to the next. From the frustrated expression on a number of the crew's faces, he wasn't the only one, and Hardy was starting to get that impatient look. Fortunately, the XO piped up and asked Davis to go back a slide and clarify a point she had just made. As she looked at Bair to provide further explanation, Jerry saw him mouth the words: "Slow down." Emily nodded and her pace noticeably slowed.

It was only after she got to the detailed technical specifications of the ROVs that she seemed to reach her comfort zone. Slowly and deliberately, she went over every system and explained its function in detail. She also went over each step in the launch and recovery processes with the same degree of detail.

Jerry was furiously writing notes as he listened, and he couldn't help but be impressed with Emily's technical competence. Every question posed by a crew member was answered thoroughly and professionally. Even Hardy was getting into the briefing, leaning forward in his chair as Emily highlighted the various features of her vehicles. Patterson, on the other hand, seemed bored with the whole thing. Toward the end of the presentation, there was a lot of discussion on the sampling system and how it operated.

"Dr. Davis, since many of the sediment and water samples may be radioactive, how do we safely get them back to nucleonics, where the analysis equipment is installed?" asked Ho. "I'm concerned about the risk of spreading contamination throughout a good chunk of this boat."

"I understand your concern," replied Emily. "The sediment and water sampling systems are encased in individual watertight containment modules and are removed from the ROV as complete assemblies. They've been pressure-tested to four hundred pounds per square inch. The test pressure is greater than the ROV's maximum design depth."

"Good," said Hardy. Then, turning toward Jeff Ho, he continued, "Engineer, only your people will be allowed to transport the sample modules from the torpedo room to Nucleonics. And I expect radiation surveys to be made along the entire route to verify that there was no leakage."

"Aye, aye, sir," responded Ho.

"Any other questions?" demanded Hardy. When none were forthcoming, he said, "All right, then, we'll man ROV launch stations in half an hour. Dr. Davis, make sure the XO has a copy of your brief so it can be uploaded to the network for reference by the crew. Dismissed."

As people filed out of the wardroom, a number of the officers and chiefs paused to compliment Davis on her presentation. Patterson appeared annoyed by the attention that Emily was getting and left in a huff, nearly running over Cal Richards in the process.

Jerry stayed behind in the wardroom and waited for an opportunity to talk to Emily. It took a few minutes before he was able to get near enough to speak without having to raise his voice. "Great presentation, Emily. Even the Captain seemed to like it. I'd interpret that as a rare compliment."

"Thanks, it did seem to go well. Still, I'm just glad it's over."

"How are you doing with your little issue that we talked about yesterday?"

"Better, thank you. I'm still somewhat nervous, but the XO was very helpful in talking me through it. Thanks again for all your help," replied Emily sincerely.

"Glad to be of service, ma'am." Jerry said with a mock bow. He then took a quick look around the wardroom to make sure Patterson wasn't within earshot. "Switching topics, I noticed that Dr. Patterson didn't look too thrilled during your presentation. You'd think she would be more interested, seeing as these ROVs of yours are key to the success of this mission."

"Well, Jerry, in her defense, she has seen this brief over a dozen times," said Emily apologetically. "I'm sure it starts to get a bit stale after the fourth time."

"Yeah . . . well, I see your point. I guess I'm just reacting to her sandpaper approach to interpersonal relationships. She damn near ran over Mr. Richards getting out of the wardroom."

"She's still upset with Captain Hardy. They had a terrible fight after the meeting yesterday and apparently Hardy read her the riot act on what she can and cannot do in regard to this mission. From what little she has told me, she'd turn this sub around right now if she hadn't committed herself in front of the President." Emily paused while she finished putting her laptop away. She then looked Jerry in the eye and said, "Dr. Patterson doesn't take it well when people oppose her. She's used to being in charge and she's used to getting her way."

"Sounds vaguely like my commanding officer," remarked Jerry sympathetically. "But if we are going to pull this mission off, we all need to learn to play nice."

"Teamwork is not something Joanna Patterson is good at. Just ask about a half dozen *former* White House staffers," replied Emily with a slight hint of humor.

"Wonderful! And Captain Hardy's afraid of joining them."

"That's about how I see it, Mr. Mitchell."

"Well, then, with that cheery thought in mind, Dr. Davis, shall we head off to the torpedo room and prepare your vehicles for their test runs?"

"Certainly." She brightened as Jerry changed the subject. "But I need to get something to drink. My throat is dry after all that talking." The hoarseness of Emily's voice reinforced her statement.

"Sure thing. We can swing by the galley and grab a cup of bug juice on the way," said Jerry.

"Ewwww, that sounds disgusting! Why do you guys have to be so gross?" complained Emily.

"Sorry, Navy tradition. How about we grab you a cup of cheap Kool-Aid? I believe they are serving green and purple today."

"Huh? What's with the colors? Don't you Navy types believe in flavors like the rest of the us?"

"In theory, there are flavors. I think the green is supposed to be lime and the purple is grape. But they pretty much taste the same, so we go by colors. That's what you get when you buy from the lowest bidder."

Making their way to the galley, Jerry and Emily picked up their drinks and then headed forward to the ladder that led to forward compartment lower level and the torpedo room. Since the ladder ended up in the twenty-one-man bunkroom, Jerry went down first to make sure no one would be "surprised" by Emily's appearance. With the coast clear, Emily quickly made her descent and the two of them entered the torpedo room.

Senior Chief Foster already had the entire torpedo division assembled when Jerry and Emily arrived. Foster was reviewing the ROV launch procedures with the men and paid little attention to the two as they headed over to the ROV control area.

Emily sat down at the control and display pallet and powered up the computer systems. Jerry looked around the space as she went through the initial system checks. He focused on the two ROVs in their support cradles and his eye caught the stenciled H and D on the vehicles. He asked, "Emily, I have a question for you. What do the 'H' and 'D' stand for on the ROVs?"

"Oh, that's just my way of telling them apart. The 'H' stands for Huey and the 'D' stands for Duey."

Jerry just stood there and stared. The quizzical look on his face made Emily chuckle.

"You mean to tell me you named those two vehicles after Donald Duck's nephews?"

"Ahh, well, uh . . . yes . . . and no," answered Emily, whose face started to blush.

"Okay, that was as clear as mud," replied Jerry sarcastically. "C'mon, what do the letters really stand for?"

"I told you," said Emily defensively. "My babies are named after two of the maintenance robots from the 1971 science fiction movie *Silent Running*. The robots were named after Donald's nephews."

"*Silent Running?*" asked a befuddled Jerry. "Isn't that a submarine movie?"

"Oh, no! It's classic sci-fi!" Emily's face brightened, and she became more animated as she described the movie to Jerry. "There were these three spaceships carrying the last existing forests in domes, awaiting the message to return to Earth and renew the world following a devastating nuclear war. And on each ship there were three maintenance robots, and on the *Valley Forge* the three robots were named Huey, Duey, and Louie."

Jerry could only stare in utter amazement as Emily just kept babbling on about this movie. She had the same unrestrained zeal for science fiction that his sisters had for shoes, jewelry, and boys. Jerry was now absolutely convinced that Emily Davis was a geek, a nerd—another brilliant engineer who didn't appear to have a life. She went on for ten more minutes and finally concluded by describing how the tragic hero kills himself with a nuclear bomb. "It's a wonderful movie with lots of depth and emotion all tied together in a futuristic spaceship motif. You really should see it sometime."

"Let me get this straight," Jerry said with deep concern in his voice. "Your favorite movie is about a ship. It has two robots named Huey and Duey. The movie has an environmental theme to it. Its title is *Silent Running*, which is something we will probably be doing a lot of. And at end, the hero is killed by a nuke. Are you trying to tell me something here?"

"What?" It was now Emily's turn to be confused. But after a few moments, her eyes widened, her mouth dropped, and she sputtered, "Oh. Oh! No, no, I didn't mean anything like that at all, Jerry!"

"Good! I'm glad to hear it, because I don't like your ending." Both of them laughed over Jerry's response. The sound was so loud that all of the torpedomen stopped and looked over at the two of them. Foster had absolute disdain on his face.

Before Jerry could explain, the 1MC announced, "Man ROV launch stations."

Pulling himself together, Jerry looked over at Foster and ordered, "Senior Chief, please start loading Huey into tube three."

Perplexed, Foster replied, "Excuse me, sir?"

"The ROV with the 'H' on it, that's Huey. Please load it into tube three."

"Aye, aye, sir," Foster said coldly.

Foster turned and signaled TM1 Moran, who opened the breech door for tube three remotely from the weapons launching console. Greer then inspected the tube with a flashlight, while Foster and the other torpedomen positioned the loading tray with the ROV so it lined up with tube three. The hydraulic rammer was connected, and Huey was slowly pushed into the tube, stern first and upside down. Emily showed the torpedomen how to thread the fiber-optic cable through the small penetration in the breech door and made sure there was enough slack so the cable could be hooked up to the connection box on the inboard side of the tube.

Foster and Lee then attached the deployment drogue to the nose probe on the ROV and slipped the retrieval cable through a larger breech door penetration and attached it to the drogue body. Finally a breech support ring was installed in the tube, which firmly secured the ROV and would prevent it from moving inadvertently. After the loading had been finished, Emily and Jerry inspected the ROV to make sure everything was in order. For Jerry, this was more of a quick course on what to look for when double-checking to see that a ROV had been loaded properly.

Satisfied that everything was correct, Emily asked Moran to shut and lock the breech door. She then took the fiber-optic cable, crimped on a connector, and hooked it up to the connection box. While the loading process went well, it still took twenty minutes to complete and it was clear from the torpedo room phone talker that the Captain was getting impatient.

Jerry and Emily hurried back over to the control pallet, and while Jerry put on his headset, Emily brought Huey to life. After a quick diagnostic check, she informed Jerry that everything was functioning normally and that Huey was ready to go. Jerry then reported to the control room, "Control, U-bay. ROV has been loaded and tested. Test satisfactory. Request permission to flood tube three, equalize to sea pressure, and open the outer door."

The Chief of the Watch in control acknowledged the request and relayed it on to the OOD, who in turn asked the Captain. It didn't take long before "Permission granted" was passed back to Jerry. Looking over toward Moran, Jerry called out in a loud voice, "Launcher, flood tube three, equalize to sea pressure, and open the outer door."

"Flood tube three, equalize to sea pressure, and open the outer door, aye, sir," replied Moran.

Looking back down at the checklist, Jerry marked off the step with a grease pencil. He then looked at the ship's speed, the digital display read five knots, and he requested control to slow to two knots—bare steerageway.

"Sir, tube three outer door open," reported Moran.

"Very well," said Jerry. Now all they had to wait for was for *Memphis* to slow down enough so that the ROV could leave the tube without damaging itself in the process. It took a few minutes, but as soon as the speed indicator read two knots, Jerry contacted control again.

"Control, U-bay. Tube three outer door is open, all launch conditions have been met. Request permission to launch the ROV."

As Jerry was waiting for permission from control, Dr. Patterson walked into the back of the torpedo room. He waved her over and offered her his chair. Jerry was surprised to hear her say, "Thank you."

Control relayed the Captain's permission, and Jerry looked over at TM2 Boyd at the winch controls. "Winch operator, release the brake."

"Release the brake, aye. Sir, the brake is released," said Boyd.

"Very Well." Jerry then turned to Emily and said, "It's your show now, Dr. Davis. Launch Huey."

"Right. Engaging thruster," she said.

"Louder, Emily. Everyone has to hear you," chided Jerry.

"Engaging thruster," repeated Emily in a louder voice.

"Cable paying out," reported Boyd.

"Very well," acknowledged Jerry.

The display console showed Huey slowly backing out of the tube. Once clear of the submarine's hull, the ROV swung around in a lazy arc, righting itself, and assumed a position twenty feet below *Memphis.*

Emily announced that Huey was in the tow position. This was confirmed by Boyd, who reported that the cable was holding. Jerry then ordered the winch brake engaged and informed control that they were ready to begin the tow test. Slowly but steadily, *Memphis* increased speed from two to eight knots. At each half-knot increment, Boyd reported the tension on the cable. The stresses were within the specifications provided by Draper Labs. With the tow test completed, Jerry requested that the boat's speed be reduced to five knots in preparation for the next phase of the trials.

While *Memphis* was slowing down, Seaman Jobin noticed that some water drops were coming from the fiber optic penetration in the breech door. Surprised, he called out to Emily, "Doctor Davis, ma'am, there are some drops of water leaking from the fiber-optic penetration in the door. Is it supposed to do that?"

Jerry took off his headset and walked over to tube three. So did Foster. As they were moving toward the tube, Emily said, "I was warned that the penetrations through the breech door might weep initially. As long as it is just droplets, it should be fine."

Both Jerry and Foster looked at the very slow but steady drip from the seal around the penetration. Their instinctive dislike of any seawater entering the boat fought against Dr. Davis' known engineering credentials. "Senior Chief?" Jerry asked hesitantly. Foster looked at his division officer with an equally questioning expression and shrugged his shoulders. "I have no idea if this is normal, sir. But it doesn't look too bad."

"Okay, then, let's continue the test," said Jerry as he stood up. "Jobin, keep an eye on it. If it gets any worse, sing out."

"Aye, aye, sir," replied Jobin.

"What's next, Dr. Davis?" asked Jerry.

"It's time to let Huey go for a short swim." After pushing a few buttons and then pulling back on the joystick, Emily announced, "Detaching from the drogue."

Jerry watched as Emily activated the forward-looking sonar and the video camera. Instantly, the sonar display showed the outline of *Memphis'* hull, but only a vague shadow could be seen on the video screen. She then turned on the two 150-watt underwater lights and the greenish underside became clearly visible.

"Whoa! Way cool," remarked Jerry softly.

Emily drove Huey about five hundred yards away from *Memphis* and then back. Satisfied that everything seemed to be in working order, she told Jerry it was time to recover the ROV.

Jerry nodded and called to control. "Control, U-bay. Preparing to recover the ROV. Request permission to flood down, equalize, and open the outer door on tube one."

Permission was granted, and Moran proceeded to open tube one's outer door. Normally it would not be possible to open both the outer doors in the same tube nest, but Foster had disabled the mechanical interlock. This was necessary since tube one contained a retractable arm that would be needed to assist in the recovery of the ROV into tube three below.

"Activating docking beacon," announced Emily. The very-high-frequency acoustic beacon provided precise information on the drogue's location to the ROV's navigation system. This enabled it to find the drogue and dock. As Huey approached the drogue, Emily tweaked the course with slight nudges of the joystick. Once the nose probe of the ROV edged into the drogue, mechanical clamps latched onto it and held the ROV securely.

Turning off the sonar, video camera, and lights, Emily reported, "Huey is docked and ready to be retrieved."

"Very well," said Jerry as he moved over to the retrieval arm station. He turned on the black-and-white video camera and lights and then extended the arm. "Winch operator, slowly reel in the ROV to my mark." Boyd acknowledged Jerry's order and began to reel in the cable. Jerry watched the video screen intently, waiting for the first sign that the ROV was near the outer door of tube three. He wished he had as clear a view as Emily did from her vehicle's video system, but the arm used considerably less advanced technology. Soon the ROV's form emerged from the shadows. Jerry shouted, "Mark!" and Boyd stopped the winch. He then tried to reach Huey with the arm, but the ROV was still too far away. It took a couple of tries before Jerry got a good grip on Huey's hull. As Boyd started reeling in again, Jerry moved the ROV into place so that it entered tube three cleanly. As Jerry was stowing the retrieval arm, Boyd called out, "Breech ring contact."

With a sigh of relief, Jerry ordered, "Launcher, close the outer door on tube three, drain the tube, and open the breech door." He felt like clapping and Emily had a cautious smile. One down, one to go.

Jerry turned to Foster and said, "Senior Chief, have the men pull Huey from the tube and prepare Duey for its test run as quickly as they can."

"I know what to do, sir," replied Foster icily.

"Very well, Senior. Carry on," responded Jerry casually.

The second test run went more smoothly than the first, and Jerry thought his guys were starting to get the hang of deploying and recovering the ROVs. After Duey was recovered, Jerry sent some of the division off to dinner while the others washed down the two ROVs. The first group returned to perform some of the required maintenance, under Emily's watchful eye, while the others went to the second sitting.

Both Emily and Dr. Patterson were very pleased with the test runs, and both were confident that the ROVs would perform as expected once *Memphis* reached the Kara Sea. After everything was completed, and Emily had tucked her babies in for the night, Jerry grabbed a cup of coffee in the wardroom and started studying for his next watch.

All in all, Jerry thought, the day had gone remarkably well. The ROVs had performed to spec, Emily was happy with how things went, and both Hardy and Patterson had been civil. Foster was still a pain in the ass, but he had gotten the job done, and that counted for something. Jerry hoped that maybe, just maybe, this crew had turned the corner and that things would improve in the coming days. Jerry even dared to consider the possibility that this mission might not be as bad as he had originally thought. Only time would tell.

Drill Team

The obnoxious wailing woke Jerry from a dead sleep and for a moment he thought it was his alarm clock, but as he reached for it, he woke up a little more. It was loud, way too loud for his alarm clock. As his brain began to function, Jerry recognized the sound. It was the Collision Alarm. There was a flooding casualty somewhere on board the boat.

Berg and Washburn were already out of their bunks and pulling on their poopy suits. As Jerry got up, the alarm stopped and he heard the Chief of the Watch's voice over the 1MC announcing system. "FLOODING IN THE ENGINE ROOM! CASUALTY ASSISTANCE TEAM LAY TO THE ENGINE ROOM!"

Nobody in the stateroom slowed down, and Jerry rediscovered that quickly dressing in a cramped space with two other people took a lot of practice all by itself. He inflicted a nasty blow to Washburn's rib cage when Jerry's elbow stuck out a bit too far, and he almost put on Berg's shoes. As he dressed, Jerry went over his assignment for the different emergency stations. For flooding, he was supposed to muster his division in the torpedo room.

Officers were pouring out of their staterooms like ants from a kicked-over hill. Jerry hurried toward the ladder and slid down the handrails to reach the torpedo room below. Most of the TMs and FTs were already there, including Senior Chief Foster. As he took stock of his spaces, Jerry thought to check his watch. It was 2:23 in the morning.

It was only a drill, of course, so there wasn't a fountain of cold seawater endangering *Memphis*. FT3 Larsen was wearing the sound-powered phones that allowed him to pass information on to everyone in the torpedo room as to what was going on in the engine room.

Jerry was ready to sit tight and wait when Foster started grilling the torpedo gang. He pointed to the aft bulkhead. "Seaman Jobin, what do we do if water starts coming under that door? Petty Officer Boyd, how do we fire torpedoes if we lose the high-pressure firing air reducer?"

A door on the aft bulkhead led to a passageway on the lower level, but it wasn't watertight, so there was little they could do to stop the flow of water. There were, however, emergency procedures for restoring high-pressure firing air, should the reducer fail.

As Boyd simulated setting up the starboard tube nest for a shot, Emily Davis came down the aisle between the torpedo storage racks.

"Is this your damage control station?" Jerry asked.

"What's that?" Emily asked in return. She seemed nervous.

"The XO was supposed to assign you stations. Places where you're supposed to go in an emergency," he explained.

As he spoke, the lights suddenly went out. Battery-powered battle lanterns cut in automatically, creating cones of light filled with angular shadows. Jerry was a little startled, but Davis screamed and headed back toward the door.

"It's all right!" he called. "They're just isolating some of the electrical circuits to keep them from shorting out."

Davis froze, either because of Jerry's explanation or because the path before her was dark as well. "It's just part of the drill." It was hard to sound soothing without also patronizing her, but she was probably too scared to notice. She held her place between the racks, undecided about which darkness was less threatening. Finally she turned and felt her way back toward Jerry.

TM1 Moran brought over a sound-powered phone headset. "Here, ma'am. Maybe you'd like to listen in on the DC circuit." He helped her with the headphones and the unfamiliar microphone. Moran then explained how the phones worked; that the energy of her voice created the current that powered the circuit. She grasped the principle instantly and was also interested in the activity on the circuit. "Just don't press the 'Talk' button on top of the mouthpiece," Moran instructed.

Just as Davis started to calm down, the lights came on, and the 1MC announced, "Secure from drill."

Another voice, the Captain's, came on the 1MC. "That was disgraceful. It took eight minutes for the Casualty Assistance Team to get on scene and twelve minutes to secure the flooding and begin dewatering. Do I have to remind everyone that there is only one watertight bulkhead inside the pressure hull?" It was one of the first things any submariner learned about the *Los Angeles* class. Only the forward bulkhead to the reactor compartment was fully rated to test depth. The Captain's caustic reminder was more than a little insulting.

"This was a simple one. In a real flooding casualty, we would have lost vital systems, and the accumulating seawater would have taken out others. But if you prefer standing hip-deep in cold salt water, we'll let you try it.

"So far, this crew has not demonstrated it is ready to respond to an emergency properly. Until it is, expect more drills. That is all."

Hardy gave them forty-five minutes before hitting them again. This time it was the general alarm klaxon, followed by "FIRE. FIRE IN THE PORT AC SWITCHBOARD. ALL HANDS DON EABS!" The ventilation fans and lights died immediately, and Jerry had to fumble for a flashlight he kept by his bunk. Berg and Washburn also used them in what now seemed to be an even smaller stateroom.

Slowed by the darkness and the need to plug into an EAB manifold to breathe, Jerry found his division already mustered in the torpedo room. Larsen had the phones on again and Foster had started a training session on the emergency air breathing system. Jerry stood and listened carefully. Foster knew the ropes, and while he might hate Jerry, he took care of his men.

Emily came down the aisle again, carefully holding a flashlight so that it pointed at the deck immediately in front of her. "I asked Lieutenant Commander Bair," she announced, "and he says I should report here, since this is where my . . . ROVs . . . are . . . located." Her words trailed off as the light showed nearly a dozen men standing around with masks on. Her puzzled look told Jerry that she didn't have a clue as to what was going on. Walking over to her, Jerry removed his mask and said, "Good morning again, Dr. Davis. If I may be so blunt, where is your EAB mask?"

"My what?"

"Your emergency air breathing mask, like this one." Jerry held up his mask so that Emily could see it clearly. "There are two such masks in your stateroom: one for you and another for Dr. Patterson. If you hear the 1MC announce 'Don EABs,' please take the mask out of the bag, put it on, and make sure you have a good seal. You then plug the mask into an air manifold that looks like this." Jerry pointed up into the overhead at a red-colored pipe with four plugs protruding from it.

"I'm sorry. I didn't realize I was to participate that much in the drills," Emily apologized.

"The EAB system's purpose is to enable you to continue breathing in a toxic atmosphere. That usually happens when there's a fire on a submarine. You need to learn how to use the EAB mask properly so that you are prepared in case something does go wrong," Jerry explained firmly. "In fact, why don't you sit in on Senior Chief Foster's training? He's going over the basics right now." Just as he was about to lead Emily over, it finally struck him that Dr. Patterson wasn't here with her.

"Where is Dr. Patterson? What's her emergency station?" asked Jerry.

"She's still in bed," answered Davis. "She says these drills are silly and refuses to have anything to do with them."

"What?" exclaimed Jerry.

Everyone looked at Emily with as much surprise as their division officer. Even Foster stopped his instructions in mid-sentence. Nobody on a sub ignored casualty drills.

Hardy's voice over the 1MC announced: "Secure from drill. All hands remove EABs. If that had been a real fire, I'd be heading for the nearest port and hoping we'd make it. It took too long to isolate the circuit and once again the Casualty Assistance Team was too slow. Count on doing this again until you do it right." The lights came on and Jerry wearily headed back to bed.

Hardy hit them with a reactor scram at five, and then an engineering casualty during breakfast. As that drill ended, Jerry heard the General Alarm and the 1MC announcement, "MAN BATTLE STATIONS TORPEDO." Jerry was the Officer of the Deck under instruction for this drill, so he hurried to the control room.

He came into the space on the tail end of yet another argument between Hardy and Patterson. ". . . tired of these games. I've got work to do, and these drills keep slowing us down."

"Doctor, I will drill this crew until I am satisfied with their performance. If our only job is to get you north, then how I run my boat is none of your business." He spoke calmly, almost casually.

"Captain Hardy, you will stop these pointless drills!" Patterson's voice was more than firm.

Hardy paused before answering. For a moment, Jerry thought he was going to comply. Then his expression hardened. "Respectfully, ma'am, I refuse." As Patterson started to protest, he cut her off. "And in the future, Doctor, for the safety of this boat, you will participate in any casualty drills." She didn't answer him immediately and he continued. "Do not mistake me, Doctor. It truly is the safety of the boat—and the mission—that is at stake here."

Patterson, almost expressionless, looked at Hardy for a moment, then nodded silently in agreement. She turned and left the control room.

Jerry realized he'd been holding his breath. So there were limits, things even Hardy couldn't be bullied into doing. It made Jerry a little more hopeful, but he wondered what price they'd pay for Hardy's defiance.

The drills continued throughout the day, with Hardy mixing accidents, engineering casualties, and battle drills almost continuously.

Drills are a normal part of submarine life, but Hardy was merciless in his pace, as well as in his critique of the crew's actions. Even the smallest infraction brought blistering condemnation. The best the crew could hope for was a plain: "Secure from drill." If Hardy didn't have anything bad to say, he wouldn't say anything at all.

Jerry watched as the crew took grim satisfaction in the lack of praise. During one of the engineering drills, he overheard one of the nuke electronics technicians say proudly, "Even the old man can't find anything wrong with that one."

But if there was any criticism from Hardy, the department head and division officers echoed it, passing it down the chain of command. When the machinist mates didn't deal with a feed pump casualty quickly enough,

Hardy held a "washup" in the wardroom—for all the officers. After reviewing the casualty in detail and pointing out each and every thing that had gone wrong, Hardy laid into Lieutenant Commander Ho, the Engineer.

"Your people aren't properly trained or supervised. You tell Jackson, Hughes, Train, and even Chief Barber that their performance is not satisfactory, nor is yours for letting it happen."

Ho stood at attention in front of the entire wardroom while the Captain lambasted him for several more minutes. He managed to work in an "Aye, aye" or "Yes, sir" where appropriate, but Hardy never gave him the chance to explain or even apologize.

Jerry listened to it with the rest of the wardroom, embarrassed for Ho, and remembered how different his old squadron commander had been. He suspected that the difference in command styles was not because one was an aviator and the other a submariner.

After Hardy left the wardroom, Jerry watched as Ho turned on Al Millunzi, the Main Propulsion Assistant. His division maintained and operated the feed pump in question and had muffed the drill. "What were your people thinking, mister? Or were they thinking at all?" Ho spoke loudly, much more loudly than he had to, and Jerry saw him glance in the direction of the passageway, as if he wanted to make sure Hardy heard him berating the MPA.

Millunzi immediately came to attention and didn't respond as Ho criticized his leadership, his technical knowledge, and even his dedication to the Navy. "I'll expect nothing less than perfection from you and your men, mister. Now, go make it happen!"

The lieutenant, red-faced, nodded silently and left the wardroom. Jerry felt sure that Chief Barber and M division were next in line for "verbal admonition."

As the crew demonstrated their competence with the basic drills, Hardy and the XO increased the complexity. Engineering casualties caused flooding. Toxic smoke from a simulated insulation fire in forward compartment middle level caused dozens of simulated casualties, including Jerry and his men, who were told to lie in place and wait to be treated.

The rescuers appeared quickly, all wearing EABs and their fire-fighting suits. As the leading "rescuer" reached down to pick up one of the casualties, the XO stopped him. "Wait a minute, Brown. Is your mask on properly?"

Machinist Mate Second Class Brown nodded, "Yes, sir." His answer was muffled by the mask.

"Good," the XO replied. "And can you see all right?"

"Yessir, as well as the mask allows," responded Brown.

"Do you have a nifty with you?" Bair asked innocently. The nifty is the handheld Navy infrared thermal imager (NIFTI), which is used by firefighters to locate a fire in thick, obscuring smoke. It can also be used to find personnel casualties by their body heat.

"Uh, no, sir. The fire-fighting teams have both of them."

"Well, that's no good! This compartment is filled with toxic smoke. It's not only poisonous, it's nearly opaque." Bair pulled out a small green trash bag and slipped it over Brown's head. He then passed bags to the rest of the team. "Here, all of you put these on, just like Brown."

As they pulled the bags over their heads, a muffled curse came from somewhere in the group. "I can't see shit!" exclaimed an anonymous voice.

"I can't see shit, sir!" the XO replied, amused. "If you can guarantee that fires will never have smoke, I'll let you take off the bags."

"Permission to proceed, sir," Brown said in a tone that managed to mix frustration with proper respect for the XO's rank.

Bair nodded approval, and then, remembering they couldn't see him, said, "Proceed."

The rescuers were required to actually "examine" each casualty, then bodily lift the "unconscious" man from the space and evacuate him to a safe portion of the sub. Stumbling, moving carefully to avoid the angular equipment that filled the space, the rescue team had only evacuated half of the casualties in the torpedo room when Hardy came clattering down the ladder from the deck above.

"What's going on . . ." he started, but then stopped himself as he realized what the XO had done. He saw Bair checking his watch and asked, "How long have they been at it?"

"Ten minutes, sir. They've cleared five casualties so far."

"Leaving the other five breathing toxic smoke for ten minutes," the Captain said harshly. He pointed to the men, including Jerry, still lying "unconscious" on the deck. "Well, we might as well stop the drill, because these men are all dead."

The rescue team did stop, and some of the men started to remove their bags, but Hardy yelled, "No! Belay my last! Leave the bags on and keep going. You obviously need the practice. Next time you might not have ten minutes."

The crew had now been subjected to over fifteen hours of intense drilling, and both Bair and Master Chief Reynolds argued strongly for a break to let the crew catch its breath and have a meal in peace. Hardy deferred to the petitions of the XO and COB and allowed the crew to eat dinner without any interruptions, in stark contrast to both breakfast and lunch, and everyone welcomed the three-hour respite.

The meal, however, was not according to the menu that was listed in the plan of the day. Washburn apologized profusely to both the wardroom and the crew's mess for having to serve sliders and fries, instead of the much-anticipated surf 'n' turf. His mess cooks just didn't have enough time to prepare the steaks and lobsters with all the drill activity. Although there was a little grumbling, no one blamed the supply officer. Most of the crew was just grateful to have a quiet hot meal.

Half an hour after dinner, though, the drills returned with a vengeance. "FIRE IN THE TORPEDO ROOM! ALL HANDS DON EABS! CASUALTY ASSISTANCE TEAM LAY TO THE TORPEDO ROOM," blared the 1MC. Followed immediately by the *BONG, BONG, BONG* of the general alarm. Jerry grabbed the EAB mask on his bunk and started to walk quickly to his spaces. He had taken only a few steps, when he nearly collided with Emily Davis, who was exiting the wardroom. "Stay here!" Jerry yelled as he literally pushed her back into the wardroom. Confused by Jerry's actions, Emily watched as he turned the corner on his way to the torpedo room. The other junior officers scampered by, going as fast as they could to their damage control stations. Not knowing what to do, Emily shut the wardroom door and sat down on the couch.

Jerry reached the crew accommodations just aft of the torpedo room and found a number of TMs and FTs in fire-fighting gear rigging a fire hose. He slipped on a Nomex flame-retardant jumpsuit and the protective headgear and gloves as quickly as the very cramped quarters would allow. Once finished, he moved up to the man with the sound-powered phones to report to control that he was in charge at the scene. But as Jerry got closer, he was surprised to see that it was FT1 Bearden manning the phones. Looking around, he saw no sign of Senior Chief Foster.

"Petty Officer Bearden, where is the Senior Chief?"

"I don't know, sir. He should have been here by now." Bearden's response did not encourage Jerry at all. "I'm on line with control. Do you want me to report that you are in charge at the scene?"

"Yes, please." As Bearden made the report, Jerry looked around the area and saw that the team was just about ready to make its entry into the torpedo room. He then noticed that the red ball cap that Bair was wearing, the "badge" of a drill monitor, had a Fokker triplane embroidered on the front. The XO also had a grin on his face that would do justice to the Cheshire cat. Jerry poked Bearden on the shoulder and asked, "What's with the XO?"

Bearden turned, looked, and then Jerry saw his shoulders sag. Facing his division officer, Bearden said dejectedly, "Ahh shit, sir. We're screwed."

"What's wrong?"

"The XO is wearing his Red Baron hat. It's his way of telling us that this drill is going to be a ball buster. Every time he's worn that hat, the drill has always been complex and hard. Very hard."

"Wonderful," replied Jerry sarcastically.

An unidentifiable rating then handed Jerry a training NIFTI. Actually, it was just a small coffee can with both of the ends removed and painted white, but it was good enough to keep one of the XO's stupid green garbage bags off his head.

Positioning the hose team, Jerry turned to have Bearden report that they were making their entry. Only, he wasn't there. Looking frantically for his phone talker, Jerry spotted Bearden and Foster at the end of the line, apparently arguing about something, given Foster's animated hand motions. Angrily, Bearden took off the sound-powered phones and handed them to the Senior Chief. It seemed to take Foster a very long time to get the phones on, adjusted, and checked back into control. Jerry figured that that little stunt had cost them almost a minute. The XO certainly didn't look happy.

Once Foster finally reached Jerry, he ordered the senior chief to report to control that the team was entering the torpedo room. As Jerry opened the door, all the lights went out in the compartment and everyone, save Jerry, had a bag put over their head. Holding his coffee can up to his face, Jerry was allowed to see a flickering reddish light from the aft port side of the room. Great, thought Jerry, the fire is over by the warshot Mk 48s. I bet we only have a limited amount of time before the XO has one of the weapons cooks off. Bearden was right. This will be a ball buster.

Advancing slowly, crouched down and waddling, Jerry led his team up and around the center torpedo storage rack. As they came up to the weapons launching console, Jerry saw TM3 Lee lying on the deck. Jerry directed the last two members of the team to remove Lee from the torpedo room as quickly as they could. Foster grabbed another sound-powered phone set from its storage box and tried to find the jack; the first set he had been wearing wasn't long enough to reach the fire's location. Jerry reached over, took the connector, and plugged it in for him. The senior chief seemed to double-check the connection, but Jerry wasn't about to be blindsided again and he rechecked the connection himself. It was secure.

Continuing on around the center stow, the team came across a red strobe light that marked the location of the fire. The only thing back in that corner was one of the AC power distribution panels. Turning to Foster, Jerry yelled, "To control, the fire is near panel P-4. Recommend electrically isolating the panel." Foster repeated the report precisely and forwarded it to control. Jerry waited about fifteen seconds and then directed the hose team to shift to high-velocity fog and start fighting the fire. He waited the extra time to allow control to pass the word to isolate the electrical panel before he started spraying it with lots of seawater.

Bair walked over to the strobe light, increased the frequency of the flashes, and moved it closer to Jerry's team. "The fire is getting worse and it's starting to get really hot in here," he said loudly. Immediately, Jerry yelled to Foster, "To control, the fire is getting worse. We need a second hose team." Preoccupied with fighting the simulated fire, Jerry didn't hear Foster's repeat back. After about thirty seconds, Jerry became concerned that he hadn't heard anything from control about sending in a second team. He was about to ask Foster if control had responded when the 1MC roared to life, it was the Captain's voice and he sounded agitated: "TEAM LEADER, CHECK YOUR SOUND-POWERED PHONE CONNECTION!"

Jerry spun around and looked over at the sound-powered phone jack. The plug was halfway out of the socket. Reaching over, he angrily screwed the plug back in. "Senior Chief, verify that you are back online with control and then pass on the word that we need a second hose team down here."

"Yes sir," replied Foster smugly.

No sooner had Jerry turned his attention back to the fire than the XO turned on a white strobe light and pointed it at the team. "It's extremely hot in here. You can't stand the heat any longer," shouted Bair as he pushed Jerry's team back from the strobe lights.

Jerry felt frustrated, as there was little he could do without the second hose team. The XO wasn't cutting them any slack either, and unless Jerry took measures to protect his team from the heat, the XO would start having them pass out on him. With a hard sigh, Jerry ordered the nozzle man to select low-velocity fog. He then ordered the team to start backing away from the advancing fire. Moments later, the 1MC announced, "SECURE FROM DRILL. ALL HANDS REMOVE EABS."

Jerry stood up and ripped the EAB mask off his face. He was angry, very angry. He looked around to find Foster when Hardy came stomping into the room with Lieutenant Cal Richards in tow. "That was absolutely deplorable," screamed Hardy. "If this had been a real fire, we'd be in three-section duty on the bottom with *Thresher* and *Scorpion*"—a sarcastic reference to the only U.S. nuclear-powered submarines that had sunk with all hands.

"Mr. Richards," ranted the Captain, "this team reacted so slowly to the fire that my grandmother with a garden hose could have done better. If you haven't realized it yet, there were four warshots with six hundred and sixty pounds of high explosive each sitting in the middle of that fire!"

Turning toward Jerry, he continued to lash out. "What excuse do you have for your incompetent communication practices? You were out of touch for nearly two minutes! And in that time you let the fire get so bad, so out of hand, that the weapons in the racks cooked off!"

Shifting back to Richards, Hardy finished his tirade in typical form. "WEPS, I'm holding you personally responsible for this abysmal performance. It's clear that you have been derelict in your duties as a department head, since these imbeciles are less capable than basic sub school students. I can only assume that you are gundecking your training!" Cal Richards was pasty-white with fright, as Hardy was using words usually reserved for courts-martial offenses.

"XO, you and the WEPS come with me," Hardy shot out as he turned to leave. "We need to plan remedial drills for the Weapons Department. The rest of you, clean this mess up." With that, Hardy and the still silent Richards left the torpedo room.

Bair let loose with a heavy sigh, looked at Jerry, and said, "Clean up and stow the DC gear, Mr. Mitchell. We'll discuss the drill later."

"Aye, aye, sir," responded Jerry quietly.

Turning to leave, Bair gave Jerry a friendly slap on the shoulder and then headed off for the CO's stateroom. As the XO slowly walked out of the torpedo room, Jerry sensed his weariness.

"Okay, folks, let's clean up," Jerry said as he reached down and unplugged the two strobe lights. He then peeled off his fire-fighting gear and gave it to TM3 Lee.

As the rest of torpedo division started to secure the phones and the rest of the DC gear, Jerry quietly made the rounds to see how his people were doing. Most were downcast, resigned to the inevitable additional drills. Some made jokes that a three-section watch rotation with *Thresher* and *Scorpion* would be easier than what they had right now. Bearden looked just plain mad.

Jerry was furious that the entire department was being forced to suffer because of one man's bad attitude. While the thought of confronting Foster was not all that appealing, Jerry had to do something before he destroyed what little morale the division had left. Jerry, working hard to keep calm, said, "Senior Chief, can I see you a moment, please?" He held up a clipboard, as if he wanted to speak about some paperwork issue.

Foster followed Jerry forward to an unoccupied corner of the torpedo room. Speaking softly, Jerry said carefully, "You intentionally broke that phone connection, Senior Chief."

"So?" retorted Foster. "I was just imposing another casualty."

"After I'd double-checked the connection? And on your own?" He challenged Foster. "The XO decides what drills to run. Did he tell you to impose that particular casualty?"

"No." The Senior Chief pointedly did not add "sir."

Jerry was direct. "So why did you do it?"

"To see how you'd handle it. And you didn't."

"To make me look bad in front of the Captain seems a better explanation."

"You can do that all by yourself."

"But you don't mind sticking out your foot now and then."

"This conversation is over," Foster announced in a voice loud enough to be overheard.

"Not yet it isn't, Senior Chief! Not until I say it's over," countered Jerry forcefully.

"Give me a break." Foster didn't even try to speak softly. "You can't hack it." He was impatient with the conversation and turned to leave, but Jerry kept talking.

"I'd have a better chance of hacking it if you were working with me—or at least not against me. And we do have a mission to accomplish," he reminded Foster.

"A junket for Broomhilda? This is one mission I want to fail. And why should you get a second chance? It's just more politics." Foster sounded disgusted with the word. "The only mission I've got is to make sure that you don't stay in submarines, and better still, to get you out of the Navy altogether."

"Well, Senior Chief, my mission is to obey the orders of a duly elected Commander in Chief and the chain of command, even if I think they are politically motivated. And if you do anything like this again, I'll drag your ass in front of the XO personally. Is that absolutely, positively, crystal clear, Foster?" replied Jerry loudly and sternly.

Momentarily taken aback by the vehemence Jerry displayed, Foster smiled and said, "You don't have the guts, flyboy."

Foster threw that last sentence over his shoulder as he walked away from Jerry, past the rest of the division, and out of the room.

After the senior chief's abrupt departure, the men busied themselves with their assigned duties silently. Jerry remained isolated and tried to understand what had just happened—and why. He had never seen such open insubordination before, and he certainly didn't know how to handle it—short of officially putting Foster on report, of course. Jerry was pretty sure the XO would back him up, but given Richards' present state of mind, he would almost certainly support Foster. Regardless, it would be very messy if Jerry tried to bring charges against Foster. And how would Captain Hardy react? Very likely negatively, and that would end his second chance for a naval career for sure. "Damned if I do, damned if I don't," muttered Jerry to himself. A sudden movement caught Jerry's eye, breaking his concentration. It was FT1 Bearden.

"Sir, the guys have finished cleaning up and all the DC gear has been properly stored. May I dismiss the men who are not on watch?"

"Yes, yes, of course," said Jerry with a slight smile. "Thank you, FT1."

Bearden fidgeted about for a moment, reluctant to speak, and then quietly he said, "Mr. Mitchell, I never should have let Senior . . ." Jerry sharply raised his hand, silencing the petty officer.

"It's not your fault, Petty Officer Bearden," stated Jerry sincerely. "It's not your fault. Understood?"

Bearden nodded stiffly as Jerry clasped his shoulder.

Drained physically and emotionally, Jerry started to make his way back to his stateroom. As he walked, he wondered if he had done the right thing. Well, he thought, that's behind me now. For good or ill, the conflict between him and Foster was now out in the open. Right now, Jerry could only hope and pray that Foster wouldn't call his bluff.

⑩ Using the System

The drills continued unrelentingly throughout the next day. Hardy did let the crew have lunch, although he used the time to critique each drill in detail over the 1MC. The Captain was unsparing in his remarks.

". . . and Petty Officer Gregory didn't remember to align the valves on the drain pump manifold properly, so the trim pump was unable to dewater the engine room. Progressive flooding drove us below our crush depth, killing everyone aboard. Mr. Lopez, it's your responsibility to properly train Petty Officer Gregory, so those deaths are on your head, as well as his.

"Also, Mr. Lopez, there were serious training deficiencies noted during the fire drill we held this morning. As the Damage Control Assistant, you are to ensure that every member of this crew has adequate knowledge of the DC gear on this boat—and that includes the EAB system. During the fire drill, several of the crew didn't properly seal their EAB masks after hooking them up. Toxic gas leaked in and they all died."

Hardy paused for a moment. "In the four drills we held since breakfast, everyone aboard this boat has died at least twice. You are supposed to be professional submariners and I'm not going to throw softballs at you. We will continue to conduct emergency drills until you get it right. That is all."

Jerry sat in the wardroom and half-listened to Hardy's lecture as he tried to eat. He felt really bad for Frank Lopez as Hardy went on and on about his lack of professionalism. Looking down the table at Lopez, with his shoulders slumped over his meal, Jerry could empathize with him. He himself had earned similar treatments from Hardy—as had every officer present. But right now, Jerry had a bigger problem than the Captain.

Foster's animosity and insubordination would be a crisis on any ship, but right now, on this boat, it was an unmitigated disaster. Bringing it into the open hadn't clarified the problem or given him anything that would help him solve the conflict.

The rest of the wardroom looked upset, worried, or just plain scared.

Hardy's leadership style got results, but at a very high price. He ruled *Memphis* by fear, and he wasn't afraid to name names over the 1MC. Jerry had been taught to praise in public and chastise in private, but Hardy seemed to reverse the procedure. Then Jerry corrected himself. He'd never seen Hardy praising anyone, so with that kind of policy it didn't really matter what the order was.

Of course, Jerry had heard about "screamers" in the aviation community and throughout the Navy at the Academy. As long as their units produced, the higher-ups didn't intervene. Their view was that a captain had the right to run his command as he saw fit. But it was awfully hard on the help.

After he finished his harangue, Hardy came into the wardroom, followed closely by Bair, who looked torn. The junior officers started to rise, but Hardy stopped them with a curt "As you were." Hardy and Bair took their seats at the table, and it seemed to Jerry that the wardroom was even quieter than before. As he was served lunch, Hardy cast an icy gaze over the officers. Some actually hunkered down farther as he looked at them.

When he finally broke the silence, Hardy spoke calmly, but his voice seemed deafening, and although calm, his tone was harsh. "Since we've got people dying when they use damage control equipment, after lunch I want all departments and divisions to review EAB mask procedures. Mr. Lopez, you will personally conduct the training with each man aboard. That may take a while, but I'm sure all of you have other casualty procedures you may want to practice."

He got up suddenly and left the wardroom without eating a bite. A few moments passed, then everyone let out their breath all at once. Jerry started eating again, although quietly. Like him, the other officers seemed to be preoccupied.

Finally Bill Washburn, the Supply Officer, spoke. Tentatively, he asked, "XO, sir, do you think you could ask the Captain to guarantee us a few drill-free hours? My people need to be able to work and right now . . ."

"I'm sorry, Bill, I've already brought that up with the Captain. He is insistent that the crew be ready to drop everything at a moment's notice, at any time, day or night."

"But at sea, we don't face nonstop emergencies. And I'm not talking about missing sleep. My people need to move stores, to cook. I can't plan menus because I don't know when my people will be called away. If this goes on for much longer, I'll have to start feeding the crew battle rations."

"Then that's what you'd better do," Bair replied bluntly.

"It's not just the cooks, sir." Jeff Ho, the Engineer, was more forceful. "I've got a lot of cranky machinery to take care of. My men could work full-time just keeping the plant from flying apart."

"Are there any big problems?" Bair asked.

"No, sir, nothing major yet."

"This isn't our first deployment," the XO reminded them. "We always have drills our first few days at sea." He waved down a few who started to protest. "I know they've never been this frequent or this difficult, but that is his call. If you want the drills to stop, give him what he wants."

Bair pushed his plate away. "Let's get organized for that shipwide training session. Muster everyone in their spaces as soon as the meal is finished, and I don't want to hear that Mr. Lopez is kept waiting. He's got a lot of ground to cover, and this cannot take all afternoon."

A chorus of "Aye, ayes" followed him out of the wardroom as the XO left and Jerry automatically started to head for the torpedo room. He had to make sure. . . .

He paused. Of what? That Foster would still follow his orders? That the torpedomen and fire-control technicians would? They'd all seen Foster tell him off. It was impossible to go about business as usual when his own division chief had said he wanted the mission to fail, that he wanted Jerry to fail.

This conflict was way out of control. Jerry needed help, desperately, but from whom he couldn't say. Not from the Captain, certainly, and even the XO couldn't do much to adjust Foster's attitude.

The chief petty officer, is, by tradition, "the backbone of the fleet." The typical CPO had a ton of experience and was often the most competent technician in his field onboard. But chiefs also wore the khaki uniform, making them a critical part of the leadership structure. It was the chiefs who made things work. Pairing a junior officer with an experienced chief was a good system; practical, effective, and enshrined in naval tradition.

Which folded like wet Kleenex when the chief in question didn't go along with the plan. None of the officers could help, and he couldn't go to his division. They looked to him to fix this problem. He couldn't possibly ask another chief for help—or could he?

Master Chief Reynolds was the Chief of the Boat, the senior enlisted man aboard. As the COB, he was the official, sanctioned, box-in-the-org chart link between the officers and the crew. In sub school, they told him that a junior officer couldn't go wrong if he asked the COB for help. It was worth a try.

Reynolds worked for the XO, but he often helped the nonnuclear machinist mates, or auxiliarymen, under Lopez, and Jerry was pretty sure he'd be in their spaces. As he hoped, Jerry found Reynolds in the auxiliary machinery room in forward compartment lower level, aft of the torpedo room. He was reviewing the maintenance records on the emergency diesel generator.

"Master Chief, do you have a few minutes?"

Reynolds straightened up. He was a huge man, seeming to fill the space, although he, Jerry, and the watchstander were the only ones in it. In spite of his size, he was not intimidating, and Reynolds' weather-beaten face was relaxed and friendly. His tone was friendly as well. "Of course, Mr. Mitchell." He turned to the auxiliaryman watchstander and said, "I've got it for ten minutes. Go get some coffee." The young sailor quickly left.

He settled down on top of a pump housing, offering Jerry the only chair in the space. "I have a hunch I know what you want to talk about," he said as Jerry sat down. "Or 'who,' actually," Reynolds added.

Jerry was a little surprised. "Exactly what have you heard?" he asked carefully.

"Everything," replied Reynolds matter-of-factly. "There aren't any secrets on a submarine. Well, not for more than thirty seconds anyway. And Senior Chief Foster hasn't been secretive."

"Master Chief, I've tried talking to him in private, and he blows me off. He sabotages my work, and now the division's work. He has intentionally caused us to fail in two drills, and he's destroying what little is left of my division's morale. He says he wants the boat's mission to fail and he wants to make sure I don't get my dolphins."

"So I've heard," Reynolds remarked. He sat quietly, letting Jerry talk.

"I've got my qualification to work on, we don't know half of what we should about those ROVs, I'm still learning my regular duties, and I've got to keep at least one eye on Foster to make sure he doesn't blindside me." Jerry was frustrated and angry. "The blowup this morning is the worst yet. I don't know what to do about him."

"How can I help?" Reynolds asked.

"What's his problem? Why is he doing this?" Jerry asked, almost pleading.

"He thinks you're a lightweight," Reynolds answered, "someone who was assigned to this sub because of his political pull."

Jerry shrugged. "I guess that's true, to a certain extent. I wanted subs, and I used my uncle's influence to get the Navy to listen. But I've pulled my weight since I got here. Others aboard were unsure of me too, some were even hostile, but they've changed their minds. Why not Foster?"

"A long time ago, Foster applied for a direct commission program. He was turned down because he didn't have a college degree. When he tried to apply for a college program that would give him a commission, they told him he was too old. He applied for a waiver and was denied."

Jerry listened, then thought for a moment before replying. "So why should I get a second chance when he didn't get any at all?"

"That's pretty much it," agreed Reynolds.

"What do I do about it?" demanded Jerry, almost angry, but really just frustrated.

"You can't shoot him," remarked Reynolds, smiling.

"I was considering it," Jerry confessed. "But seriously, I can't take him to mast, and I don't want to. And I can't think of any other punishment or any way to force him to change his attitude."

"You're right. There isn't any," Reynolds confirmed. "You can't just change a man's feelings. He's got to do that. You're going to have to convince him that you're more than a political hack. Then he may fall into line."

"I'd just settle for him leaving me alone. He's supposed to be working with me, but at this point I'd be happy if he'd just stopped working against me."

"Could you use some help?" Reynolds suggested.

"I'd love any help, from anywhere. What do you have in mind?"

"Well, Senior Chief Foster is supposed to be helping you become a good division officer—and that includes your qualifications. Since he's not willing, maybe I can fill in."

Jerry's spirits soared. "Master Chief, there's no 'maybe' involved. I know I'll qualify with you helping me."

"It's not enough, Mr. Mitchell. Qualifying isn't going to make Senior Chief Foster respect you. You need to demonstrate to Foster that you are a good officer. One that looks after his men, goes to the mat for them when he needs to, and puts their best interests before his own. Except for the XO, and maybe one or two others, there aren't many good officers on this boat. But if you don't qualify, you won't get very far in the submarine force. So, we'll start there."

"I'm grateful." He reached out, and Reynolds took his hand and shook it. Jerry said, "Thanks, thanks a lot."

"Come by after you get off the noon-to-six tonight and we'll see what you've got left in that qual book."

"Right, COB, I'll be there and thanks again."

Jerry left, headed forward with what would be a spring in his step, if he had the headroom.

MASTER CHIEF REYNOLDS watched him leave, then sighed. He paused for a moment, looked at his watch, and headed up and forward to the chiefs' quarters. Along the way, he saw FT2 Boswell, one of the men in Jerry's division. He told Boswell to find Senior Chief Foster and ask him to join Reynolds in the Goat Locker.

Reynolds got there ahead of Foster, and chased out two chiefs sucking on coffee and pretending to do paperwork.

Foster showed up a minute later, to find Reynolds waiting for him. "What's up, Sam?" he asked, dropping into a chair.

"I want to know when you're going to let up on Mitchell," Reynolds said flatly.

Just hearing Jerry's name changed Foster's demeanor. Angrily, he answered, "That no-load? I'll have him begging for mercy by the time we're back!"

Foster's statement was no surprise to the COB. He'd heard the Senior Chief say the same thing or worse in the chiefs' quarters. Foster hated Mitchell and wasn't quiet about it.

"Everyone else is willing to cut the kid some slack. Why don't you ease up?" Reynolds made the last sentence a suggestion, not a question.

"Because I'll be damned if this Navy's going to be ruined by someone with the political pull to change the rules."

"Even if you have to ruin your division, or this boat, to do it?" Reynolds voice was hard.

"I don't know what you mean," Foster answered.

"I was on the phone circuit during that Otto fuel spill drill during sea trials. I know what you did. And even if I didn't, your last blowup with Mitchell is all over the boat. You admitted to tanking the drill on purpose."

"So what? The kid's worthless. He can't lead, and now the division knows it."

"Nobody can lead when his next-in-line is backstabbing him. I don't see you doing the Navy any favors. I see you taking cheap shots to work off an old grudge."

Foster took a different tack. "What did he do? Come running to you?"

"Which is exactly what any officer on this boat should do when an enlisted man's behavior is unsat."

"But he couldn't take care of it himself, could he?" Foster sounded smug.

"He did take care of it, by talking to me," Reynolds explained. "It's the COB's business to deal with bad actors."

Reynolds leaned his massive frame forward, emphasizing his words. "You've disobeyed lawful orders from a commissioned officer, as well as being openly insubordinate. You've deliberately interfered with ship's drills and you've disrupted discipline in your division. If you were a first class or below, you'd be at Captain's Mast, minus at least a stripe. But we don't do that to chiefs, because they're supposed to be better than that."

Foster was grim, but not contrite. "You can't make me kiss up to that . . ."

Reynolds cut him off. "What I expect is for you to earn your pay and do your work. Nothing less and nothing more." Foster looked unconvinced, and the Master Chief continued.

"The only reason Hardy hasn't noticed your private war is that he's too busy sweating Patterson and the mission. If I do not see a change in your behavior immediately, I'll bring this to the Captain's attention myself."

Foster was still unmoved. "Hardy's hated Mitchell since he came aboard."

"I'll just mention the part about how you want our mission to fail.

Remember, you not only told it to Mitchell, but the rest of the torpedo division. Add to that your sabotaging of the drills, insubordination, and failure to obey a lawful order, and I think I could make an excellent case against you. If he heard half of that, Hardy would have your ass off this boat in twenty-four hours and you'd be facing Commodore's Mast."

Both of them knew that was no idle threat. Captain's Mast, or more formally, "nonjudicial punishment," was used to discipline enlisted members who broke the rules aboard ship. Insubordination, unauthorized absence from the ship, dereliction of duty, or a dozen other offenses could be punished by extra duty, restriction to the ship (when next in port), fines, or in extreme cases, the malefactor would lose a stripe and the associated pay.

Officers and chiefs could not be disciplined by Captain's Mast. They went before the squadron commander, which was similar, but it wasn't a "family matter" any longer. It made the ship look bad, which made the Captain of that ship look bad. Hardy would not be pleased at all. People who wore khaki weren't supposed to need this kind of disciplinary action, so anyone who appeared before the squadron commander could expect no mercy.

Considering the charges Reynolds had listed, Foster would expect a reduction in rate, and to be permanently beached. The financial loss would be accompanied by a succession of crappy duty assignments until he eventually retired.

The two chiefs studied each other. Foster tried to gauge how serious Reynolds really was, and Reynolds watched the wheels turn as Foster processed the Master Chief's threat.

Foster finally said, "I won't stand for him being in my Navy."

"It's not your Navy, and it's not your place to make that decision," Reynolds reminded him. "The only one I see breaking the rules here is you. And I won't let you wreck *my* boat."

"I won't help him."

"No, I'll do your job," said Reynolds harshly. "Your new job is to stop tripping him up. And you will follow the lawful orders of any commissioned officer aboard this vessel." The COB stood up suddenly. "I've told you what's wrong, what needs to be to fixed, and what will happen if it doesn't get fixed. Consider yourself counseled, Senior Chief."

He left Foster alone in the chiefs' quarters, considering.

AFTER HIS MEETING with Reynolds, Jerry felt better, although he was still unsure about how to deal with Foster and his division. Finally he decided he would just go to the torpedo room and muddle through as best he could. So far, the torpedo gang had done their jobs as if nothing had happened. They were smart enough to know that Foster was wrong. Jerry had to stay focused on the division, and trust his men to follow him in spite of Foster.

The XO found Mitchell as he passed through the control room. "Jerry, I'm going to put Dr. Patterson with your division for the training session. You've already got Emily Davis, so the ladies can stay together."

"Broomhilda?" Bair's order had caught him off guard. "I mean, ah, where has Dr. Patterson been for the other emergency drills, sir?"

"In her stateroom pretending to work. She's come up with one excuse after another for avoiding them, but I think I've impressed on her the value of learning how to use an EAB mask."

"How did you manage that?" Jerry was astonished, and more than a bit curious. Patterson wasn't easy to convince.

"I scared her out of her wits by telling her about *Bonefish*," said the XO with a devilish smile on his face. *Bonefish* was one of the few diesel-electric submarines in the U.S. Navy's inventory back in the '80s. She suffered a hideous battery well fire in the spring of 1988. Three men were killed and twenty-three were injured by the blaze.

"They taught us about her at sub school." Jerry shivered as he recalled the pictures they showed him of the *Bonefish* on the surface, with brownish smoke billowing from her sail. "That was one nasty fire."

"Well, Patterson never went to sub school, but when I described how those men suffocated, she became a believer. I'll make it worth your while and send Lopez to you first."

"Aye, aye, XO. She's more than welcome to join us, of course."

Bair grinned. "That's nice. I could never lie that well."

FOSTER WAS NOT in the torpedo room when Jerry came down the ladder. Emily Davis had TM1 Moran, FT1 Bearden, and FT2 Boswell going over the weapons launching console with her. Jerry called TM1 Moran over and told him about Patterson joining them for the drill.

"Broomhilda? Ah, sir, does she have to be here?" Moran almost pleaded with the lieutenant. "Marcie's okay," he said, indicating Emily Davis, "but Broomhilda's just going to make a fuss."

"Not our call, TM1." Then, doing a double take, he asked, "Marcie?"

Moran nodded toward Davis, as she quizzed the two FTs about the panel. "Short, straight dark hair, big glasses, kinda quiet, and hangs around with a dominating Patty, of a sort. And she called me 'sir,' sir."

Jerry closed his eyes and rubbed his forehead as he thought about the allusion Moran had made concerning the mousy Peanuts character and Emily. The image of Marcie following Peppermint Patty around was way too accurate a comparison. He had to admit that Moran had her pegged. Puffing out a sigh, Jerry said, "Whatever works, Petty Officer Moran, just expect one more for the training. And pleeease, don't call her Broomhilda—at least while she's here."

"Yessir."

It wasn't until he had left that Jerry realized how normal Moran had acted.

There was a clattering on the forward ladder and Senior Chief Foster came down from the Goat Locker. Jerry decided the only way to deal with this was to act like he was in charge, because he was. "Senior Chief, we're just about set up for the training session. Dr. Patterson will be joining us, and Lieutenant Lopez will start with us."

Foster stepped away from the starboard tube nest, started to reply, "I don't . . ." but was interrupted by footsteps behind him. He quickly moved out of the way as Master Chief Reynolds came from the after crew accommodations.

"I heard Dr. Patterson was joining you. I thought I might stand by, in case you needed a hand, sir." Reynolds started the sentence facing Jerry, but finished it by looking at Foster. Jerry was sure everyone in the room had seen it, including the Senior Chief. Reynolds' support might not have been necessary, but Jerry welcomed it all the same. He struggled to suppress a smile.

"Senior Chief, would you please double-check the preparations?" Jerry asked as casually as he could.

"Yes, sir," Foster answered coldly, managing to look daggers at both Jerry and Reynolds.

Patterson then entered the room by the same path the COB had taken. She paused halfway down the small passage between the center and starboard racks and said, "Lieutenant Mitchell? Emily? Since you're here, this must be the torpedo room," she said jokingly.

"As if the rack of torpedoes on the port side and the ROVs on the starboard wasn't a dead giveaway," muttered Moran under his breath. Jerry hoped she hadn't heard that.

Patterson walked up to Jerry and seemed to gather herself. "Lieutenant, I'm supposed to learn about the emergency air masks with Dr. Davis and the rest of your division."

Mitchell was impressed. Patterson was actually being polite. What did the XO tell her?

Lieutenant (j.g.) Frank Lopez appeared, quickly descending the forward ladder.

"The XO says I'm supposed to start in here. Are you ready?"

"Yes, Frank, we're all set."

"For the benefit of our guests," Lopez began, "I'll go over the basic mechanics of the emergency air breathing system before we discuss the procedures on how to use it." Lopez picked up a mask and started to go over the various parts. He explained that the mask was made of flexible rubber, with a clear Plexiglas faceplate and that all masks were the same size. There were four straps that pulled the mask tightly against the face and could be made to fit anyone. Lopez then cautioned Dr. Patterson to make sure her long hair was pulled back when she put the mask on. Otherwise the hair would prevent a good seal.

The air, not oxygen, was provided by the ship's low-pressure air system and there were 169 EAB manifolds located throughout the boat. You could always find a manifold by looking for the red squares with a black triangle on the deck. He pointed to the one below him and asked Emily to run her hand over the triangle. It was noticeably rough, like coarse sandpaper. Lopez explained that this was how you could find the square in the dark with your hands, or even with your shoes.

He then went to the end of the hose and showed them the conical plug. Reaching up to the manifold, he demonstrated how the plug could easily be inserted into the manifold, even though there was one hundred-pound air in it. To release the plug, he pushed on the outer ring on the female connector and the air pushed the plug out.

The air was not allowed to just flow into the mask. That was much too dangerous. Instead, air was passed to an individual only as it was needed by a demand regulator, which was attached to a person's belt. It was the same type of regulator that scuba divers used and it was very reliable.

Emily was intrigued by the simplicity of the EAB mask, but she also looked nervous. Jerry guessed she was still dealing with being submerged.

Lopez turned to Patterson and Davis. "Ladies, the torpedo gang are all familiar with the mask and the procedure. If you'd like, I'll put them through it first while you watch, so you can see how it's done."

He pointed to Jerry. "You first. You can set a good example."

Jerry took the mask and placed it over his face. He grabbed the top two straps and pulled on them. He then grabbed the bottom two straps and pulled tightly. He repeated the process again to ensure a good seal.

"Now watch as he tests to see that the mask has a good seal with his face," said Lopez.

Jerry inhaled and the mask flattened noticeably against his face.

"See that? If you inhale, the reduced pressure in the mask will cause it to be pushed against your face. That's how you know the seal is airtight. Okay, Jerry hook up."

Jerry took the plug and inserted it into the manifold. There was a momentary *hiss* as the plug was locked into the connection. Taking a deep breath, there was a brief sound of moving air, identical to that made by Darth Vader.

"Hear that sound? That is the demand regulator releasing air at the correct pressure when it senses the reduced pressure in the mask. If one hundred-pound air were released directly into the mask, it would burst your lungs. Thanks, Jerry."

Jerry removed the mask, unplugged it and wiped the inside of the mask with a cleaner.

"There isn't enough air in the mask for you to re-breathe," cautioned Lopez. "So if you need to move from one manifold to another, be sure to take a deep breath and hold it. Pop the connection and move quickly, but carefully to the next manifold. Any questions?"

Patterson and Davis both watched carefully. Jerry then handed the mask to Foster, who tested and donned it expertly.

After several more of the torpedo gang had gone through the procedure, Patterson raised her hand. "I'd like to try it now."

Jerry was amazed all over again. Patience? Politeness? He watched as Lopez handed her the mask.

"What am I supposed to do first?" she asked. "Aren't you going to set it up for me?

Lopez shook his head. "No ma'am. You have to do it all by yourself."

Patterson looked puzzled, and the lieutenant continued. "What if you were alone? What if we were unconscious?" His tone changed, becoming more intense. "In an emergency, all our lives depend on each other. You have to know how to do this," he said flatly.

Nodding, she took the mask and started to check it. Lopez guided her through the process telling her what to do, but making her handle the mask, test the seal, and make the attachment. In the end, she was wearing the mask and breathing regularly, a huge smile visible through the face-plate.

She took it off and handed it to Lopez, who turned to Davis. "Your turn, ma'am," he said, offering her the mask.

Davis quickly shook her head, "I'd like to watch some more, first."

The officer answered, "All right," and turned to FT3 Larsen. "Then you're next. Let's see if you can do it as well as a civilian."

Dr. Patterson, arranging her hair, came over to Jerry. "I've never done anything quite like this," she remarked. Then, more softly, "Did those poor men really suffocate on the *Bonefish*?"

"Yes, ma'am, they teach us all about it in sub school. That submarine didn't have this kind of safety equipment, though," he added encouragingly.

She shuddered, then changed the subject. "Is Senator James Thorvald from Nebraska, your uncle?"

"Yes, ma'am, my mother's oldest brother," Jerry replied.

"I've met him a few times on the Hill. This is what, his fourth term? He's got a decent record on the environment—for a Republican," she said with a smile. "I understand he gave you some help getting this assignment."

"Some, ma'am, he didn't tell me the details." Jerry was vague, hoping she'd stop talking about it.

"Oh well, normally it involves making the Pentagon brass do something they don't want to do. Let's see, I'm pretty sure he's on the Senate Armed Services Committee. Which means if the Navy doesn't give him what he wants, he can make life hard for them when they come before the committee."

Jerry was becoming more and more uncomfortable and noticed that several of his men, including Foster, were listening to Patterson.

"You're lucky the senator is on Armed Services. If it had been Small Business or Agriculture, you probably would have been out of luck. But in that case, your uncle might have found a friend on one of the committees that handles defense, like Intelligence or Appropriations, and asked for a favor. There's almost always a way to make the system work for you."

"If you've got friends in the right places," someone muttered.

Jerry ignored the comment and tried to explain. "I just asked if he could help, and he said he'd make a few calls."

"And that's probably all it took." Patterson explained. Jerry had never seen her this at ease. She was in her element. This was her world, the world of political give-and-take, and she was very comfortable in it.

"This goes on all the time. For something as simple as this, he probably called the Secretary of the Navy's office and talked to one of the staffers there. Who made the final decision on your case?"

"The Chief of Naval Personnel," Jerry answered quietly.

"Does he work for the Secretary of the Navy?"

"No, ma'am, not directly. He reports to the Chief of Naval Operations, who works for the secretary."

"Oh, okay, then, the secretary's staff calls the Chief of Naval whatever and he calls the personnel person."

To ordinary officers and sailors, "BUPERS," the CNO, and "SECNAV" were not people but mighty beings who could be petitioned and who would, for perverse reasons, grant or deny those requests. The idea of Uncle Jim calling and twisting their arms was unsettling. They had bigger things to worry about. They had a Navy to run.

In spite of the distracting conversation, Lopez had pressed on with the EAB drills. "That's the last of the torpedo division," he announced. "Dr. Davis, it's your turn next. You'll have to take your glasses off. They aren't wire rims and they'll prevent you from getting a good seal."

Still listening to Patterson, Jerry watched as Davis stepped up, fumbling with the mask as she went through the procedure. He was surprised. Subconsciously, he'd expected her to be more familiar with the gear, being an engineer and all that.

Patterson was still talking about his uncle. "I'm sure it was a simple

thing for your uncle to arrange. I'm dealing with him on an environmental issue. We want him to come over to our side on the Superfund Act this year,
but it's going to cost us. Possibly some farm subsidies or he might hold out
for some construction contracts for his state. That gets messier because . . ."

"Excuse me, ma'am, but is that really how business is done?" Senior
Chief Foster had come over to join the conversation. Although he looked
calm, Jerry knew him well enough to see how agitated he really was. Foster's
face was a little redder than usual, and his movements were small and tightly
controlled. "Shouldn't that kind of thing be decided on its own merits?"

Foster spoke with a soft intensity Jerry had never heard before. This
guy really lived by the book, and he didn't think much of those who broke
the rules. Evidently he took it all very personally.

Patterson was momentarily surprised by the questions, but seemed to
have a ready answer. "Merit matters, of course. But any new law needs
friends, powerful friends. Usually there's a price for that support."

"And you don't think there's a problem with that?" Foster said disapprovingly.

"I don't try to fix the system. I just try to make it work."

Foster voice was harsh. "Even if it's corrupt?"

Dr. Patterson, obviously offended, started to reply, but was interrupted
by a scream. "I can't breathe! Take it off! There's no air!"

They all turned to see Emily Davis on her knees, frantically pulling the
mask off her head. Reynolds, as well as several of the torpedo gang, hovered
around her, while Lopez checked the connection. "She's got air!" he announced.

Davis seemed to have trouble getting the mask off, but her hands
weren't pulling at the right spot. Reynolds reached out and neatly slipped it
off, leaving her gasping, her face streaked with tears. She fumbled to put her
glasses back on.

"I'm sorry. I couldn't breathe. I couldn't see anything. There was no air
coming in." She was shaking, leaning forward to support herself with her
hands as well as her knees.

Puzzled, Lopez checked the faceplate. It was clear. Reynolds helped
her to her feet.

"I'm sure the mask is all right," Lopez said reassuringly. "I watched you
make the connections and you did just fine." He paused for a moment, then
added, "And what about the others who used it? It worked fine for them."

"Maybe it was just funky," joked Jobin. "Everybody knows Lee's breath
reeks."

"Don't joke about it," Davis gasped. "I really couldn't breathe!" She
looked menacingly at Jobin, who did his best to shrink behind the others.

"All right," said Lopez, "we'll do it differently. I'll hook it up first, see?"

He plugged the mask into the manifold, pressed it to his face, and breathed deeply. Emily heard the regulator release air into the mask. Pulling the mask away, Lopez handed it to her. "Just hold the mask up to your face and make sure you can breathe first. Then you can adjust the straps."

She took the mask as if it was coated with acid and placed it over face. She took a breath and felt her lungs fill with the dry air. After careful consideration, she looked at everyone surrounding her, sighed, took off her glasses, and then pulled the mask on.

The compartment was absolutely silent, and Reynolds said, "Step back, guys. Give her a little room."

As they stepped back, Jerry watched Emily. Her body had that same posture of tight control he'd just seen in Foster. She stood perfectly still, took three deep breaths, then said, "All right! It works this time." She quickly ripped the mask off the next instant and handed it to Lopez.

The lieutenant handed the mask to Foster and said, "The Torpedo Division is done. I've got the rest of the crew to check, so I'm outta here," he said resignedly.

Lopez left, followed by most of the torpedomen and FTs. Reynolds, Patterson, and Jerry remained, along with Emily. Foster was there as well, but did not stand as close. More composed now, she said, "I'm sorry. The mask was working fine the first time. I couldn't stand to have anything over my face."

She turned to Reynolds. "Thank you, Master Chief." She hugged him, and then left.

That afternoon Hardy hit them with a battle drill that combined an approach on an escorted boomer with an engineering casualty that almost caused a low-water alarm in one of the steam generators. The crew handled it, although not perfectly.

True to his word, Washburn's cooks served battle rations for dinner: ham sandwiches, boiled eggs, and apples. It was still early enough in the voyage that the apples were fresh. Compared to normal submarine fare, this was a real step down, but Hardy didn't say a word.

After dinner, he simulated an electrical fire in the sonar room. As the auxiliarymen isolated the circuit at the switchboard forward, the entire sonar system dropped off line, leaving *Memphis* blind and deaf.

Hardy was livid until the ship's sonar officer, Lieutenant (j.g.) Tom Weyer, was able to prove that the auxiliarymen had not caused the failure. The fault lay in the switchboard, which would have been overhauled if they had not been scheduled for decommissioning.

They repaired the malfunction quickly and then continued with the drill. As they watched the crew simulate isolating and correcting the fault, Bair quietly pressed his case with Hardy. "If we keep on at this pace, we're going to have real casualties, self-inflicted ones. The crew is not getting the time it needs to take proper care of the gear. And they all need sleep. If we don't slow down, they're going to start making more mistakes due to fatigue and the training won't be worth a damn."

"I'm not convinced they can handle themselves. I can't trust them to deal with every possibility yet. If there's a casualty and they drop the ball, it's a black mark against me, not them."

"From who? Patterson?" Bair was dismissive. "She doesn't care. She doesn't even understand. We have to drill them to our standards, not hers. And sir, with all due respect, it seems like you've raised your standards a little."

Hardy sighed. "What's your recommendation?"

"Give them the night off. No drills until after breakfast tomorrow."

The Captain thought about it for almost a minute, but finally said, "All right, pass the word."

11 Blue Noses

May 18, 2005

Denmark Strait, Near the Arctic Circle

Memphis' crew arose the next day transformed. Jerry was amazed at the effect one night of uninterrupted sleep had on everyone's temperament. They even had time for breakfast and some administrative matters in the morning before Hardy started the next round of drills. The first was a slow leak from one of the primary valves that "contaminated" the area around the reactor coolant sample sink in engine room middle level. Any piping or valve that comes in direct contact with the cooling water that circulates around the reactor's core is considered a primary system component. Thus, any leak from any part of that system is as much a radiological problem as it is a mechanical one.

Millunzi's engineering laboratory technicians, or ELTs, quickly isolated the area and began their search for the offending valve. Not only did they have to find and fix the problem, but simulate decontaminating the sample sink area and the affected crewmen. Bair had sneakily written LVS or "leaky valve seat" in small print on the back of one of the harder to reach valves and he expected it would take the ELTs some time to find it. Clad in their yellow anti-contamination suits, or anti-C's, the ELTs worked methodically and found the valve in short order. And once located, they simulated torquing the valve down and then cleaning the space, all within the allotted time. The Red Baron was pleased.

Hardy didn't praise their performance, but made only a few desultory criticisms. Jerry noticed the crew smiling, almost as if he had complimented them.

There were no further drills that morning, and Jerry spent the time trying to catch up on several days of paperwork and qualifications. He kept waiting for the general alarm to sound, but after an hour or two had passed, he started to believe that Hardy might be easing up.

Because he had the twelve to six Diving Officer watch in control, Jerry ate lunch at the first sitting. The atmosphere was more relaxed than it had been for days, and he even thought the food tasted better. The talk at the table was still muted, but things had definitely improved.

Lieutenant Commander O'Connell, the Navigator, broke the relaxed quiet. "XO, sir, I've refined my figures, and it appears we'll be crossing sixty-six degrees thirty-two minutes North latitude around 1600 tomorrow."

The sixty-six degrees thirty-two minutes North latitude marked the Arctic Circle, a milestone on the way to their destination, but O'Connell said it with a formality that implied something more. . . .

Then Jerry remembered—the Bluenose ceremony. He immediately looked at the two ladies, both seated to the left of the Captain. The XO was studying them as well, and after a few moments of silence, said, "Ladies, as Mr. O'Connell indicated, we will be crossing the Arctic Circle tomorrow afternoon. I'm sure you've heard of the ritual that occurs when you cross the Equator."

He waited for moment and both of them nodded. He continued, "There is a similar ceremony when a vessel crosses the Arctic Circle. We ask permission of Boreas Rex, Ruler of the North Wind and Sovereign of All the Frozen Reaches, to enter his realm, and if we are judged worthy . . ."

"Sounds like a silly initiation, like some seagoing fraternity." Patterson's critical tone was even harsher than her words.

"Calling us a 'seagoing fraternity' is not an insult, if that was your intention," Captain Hardy replied tersely. "These traditions have a long history, and we respect them, even if you do not." He looked over to the XO, prompting him to continue.

"By *tradition*," the XO put emphasis on the word, "anyone who crosses the Arctic Circle has the option of participating or not, as they choose. Although you've made your feelings clear, Doctor, we did want to invite both you and Dr. Davis to join in the festivities."

Patterson met the XO's statement with a stony glare, but Emily Davis asked, "What's involved in this ceremony?" Her tone implied that she expected it to be unpleasant.

Bair smiled. "His Majesty's representative, Davy Jones, will board us tomorrow and receive the petitions of those who have not entered the frozen realm before. Then King Boreas arrives with his court after we cross the Arctic Circle . . ."

"Guess who was Boreas the last time we went north?" interrupted Frank Lopez.

Bair shot him a hard look, but then smiled. He continued and his smile widened. "The exact details of the ceremony are a deep secret, known only to those trusted members of the Royal Court. But essentially, the hot-blooded neophytes will petition His Majesty to enter his domain. They will then be brought before King Boreas, who will stand in judgment over them before the Royal Court and the Captain of the Royal Guard. If they are found pure of heart, they will be baptized and then admitted to his realm. All in a politically correct and tasteful way, of course," he added reassuringly.

Riiiiight, Jerry thought. He'd heard horror stories about line-crossing ceremonies since his Academy days. It could be a grotesque, almost revolting, ordeal. The presence of the ladies would certainly tone it down some, even if they did not participate. Jerry, however, found himself hoping they would, not only because it would make them more a part of the crew, but also because the more "petitioners" there were, the less time "the Royal Court" could spend on each one. Safety lay in numbers.

"There's a really nice certificate," Berg offered helpfully.

"It's an idiotic male ritual, and I will take no part in it," announced Patterson disapprovingly. As she rose to leave, she looked over at Davis, who said, "I guess I'll pass as well, sir."

As the two departed the wardroom, Lenny Berg remarked. "She'd make a fine Queen of the Snows. She already has a chilling personality." Looking at his watch, he motioned to Jerry and said, "C'mon, Jerry, we need to go and relieve the watch." Turning toward Hardy, he added "Excuse us, Captain."

Hardy nodded stiffly, but said nothing.

As Jerry and Berg headed up to control, Jerry asked, "Is it my imagination or is the CO more depressed than usual?"

"Hard to say, Jerry. He has his ups and downs like everyone else. It's just that his downs tend to significantly outnumber his ups. But if I had to guess, I'd say that the enormity of just how hosed up this mission is might be starting to sink in," replied Berg. He started climbing the ladder to control.

Jerry followed him up and went over to Ensign Jim Porter to begin the watch turnover at the Diving Officer station. Looking around, Jerry didn't see Chief Gilson anywhere in control. This was strange, because Gilson had the watch officially. Jerry was still standing it under instruction.

"We pumped sanitaries during the last watch, and we're still making water with the 10K evaporator," said Porter during turnover. "The trim appears to be good, but at sixteen knots it's hard to tell. You'll probably slow down during your watch to make sure that the boat has a satisfactory one-third trim." Porter was referring to the fact that at higher speeds, a submarine can carry more water in its variable ballast tanks because of the greater hydrodynamic forces generated by the fairwater and stern planes. By slowing down, to ahead one-third, these forces are reduced considerably and Jerry could figure out whether the sub was heavy or light and if the distribution of water among the tanks was correct to maintain a good fore and aft balance.

"If you don't have any questions, then I'm ready to be relieved," stated Porter.

Jerry looked around the control room again; still no Gilson. "Jim, I'm sorry but I can't assume the watch without. . . ."

"*Yes you can*, Mr. Mitchell," thundered Reynolds, who appeared suddenly from the navigation equipment space behind control.

"C-COB?" Jerry stammered, quite confused.

"I'm taking the watch for Chief Gilson. I want to see how well you can balance this boat," replied Reynolds firmly. "I'll be here in case something goes wrong, but you have the watch, sir."

Surprised, Jerry just stood there and stared at the huge man. Reynolds waited a moment, then motioned toward Porter and said, "You can relieve Mr. Porter, sir."

Jerry turned slowly to Porter and said, "I relieve you."

"I stand relieved."

As Jim Porter reported to the OOD that he had been properly relieved, Jerry sat down at his station and looked at the indications on the ship control panel. After a few minutes of careful watching, he couldn't determine if the trim was good or not. Porter was right; they'd have to slow down first. Looking over his shoulder, Jerry saw Master Chief Reynolds leaning up against the bulkhead next to the plotters. He seemed far away, even though it was only about twenty feet.

After all the stations had changed over, Berg announced, "Attention in control, my intention is to slow to ahead one-third and conduct a baffle clearance maneuver to the right. Once the maneuver is completed, I'll let the Diving Officer check the boat's trim before we resume our transit speed. Carry on."

Berg then informed the sonar supervisor that they were slowing and coming to the right to check the baffles, the spherical array's blind zone behind the sub's propeller. After he had hung up the handset, Berg ordered, "Helm, ahead one-third."

"Ahead one-third, helm aye." Reaching over to the engine order telegraph, the helmsman twisted the dial to AHEAD 1/3. Almost immediately, a second dial beneath the first moved to the same position. "Sir, maneuvering answers ahead one-third."

"Very well, helm," responded Berg.

Berg waited for *Memphis* to slow down a little before starting the turn. Once the speed had dropped to ten knots, he ordered a slow turn to the right to give the sonar shack adequate time to check the baffles. With no signs of any contacts, the boat completed the circle and steadied up on its original course.

"Okay, Dive, check the boat's trim. And please be quick. We need to get back on track," said Lenny, with an unusual amount of sternness.

"Aye, aye, sir," responded Jerry. During the turn, it became clear to him that the boat was heavy, but he couldn't tell by how much or where. Since a submarine heels into a turn, the stern planes and the rudder interfere with each other and it's really hard to judge just how much influence is being exerted by the stern planes to maintain depth. Once *Memphis* steadied up on her course, this would no longer a problem.

Looking at the positions of the stern and fairwater planes, Jerry deduced that the boat was heavy overall and heavy forward. "Chief of the Watch, when was the last time that a compensation for potable water was done?" asked Jerry.

"About an hour and a half ago, sir."

"Very well. Chief of the Watch, please compensate for one and a half hours of potable water," ordered Jerry.

"Compensate for one and a half hours of potable water, aye, sir," replied MM1 Anderson. Jerry watched as Anderson positioned switches on the ballast control panel that remotely opened valves and created a clear path from the variable ballast tanks inside the submarine, through the trim pump, out to sea. "Pumping, from auxiliaries to sea," reported Anderson. Jerry acknowledged the report.

It took a few minutes for Anderson to complete the compensation. As he was repositioning the valves, he said, "Diving Officer, thirty-eight hundred pounds from auxiliaries and twelve hundred pounds from forward trim have been pumped to sea."

"Very well, Chief of the Watch," responded Jerry. After another ten minutes and another four thousand pounds pumped overboard, Jerry was about to announce that he had a satisfactory one-third trim when he noticed something odd. The stern planesman was holding his planes steady at five degrees down. This indicated that the boat was heavy aft and that the planes were trying to hold the stern up. Glancing at the fairwater planes, he saw that they were in the rise position and that the boat was maintaining the ordered depth of two hundred feet. I must have screwed up somewhere, Jerry thought. I've made her too heavy aft.

"Chief of the Watch," Jerry said. "Shift four thousand pounds from after trim to forward trim."

"Shift four thousand pounds from after trim to forward trim, aye, sir."

"Something wrong, Dive?" inquired Berg.

"Yes, sir, I think I messed up the fore and aft trim a little," replied Jerry, somewhat embarrassed.

"Very well, fix it so we can get going again."

"Aye, sir." He glanced over at the COB, but Reynolds' face was a mask.

After Anderson had moved the four thousand pounds of water from the aftermost part of the ship to the forward-most part, Jerry looked at the indications to see if he had corrected the problem. At first, it looked like it had indeed done the trick. But within minutes, the stern planes were now holding steady in the rise position and the fairwater planes in the dive position. All this told Jerry that he was now heavy forward, that he must have moved too much water. However, the plane positions were suggesting that he had to move almost as much water back aft as he had just shifted forward. "I don't understand why this isn't working," muttered Jerry to himself as he scratched his head.

"Chief of the Watch, shift three thousand pounds from forward trim to after trim."

"Shift three thousand pounds from forward trim to after trim, aye, sir."

"Diiiive, would you please explain what the hell is going on?" Berg demanded, clearly annoyed.

"Uh, sir, I seemed to have overcompensated. I'm working on it now. Please bear with me."

"Grrrr," growled Berg.

Jerry felt more and more uncomfortable and stressed. He completely understood Lenny's irritation, but what bugged Jerry more was his apparent inability to balance the boat. And why was the COB standing back there like a damn statue when he really needed the man's help?

With Anderson's report that the pumping was completed, Jerry stood up, leaned forward, and stared at the fairwater and stern planes indications. Standing there, he willed the indicators to zero out, but once again the stern planes went to a modest dive angle, while the fairwater planes drifted upward on the rise side.

"Son of a bitch!" hissed an exasperated Jerry. "What is wrong?" Turning around, Jerry was finally going to ask the COB for help, but he was gone! He was nowhere to be seen! On top of that, Berg was on the periscope stand, arms folded across his chest, glowering at him. Jerry felt helpless and was now uncertain as to what needed to be done to remedy the boat's trim. He was thinking about being relieved when he heard the noise of people moving.

At first, it was rather subdued, similar to what one would expect at watch changeover, but it grew in volume. Then a long string of men emerged from the navigation equipment space behind him. One by one they walked past him on their way down the ladder to forward compartment middle level.

Some of the men waved as they went by. Seaman Jobin said, "Hey, sir!" All were smiling. At that moment, Jerry knew he had been tricked. He had fallen victim to one of the oldest pranks in the submarine force: the Trim Party.

For operational and safety reasons, a submarine's trim must be finely balanced. Moving a significant amount of weight from one end of the submarine to another will have noticeable affect on the boat's fore and aft balance. In a trim party, a large number of men cram themselves into a space as far aft or forward as they can get; in this case, in the extreme after end of the engine room or the torpedo room. When the Diving Officer compensates for the extra weight by moving water to the other end, the men start moving to the other end as well. This causes the boat to "see-saw" back and forth, apparently without reason, much to the annoyance of the Diving Officer.

A seasoned Diving Officer would have recognized what was going on and simply used the planes to maintain an even keel and waited for the individuals involved to get bored and quit. But rookie Diving Officers are easier to deceive and so often became the prey of a merry band of mischievous submariners. As the long procession continued, Jerry felt his cheeks ablaze with embarrassment. Sitting down, he watched as the steady stream of men seemed to go on forever. Finally, as the last man walked past, Jerry heard the sound of clapping from behind him.

"Outstanding trim party, Jerry," Lenny chortled, barely able to contain himself. "That has got to be one of the biggest, longest parties I've ever seen. What do you say, COB?"

"Yes, sir, Mr. Berg, easily in the top three," replied Reynolds. The huge grin on his face made it clear to everyone present that he had thoroughly enjoyed Jerry's initiation.

Getting into the spirit of things, Jerry stood up and bowed. "Thank you, thank you, very much. For my next trick, I'll go down to the torpedo room and have myself impulsed out of a tube and swim to Keflavik!"

"Nah, that won't be necessary. We're getting plenty of entertainment value out of just giving you grief," responded Berg.

"Heaven forbid that I should deny you your diversion, sir," Jerry replied sarcastically.

"Quite so," said Lenny. "Now, why don't you finish fixing up the trim, huh?"

"Yes, sir, at once, sir." Before he turned back to the ship's control panel, Jerry looked at Reynolds and waved an accusing finger at him. Feigning a shocked expression, the COB merely shrugged his shoulders and tried to look innocent. The merry twinkle in his eyes, however, spoke loudly of his guilt.

Without the malicious interference of half the crew, Jerry was able to quickly get a satisfactory trim and *Memphis* increased speed to sixteen knots.

Except for a single fire drill, the remainder of the watch was quiet and Jerry and Reynolds went over a number of the finer points of being a good Diving Officer.

After a quick dinner, Jerry stopped by the ship's office. He had some paperwork to drop off, but he also had an important question for YN1 Glover.

The yeoman had "Abbey Road" playing when Jerry knocked on the door. It was open, but the ship's office was Glover's domain, and Jerry had seen the XO knock before he stepped inside.

Glover thanked him for the paperwork, and then Jerry asked his question. "How many of us will have to go through the Bluenose ceremony?"

The yeoman smiled. "Thirty-one. We've actually got forty who haven't made the trip with us, but nine have entries in their service records. That's not counting the two ladies, of course."

"You knew, just like that?" Jerry asked.

"The XO asked for the numbers yesterday." Glover explained.

Jerry felt relieved. "That's a quarter of the crew," he observed.

"Well, we've stayed pretty close to home in the past year or so, mostly doing Manta trials."

"It'll be nice to get it over with," remarked Jerry.

"Oh, you'll do fine, sir. Although I've heard that they're working on a special procedure for new officers that used to be aviators." He smiled and Jerry couldn't be sure if he was serious or not.

As the evening wore on, Jerry started to hear Bluenose stories creep into the crew's casual conversation. Those who had crossed before shared their experiences, suitably embellished to amaze the recipients. The trick was to exaggerate outrageously, but still make it sound plausible. Even if the listeners knew the story had to be untrue, a good storyteller could create uncertainty in their minds.

He heard the story about Boreas and the admiral and several variations on ways to get ice cubes from one end of the boat to the other before they melted. Jerry was advised to pick one and practice, just in case Boreas wanted to test his skill.

The actual preparations were secret, of course, as were the exact trials that the "warm bodies" would have to endure. Jerry figured it wouldn't do any good to ask, but Ensign Jim Porter, the Electrical Officer and most junior officer aboard, kept on asking. Either out of fear or just plain curiosity, he grilled his division, then the wardroom, trying to find out exactly what would transpire.

Early the next day, Thursday, Porter spotted Frank Lopez and Master Chief Reynolds in the wardroom. They were working on A division paperwork, spread out on the wardroom table, but had paused, and he sat down. Jerry, on his way to see the XO, knew what was coming and stopped to watch.

"Mr. Lopez, Master Chief, how many Bluenose ceremonies have you seen?"

"More than a few," the COB said vaguely. Lopez simply replied, "Just one, on this boat's last northern run."

Porter pressed his point. "Master Chief, are the ceremonies the same on every boat? Who decides what happens?"

"Why, King Boreas, of course," said Reynolds, laughing.

"Come on, Master Chief," pleaded the Ensign, "somebody on *Memphis* must be in charge of organizing the Bluenose ceremony this evening. Who is it?"

"Son," growled Reynolds menacingly, "talk like that will get back to Boreas. And if he doesn't find you pure of heart, he may not let you in, and then you'll have to swim home."

Jerry was startled by a harsh voice almost directly behind him. "How much of this foolishness do I have to put up with?" Patterson exclaimed. " 'King Boreas,' my foot."

Jerry quickly stepped out of the way, almost physically pushed aside by the force of her words.

"We have more important things to worry about than some male bonding ritual. All I hear about is how much work it takes to run one of these things, and if you don't do everything exactly right, someone—probably all of us—will die."

As Patterson talked, she poured herself a cup of coffee. When she paused to drink, though, it set her off again. "And the food on this ship! Hasn't the Navy ever heard of low-fat cooking? And this coffee tastes like it came out of a paint can. In fact, this whole boat smells like the inside of a paint can!"

She was shouting now and didn't even look at Jerry or Lopez or Reynolds. A few other officers, including the XO, clustered at the door, but didn't seem eager to come in.

"There's no space. I'm constantly bumping into people or things I'm not supposed to touch. There's no privacy and too much noise. I can't get in touch with my office. I can't even make a phone call! I cannot imagine why any of you stand for it!"

Master Chief Reynolds, like the others, listened to her tirade. When she paused, he asked, "If you hate being on board so much, why are you here? Why didn't you send someone else?"

"Because it was my idea. Because I'm the best-qualified person to do the job and to see that it is done properly," she replied intensely.

"That's what every sailor on *Memphis* would say, if you asked them. They volunteered for sub duty, and they had to work hard just to get here."

When she didn't answer, Reynolds added, "It's a much easier life ashore, and the pay's a lot better too, especially for men this well trained. Each and every crew member chose to be here, in spite of all the discomforts and the separation from their loved ones, because they know it's a job that needs to be done. And they want to make sure the job is done right. Patriotism isn't dead in this Navy, Dr. Patterson, of that I can assure you."

Patterson remained silent for a moment, her eyes fixed on the COB. "You should have been in politics." A slight smile flashed across her face as she softened. "I see your point, Master Chief. And . . . I admit that I may have misjudged the people on this sub."

The COB responded, "You can work with these men, if you'll only give them a chance. And if you're willing to work with them, then play with them as well. Don't the people in the White House have a party every once in a while?" asked Reynolds with a grin.

Patterson sighed, steeling herself, then turned to the XO, standing in the doorway. "Commander, is that invitation to the Bluenose ceremony still open?"

"Of course, ma'am," replied Bair. "We'd be honored if you would join us."

At 1515 that afternoon *Memphis* came to a complete stop and Davy Jones was brought aboard. Jerry watched as an elderly man dressed in a white robe and bedecked in seaweed, actually plastic ivy, climbed down from the forward escape trunk. In his hand was a scroll case, encrusted with seashells and starfish. Bair greeted him at the trunk and escorted the King's herald to the CO's stateroom to examine the petitions of the neophytes. An hour later, the submarine officially crossed the Arctic Circle.

"All warm bodies are to muster in the crew's mess," squawked the 1MC. "The honor guard is to muster by the forward escape trunk, to welcome His Majesty aboard."

Jerry, Emily, Patterson, and the other warm bodies were herded into the crew's mess. Most of them looked nervous, some were afraid. Emily was also a bit apprehensive, but Patterson looked calm and collected.

Everyone, as ordered, wore swim trunks, and the ladies were attractively but modestly attired in one-piece suits and a pair of shorts. Patterson's was blue, Emily's green with stripes. Both were new, obviously purchased for this special occasion.

Jerry couldn't help but notice that Joanna Patterson was rather attractive in a one-piece bathing suit. With her ash-blonde hair in a ponytail, she looked far more feminine than usual. At that thought, Jerry looked away, as he didn't want to get caught staring at her. She would probably grow fangs and bite his head off.

Emily, on the other hand, was striking. Although she was smaller than Patterson, she had one hell of a figure. Remembering that these two ladies were the only females on board and that he hadn't seen any other members of the fair sex for some time, he tried to be objective in his appraisal. Sidelong study of both confirmed that they were lookers. Jerry caught some of the others studying their guests as well and hoped this wasn't going to complicate things.

Unexpectedly, Emily turned and her eyes met Jerry's. For a brief moment, they simply looked at each other, and then Emily suddenly blushed and turned away. Jerry was also embarrassed and wondered if she had read his thoughts—or if they were written all over his face. He didn't have long to think about it, for a loud voice announced: "ALL STAND FOR HIS MAJESTY, BOREAS REX, RULER OF THE NORTH WIND AND SOVEREIGN OF ALL THE FROZEN REACHES."

From the back of the crew's mess, King Boreas walked in wearing a very regal-looking red and gold cape; a seashell crown rested on his noble brow. His Majesty sported a huge white beard, which must have required a master engineer to construct, since it was made from cotton balls. It didn't take Jerry very long to see that Master Chief Reynolds had the honor of playing Boreas on this run. Jerry felt a little relieved that the COB would be in charge, but that would soon change.

Following Boreas was his Royal Consort, the Queen of the Snows. Jerry had no idea who was playing the role of the Queen, but whoever it was, they did a pretty good job. The white wig with sparkling garland, matching boa and handbag, and a pair of pink fish sunglasses made whoever it was look more like a cheap movie actress. In tow behind the Queen was the Royal Baby. This kid was a real whiner and acted more like a chimpanzee than a baby. As the royal offspring got closer, Jerry saw that it was Lenny Berg. Behind him were Bill Washburn as the Prime Minister, dressed in a simple toga and carrying a satchel of scrolls, and Senior Chief Foster as the Captain of the Guard. Foster was in some sort of brown leather biker outfit, complete with a real-enough-looking short sword and scabbard. It made him look quite menacing, as it was intended to.

With his two roommates, his division chief, and the COB making up most of the royal entourage, Jerry suspected a conspiracy against him. He then remembered Glover's earlier comment about a special procedure for new officers who used to be aviators. I'm toast, Jerry thought ruefully.

As Boreas walked haughtily down the small aisle in the crew's mess, he carefully gauged the hot-blooded neophytes. As he passed Jerry and the two women, he paused a moment to examine the three more closely. A deep frown appeared on his face. As the rest of the Royal Court went by, each looked directly at Jerry. The Queen also stared intently at the two ladies, flicking her boa around in an agitated manner. Foster had the most wicked expression Jerry had ever seen, a devious cross between a sinister sneer and a gloating grin. All this confirmed Jerry's growing fear that he was going to be *the* special guest at today's festivities. Right now, he thought, it sucks to be me.

Hardy was waiting up at the front of the mess, and as Boreas approached, he bowed and announced, "Welcome, Your Majesty, to my ship. My crew and I are honored that you have consented, once again, to grace us with your presence."

"Greetings, Captain," boomed Reynolds. "It has indeed been too long since we last met. And I am pleased to see you and those of the Royal Order of the Bluenose once again in my realm."

"Thank you, Your Highness. We are but humble servants whose duties have blessed us with the opportunity to travel yet again to the far north." Hardy was laying it on pretty thick and Jerry saw that he wore a broad smile as he played his role. This was a side of Hardy that Jerry had never seen.

The pleasantries continued as Boreas introduced the remaining members of the Royal Court. Each offered his respects to Hardy, then assumed his place behind the King. After the introductions were completed, Bair and Davy Jones showed up at Hardy's side with Jones carrying the sealed scroll case. Kneeling before Boreas, he offered the case to the King. "Excuse me your Majesty. Sire, here are the petitions of all the warm bodies present."

"Ahhh, thank you, my loyal herald," replied Reynolds loudly. "You are quite right. We must proceed with the business at hand." Taking the petitions, he handed them to Washburn, who, along with Foster, began to examine them. Reynolds then clasped Hardy on the shoulder and pulled him over to Patterson and Davis. Gesturing toward them with his massive hand, Reynolds asked, "Before we begin, Captain, perhaps you would care to explain this? It is most irregular for females to be aboard a submersible vessel, is it not?"

"Uh, yes, Your Majesty, you are correct." Hardy's response seemed awkward, shuffling his feet, as if he were reluctant to answer the King's questions. "You see, Sire, my ruler ordered me to bring them along in the pursuit of our duties. They are crucial to my ship's ability to fulfill his wishes."

"I see," Reynolds said sternly. "We shall have to review their petitions closely."

Returning to the front of the mess, Reynolds drew himself up and formally addressed Hardy. "Captain, as these warm bodies are under your command, I desire to know your assessment of their worthiness to enter my realm."

"Of course, Your Majesty." Hardy turned to face the warm bodies, a hard look on his face. Then, with a slow wave of his arm, he shouted, "Sire, they are all unworthy bastards!" The force of his statement caused Emily to audibly draw in her breath. Hearing her gasp, Hardy looked directly at her. "Correction, Your Highness, all but two are unworthy bastards! Those two are unworthy wenches!"

Patterson erupted indignantly, "Now, see here, Capt . . ."

"SILENCE!" roared Reynolds. His bellow was so loud that it actually echoed inside the crew's mess. Even Patterson was taken aback by the sheer power in his voice. Reynolds then looked around menacingly at everyone, to make sure they understood that he meant business. Sighing, he turned once again to Hardy. "Captain, I appreciate your candor in this matter. But as their lord, you must make at least a perfunctory attempt at defending them."

"Of course, King Boreas. My apologies." Hardy then proceeded to testify that these warm bodies hadn't sunk the ship yet, although their ignorance had nearly succeeded on numerous occasions. Furthermore, they were barely adequate in the performance of their duties and their exercises. Hardy ranted on for a few more minutes about their general inability to do anything right and concluded that they were totally unworthy in and of themselves. Their only credible defense, Hardy concluded, was for them to throw themselves at the mercy of the King's court. Reynolds listened with rapt attention, looking very sagelike in his robes and fake beard.

"Very well, Captain. I concede their unworthiness," stated Boreas. "However, I am willing to be merciful to these warm bodies and allow them one last opportunity to prove that they are indeed worthy to enter my domain. We shall begin the . . ."

All of a sudden, there arose a commotion behind Reynolds. Washburn and Foster appeared to be shocked and angered by one of the petitions and their agitated discussion interrupted the King. A very annoyed Boreas turned toward his two courtiers and swore, "By my beard, you try my patience! What are you two babbling about?"

Both Washburn and Foster quickly came over with the petition and presented it to Boreas. "Your Majesty," spoke Washburn hesitantly as he knelt before Reynolds. "There is a warm body present that has openly admitted to being affiliated with a most heinous association. I—I—" Washburn seemed unable to finish, so appalled by what he had read.

"Please go on, Prime Minister," commanded Reynolds. Jerry had a sinking feeling that there were talking about him.

"Sire," spoke Foster with significant disgust. "The warm body in question is an aviator."

Jerry watched as Reynolds' hands curled up into clenched fists. Slowly and rigidly, he turned around and cast a chilling gaze on the warm bodies. "Do you mean to tell me there is a member of that league of arrogant scoundrels who routinely trespasses on my realm without so much as a 'By your leave!' " Reynolds was shaking as he spoke and Jerry noticed that everyone near him had started to move as far away as they could, given the tight quarters.

"WHERE is this wretch, my Captain of the Guard?" demanded the

King angrily. Foster wasted no time in pointing Jerry out. With slow, deliberate steps, Reynolds marched toward him.

Oh shit, this is not going to be good, Jerry thought as Reynolds approached and towered over him. Jerry gulped as two large hands grasped his arms and lifted him off the deck. Once the two were at eye level, with Jerry dangling almost a foot off the deck, Reynolds spoke in a hushed voice through clenched lips, "You have much to account for, flying man!"

Jerry could only nod his head, amazed at Reynolds' strength and a little afraid of what was to come. Reynolds gently put Jerry back down and released him. Both Davis and Patterson watched in awe, their eyes the size of saucers, as they witnessed Reynolds easily lifting Jerry off his feet. Turning away with a graceful swing of his cape, Boreas commanded, "Let the trials begin! Captain of the Guard, escort these unworthy warm bodies to the torpedo room."

For the next two hours, Jerry and the other warm bodies underwent the trials as prescribed by King Boreas. None of them were particularly harmful to the body. Most were simply uncomfortable, but everything revolved around being cold, somehow, somewhere.

The first trial was relatively simple. All a warm body had to do was crawl down the twenty-two-foot length of a torpedo tube and rub their nose on the muzzle door. Of course, with the forward end of each torpedo tube exposed to the sea, the temperature in the tube was a bit on the nippy side. It was a cold trip down and back, as well as a little claustrophobic.

The part that Jerry hated the most was backing his way out of the tube once he had reached the muzzle door. In order to get anywhere, Jerry had to arch his back so that he could shuffle backward. This brought his bare back in contact with the frigid guide rail at the top of the tube. He yelped more than once.

As Jerry had been warned earlier, many of the trials involved the use of ice in a number of very unpleasant ways. In one particularly devious trial, he had to transport two ice cubes placed under his armpits from the back of the engine room to the spherical array access trunk: the full length of the boat. "This will clip his wings," remarked the Royal Baby as he placed the ice under Jerry's arms. Unfortunately, the ice cubes on his first attempt were too small, and they melted before he could finish the course. Obviously, Jerry was still too hot-blooded to enter the frozen realm. He was sent back to the engine room to try again.

Midway through the trials, he had had significant doubts whether he'd make it. The low point was during Captain Hardy's favorite game: bobbing for ice cubes. In this trial, Jerry was pitted against another warm body and the two would submerge their faces into a large container of water filled with ice cubes. The first to grab an ice cube with their teeth won. The loser had to keep on playing till they defeated someone. Jerry proved to be particularly inept at this game, and ended up going seven rounds before finally managing to beat a junior petty officer from E Division. Even Patterson beat Jerry. It was with a bruised and frozen ego that Jerry heard the crew cheer, "Broomhilda! Broomhilda!" as Patterson emerged first with an ice cube clutched firmly in her mouth. He'd be hearing about this ignominy for the rest of the patrol.

With most of the trials over, the warm bodies started to congregate in the auxiliary machinery room for the baptism. As Jerry entered the twenty-one-man bunkroom, just forward of the auxiliary machinery room and aft of the torpedo room, the Prime Minister and the Captain of the Guard brought him up short. "His Majesty, the King, requires your presence, warm body," said Foster malevolently. Washburn and Foster then grabbed Jerry's arms and led him into the torpedo room.

"Ahhh, excellent. You have found him," remarked Reynolds, pleased. "Well, done. Well done. Bring him here."

Jerry was ushered up to King Boreas, where the Captain of the Guard pushed him to his knees. "Show the proper respect to His Majesty, knave!"

The rough handling by Foster was starting to anger Jerry. Foster's behavior was becoming abusive and even in such ceremonies there were limits. Jerry sensed that Reynolds also knew that Foster had gone overboard and ordered him to back off. "Stand easy, my Captain!"

Foster moved away from Jerry, who was allowed to rise and face the King.

"According to the reports of the Royal Court," began Reynolds, "you have acquitted yourself well in the trials. But there is still one issue that I need to have satisfied before I grant you entry into my realm." Turning away from Jerry, he paced about a bit, rubbing his beard slowly, as if he were trying to find the right words.

"What issue would that be?" asked Jerry. Belatedly he added, "Your Majesty" after Foster glared at him.

"It's rather simple really," said Reynolds, pausing as he faced Jerry. "Are you an aviator or a mariner?"

"I was an aviator, but I'm no longer qualified to fly. I'm now a submariner."

"He lies, Your Highness!" screeched Foster. "I recommend that he be given the truth serum!"

"Hmmm, perhaps you are right, Captain." Reynolds then motioned to Washburn to come forward. In his hands was a steel bucket. "Prime Minister, administer the serum to this warm body so that we can see if he is indeed telling us the truth or not."

Washburn lifted the bucket, handed it to Jerry, and ordered, "Drink!" Jerry took the bucket and looked closely at the contents. The liquid inside had a dark orangeish-brown color and it had an oily sheen to it. A light brown foam clung to the edges. It looked absolutely disgusting and it smelled just as bad.

"I said, drink!" repeated Washburn forcefully.

Hesitantly, Jerry slowly lifted the bucket to his lips and took a drink. Almost immediately he began to cough and sputter as he gagged on the foul-tasting elixir. He coughed so hard that he nearly spilled the rest of the serum onto the deck. Washburn deftly recovered the bucket from Jerry's shaking hands and said, "The serum has been administered, My Lord."

"Very well, Prime Minister. It will take but a few moments for it to take effect."

A few moments, my ass! thought Jerry as the coughing finally subsided. It's having one hell of an effect right now. Jerry didn't know all of what they had mixed together in that bucket, but from that one vile gulp he was certain that soy sauce, vinegar, and some sort of carbonated drink were included. What sick mind had devised this concoction? They should lock him up before he hurts someone, Jerry lamented.

"I ask you again: Are you an aviator, or a mariner?" Reynolds' voice was louder and firmer than the first time.

More than a little irate with the whole Bluenose business, Jerry replied firmly. "Your majesty, I am *now* a mariner. I sail on and under the sea, not over it."

"More lies. It is well known that aviators do not pay their respects to King Boreas. And you were an aviator," growled Foster.

"That is incorrect, Captain of the Guard," replied Jerry sternly. "Aviators like myself fly from ships. When the ship crosses the Arctic Circle, we pay proper homage like anyone else." Foster appeared almost apoplectic, shocked that Jerry would dare challenge him.

"That may be true," interrupted Reynolds, "but explain to me why those in their flying machines do not pay their respects and violate my domain with wild abandon? Even though I send my fiercest winds, they ignore my challenge and come and go as they please."

Jerry looked at Reynolds and tried to figure out why he was doing this. It seemed like he was really trying to make a point, but what? And to whom? It should be obvious to Reynolds that this sort of ceremony wouldn't be possible in a tactical aircraft, and Jerry just didn't know if the charge Foster was leveling against all aviators was accurate or not. Maybe the aviation community had some kind of ritual that he wasn't aware of. So, why would Reynolds emphasize the lack of respect by aviators? Was this just one of those legendary trumped-up charges brought against people during these ceremonies to which there was no right answer? Or was Reynolds trying to get him to admit to something under pressure—to someone who needed to hear it. His gut feeling said it was the latter.

Jerry stood as erect as he could and slowly, evenly addressed Reynolds' question. "Your majesty, I was an aviator. And I was a good one. But due to an accident that was not my fault, I can no longer fly. I wanted to stay in the Navy, but I also wanted to belong to an elite group, a group that had some of the best people in the service. I tried to transfer to submarines, but I was told no. Not because I wasn't qualified, but because it would cost too much and that the Navy wouldn't get a good return on its investment." Jerry found his gaze slowly shifting toward Foster as he continued speaking. "I didn't like the answer I received; it seemed to me to be arbitrary and capricious. The higher-ups just didn't want to be bothered by a baby aviator with a broken wing. I forced the issue through family political connections because I don't believe in giving up on something important just because it's hard to achieve. And now I'm here."

Taking a deep breath and returning his attention to Reynolds, Jerry concluded his little speech. "Now Your Highness, as for the disrespect shown by aviators: I can't speak to the actions of others. I can only speak for myself. In that regard, I am here, now, willingly paying the proper respect and deference due to your exalted position and humbly seeking your permission to enter your realm. These actions should be the point of debate for the Royal Court, not my past status."

That twinkle in Reynolds' eyes told Jerry that he had made the right choice. "Well said, lad. I accept your explanation." Turning toward the Prime Minister and the Captain of the Guard, Reynolds inquired, "Are there any other charges against this warm body?"

"None, sire," said Washburn with a huge smile. Foster said nothing, but shook his head no.

"Very well, then, young mariner, join the other warm bodies and we shall conclude the ceremony." Jerry bowed and left the torpedo room.

The baptism was the climax of the Bluenose ceremony. Each warm body stepped into the shower area in the crew's head and was liberally doused with unheated seawater from one of the small garden-hoselike fire-fighting connections. Jerry watched as Emily was drenched with freezing water. Her screech was so loud, it was picked up by one of the ship's self-noise monitoring hydrophones. When it was Jerry's turn, Reynolds himself took the hose and gave him an extra-long soaking. Jerry stood there and endured it, determined to not cry out. Shaking violently, Jerry was led to the auxiliary machinery room, where he was allowed to dry off, and a petty officer painted his nose a very deep shade of blue. He was now a true and trusted, ice- and brine-encrusted Bluenose.

The celebratory feast, in spite of the pomp and circumstance, was really just another excuse to give the new Bluenoses some more grief. The dinner was served cold, naturally, and Jerry thought the menu was about as disgusting as the truth serum. The salad was half-frozen cooked spinach with anchovies, pickled relish, some kind of squishy nut, and spearmint dressing. The main course consisted of sardines in peanut butter sauce, cold mashed potatoes with hideous gelatinous sardine gravy, and frozen snow peas. Dessert was a snow cone made from the water drained from cans of tuna fish. In addition to the chilly and revolting cuisine, the new Bluenoses ate their dinner while sitting on ice held in large sheet cake pans. By the time the ceremony had finally concluded, and King Boreas and his court retired, Jerry's butt was numb with cold.

Slowly waddling back to his stateroom, Jerry was congratulated on surviving his initiation. He acknowledged their greetings with a stiff nod, but all he cared for right now was a hot shower. Grabbing a towel from his stateroom, he headed for the officer's head. Once at the shower stall, he turned on the water and waited for it to warm up—it didn't. Jerry moaned and cursed the general unfairness of it all, as the XO had secured the hot water until further notice. He had to get the salt off his body, so with a deep, resigned sigh, Jerry jumped into the cold fresh water.

Up in their stateroom, Patterson and Davis were desperately trying to warm up from their ordeal. Emily was still shaking uncontrollably, despite being wrapped up in two blankets. Patterson walked around their tiny room, shivering, upset, and annoyed that there was no hot water. Suddenly there was a knock at their door.

"Yes!" yelled Patterson, "Who is it?"

"Messenger of the Watch, ma'am, with a gift from Master Chief Reynolds."

Patterson flung open the door, poised to tell the messenger just what he could do with the master chief's gifts, when she saw the sailor holding a tray containing two large steaming mugs. "What is this?" she asked.

The sailor smiled. "Hot tea fortified with a little depth charge medicine, ma'am. COB said you two earned it."

Patterson grabbed one of the mugs and took a sip, "Oh, my God! A Hot Toddy! Bless you." She grabbed the other mug and handed it to Emily, who seemed more content to just hold the hot ceramic in her hands.

"Where on earth did you find brandy?" questioned Patterson through sips of the prized beverage. "I thought the Navy didn't allow alcohol to be consumed on board ships."

"That's true, ma'am. But we do carry some alcohol for medicinal purposes, and as the COB pointed out, you two aren't Navy, so the rules don't apply to you."

"Well, thank you for the hot drinks. We do appreciate them," replied a grateful Patterson.

"Oh, ma'am, one more thing." The messenger moved a little closer and whispered in a hushed voice, "The XO wishes to convey his compliments and says that by the time you are done with your tea, the hot water will be back on line."

Patterson thanked the messenger for the news and shut the door. Shuffling over to the desk, she sat down and slowly sipped her drink. As the warmth poured back into her body, Patterson looked over at the huddled mass on the bunk and said, "You know, Emily, for military types, these guys are okay. Criminally insane, but okay."

Davis could only nod her assent.

 The Casualty

May 21, 2005

•••

Norwegian Sea, Near Jan Mayen Island

Jerry stood at the sink in the officer's head, fiercely scrubbing his nose. And yet despite his efforts of the past two days, it was still a very noticeable shade of blue. Only now it was sore as well.

"Hey, Jerry, go easy on that weather vane of yours," quipped Berg as he stepped into the head. "You might as well get used to it. Your nose is going to be blue for a while."

"How long?" asked Jerry testily. "And what the hell kind of paint did you guys use, anyway?"

"No, no, nooo, Jerry, my man. We didn't use paint at all." Berg dramatically paused as he started shaving.

"And!?!" said Jerry. He was in no mood for Lenny's usual riddles this morning. His nose hurt, he was tired, and he had to hurry up if he wanted to eat breakfast before the second ROV test prebrief.

"Huh? Oh yes. Let me see now," Berg's façade of temporary forgetfulness only annoyed Jerry further. "We used tried-and-true Prussian blue dye on the noses of the warm bodies. You know, the dye we use for checking valve bodies and stems."

Jerry vaguely recalled the maintenance procedure, but he didn't initially catch Berg's key word: dye. When he finally did, his eyes opened wide and he gasped, "You used a permanent dye? How long will the color last?"

"It's not just any dye," protested Berg. "Prussian blue is one of the first synthetic colors ever made. It has a very honorable history in the textile industry and art since the early 1700s. Its name is derived from one of its earliest uses: the dyeing of Prussian military uniforms."

"How long?" growled Jerry

"Don't worry, it'll fade." Berg hesitated as he applied his aftershave and then added, "Eventually."

"Eventually. Could you be a wee bit more precise than that?"

"Sure. How about a couple of weeks?"

"Arrgh!" snarled Jerry as he marched back to his stateroom.

"Hey, shipmate, chill," admonished Berg as Jerry left.

Jerry regretted snapping at Lenny. He knew he shouldn't take his frustration out on him. Lenny had played only a minor role in his Bluenose initiation, as did Washburn. But what bothered Jerry more was the way the COB went after him. Between the trim party and the extra attention during the ceremony, he felt like Reynolds was doing everything in his power to make him look like an idiot. On the other hand, the COB had certainly made good on his promise to help him with his qualifications. Jerry had already completed his Diving Officer requirements and was ready for his qual board. Reynolds' mentoring had gone a long way toward speeding up the process. That and the extra watches he stood didn't hurt, either. Still, Jerry was getting mixed signals and he no longer understood just what Reynolds was doing, or why.

Jerry scarfed down breakfast like a tornado going through a trailer park. And just in time, too. As soon as his dishes had been cleared away, the wardroom door opened and Emily, Patterson, Foster, and others started pouring in. Hardy and Bair brought up the rear, and they squeezed into their places.

Jerry was relieved to see that several others had the same shade of blue nose as he did. Until he'd seen them, his nose had seemed as big as the bow array. Emily's and Patterson's appeared more subdued, but he suspected they may have used makeup.

Emily's briefing was much shorter than the previous one, as it was mostly a review of the procedures. There were a few questions on ROV limitations and handling issues, but Davis dealt with them quickly. After less than half an hour, when everything had been covered, the XO spoke up.

"All right, everyone, that last piece of business to go over is the watch rotation for the two test runs. Mr. Richards, do you have your teams lined up?"

"Yes, sir," responded the Weapons Officer. "Team one will handle the first test run and will switch with team two as soon as the first ROV is recovered and secured. Also, each team will be assigned to the same ROV for the duration of the patrol."

Jerry saw that both Emily and Patterson looked confused, and it didn't take long for Patterson to interrupt. "Excuse me, Commander, I don't understand why we need teams. During our first two test runs, Mr. Mitchell employed all of his people and they handled the tests very well. Why do we have to split them up into two teams?"

"It's a simple matter of logistics, Doctor," replied Bair matter-of-factly.

"After reviewing the plan of operations that you and the Navigator submitted, it became clear that we'd have to go to port and starboard sections just to conduct all the ROV missions you want. If we stood the whole torpedo division up for each run, they'd be exhausted in only a few days. Tired men make too many mistakes."

Hardy nodded his head in agreement and added, "Dr. Patterson, you've planned a very aggressive schedule with over two dozen missions within a three-week period. If we're going to be successful, we must pace ourselves. Even so, this will be a hard rate to maintain."

Jerry watched and listened as Hardy and Patterson went back and forth over the mission details. It was remarkable to see them being so civil, when only a week ago they were screaming at each other. There was still some tension, to be sure, but it seemed to be held in check. Patterson was very goal-oriented, and as long as she believed that Hardy was helping her toward her goal, things went smoothly. But if she felt he was being obstructive, she could become a holy terror in a heartbeat.

It struck Jerry that Dr. Patterson was one of those people who was good at visualizing what needed to be done. But for all her knowledge and political savvy, she wasn't very good at figuring out how to do it. One might say that she was process-impaired. This was, however, Hardy's forte. Give him an objective and he'd get you there. Just don't tell him how to do it.

Jerry's amateur psychoanalysis came to an abrupt end when the XO addressed a question to him. "Mr. Mitchell, how are the maintenance arrangements coming along?"

"Huh? Oh, excuse me, sir. I've discussed our maintenance support needs with all of the department heads and they have specialists in sonar, navigation, and electric propulsion ready to assist my division as necessary."

"Good. Anything else?"

"Ahh, yes, sir. I have one concern," said Jerry hesitantly.

"And what is that?" said Hardy and Patterson in unison. Both momentarily looked at each other, more surprised than annoyed, and then they returned their attention to Jerry.

"Well, Captain, ma'am, my guys can perform the routine maintenance between the runs—that shouldn't be a problem—but I don't know if we'll be able to do much if something major breaks. I mean, we've only had a week to study the plans and there has been no formal training on these vehicles. And what little we do have on emergency repair procedures is not exactly up to Navy standards. No offense, Dr. Davis."

"None taken, Mr. Mitchell," replied Emily politely. "But if something does break down, then it's my job to fix it. I designed and supervised the modification of the ROVs, and I'm responsible for their health and well-being; with your division's help, of course."

"I appreciate your candor, Mr. Mitchell," said Patterson firmly, "but Emily has gone over the mission requirements and determined that the probability of a mission critical failure is quite low."

This pronouncement caught all the Navy people off guard, and Jerry had to resist the urge to sigh. Assuming the odds of a major failure was low based on calculations with little or no operating history was risky business. He had seen an early draft of the mission plan, and the proposed ROV operations tempo was harsh. With little time for maintenance between each run, the whole concept of operations begged for a major problem to occur. By the look of several other crew members, it was clear that they shared his skepticism.

"Final item," Bair declared suddenly, breaking the awkward silence. "During the second ROV test, Mr. Mitchell will observe the evolution from the control room."

"Sir?" asked Jerry, slightly perplexed.

"It's important that you see what goes on in control during a ROV deployment. It will give you an appreciation for what the ship control party has to do to support a launch and recovery. This will also improve your understanding of our information needs."

"Yes, sir."

Hardy then stood up and spoke firmly, "If there are no further questions, we'll man ROV stations in half an hour." It was not a request, and by definition there were no other questions. "Very well, then. Dismissed."

Jerry stood and waited for Hardy and Patterson to leave. Once the herd had thinned out a bit, he left the wardroom and headed toward the torpedo room. He had taken less than half a dozen steps before Emily entered the passageway and called to him.

"Hey, Jerry, wait up a moment, please."

He stopped, turned, and waited while she caught up with him. "Are you feeling okay? You were pretty spaced in there for a while."

"Yeah, I'm fine," answered Jerry. "I was momentarily mesmerized by your lovely blue nose."

Emily immediately reached over and cuffed Jerry lightly on the head.

"Oww! Geez, pay the lady a compliment and she whacks you one."

"A woman's prerogative," Emily replied tersely. "And stop acting like you've been mortally wounded. I didn't hit you that hard."

"Yes, ma'am. I'll gladly accept any further abuse in stoic silence."

Emily sighed, shook her head, and said, "Why is it that men always resort to sarcasm?"

Concluding that silence was the better part of valor, he quickly escorted Emily past the twenty-one-man bunkroom and into the torpedo room. Once inside, he gently directed her toward the ROV and Manta control area.

"All right Emily. What's bugging you?" Jerry asked firmly.

She reluctantly looked at him. There were tears welling in her eyes and she blurted out, "Do you really not trust me, Jerry?"

Shocked and surprised, Jerry could only wonder: Where the hell did that come from? Confused, he asked, "What are you talking about, Emily?"

"During the brief, when you raised your concern on the repair issue, I saw the look on your face when I said I could take care of any major repairs. And when Dr. Patterson said I had calculated that there was a low chance of a critical failure happening, you didn't seem to believe her. I can only conclude that you don't trust me."

Oh boy, Jerry thought, as he finally understood the problem. Mom warned me about this gender communications gap, he thought to himself. Struggling to answer Emily's accusation without digging himself a deeper grave, Jerry motioned for her to sit down.

Then, after taking a deep breath, he carefully and slowly offered his explanation, "Listen, Emily, there is something that you have to understand. Navy people are trained to be conservative when dealing with equipment; submariners even more so. For example, when we conduct a reactor startup, we calculate the precise height that the control rods have to be raised before the core goes critical. There are a lot of variables that go into this calculation, and it takes several highly trained operators to do the math, and then it is triple-checked. And yet when we begin the startup, we operate under the assumption that the core could go critical the moment the Reactor Operator begins shimming the rods out."

Emily's scrunched brow told Jerry that she wasn't quite making the connection.

"There are always places where a mistake could be made, and the results of such an error could be catastrophic. I admit there are a lot of coulds, possibles, and ifs in what I just said, but we can't afford even one serious reactor accident."

"But you trust your people, don't you?"

"If they are qualified for their watch position, absolutely. But we all know that a mistake could still be made if we become complacent and just assume that the calculation was done correctly. And this, mind you, is how we treat an engineering plant that most of us have had years to become familiar with and can operate competently. We can't say the same thing for your vehicles."

Embarrassed, she looked down at the deck and shook her head no.

"Okay, then, please don't confuse our lack of trust for your ROVs, as a lack of trust in you. I believe the crew trusts you. I know I do, but your ROVs have had so little operational time that most of what you and Patterson have said they can do is still on paper."

A small smile flashed quickly across her face as she wiped her eyes on a Kleenex that Jerry had magically produced. "Thanks. I guess I'm taking any criticism of my babies, real or implied, a bit personally. I'm sorry that I accused you of not trusting me."

"Don't worry about it, Emily," responded Jerry reassuringly. "When a person pours their heart and soul into a project, they get attached to it."

For a brief moment, Jerry relived that fateful day when his F-18E/F Super Hornet spun out of control and blew up. He remembered saying he was sorry, over and over again, and feeling like he had just lost a friend. Jerry shook his head a little, as he tried to purge the memory from his brain. He saw the quizzical look on Emily's face, smiled, and said, "Sorry, got lost there for a moment. Anyway, I want you to know that I understand where you are coming from and that I know how important those ROVs are to you."

"Thank you, Jerry, I appreciate your empathy," she said as she rose. She started to give him a peck on the cheek, but then reconsidered. Jerry saw her stop, but smiled almost as if she had kissed him. Both turned to their assigned tasks.

As she went about powering up the control console, Jerry surveyed his spaces and noticed that Huey was prepped and in position to be loaded. Looking at his watch, he saw that there were only a few minutes left before they manned launch stations. Less than a minute later, Senior Chief Foster, Petty Officer Willis, and Seaman Jobin entered the torpedo room and moved toward the ROV. They were the bulk of ROV team one; Petty Officer Boyd was already there, since he had the torpedo room watch.

"MAN ROV LAUNCH STATIONS," announced the 1MC. The Captain was precisely on schedule.

"All right, people. Let's get this vehicle into tube three," ordered Foster. Jerry got out of the way. Despite the smaller number of men working on the ROV, Foster managed to get it into the tube and hooked up in about the same amount of time as during the first test trials. Ten minutes later, Huey was outside swimming around. Once everyone was clear of tube three, Jerry walked up and shined his pocket flashlight on the fiber-optic penetration in the breech door. The leak they had seen during the first two tests had noticeably decreased to a slow drip. Satisfied, Jerry returned to his place back by the control console.

Emily ran Huey through her test regimen. After fifteen minutes, the mechanical arm in tube one reached out and gently hauled the ROV back into tube three. The test had gone flawlessly, and Emily was clearly pleased. Foster and company pulled the vehicle from the tube and pushed it into the outboard stow of the lower centerline rack. After the restraining straps were in place and the vehicle secured, team two stepped up and prepared to do the whole thing all over again with Duey.

As team one departed, Jerry turned to follow them. He stopped momentarily, waved to Emily, and then called over to TM1 Moran, the senior man on team two. "Petty Officer Moran, I have to be in control for this test run. You're in charge down here."

Moran poked his head up from behind Duey, looked over to his division officer, and said, "Yes, sir." He immediately went back to work preparing the ROV for loading, while Jerry made his way to control.

Jerry took the steps up the ladder to control from middle level two at a time. Tim Weyer was the Officer of the Deck and with him on the periscope stand were Hardy and Richards. He made his way over to the fire-control area and sat down at the third position, the closest one to Richards, who was manning the sound-powered phones. Bair suddenly popped out of the sonar shack and walked quickly over to the stand.

"Captain, that last sonar contact is classified as biologics. It sounds like a pod of humpback whales was just passing by, likely heading out toward deeper water."

"Very well, XO," growled Hardy, his tone reflected his annoyance. "Please schedule remedial training for sonar division, XO. We can't afford to have improperly trained sonar techs getting spooked by whales once we are in area."

"Yes, sir," replied Bair flatly.

"As for the two of you," snapped Hardy at Weyer and Richards, "I strongly suggest that you get your collective acts together and pay more attention to your people's less-than-adequate proficiency. This error is inexcusable. Am I clear, gentlemen?"

Wincing at the Captain's criticism, Weyer and Richards uttered their barely audible responses. Jerry found himself wishing that he could just slink back down to the torpedo room.

After sitting for half an hour, Jerry found himself fidgeting. What was taking Moran so long? They should have requested permission to launch by now. Hardy was pacing around the periscope stand and was obviously on a slow boil. Jerry feared he would lose his patience any moment now. Fortunately, he overheard Richards as he spoke into the sound-powered phones, "Request permission to flood tube three, equalize to sea pressure, and open the outer door, aye, wait. OOD, the torpedo room reports they are ready to launch the ROV and request permission to flood tube three, equalize to sea pressure, and open the outer door."

Weyer looked at Hardy, who nodded curtly. Turning to Richards, he said, "Permission granted."

Down in the torpedo room, Moran was sweating. It had taken longer than he had expected to get the ROV into the tube. He was sure that the CO was pissed as hell, and he was sure he'd hear about it later. But at least his

on her EAB mask when he reached her. Grabbing her head with both of his hands, he put their two facemasks together. She looked terrified, but there was no time for comforting words. She needed to get out of here—now! Jerry yelled as loud as he could through his mask, "EMILY, YOU NEED TO LEAVE. FOLLOW THE BULKHEAD TO THE DOOR!" Without waiting for her reply, Jerry jerked her to her feet and placed her right hand on the bulkhead. He then grabbed her left hand and put it on her EAB connection. "ON THREE, YOU PULL THE PLUG AND GO! ONE! . . . TWO! . . . THREE!" Even though her hands were shaking badly, she managed to unplug her connection and started walking along the bulkhead.

More sparks popped out from the flames, but this time the lights blinked as well. An electrical fire! Jerry moved as fast as he could over to the power distribution panel. He swung the panel door open and started opening the breakers inside. Since he didn't know exactly what was on fire, he opened all of them in the hope that it would cut out the equipment that was burning. As he stood there, he felt the boat developing an up angle; they were coming shallow. Soon they would be at a depth where they could emergency-ventilate the torpedo room and get rid of the smoke.

Jerry considered grabbing a fire extinguisher and heading toward the fire. But he realized that it was more important for him to report to the XO that he thought they had an electrical fire on their hands, and that he had already opened the breakers. Once again, Jerry took a couple of deep breaths, unplugged his EAB, and started making his way back toward the berthing area. When he reached the ROV control consoles, he stopped to plug into the emergency air supply nearby. As he was feeling around for the EAB manifold, he bumped into somebody—it was Senior Chief Foster. Once Foster realized who it was, he tried to go around Jerry, but Jerry held him back. "OUT OF MY WAY! I DON'T HAVE TIME FOR YOU," snarled Foster. "WE HAVE AN ELECTRICAL FIRE. I HAVE TO . . ."

"I ALREADY TOOK CARE OF THE BREAKERS, SENIOR CHIEF," shouted Jerry angrily as Foster pushed against him.

"WHAT?" Foster seemed shocked by Jerry's report.

"I SAID, I ALREADY OPENED ALL THE BREAKERS ON THE P-PANEL. I'M GOING TO INFORM THE XO." Feeling a tad smug, Jerry unplugged himself and continued his search for Bair. Foster just stood there, dumbfounded.

He found the XO right where he expected him to be, leading the fire-fighting team. They were all crouched down, advancing slowly toward the forward part of the torpedo room, under the cover of a low-velocity water fog to keep the heat down. Jerry crawled up to Bair's side and plugged himself into his EAB fitting. Carefully and deliberately, Jerry reported his observations and corrective actions to his superior. The XO listened, and after Jerry had finished, gave him the thumbs-up sign. Bair then raised the NIFTI back up to his faceplate and motioned for the fire-fighting team to resume their advance and began spraying the burning console with high-velocity fog. Jerry detached himself and backed off. He would only be in the way now. With the power supply to the weapons launching console isolated, the fire was quickly extinguished.

The uncontrolled leak that caused the fire had also died down. Once the muzzle door had been shut, the torpedo tube depressurized rapidly and the dangerous pressure-driven spray quickly diminished to an inoffensive trickle. The danger to the boat was over.

⓭ Recovery

Memphis bobbed around at periscope depth for forty-five minutes while the smoke was cleared from the forward compartment. The atmospheric monitoring equipment indicated that the carbon monoxide and carbon dioxide levels in the boat were once again within safe levels. But Hardy made everyone wait another ten minutes while he had the atmosphere tested manually. Finally, the 1MC announced to the crew that they could take off their EABs.

Jerry removed his mask and was immediately greeted by the stench of burnt electrical insulation. The smell was so pungent that he briefly considered putting his mask back on. Throwing his EAB onto the centerline storage rack, he walked over to the starboard tube nest. Boyd and Greer had finished draining tube three, and were examining the inside of the breech door as Jerry approached.

"Any ideas as to what happened?" he asked.

"Not a clue, sir," answered Boyd frankly. "Oh, it's obvious that the gasket failed catastrophically, but I can't tell you how or why."

"Can we still use the tube?"

"Sure. We can screw in the metal plug and seal the penetration, but we won't be able to support ROV ops."

"I see," Jerry said. It was not going to be a pleasant experience when he'd have to tell Patterson that the tube might no longer be capable of supporting the mission. She might blow a gasket herself. "Well, go ahead and put in the plug. I want this door watertight. And find me some of that gasket, we need to figure out what happened."

"Aye, aye, sir," replied Boyd.

Jerry surveyed his damaged room. In the poor light, he couldn't tell if what he saw was burned equipment and structure or if it was just soot from the fire. Turning his flashlight to the weapons launching console, he was surprised to see that it was largely intact. He half-expected it to be a charred ruin. Jerry had just started walking over to make a closer inspection when the lights came back on. Over at the power distribution panel, he saw Foster and FT3 Larsen, the latter on the sound-powered phones. He was probably talking to maneuvering, Jerry thought, making sure that it was safe to close the breaker for the lighting circuit. With better illumination, the real state of the torpedo room became readily apparent.

The forward part of the room was pretty bad off. The damage to the launching console was worse than he had first thought, and the area between the tubes was badly burnt as well. The rest of the room, however, just looked dirty from all the smoke. Foster left the P-panel and marched down to the console, his feet sloshing in half an inch of cold seawater still on the deck. Jerry watched as the senior chief wiped off part of the control section and surveyed the damage. He looked tired and dismayed.

Slowly, Jerry walked up behind Foster and asked, "How bad?"

"Real bad," replied Foster as he shook his head ruefully.

"Can it be repaired at sea?"

"Uhh, I don't know . . . sir." Foster closed an access panel and then turned to face Jerry. "And I won't know for sure until we have stripped this console to parade rest. But I can say this much: I wouldn't hold out much hope."

Jerry nodded his acknowledgment and the two of them just stood there, an awkward silence between them. It was a little too much for Jerry.

"How's Moran?"

"He was badly bruised when he got slammed into the tubes by that jet of water, but Doc says he'll live," said Foster wearily.

"You did well getting him out as fast as you did, Senior. Thank you."

Foster was startled by the sincerity of Jerry's compliment. And for the second time that day, he was at a loss for words.

Jerry was about to suggest that Foster go and get some dry clothes on, when Emily walked into the torpedo room. He was glad to see that she had not been hurt. He regretted being so rough on her during the fire, but he had to do it. He had to get her to safety. As Emily got closer, he could tell that she was awestruck by all the damage. But what Jerry initially took as an aftereffect of shock turned out instead to be unbridled rage.

"What did you idiots do?" demanded Emily. Her whole body shook as she spoke.

Completely taken aback by her accusation and vehemence, Jerry was barely able to muster a weak, "Excuse me?"

"You heard me, Mitchell! Why did those stupid Neanderthals of yours play around with the cable fitting! If they had just left things alone, this wouldn't have happened and my baby wouldn't be stranded out in the middle of the Norwegian Sea!"

Both Foster and Jerry were utterly amazed that the ranting woman in front of them was the mousy, quiet Dr. Davis. In different circumstances, the extremes of Emily's behavior would have been humorous. But right now, any sign of joviality would be ill advised. With one of her precious ROVs stuck outside, she had the temperament of a mother grizzly bear whose cub was threatened.

"Emily, I can assure you that my guys did not cause this casualty . . ."

"Don't give me that patronizing bullshit, you son of a bitch! Your men cut him loose!"

Jerry felt his jaw tighten and he found himself becoming angry as well. He was cold, wet, and coming down from an adrenaline high. He really wasn't in the mood to deal with someone who couldn't separate the cause of the accident from proper corrective actions. And while Jerry liked Emily Davis a lot, he wasn't about to put up with her irrational tirade.

"Now, wait one damn minute, Dr. Davis! My men did not cause that fitting to fail. They responded properly to the casualty that followed. And I stand one hundred percent behind their actions, even though it meant cutting the drogue umbilical cable and stranding the ROV. In the grand scheme of things, Doctor, the lives of my men are considerably more important than your vehicle!"

It was Emily's turn to be surprised. She simply stood there, her mouth hanging open, as Jerry's stern message sunk in. Slowly, she nodded her head, the anger on her face replaced by anguish. "But what about Duey?"

Before Jerry could answer, another angry voice repeated the question. "Yes, Lieutenant, what about the ROV? Can it be recovered?"

Jerry looked up and saw Patterson and Hardy approaching them. Inwardly he groaned. It would be nearly impossible now to keep the situation under control with the two hottest heads on the boat joining the discussion. Jerry knew that they would both be upset, but for vastly different reasons. Hardy didn't disappoint him as he butted in. "The question of the ROV's recovery will have to wait, Dr. Patterson. What I need to know, Mr. Mitchell, is the name of the individual who is responsible for this debacle—and nearly cost me my boat!"

Jerry heard Foster swallow hard behind him. Jerry knew it would be so easy to blame him for this whole incident. According to Greer and the others, Foster was the senior member present when the casualty occurred. And Davis would almost certainly back his claim. It was the *Memphis* way of doing business after all, pass the blame onto someone else. But that was not how Jerry was brought up or trained by his instructors at the Academy and by Commander Casey. When he signed on to *Memphis* and assumed the duties as the Torpedo Division Officer, he became responsible for whatever happened in this room.

"I'm waiting, mister!" snarled Hardy.

"Yes, sir," replied Jerry, stalling as he built up his courage. "Based on my knowledge of the events that led up to the casualty, sir, I really can't give you the name of a particular individual at this time."

"That is totally unacceptable, Lieutenant!" screamed Hardy, his face and neck bulging with anger.

"I'm sorry, Captain, but there is no way I can name an individual with any degree of confidence," replied Jerry firmly, but with respect. "We had a fitting, not installed by the ship's crew, fail at two hundred feet when it is rated for considerably deeper depths. We had a control console that is supposed to be splash-proof, short out and burst into flames. Without investigating how and why these incidents occurred, I can't tell you if one of my men is responsible or if the fault lies with SUBASE personnel or even Draper Labs."

Hardy, completely unconvinced by Jerry's argument, seethed and through clenched teeth said, "One last time, Lieutenant Mitchell, I'm ordering you to tell me who is responsible for this disaster!"

"Very well, Captain. If you want a name, then use mine. Because I'm responsible for what goes on in my torpedo room."

An eerie silence descended on the group as all of them were surprised by Jerry's forceful response to Hardy's demand.

"Umm, Captain," interrupted Patterson. "While this incident is of some importance *to you*, we do not have time to play your petty blame game when there are larger issues to consider. Can the ROV be recovered and can we continue on with our mission?"

Jerry recognized the snide "mission commander" tone in Patterson's voice and knew that Hardy was in a poor position to negotiate since she had kept her questions strictly within the boundaries he had set for her. Recognizing the right answer when told, Hardy motioned for Jerry to address her questions.

"In regard to your first question, ma'am. Yes, I believe we can recover the ROV. As to the second, again, I don't know. If we can't determine the cause of the failure, then we can't safely use the tube to support ROV ops. Since no other tube is configured to deploy the ROVs, that would constitute a mission-critical failure." Jerry intentionally used Patterson's own words from that morning's briefing to drive his point home.

"I see. And if you can determine the cause of the failure?"

"If we can isolate the root cause—and if we can correct it—we should be able to support ROV deployments, barring any complications from the fire. As to whether or not we continue the mission, that is a decision that you and the Captain need to make."

"Fair enough, Mr. Mitchell. Now, how do you propose we recover the ROV?"

Jerry turned toward Emily and asked, "Emily, did you keep the emergency retrieval hardware and software of the NMRS in your ROVs?"

"Certainly. Once the ROV detects a loss of signal continuity with the control console, it assumes that the fiber-optic cable has been severed and returns to the launch point. Once there, it emits a series of *knock, knock* pulses to alert the submarine that its back and waits for the homing beacon to be activated. But Jerry, without the drogue, we don't have a homing beacon and we can't position the ROV properly for it to be recovered by the mechanical arm."

"Then, I guess someone will have to go outside and manhandle Duey into position."

"Wait a minute," Hardy protested. "I will not authorize a dive that requires decompression. And at two hundred feet your bottom time is only a few minutes before decompression is necessary."

"Actually, Captain, it's five minutes," boomed Reynolds as he came down the starboard aisle between the storage racks. "And I agree with you, sir, a decompression dive is risky business even with seasoned divers. With inexperienced divers, it would be unacceptably risky. But somehow I don't think Mr. Mitchell had a deep dive in mind, did you, sir?"

"No, COB, I didn't," smiled Jerry.

"Very well, then. What is your plan?" Hardy was now as curious as the others about what Jerry had in mind.

"We'll position *Memphis* as close as possible to the launch point, but we'll be at periscope depth. Once we know Duey is nearby, the divers will go out and call him up to our depth. We can then push it into position where the mechanical arm can grab it."

"But Jerry, how will you call Duey?" asked Emily. "None of your hull arrays can transmit at a frequency that Duey's sonar can pick up."

"True enough. So we rig a portable power supply to one of the spare drogues and the divers lift it over the side and point it down toward Duey. If we do this right, the ROV will be less than three hundred yards away and its sonar should be able to detect the homing beacon."

As she listened to Jerry's scheme, Emily's face became bright with hope. "Yes, Yes! That should work. Oh Jerry, you're brilliant!"

Jerry was uncomfortable with her enthusiasm. "Let's hold off on the 'brilliant' stuff until after we get Duey back, shall we?"

Hardy was silent as he considered Jerry's idea. His wrinkled brow and clenched jaw showed his reservations, his uncertainty that the risk was justifiable. Finally he approached Reynolds and asked, "COB, what would your bottom time be for a dive of seventy feet?"

"Let's see, seventy feet with no decompression would give us about fifty minutes, sir. That should be more than adequate for the job."

Hardy started pacing as he continued to mull over Jerry's proposal. As he walked, Reynolds kept feeding him more information. "We have the proper dive gear, and there is very little current to speak of. We have plenty of daylight left, so visibility shouldn't be a problem. The only way we could reduce the risk further would be to go diving in a swimming pool."

"Very well, COB. I'll authorize the dive," conceded Hardy with a sigh. "I trust you'll be the lead diver, but who will be your partner on this dive?"

"Mr. Mitchell, sir."

"Mitchell?" Hardy sounded incredulous.

"Yes, sir," Reynolds answered politely. "He's a certified Navy diver, he possesses the best knowledge on the ROVs of any diver onboard, and I believe he has some ice diving experience. I'd say that makes him perfect for the job."

Patterson, Hardy, and Emily all looked at Jerry as if he was some sort of circus freak. All that undesired attention made him feel a little uncomfortable, so he tried to explain. "I did some ice diving in Wisconsin and Minnesota as a kid. It's really quite a unique experience diving under an ice canopy . . . and . . . ahh, just forget it."

Patterson and Emily both laughed, while Hardy slowly shook his head. "All right COB, I'll get *Memphis* in position while the two of you get ready."

"Aye, aye, sir," responded Jerry and Reynolds in unison.

"I'll break out the gear, Mr. Mitchell, while you finish giving your people their instructions," said Reynolds.

"Okay, COB, I'll be with you in a moment," Jerry replied. Turning to Foster and Emily, he briefly discussed with them what they had to do to support the dive. Foster reassured him that tube three would be ready to receive the ROV, and Emily said it would take her twenty minutes to put together a portable power supply and connect it to one of the spare drogues.

Jerry found the COB at the far forward end of the torpedo room, removing the diving gear from their storage lockers. The paint on the lockers had been fried, but the lockers themselves were in good condition, as were their contents. Jerry was relieved to see that they had good crushed neoprene drysuits to wear, but they didn't have any insulated undergarments. This meant that he and the COB would get cold during this dive. It might take thirty minutes or so before they started to really feel it, but they'd still need a hot shower afterward.

After breaking out the gear from the lockers, it had to be moved to the crew's mess, where they would suit up. Reynolds had several sailors lug the equipment up while he and Jerry went to their staterooms to change. Digging around in his locker, Jerry found the cotton sweatshirt and pants he'd brought and put them on, along with two pairs of socks. Back in the crew's mess, Jerry found Reynolds already slipping into his drysuit. He tossed Jerry a container of talcum powder, which he applied liberally to the legs and arms of his suit before putting it on. After adjusting the neck, wrist, and ankle seals, Jerry put on his rubber boots and made sure that the boot and ankle seals overlapped. He did the same with the hood.

Reynolds then ran Jerry through the checklist to make sure the tank, regulator, gauges, and buoyancy compensator were all in working order. With that completed, all they could do was sit and wait for the sonar techs to find the lost ROV. They didn't have to wait long. Fifteen minutes later, control called down to the crew's mess to inform the divers that the ROV was close by and that it was up to them to bring it home. As Jerry and the COB started putting on their tanks, Bair came into the mess deck and told them that the starboard torpedo nest muzzle and shutter doors were already opened and that the mechanical arm had been extended. The floodlight on the arm would also be on and they were to use it as a navigation aid, if the visibility was not as good as they expected. He then wished them luck and issued a stern warning not to do anything heroically stupid.

As they picked up their masks, gloves, fins, and flashlights, Reynolds looked over to Jerry and said, "Time for you to become a true Bluenose, Mr. Mitchell."

The wide grin on the COB's face left Jerry feeling a bit uneasy. "Why do I get the impression that I should feel honored?"

"Because it is a true honor to actually swim in the realm of King Boreas. An honor that goes far beyond merely being sprayed down with seawater during the baptism."

"Really? Well, I'll take your word for it, Your Majesty. Just no more of that Prussian blue crap," warned Jerry adamantly.

Reynolds laughed as he climbed the ladder up into the forward escape trunk. For a moment, Jerry wasn't certain that the COB would fit through the hatch. He was such a big man to begin with, and he now had most of his diving gear on as well. But with surprising ease, the COB deftly navigated the hatchway. After all their other gear had been handed up, Jerry started climbing up the ladder.

"Press your chest onto the ladder, sir. That way you won't snag the hatch seat," coached Reynolds. Once Jerry's tank was clear of the hatchway, Reynolds reached down and bodily pulled him up into the escape trunk. After being set down on the grate, Jerry called down, "Is that drogue and power supply ready?"

"Right here, sir," responded Boyd. Jerry then heard a guttural, "Umph!" Followed by, "Sir, if you don't mind, I could use a little help."

Reynolds knelt on the grate and helped Jerry grab the large box in Boyd's arms. It was rather heavy, and even the COB had to exert himself to lift it into the escape trunk. "Son of a buck!" Jerry exclaimed. "I thought Davis was going to make this thing portable!"

"Well, sir, it is—kinda. You can move it."

Jerry was unimpressed and showed his concern. "Petty Officer Boyd, if we take this thing out of the escape trunk, we'll go straight to the bottom."

"Uhh, yes, sir, we know, sir," replied Boyd with a smile. "That's why we made sure there was enough umbilical cabling so you don't have to remove the power supply from the escape trunk. Dr. Davis says all you have to do is point the drogue down over the starboard side and push the black button. As long as the button is depressed, it'll keep transmitting the homing beacon."

As Jerry pulled the cabling into the trunk, Boyd and Greer lifted the drogue and pushed it up into the trunk for the two men to grab. As they lifted the drogue, Jerry noticed that it weighed almost as much as the power supply. There were two metal gas bottles taped to it, too, one on each side. "What the hell are these for?" he asked, pointing to one of the cylinders.

"It was Dr. Davis' idea, sir. They're empty. She said their buoyancy should make the drogue easier to handle once you're out in the water."

"Would you please thank her for us, TM2? And we'll see you when we get back."

Once everyone was clear, Reynolds shut and dogged the lower escape trunk. With the hatch closed, Jerry repositioned the drogue and the cabling so that he and the COB had at least a little room to don the rest of their gear. "It's a bit tight in here, isn't it?" remarked Jerry tensely. As Jerry started to put on his fins and gloves, Reynolds saw that he was agitated, uneasy. As the COB put on his fins, he glanced over at Jerry and asked, "Nervous?"

Jerry let out a brief sigh and then admitted, "No COB, I think a better word is 'scared.' I've never left a submerged submarine before, and I've never made a dive hundreds of miles from the nearest shore."

"That's okay, Mr. Mitchell. It's all right to be a little scared. I actually prefer it that way because I know you'll be more careful. Now, once we get out there, we stay in each other's sight at all times. There is no reason for us to be apart, understood?"

Even though Jerry was an officer and Reynolds a senior enlisted man, Jerry knew that the COB had the authority of experience, and in this situation, he gave the orders. "Understood, COB."

"Okay, then," said Reynolds as he opened the valve. "Let's get wet!"

Below the grate, Jerry heard the rush of seawater as it quickly began to fill the escape trunk. He could feel the temperature inside dropping sharply on his face as the water rose up over his feet. Reynolds reached down and scooped up some seawater and swished it around in his full face mask. As he put it on, he leaned over to Jerry and shouted, "If you think the dousing I gave during the Bluenose ceremony was bad, you ain't seen nothing yet!"

Jerry did the same, but waited until the last minute before pulling the mask down over his face. As he adjusted the straps, the frigid arctic water rose over his head. Suddenly, a sharp chill clawed its way down Jerry's back, as a few drops of seawater slipped between the facemask and his dry suit. The unexpected cold caused Jerry to inhale sharply. Reynolds shook his head, a broad smile on his face. Moments later, the trunk was filled with water and Reynolds opened the upper hatch. A small amount of air bubbled its way to the surface.

Reynolds exited first and then reached down for the drogue. Jerry handed it to the COB, and after making sure that the umbilical cable wouldn't get caught on anything, pulled himself out onto *Memphis'* hull. The sea that greeted Jerry was grayish-green in color and the visibility wasn't too bad. The sail of the submarine was clearly discernable, but the rudder was harder to make out. Looking up, he could see the ocean surface. The sun was bright and rippled by the low waves. Jerry heard a long, low moaning sound in the distance: whale song.

Jerry's heart rate increased significantly, as did his breathing. He had to force himself to breathe more slowly, and he tried to think about things that would soothe him. He had to calm down or he would expend his air too quickly. Reynolds motioned with his light for Jerry to follow and they swam past the sail, looming darkly to one side. When they reached the weapons shipping hatch, a dull glow could be seen over the starboard side. It was the light on the retrieval arm.

Jerry tapped the COB on the shoulder and motioned for him to give Jerry the drogue. Reynolds passed it to him, and with the drogue firmly under his arm, Jerry swam about twenty feet away from *Memphis*. He then pointed it down and pushed the button. He had no way of knowing if the homing signal was being transmitted or not. The frequency of the pulses was about twenty times higher than the human ear could possibly hear. All he could do was keep his position in the water and press the button.

After about five minutes, Jerry's eyes made out a very dim, ghostly cloud that seemed to be coming toward him. He pointed his flashlight at Reynolds and then swept it down in the direction of the faint glow. Reynolds looked downward for a few seconds, and then he suddenly looked back up at Jerry and gave him the "okay" sign.

As Duey came up, Jerry could see that it was still too far away from the sub, so he kept on transmitting the homing signal. He hoped that as Duey got closer it would adjust its speed as it tried to find the docking signal. True to its programming, the ROV did indeed slow as it got closer and closer to the drogue. This gave Jerry an idea.

Signaling for Reynolds to follow, Jerry started swimming down toward the starboard tube nest. Holding the drogue about two feet from *Memphis'* hull, Jerry and Reynolds watched as Duey obediently followed the homing signal. When it was about ten feet away, the bright lights on the ROV turned themselves off. The light and the camera assembly then retracted itself back into the ROV's body and Duey seemed to coast the remaining few feet. Reynolds then reached out and wrapped his huge arms around the ROV's midbody. Jerry released the drogue, which bounced harmlessly against the acoustic tiling on the submarine's hull, and he too grappled with Emily's lost "baby."

For the next fifteen minutes, the two of them wrestled with the ROV as they tried to get it into the reach of the mechanical arm. After a lot of tugging, pushing, and shoving, they finally managed to coax the vehicle toward the open torpedo tubes. All of a sudden, they felt a jolt and heard a sharp metallic noise as the retrieval arm finally captured the ROV. Both men quickly moved away from the vehicle and watched as Duey was gently guided back into torpedo tube number three. Just to be sure, they stayed until both shutter doors were closed. Then they retrieved the drogue and made their way back to the forward escape trunk.

Once they were safely inside, Reynolds shut and dogged the outer hatch. As he opened the drain valve, Jerry finally felt himself relax. He also realized that he was shaking. The cold had set in faster than he had originally thought, particularly around his hands, feet, and face. On top of that, his body ached from the exertion of playing tug-of-war with a recalcitrant ROV. When the air bubble in the escape trunk was large enough, Reynolds spit out his mouthpiece, and with shivering blue lips said, "Not too shabby for your first dive, sir."

"Thank you, COB. It was an honor," replied a very tired Jerry.

Seven minutes later, Reynolds opened the lower hatch and the two of them wearily lower their gear—and themselves—onto the deck. With a little help, the two slowly walked to the crew's mess. Jerry and Reynolds had just plopped down onto a couple of chairs when Bair showed up.

"Well done, you two! I guess I don't have to tell you that Doctors Patterson and Davis are ecstatic over your successful recovery of the ROV."

Jerry could only nod in response to the XO's compliments. He was pleased they had succeeded, particularly for Emily's sake, but he really needed to warm up before he could celebrate.

"For your outstanding efforts, I'm awarding you both a fifteen-minute hot shower. Otherwise, we wouldn't be able to thaw you guys out until tomorrow morning." Jerry appreciated the XO's humor almost as much as the idea of a long hot shower. As the two divers started to remove their gear, Bair slipped over to Jerry and whispered, "The Captain wants to see you in his stateroom in forty-five minutes. Don't take too long, okay?"

Somehow Jerry knew this was going to happen. Hardy still wanted to pin the blame for this disaster on someone, and he expected Jerry to give him that someone. Again, Jerry nodded his acknowledgment of the XO's message. Twenty minutes later, hot fresh water was pouring over his cold body.

Jerry was still getting dressed when he heard a knock at the door. "It's Emily Davis, Jerry."

"Wait one," he answered and quickly pulled on his coveralls and zipped them up. Still in his stocking feet, he opened the door. "Please come in."

He motioned her to a seat, but she shook her head and remained standing. With Hardy waiting, he felt a little rushed, and sat down to put on his shoes.

"Jerry, I want to apologize for the things I said earlier."

"Emily, you were upset. Nobody's mad at you. We understand how much those ROVs mean to you. They're important to us, too."

"And I knew that too, but I still yelled at you. I guess it was because I was still afraid. The roar of that water coming in, the smoke and fire, and there was no way to get away from it. It was my worst nightmare." She shivered, holding her shoulders. "I'm still shaking."

As he listened, Jerry finished dressing and took a moment to check his appearance in his mirror. He had to report to Hardy shortly, but he didn't want to look like a slob when he did.

Jerry turned to face her and tried to sound as positive as he could. "But you got through it, just like we all did. We were all scared. We all got through it because of our training. And next time, if there is one," he added reassuringly, "you'll be better prepared for it."

Jerry stepped toward the door and Davis moved to one side. "Excuse me, but the Captain's waiting."

Followed by Davis, he climbed the ladder to the upper level, heading for Hardy's stateroom. Dr. Patterson was in control when she saw Jerry climbing up the ladder and stepped out to meet him.

"Lieutenant Mitchell, thank you very much for recovering the ROV. You and Master Chief Reynolds risked your lives for our mission. I won't ever forget that."

Patterson spoke so warmly that Jerry fought to keep the surprise from his face and had to pause a moment before answering lamely, "Thank you, ma'am. I'm glad we were successful."

"I was afraid the whole time you were out there. For you two, of course, and for the mission, and for what almost happened in the torpedo room. I promise never to complain about drills again."

"Mr. Mitchell!" Hardy's impatient call interrupted Jerry's weak reply.

Leaving the two women, Jerry took the few steps necessary to reach the Captain's stateroom.

Out of habit, he knocked on the doorjamb as he answered, "Lieutenant (j.g.) Mitchell reporting as ordered, sir."

"Get in here and close the door behind you." Jerry did as he was told and stood, unprompted, silently at attention.

Hardy sat in his chair, outwardly relaxed, but his face showed the strain of the past few hours. "Mr. Mitchell, this entire sorry episode is further evidence of your poor leadership and lax control. A small leak becomes a fire which almost costs us mission-critical equipment, and the only way to save the situation is to risk the lives of two members of my crew."

"Yes, sir." Jerry couldn't think of what else to say, but evidently it wasn't what Hardy was looking for.

" 'Yes, sir?' Is that the best you can do?" Hardy stood up, as if to pace or somehow burn off nervous energy, but there was little room. "We could have lost this submarine and the lives of everyone aboard. Even after the danger to *Memphis* was ended, we had to take more risks to get the ROV back.

"You could have failed and left us short an ROV. You and Reynolds could have failed and died, which would have left us short an ROV and two crew.

"And I'm the one who'd have to go back and explain everything to a lot of very disappointed flag officers." Hardy sat heavily in his chair, looking drained. "It's easy when you've only got yourself or a small group to be responsible for. I'm responsible for this boat, and all the men aboard and everything they do, and the mission on top of that. If anything goes wrong on *Memphis*, I'm the one who will have to account for it."

Hardy paused, then continued in a more businesslike tone. "So I want to know exactly who screwed up. I'll make sure he never makes that mistake again, and everyone else will see what happens to those who do make mistakes."

Jerry was appalled. Moran had screwed up, but he wasn't the root cause of the casualty and he certainly didn't merit the kind of punishment that Hardy seemed to be planning. He quickly answered, "Sir, Petty Officer Moran had been told by Dr. Davis that the fitting would leak a little. In fact, she told that to Senior Chief Foster and me as well. When it started to leak faster, Moran immediately called Senior Chief Foster to come and look at it, since he had observed the fitting during the first trial. Before Foster could do anything but look at the fitting, the gasket failed for reasons still unknown."

Jerry didn't mention that these highly trained men each failed to act because they were afraid to make a mistake. Better to do nothing than goof and get punished. Better still to find someone in authority, so it's not your fault. In the meantime, of course, things went to hell.

"And while everyone's running around deciding what to do, the sub and the mission and everyone's life is in jeopardy. Successfully recovering from a casualty is not an acceptable substitute for safe procedures in the first place."

Jerry screwed up his courage, but he found it easy to say. "Sir, with all due respect, I do not believe Moran's actions merit any punishment. He acted as soon as he saw a problem."

"Then why did we almost lose the boat?" Hardy countered angrily. "Don't think that defending him will reduce your guilt in this business. You are ultimately responsible for everything that happens in your division. Just as I am responsible for everything that happens on *Memphis*." He sighed heavily. "Get your division in order, mister. We were lucky this time. There will be no next time."

"Aye, aye, sir." Jerry responded dutifully.

"Get out."

Jerry got out quickly and immediately headed down the two decks to the torpedo room. Almost all of the division was there, working on the space. While it had been dewatered, there was a lot of cleanup left, as well as the repairs to the weapons launching console and the ROV.

Hardy was right. Jerry did have to get the division in line.

Senior Chief Foster was working on the console with FT1 Bearden when Jerry entered the torpedo room, "Senior Chief, I need to talk to the entire division right now for a few minutes. Please call them together. And make sure that door to berthing is closed," he said, pointing to the opening in the back of the space.

Puzzled, Foster nodded and barked an order to Jobin. "Get Davidson and Willis out of berthing. And Larsen, close that door."

The rest of the division was curious as well and stopped work to gather around their division officer and senior chief. By the time Larsen had closed the door, isolating them from the passageway and the berthing area, the other enlisted members had arrived.

Jerry waited until they were all present and close by, so he didn't have to raise his voice. He suddenly realized he should have rehearsed his talk a little, but he knew what he had to say.

"I've just come from Captain Hardy." He could almost see everyone, especially Moran, tense. "There will not be any disciplinary action, and I want to personally commend everyone for the way they acted."

There were a few audible sighs, and Jerry did feel the division relax. "Everyone did exactly what they were supposed to do, and we helped to save the boat and the mission. But we can do better."

Jerry stopped for a moment, then spoke carefully. "We had a small leak that grew to a big one and ultimately became a fire. The casualty could have been stopped earlier, but the watchstander"—he avoided using Moran's name—"was unsure of what do. He didn't want to make a mistake." Jerry carefully did not look at Moran, but he did see some others in the division nodding, and Jobin silently mouthed, "Damn straight." Foster looked thoughtful.

"We don't always have that much time during a casualty, and we almost didn't have it today." Trying to speak to the entire division, he continued, "I trust your judgment, and if any of you see a problem, I want you to deal with it. Immediately. Call for help, but from now on, don't wait for it.

"Whatever happens, right or wrong, as long as you're acting in the best interests of *Memphis*, I'll do my best to protect you." It was a strong statement, but he'd kept Hardy from persecuting Moran, and could only hope he could do it again.

"That's all I've got. Do your best, and I'll back you up." He nodded to Senior Chief Foster, who ordered, "All right, everyone, back at it! We've still got a lot of work to do to get this place squared away."

Jerry watched as the torpedo gang returned to work. He turned to Foster, reluctant to ask what should have been a routine question, but he was the man to ask. "Senior Chief, what's our status?"

"I've got the FTs working on the panel, of course, and Moran, Greer, and Boyd are working on the ROVs. Everyone else is giving the space a field day, sir." Foster paused and then added. "As soon as Bearden and I have checked out the console, I'll find you and fill you in."

"Thank you, Senior Chief." Jerry responded automatically, and Foster turned to go back to the badly damaged console.

Jerry was surprised by Foster's complete, polite report. It was the last thing he'd expected. He was so used to Foster's hostility that its lack confused Jerry, and he looked for some hidden trick on insult, but he couldn't find one.

14 Growing Pains

Jerry awoke late the next morning, stiff and sore, his aching body reacted poorly to his movements as he extracted himself from his rack and stood up. He hadn't felt this out of shape since his days at the Academy, when he first started running track. I really need to hit the gym more often, Jerry thought to himself as he shuffled his way to the head. After getting dressed, a process that took longer and was more uncomfortable than usual, Jerry slowly walked to the wardroom.

"It's alive! It's alive!" wailed Lenny, as Jerry stiffly closed the door.

"That, sir, is a matter of debate," Jerry lamented, wincing as he sat down. "Right now, I'd settle for the ability to perform basic functions without pain."

"A bit sore, are we?"

"No, a lot sore. I didn't think pushing an ROV around would be so taxing, but it had a mind of its own and we had to wrestle the damn thing into position so the arm could grab it. I'm really glad the COB was out there with me. He did most of the work."

"He is a rather large fellow," remarked Lenny as he made a cup of hot cocoa. "I hear he moonlights as a tow truck during the winter. 'Reynolds Wrecking Service' has a nice ring to it, don't you think?"

Jerry couldn't help but laugh. However, it was cut short by the sharp pain he felt across his chest. Nearly doubling over, he looked over toward Berg and said, "Lenny, please don't do that again. It really doesn't feel good."

"Only hurts when you laugh, huh?" asked Lenny as he set the cup in front of Jerry.

"No, it hurts *more* when I laugh, you twit!"

"Yes, I know," responded Lenny innocently as he opened the door to leave. "Have a nice day."

Jerry watched as his friend left and chuckled. Despite his sometimes-loony humor, Lenny's heart was in the right place. Sipping his cocoa, Jerry looked at the clock on the bulkhead and realized that he only had a few minutes until his next-to-last systems checkout. Ironically, it was on the ship's air-conditioning chilled water system. And while humans may not need a lot of air-conditioning this far north, many of the ship's systems, particularly the electronics, would start to fail without the cooling water this system provided. Rising slowly, Jerry went over to one of the cupboards and grabbed the bottle of ibuprofen tablets and dumped three into his palm. He swilled the pills down with the rest of his hot cocoa and traveled as fast as his body would move to his stateroom to get his qual book. If he was lucky, he might make lunch before his next watch in control at noon.

He wasn't lucky. The checkout was a grueling two hours long, and Jerry had a dozen lookups to answer. With only five minutes before he had to begin the pre-watch tour of the boat with Richards, Jerry hurried to his stateroom and snatched a package of peanut butter crackers and his notebook.

Before going on watch, the oncoming OOD makes a complete tour of the boat and conducts a general inspection of the equipment. He also learns what maintenance work is going to be done during his watch and annotates in his notebook those items, if any, that will require the Captain's permission to begin.

As Jerry and Cal Richards walked into the torpedo room, Jerry was pleasantly surprised to see that the cleanup from the fire was largely done and that both Huey and Duey had been washed down and were back in their normal storage positions. He then saw Moran and three of the TMs working on tube three, while Foster, Bearden, and a number of the FTs were stripping down the weapons launching console. Richards was also impressed and uttered a rare compliment. Unfortunately, Foster had nothing new to report on the status of the console. But he did promise to inform them of the findings as soon as he completed his survey of the damage.

After finishing their tour of the rest of the forward compartment, Jerry and Richards finally entered control and began their turnover with the Navigator, Harry O'Connell. It had been a quiet morning with no drills, and the only major evolution on the books during their watch was the "field day" the XO had scheduled. Field day, sometimes more formally referred to as Janitorial Ops, was a stem-to-stern cleaning of the boat.

Since cleaning tended to make more noise than the usual day-to-day operations, the XO wanted the boat scrubbed down before they entered the Kara Sea. After only a few questions, Lieutenant Commander O'Connell was relieved of the watch. Once the noon report had been made and the new watch section had settled in, Richards asked Jerry for his qual book and they took stock of what items were to be done next.

A little over an hour later, Bair strolled into control wearing camouflage BDUs and armed with the longest screwdriver Jerry had ever seen. "OOD, I would appreciate it if you would announce over the 1MC that field day is to commence."

"Of course, XO," replied Richards. "Chief of the Watch, over the 1MC, commence field day."

"Commence field day, aye, sir." Raising the mike toward his face, the Chief of the Watch called for the start of the boat-wide cleaning. As the announcement was made, Bair's face radiated contentment.

"Sir, may I ask where you will be hunting today?" Richards asked frankly. Jerry just stood there, staring, completely confused by his XO's attire.

"Certainly! I shall be in control over behind the ballast control panel," replied Blair excitedly, pointing toward the panel with his screwdriver. "I will, of course, endeavor to not interfere with the Chief of the Watch's duties." Looking over toward Jerry, the XO frowned and then poked him with the screwdriver, saying, "Don't stare, boy! It's impolite."

"Y-yes, sir. Sorry, sir," stammered Jerry.

The wide grin reappeared on Bair's face as he made his way over to the ballast control panel (BCP). Politely, he asked the Chief of the Watch to move aside and Jerry watched in amazement as Bair turned on a flashlight with a long articulating neck and then dove under the ballast control panel.

It wasn't long before only his boots could be seen projecting out from the space where the Chief of the Watch's legs would normally go.

The dazed expression on Jerry's faced caused Richards to burst out in laughter. "I see that you hadn't seen the XO in his dustbuster outfit before."

"No, sir, I haven't."

"Well, then, Jerry, let me fill you in on a piece of true *Memphis* eccentricity," began Richards. "The XO is on a sacred quest to find commissioning dirt. He wants to dig up a scrap of paper or any other form of trash that can be positively traced back to the boat's commissioning in 1977. It's sort of his own personal Holy Grail, which he pursues with considerable vigor."

Jerry had heard about the aggressive tendency of nuke boat XOs toward cleanliness, but this was so over the top that he had a hard time believing what he had just seen with his own eyes. It all seemed so silly that a grown man would behave so ludicrously about dirt and other refuse. As curiosity won out over awe, Jerry asked, "What's with the oversized screwdriver?"

"Ah, yes, the XO-Matic," replied Richards with a smile, as he leaned up against the periscope stand desk. "It's a modified deck plate screwdriver that has had its blade machined down into a small scoop. About the same size as a baby's spoon. It is designed to get at dirt deposits that are outside the reach of most primates, let alone normal human beings." Richards then winked at Jerry and held his index finger up to his lips, motioning Jerry to be silent. Stepping quietly over toward the BCP, Richards then loudly said, "But alas, even with his special tools, the XO has failed to find that elusive and perhaps legendary prey over these past two years."

A sound, best described as a low growl, emanated from behind the panel, "Enough of your blasphemy, Mr. Richards! I will prove to you and the rest of those heretics you associate with that commissioning dirt does exist. Furthermore, since you firmly believe that it is a figment of your Executive Officer's imagination, I shall enjoy watching you clean it up after I find it!"

Laughter erupted from the entire ship's control party as the XO continued to mutter something about the growing insubordination of the crew. As the laughing died down, Jerry felt the strained atmosphere that had existed since he had reported on board easing. The camaraderie that he had missed so much from his squadron days was slowly coming to life on *Memphis*. It was a good feeling.

The watch progressed with little diversion. There were no drills. *Memphis* was on a steady course and speed, and there were few contacts. Those they did hold on the towed arrays were all distant, and were classified as merchants. In fact, for the first time since he could remember, Jerry was downright bored. The only thing that broke the monotony was when Hardy came into control looking for Bair. All hands not holding a control stick pointed to the BCP, the XO's right foot waving about in the air. Hardy stopped dead in his tracks. He closed his eyes, put his forehead in his right hand, and slowly shook his head. Muttering something about a straight-jacket, he returned to his stateroom without even speaking to the XO.

As the time passed slowly, Jerry kept looking up at the clock, waiting and wondering when he would hear something—anything—from Foster. Halfway through his watch, Jerry couldn't stand it any longer and he called down to for a progress report.

FT2 Boswell answered the phone. "Hello. Yes, Mr. Mitchell, what can I do for you?"

"Any progress?" Jerry asked.

"Ah, sir, Petty Officer Bearden would like to talk to you." Boswell's tone was not encouraging.

Bearden came on the line. "Mr. Mitchell?"

"What can you tell me? Any good news?"

"Well, sir, it's kind of a good news, bad news situation."

"Give me the bad news first."

"Sir, we've been at that console for more than six hours so far. The Senior Chief's got half the division in here and we're not making any progress. The only thing we've found out so far is just how fried it really is."

"I see," replied Jerry despondently. "And the good news?"

"Moran's pretty sure they've figured out what happened with tube three and that it can be fixed. They're working on it now."

"Very well, keep at it. I'll be down as soon as my watch is over."

"Yes, sir, we'll keep you informed if we make any breakthroughs," replied Bearden.

Jerry said thank you and hung up the phone.

Master Chief Reynolds wandered into the torpedo room shortly after Jerry's call. Foster and Bearden had the launch panel stripped down to its underwear while other ratings worked with tech manuals or test equipment. Tools and bits of circuitry littered the deck. Moran and his TMs were huddled around torpedo tube number three. They seemed to be in better spirits than the FTs.

Senior Chief Foster looked up from his work when Reynolds came down the portside aisle, but didn't stop working. His "Good afternoon, Sam" had a strained sound.

"Is it, Bob?" Reynolds asked.

Foster shook his head emphatically. "It's a hard fight with a short stick." He stood up. "Too much has been damaged and we don't have anywhere near the spare parts. Many of the control relays are charcoal briquettes, and those that I can still recognize are completely fused. Most of the circuit boards have either melted or are so warped that they won't fit in their slots, and there are several inches of vaporized cabling. In short, Sam, this console is Tango Uniform."

"I hear Mr. Mitchell had a talk with the division yesterday," Reynolds commented matter-of-factly, as if he hadn't even heard what Foster had just said.

"Yeah, he did," answered Foster with a pained look. "And before you say you were right, I will. You were right. But I still can't stand the way he used his political connections to get here."

Reynolds asked, "Has he mentioned them once since he came aboard?"

"No," Foster admitted.

"Did they help him with all the extra hoops he has had to jump through?"

"No."

"Is he asking for anything special now?"

"No."

"So he abused the system. Once. We've all done that." Reynolds pressed his point. "And I don't think that's the real issue here, is it? This isn't about bending or even breaking the rules, especially Navy rules."

Foster sighed. "But he used his pull . . ."

"Which you would have done in a heartbeat," interrupted Reynolds. "If you'd had any. You're just pissed because you didn't have his connections."

The senior chief nodded slowly, finally acknowledging the real issue between him and Jerry Mitchell. "You're right—again. I guess I am envious of him getting a second chance."

"But he's doing a good job with it. He's working his ass off, and he's taking care of his people—like a good officer should."

"All right, COB, I hear you. You don't have to hit me over the head with a hammer."

Smiling broadly, Reynolds reached over, grabbed Foster's shoulder, and said, "As my sea daddy once told me, Bob, always use the right tool for the right job."

At 1800, as soon as he'd finished his watch, Jerry blitzed down to the torpedo room. He found Foster and Bearden still hunched over the weapons launching console.

They both looked up as Jerry hurried down the aisle. Foster straightened up, shaking his head.

"Can it be fixed?" asked Jerry simply.

"No, sir, not at sea," Foster replied. "In port, with a tender or repair shop helping, it would take us a week. And we'd have to gut the thing before we could even begin repairs. In my opinion, it would be easier to replace the whole unit than fix it." He picked up a circuit board. Part of it was blackened. "Almost every board is like this, or worse. Even the ones that aren't charred have suffered heat stress and saltwater damage."

Jerry heard the frustration and fatigue in his senior chief's voice. They had worked over nine hours just to come to the conclusion that there was nothing they could do to repair the badly damaged console. "Senior, you and Bearden did your best. I can't ask for more than that. But what I don't understand is how did seawater get inside the console in the first place? It's supposed to be splash-proof."

"We haven't been able to figure that out, Mr. Mitchell. First, we thought it could have been the gasket around the tube control panels. The FTs replaced it before we left New London, but it's clear that the fire started at the bottom of the console." Reynolds pointed toward the lower portion of the console, which was almost completely charred. The buttons used to control the torpedo tube functions were several feet higher. "There is no obvious path for the water to get inside like it did."

Jerry asked, "Can we still set and launch weapons manually?"

"Yes, we can work the tubes manually without any problems, and the emergency preset circuits still seem to be working," assured Foster, "but it'll be slow, and of course the weapon inputs won't be as precise."

"Then we'll have to be very polite to everyone we meet," Jerry answered lightly. Looking over at the starboard tube nest, he motioned his head toward tube three. "Bearden said that TM1 figured out what the deal was with tube three."

"Yeah," snarled Foster with contempt. "The rubber gasket material was old and should never had been installed in the first place."

Intrigued, Jerry raised an eyebrow and said, "Really. How old?"

"We can't be certain. There wasn't much of the gasket left for us to recover. And since we didn't install the gasket assembly, we don't know how old it was, but I found these two replacement kits in our spares locker." Foster tossed the two gasket assemblies, one at a time, to his division officer. Jerry caught them deftly and then looked at the manufacturing date: February 1999. That was way too old. Any spare part with rubber that was five years old or more was to be viewed with extreme suspicion and returned through the supply system. The part was not to be installed under normal circumstances, because the rubber would have hardened to the point where it was no longer safe to use. This was particularly true if the system in question operated under any sort of pressure.

As Jerry examined the gasket assemblies, and thought back to the casualty, a perplexed frown formed on his face. "Senior Chief, if the part was defective, then why didn't it fail during our earlier trials after we left New London?"

Foster smiled. But this time it was the normal Cheshire catlike grin that a chief displayed before explaining the obvious to an inexperienced junior officer. "Well, sir, for one thing, it's hard to predict when and how a part will fail. It's even harder when the part is defective or old. But I think the water outside of New London being some twenty-odd degrees warmer had something to do with it."

A look of embarrassment flashed across Jerry's face as he soon as he heard Foster's answer. "Okay, so much for the dumb question."

"Don't feel too bad, sir. It took us a while to figure it out," said Bearden with a chuckle in his voice.

"So, the cold water made the rubber more brittle and it cracked under the pressure," said Jerry.

"Yes, sir, it also made the rubber harder," replied Foster as he handed Jerry a piece of the fiber-optic cabling. "If you'll look at this end, you can see where the two halves of the cracked gasket gnawed on the cable. I guess the flow of water in the tube caused the gasket to expand and contract rhythmically, which in turn caused the hard rubber to literally chew through the cable."

As Jerry listened to Foster's explanation and viewed the available evidence, he couldn't help but be impressed with his guys' work and he said as much. "That was a nice piece of detective work, Senior Chief, you two and Moran are to be commended. But this still leaves the $64,000 question. Can the tube be repaired?"

The grin returned again as Foster said, "Already done, Mr. Mitchell. Petty Officer Moran and the others installed an acceptable replacement this afternoon. All we need is the Captain's permission to do a hydrostatic test of the tube. If it passes—and I'm pretty sure it will—we'll be ready to conduct ROV ops immediately."

"Bravo Zulu, Senior!" exclaimed Jerry, using the Navy expression for "Well done." "I'm sure this will make Doctor Patterson very happy." Then Jerry looked back over at the remains of the weapons launching console, and his enthusiasm waned. "That, however, will not go over well with the Captain."

"No, sir, he isn't going to like that at all," admitted Foster.

Handing the defective gaskets back to Foster, Jerry let out a deep sigh and turned toward the starboard side aisle. "I guess it's time to tell him, then," he announced darkly.

"Do you want me come along, sir?" asked Foster sincerely.

Heartened by the unexpected show of support, Jerry quickly agreed. "Yes, Senior Chief, I would. Thank you."

HARDY TOOK THEIR report in the wardroom, with the XO, the department heads, and the two ladies present. The atmosphere in the room had a court-martial-like feel to it, with Hardy sitting motionless at the opposite end, a stony expression on his face. Jerry stood stiffly before the audience and summarized the damage from the casualty, the repairs that could be made and those that couldn't, and their effects.

He started with the status of the ROVs and the torpedo tubes, primarily because they were the only good news he had to offer. Patterson listened intently as Jerry reported that the ROVs were both in fine shape. While this was encouraging, Patterson appeared edgy, shifting about in her seat as though she had sat on a burr.

"Mr. Mitchell, I'm sure Emily appreciates all you have done for her ROVs, but this doesn't help us much if the torpedo tube used to deploy them doesn't work. Were you able to repair the tube?" demanded Patterson nervously.

Jerry let a small, satisfied smile form on his face as he said, "Yes, ma'am. My guys have already completed the repairs to tube three. All I need is the Captain's permission for a pressure test to make sure everything is squared away. If the test is satisfactory, we should be able to launch and recover the ROVs without any problems."

"Splendid!" exclaimed Patterson, much relieved.

"Just a moment, Dr. Patterson," interrupted Hardy, tapping the table with two fingers. "Before I authorize any test, I need to know what caused the leak in the first place and who is responsible." The look of joy on Patterson's face immediately gave way to one of frustration. For a brief moment, it looked like she was going to protest, but Hardy cut her off with a curt wave of his hand and a stern, uncompromising stare.

Looking back at Jerry, Hardy repeated himself. "What caused the casualty, Mr. Mitchell? And who is responsible?"

"Sir," said Jerry firmly, "the casualty occurred because the fiber-optic penetration gasket failed catastrophically. And the reason why it failed is because it was very likely beyond its shelf life." He motioned for Foster to hand to the Captain a piece of the failed gasket and one of the outdated spares.

"If you'll look at the remnant of the failed gasket, sir, you'll note that rubber is hard and brittle, similar to the replacement part that Senior Chief Foster just gave you. We found that gasket assembly in the spare parts we were issued." Hardy briefly examined the two parts and quietly handed them over to Bair as Jerry continued his explanation.

"We believe that the colder water made the old rubber in the gasket assembly more susceptible to cracking, and after it had chewed through the cable, it blew apart and allowed seawater to leak into the torpedo room. And Captain, all modifications to tube three, including the installation of the gasket, were performed by SUBASE maintenance personnel." Jerry forced himself not to sound triumphant as he drove the last part home.

Hardy's jaw was firmly clenched and Jerry swore he could hear his captain's teeth grinding at the other end of the table. Jerry knew Hardy was angry and embarrassed, particularly given his tirade in the torpedo room in front of Patterson and Davis. But he had little sympathy for the man. Hardy just wanted a body to make an example of, and he naturally assumed the culprit had to be a member of his crew. Well, now he would have to carry his little witch-hunt back to New London.

Bair cleared his throat, diverting everyone's attention from Hardy, and asked a crucial question. "Jerry, you've explained how the leak started, but why did it result in a fire?"

"The short answer XO is, we don't know," stated Jerry bluntly. "After over nine hours of investigating, Senior Chief Foster and Petty Officer Bearden were unable to find out how the water got inside the weapons launching console. All they were able to find was that the fire started very low in the console, near the deck, and that it was devastatingly hot."

"How bad is the damage?" questioned Bair hesitantly.

Taking a deep breath, Jerry looked squarely at Hardy and said, "The console is totaled, sir. And there is no way we can repair it at sea. We can still operate the tubes manually and the emergency preset circuits are intact, but we've lost all remote tube functions, including those associated with the fire-control system."

A collective groan came from the naval officers present. Bair put his head in his hands and simply muttered, "Oh shit!" Hardy remarkably remained silent as Patterson and Davis looked on with puzzlement.

Tapping his fingers on the table again, Hardy motioned for everyone to become silent. "Senior Chief?" Hardy said, demanding his confirmation of Jerry's report. He simply would not take Jerry's word that the weapons launching console was kaput. He had to hear it from Foster directly.

"Sir, the console is gone," replied Foster frankly. "A shipyard would just swap out the whole thing. With a tender's help, I could replace every circuit board and relay and rebuild the console in a week or two. But out here, we just don't have the parts, and I can't scrounge or make them, either."

Hardy listened with a sour expression, the kind of expression a sub captain would be expected to have when hearing that the two working tubes he'd started with were now crippled. But then it softened, and Jerry thought that for a moment, he'd almost looked pleased.

The XO and the other department heads asked Foster, Jerry, and Cal Richards questions about the torpedoes and their ability to launch them, but the Captain remained silent. It didn't take long for them to run out of questions. The console was down hard and nothing they could do would bring it back.

Hardy's announcement filled the eerie silence. "With almost no weapons capability, the ability of this boat to perform its mission has been seriously affected." Jerry agreed with that statement, but was completely unready for what the Captain said next. "I believe we should abort the mission."

Dr. Patterson stood up abruptly, her seat tipping back with a crash. *"What?"* The others in the wardroom looked just as surprised, but remained silent out of deference for Hardy's rank. Patterson felt no such limitation.

"We can't go home because of a problem with the other torpedo tubes!" she exclaimed.

"Doctor," the Captain said carefully, *"Memphis* is a warship with no teeth. We can't defend ourselves effectively. You don't understand how important that console is. In a fast-moving fight . . ."

"And what's the chance of that happening? Are we at war? Are we likely to begin one while we're at sea?" Jerry could tell that Patterson was afraid as well as angry. If Hardy turned around and went home, she'd never get the evidence she hoped to find, and her boss, the President, wouldn't get his coup at the conference.

And Hardy had the perfect excuse. A naval vessel that couldn't fight was a liability.

Hardy stood his ground. "Dr. Patterson, this mission requires that we operate in close proximity to the Russian coast . . ."

She interrupted him again "And are we going to shoot our way in?" she demanded. "I've read our rules of engagement. You aren't allowed to shoot at anyone unless they attack you in international waters, and even then, only if you can't evade or escape. Is that correct?"

"Yes, ma'am. Only in extreme self-defense."

"And when those admirals approved this mission, they said the threat was low, that the Russian Navy was a basket case, and that this would be a 'milk run.'"

"Both the CNO and SUBLANT," Hardy clarified, "would completely understand the risks of proceeding on with the mission with a crippled weapons system."

"But the CNO and SUBLANT," Patterson echoed, "work for my boss, the President. And what he's going to hear is what I put in my report."

She paused and Hardy didn't immediately respond. Her threat was obvious and her tone made it more than clear that she would carry it out.

Finally, he said softly, "Doctor, I am ultimately responsible for the safety of this boat and everyone on board."

She spoke just as softly. "And this submarine can still do the job that we have set out to do. The accident hasn't affected our engines, the sonar works, we can still deploy the ROVs, and the chances of us actually having to shoot anyone are nil. We will continue."

Hardy looked at her for a minute, then repeated, "We will continue." He made it sound like a sigh.

Later that evening, after another tense meal, Patterson was in the head she and Emily shared with Hardy, getting ready to turn in. Exhausted from the day's events, and yet another confrontation with Lowell Hardy, she just wanted to lie down and get some sleep. As she washed her face, she found herself muttering questions to the image in the mirror, "Why does he have to be so difficult? Why can't he be more cooperative, like my staff back in D.C.? Why do I always have to fight him over everything?"

As she stewed over Hardy's constant—and annoying—references to risks, consequences, and warfare, she lost track of where she was and slammed her elbow into the shower stall. Cursing the miniscule accommodations, Patterson's frustration with *Memphis* and her commanding officer boiled to the surface and her irritation was enough to make her scream. In defiance to Hardy's edicts on cleanliness, she threw the towel on the deck, turned off the light, and quietly opened the door to her stateroom. Emily was already asleep, so Patterson couldn't turn on the light. Even though there was a tiny red light shining by the door, her eyes were not adapted to the dark, so she had to navigate her way to her rack by touch. Wearily, she tumbled into her bunk and was immediately grabbed by someone. She screamed as a large arm wrapped around her waist.

In control, Hardy and Bair were going over the revised fire-control team procedures when they heard Patterson scream. Surprised and afraid, both men raced to her stateroom, each one thinking that a member of the crew had gone off the deep end and was assaulting her. As Hardy burst into the stateroom, Patterson was over by the door to the head, bouncing on both feet and pointing vigorously at her bunk. "There is someone in my bed!" she screamed.

Bair reached over and turned on the light, ready to grab the idiot once he could see him. Davis, huddled up at the far end of the top bunk, her eyes wide with terror. In the bottom bunk was a man-sized, silver-colored suit hanging halfway out of the bunk with its empty arms outstretched toward Patterson. Immediately upon seeing her assailant, Patterson stopped bouncing and yelled indignantly. "What the hell is that thing?"

Hardy looked at Bair and both desperately tried to stifle their amusement; they failed. Within moments, both men were roaring with laughter. This only served to make Patterson angrier, which in turn caused the two to laugh even harder.

"Captain Hardy, this is outrageous!"

With tears welling in his eyes, Hardy could barely reply, "Yes, ma'am.

You're right. I'm sorry." Bair nearly doubled over with his Captain's response, and the two laughed until they were gasping for air.

"Are the two of you quite finished enjoying yourselves at my expense?" demanded Patterson, still quite peeved.

"Almost," answered Hardy honestly. And after a little more chuckling he said, "Oh God! I needed that."

Bair, finally managing to get a hold of himself, turned toward control, and shouted, "Auxiliaryman of the Watch, report to Dr. Patterson's stateroom."

Within a few seconds, a balding petty officer appeared at the door. "Auxiliaryman of the Watch, reporting as ordered, sir."

"Petty Officer Johnson, please return the training steam suit to his quarters in the crew's mess," ordered Bair.

"Aye, aye, sir." Johnson quickly walked into the stateroom, grabbed the steam suit by the arms, and began to pull it down the passageway. As he made his way to the ladder, they could hear him berating the steam suit. "Bad George! Who said you could leave your locker? Now the DCA will have to confine you to quarters for the rest of this run."

With the steam suit thumping its way down the ladder, Bair and Hardy returned their attention to Patterson, who was now standing with her fists on her hips, her right foot tapping the deck. Her expression was more of annoyance than anger, but it was clear that she didn't like being the butt of someone's joke. "So, Captain, please don't tell me that this is another example of the sick and twisted kind of humor the Navy condones?" While her expression was indignant, the effect was muted by her flowered pink pajamas.

Hardy paused for a moment and then replied, "Then I won't tell you. Good night, ladies."

Surprised by his response, Patterson watched as both Hardy and Bair left, the latter closing the stateroom door. Still annoyed, Patterson let out a growl as she turned out the lights and tumbled into her bunk. After she finally got comfortable, she thought about what had just happened and started to chuckle. Sighing, she turned over and muttered to herself, "Boys will be boys."

Cold Welcome

May 23, 2005

●●

Barents Sea, Southwest of Novaya Zemlya

The next morning Jerry had the six to twelve watch in control. He and Tom Holtzmann arrived punctually at 0545, after their pre-watch tour through the boat, to begin the turnover with Lenny Berg. The relieving process always took some time, so officers were expected to show up at least fifteen minutes before their appointed watch.

Unlike the surface navy, which had four-hour watches followed by eight hours off, the submarine force used a more abusive six hours on, twelve hours off watch rotation. After six straight hours on watch, the brain turns to Tapioca pudding and all one wants is to be relieved on time. Usually, Jerry was paired with another officer who was the same rank or senior to him. But due to his aggressive qualification schedule, Jerry sometimes found himself standing watch with Ensign Holtzmann. Although Tom was junior to him in rank, he had more experience, and was formally qualified to be an OOD.

This meant he controlled the sub's movements and actions during routine operations, and was responsible for three-quarters of a billion dollars of taxpayers' money and the 137 souls aboard. If the boat went to General Quarters or some other special evolution, then the Captain would take over. Even if the Captain walked into the control room, Holtzmann would continue to run things, as long as Hardy was satisfied that he was doing a good job.

As the Junior Officer of the Deck, Jerry was learning on the job, backing up his book studies with on-watch time and training under a qualified officer. Eventually, he'd go before a board of *Memphis'* officers. They'd question him within an inch of his sanity, and if he satisfied them, he'd be a qualified OOD.

There was no Junior OOD on the earlier midnight to six watch, so Jerry listened as Tom relieved a very sleepy Lenny Berg. Lenny showed Holtzmann their progress on the chart, reviewed the status of the ship's reactor and engineering plant, and warned him about anything coming up in the next six hours. Some of the information was repetitive, as they had just talked to the offgoing Engineer Officer of the Watch, but a little redundancy is preferred over ignorance. After a few brief questions, Tom relieved Lenny and announced the turnover formally to the new watch section.

Fifteen minutes into what Jerry had expected to be a quiet transit watch, the loudspeaker announced. "Conn, sonar. New contact bearing three zero zero. Designate new contact sierra seven six."

"Sonar, conn aye," replied Holtzmann as he and Jerry clustered around the sonar console in control. The console had only a single display, but it could repeat whatever was on the eight displays the sonarmen were looking at.

"Look," said Tom Holtzmann. "Can you see what it is?" He stepped to one side.

Jerry studied the computer screen, called a "waterfall display" because the older information "fell" toward the bottom of the screen as new data showed up at the top. The video display showed the sounds picked up by *Memphis'* passive sonars, some of the most sensitive acoustic instruments ever built. The main passive array was a fifteen-foot sphere mounted at the bow with over twelve hundred transducers. It could also transmit powerful pulses into the water when the sonar went active. *Memphis* also had groups of passive hydrophones mounted along the forward part of her hull, and the most sensitive of all were the two lines of hydrophones towed behind her at the end of half-mile-long cables.

All the sounds they picked up were collected and displayed as bright green lines or wide spots on a ten-inch by ten-inch video screen. Engineers had learned long ago that humans have a keener sense of sight than hearing and had modified sonar systems to take advantage of this natural fact. The louder the signal, the brighter the spot.

Holtzmann had selected a broadband display that was divided into three separate bands. The top one displayed only a couple of minutes' worth of data, but it was updated much more rapidly than the other two that showed more information. Every few seconds, a new line of data was added at the top, pushing the older lines down.

A dim series of spots could be clearly seen on the topmost band, while it had just appeared on the middle one below. The displayed noise was fuzzy and wide, like the line left by a felt-tip pen on damp paper. A ship, especially a noisy one, would appear as a sharper, brighter set of lines because a ship has many different pieces of machinery, all making noise. This noise-maker was much more limited, weaker.

The next spot appeared on the left side of the display, now bearing three one zero degrees, to the northwest. That meant it lay to port and behind them. As Jerry watched, a new spot appeared, and seconds later, another. The spots didn't change in brightness, but the line that they drew was angling sharply to the right. That was important. Whatever it was had a high bearing rate, which meant it was fast and close.

"What do you think it is, Mr. Mitchell?" Holtzmann asked.

The bearing rate was the key. The only thing that moved that fast was an aircraft and the only aircraft in this neck of the woods were Russian ASW planes. "A Bear or May patrol aircraft." He tried to sound confident. "It's close, too."

As if on cue, the loudspeaker squawked back to life. "Conn, sonar. Sierra seven six now bears three one five degrees, drawing rapidly to the right. Contact is classified as a Bear Foxtrot."

"Good guess, sir. Now tell me how they know it's a Bear?" Holtzmann inquired as he reached up and changed the display to one that showed narrowband data.

Jerry smiled as he admitted his ignorance. "I know it has something to do with the type of engines, but other than that I haven't a clue of what I'm looking at here."

Narrowband sensors look for acoustic noise sources that are tightly confined within a very small frequency range. This kind of noise is produced by machinery that operates in a very regular and repetitive manner—like an aircraft's engines. Both the Tupolev Bear and the Ilyushin May are driven by four large turboprop engines, but the Bear has huge contra-rotating props on each one. The extra set of blades showed up clearly on the display.

"See these four groups of doublets," Tom said as he pointed to the close lines on the display. "That signal is the sound of his propellers. Each set of contra-rotating blades generates two frequencies that are really close to each other. Only a Tu-142 Bear Foxtrot has that kind of signature. And if we can hear the sound of his props, then he's close. What should we do?"

Both planes were armed with ASW torpedoes, although there was no risk of attack this far away from Russian territorial waters. A greater danger was posed by the planes' suite of ASW sensors. They carried radar, an ESM sensor that could detect other radars, and a short-range magnetic sensor called MAD that could sense the thousands of tons of steel in *Memphis'* hull. They also carried dozens of sonobuoys that could be dropped in patterns designed to detect a sub—if the plane's crew thought there was cause to use them.

Had this plane detected them? Were they responding to a report of a Yankee nuke approaching their waters? Or were they on their way home after a training mission? If *Memphis* was detected, or if the Russians even suspected there was a U.S. sub in the area, they would flood the area with ships and aircraft.

"Set up a track, and rig for ultra-quiet," Jerry recommended.

"Should we change depth?" Holtzmann asked.

Jerry thought for a beat, then said honestly, "I don't know." Working it though, he reasoned, "If we go deep, we could get a little farther away from his MAD sensor, but if he drops sonobuoys, he'll put them on both sides of the layer, and we won't be able to hear him as clearly on the far side of the layer."

The "layer," or thermocline, was a sudden change in the temperature of the seawater that partially reflected sound waves. The depth of the layer varied from day to day, but sub sailors always made it their business to know where it was, and to use it to their advantage. Putting the layer between a sonar and the sub was like hiding in the shadows. It didn't make you invisible, but it did make you harder to spot.

He paused, then said, "I recommend staying at this depth."

Holtzmann nodded, "Do it."

Jerry stepped back to the center of the control room. "Helm, all ahead one-third, make turns for five knots. Rig ship for ultra-quiet." He turned to Holtzmann. "Should we notify the Captain?" As he asked his question, he heard his order echoed over the 1MC: "Rig ship for ultra-quiet."

"We'd be in big trouble if we didn't," replied the ensign. He picked up the phone and dialed a number. "Captain, Officer of the Deck. Sir, sonar's detected a Bear Foxtrot off our port side, drawing rapidly to the right, evaluated as close. We've reducing speed and rigging for ultra-quiet." He paused for a moment, then answered, "Yessir."

Hardy stepped into the control room moments later. He stopped at the chart table for a moment, then studied the Bear's track on the fire-control system. Silently, he headed toward the sonar displays as the watch team scrambled out of the way.

The waterfall display now showed about five minutes of track history, a single fuzzy line angling to the right, straight and steady. The Russian was continuing on his way.

The Captain returned to the plot table, then the sonar display. He started to speak but caught himself before saying anything. Finally the petty officer manning the fire-control position said, "Contact is past closest point of approach and opening."

He spoke softly—not a whisper, but not a normal speaking voice either. Jerry noticed that the control room suddenly seemed quieter. He realized that many of the familiar machinery noises were missing from the background. He also felt the boat slowing, a subtle difference in the deck's vibration.

Hardy also spoke softly. He ordered, "Maintain this speed for thirty minutes after contact is lost, then resume normal speed and secure from ultra-quiet."

"Aye, aye, sir," Holtzmann acknowledged.

Hardy left, but a minute later the two ladies entered, almost breathless. "What's 'ultra-quiet' mean?" demanded Patterson. "What's happening?" asked Davis. Concern filled both their faces. Their voices, also full of concern, were raised and sounded harsh in the quiet control room. A soft chorus of "Quiet, please" and "Speak softly" surrounded them. Even Patterson looked embarrassed as the two were hushed.

"It's just a precaution," assured Holtzmann. "Sonar picked up a Russian patrol plane and we went quiet to make sure it didn't pick us up."

"You mean it almost found us?" Concern grew to alarm on Patterson's face. She started to speak softly, then forgot as emotion filled her voice.

"No, ma'am, there's no sign of that. It passed close enough for us to hear it, but there's no indication it changed course or did anything but continue flying from point A to point B. It's headed away from us now, but just to be on the safe side, we'll lay here in the weeds for a while, just in case he did drop a sonobuoy or three."

"And they can hear us if we speak too loudly?" Emily's question was a mixture of curiosity and surprise.

"Ma'am, at ultra-quiet, we reduce speed to a creep. This not only reduces the flow noise as the boat's hull passes through the water, it also lets the engineers shut down some of the machinery. Unnecessary equipment, like some of the ventilation fans, are turned off, and some normal activities, like cooking in the galley, also stop. And all off-watch personnel are supposed to get into their racks and stay there."

"Like us?" Emily asked.

Holtzmann nodded. "Like you two ladies."

"And they can really hear us walking around and talking?" Patterson asked.

"It isn't that the walking and talking are all that noisy." Holtzmann explained. "It's that everything else is that quiet. The whir of a fan, the sound of pans clattering in the galley, or a loud conversation may be the first thing they pick up."

The XO had come in during Holtzmann's explanation. He checked the fire-control track and the chart, then turned toward the ladies. "This is the part where we lie on our bellies in the mud while searchlights pass overhead. This is where we paint our faces green and merge with the underbrush. If they find us on the way in, it's going to be harder—a lot harder—for us to get the job done.

"It's not like it was back in the '70s and '80s, when we had a huge acoustic advantage," he continued, "and we are heading straight for the Russian Navy's front yard. Not only is their Northern Fleet headquarters here, but half a dozen sub and surface ship bases and as many air bases. In other words, the entire Northern Feet's right over there." He pointed to the southeast.

"Imagine how we'd feel if a Russian submarine went snooping into the Chesapeake Bay. How would our Navy react?"

"It's going to be hard to type lying down," Patterson declared resignedly, then left, with Davis following her. As she left, Bair said, "It shouldn't be too long—this time."

The signal from the Bear faded completely a few minutes later without changing course. They waited thirty minutes, the tension gone but prudence still in charge, then secured from ultra-quiet. They resumed normal transit speed, but Jerry sensed a different mood in control: not grimmer, but quieter and more focused. From here on they could expect to encounter Russian units at any time.

IT WAS ALMOST the end of his watch before anything else happened to break the quiet. Jerry looked up from his quals book as sonar announced, "Conn, sonar, new contact bearing one six zero degrees. Designated new contact sierra seven seven. Contact is a distant active warship pinging with a medium-frequency search sonar. Probably a patrol craft."

Holtzmann told Jerry, "You make the report to the Captain this time. I'll get us quiet." As he gave the orders to reduce speed and rig the boat for ultra-quiet, Jerry picked up the phone, dialed the Captain, then repeated sonar's report.

Hardy replied, "Thank you, Mr. Mitchell. What are your recommendations?"

Jerry replied, "Continue on base course, sir."

"Because a medium-frequency sonar has a relatively short range?" Hardy prompted.

"Yes, sir."

"Wrong answer, mister!" Hardy's voice was harsh. "Order a turn to the north right now, new course zero two zero. I'll be there in a minute. See if you can figure out by then what your mistake was."

Puzzled, Jerry put down the phone and told the OOD about the course change. Holtzmann let him issue the order and then asked about Jerry's expression. "I recommended that we stay on course, but the Captain said that was wrong. I don't understand why. Russian patrol craft all have short-range sonar, and he's not even close to us."

"All true," Holtzmann replied. "But what time of year is it?" he asked.

"Summer," Jerry answered, confused by the question.

"In the Barents," Holtzmann continued. "It's a short summer up here. The weather's decent, and the Russians cram a lot of exercises into these few months. Now, we know there's a patrol craft out there pinging, but he's too far away to be pinging for us. So what's he pinging for?"

"A Russian sub." Jerry answered, beginning to understand.

"Exactly," Holtzmann confirmed. "There's a decent chance that a patrol ship is getting practice on a live sub or that a sub's getting practice with a live pursuer, probably both. Now the patrol craft can't pick us up this far away, but if there's sub around, then we are in an entirely different ball game."

Hardy arrived as Holtzmann finished his explanation. "Anything more from sonar, Mr. Holtzmann?" Hardy asked.

"Sonar reports a single pinger only. They evaluate it as a Bull Horn sonar, bearing correlates with a passive sonar contact, possibly a Grisha. But it's not a single contact. They're getting several similar passive contacts, all close together, all with a very slow right bearing drift."

"A group of ASW patrol craft," Hardy concluded, "with one conducting an active search." He stepped over to the intercom and pressed the switch. "Sonar, conn. Sort out those passive contacts and make damn sure they are all surface ships. And keep a sharp eye to the south for anything that might not be a surface vessel."

"Conn, sonar aye" came over the speaker from sonar.

Hardy turned back to face them, but his explanation was for Jerry. "Individually, a Grisha or a Parchim isn't much of a problem. A couple of short-range sonars, ASW rocket launchers, and ASW torpedoes. We can outrun one or sink it with one torpedo. But they hunt subs in packs, usually in groups of three or four. They spread out in line abreast and march back and forth across a swath two dozen miles wide. They also like to work with ASW aircraft and helicopters. Right now, they're practicing how to hunt us. We're going to do our best to avoid giving them a real target to train on."

Hardy went over to the chart table to check the new course, then the fire-control display. "Mr. Holtzmann, assume an exercise area fifteen miles on a side, centered on the pinger's current position, then add the detection range of a first-line SSN's sonars. How wide is the danger zone?" Hardy sounded like he already knew the answer.

"I'll assume an Akula II with a Skat-3 sonar suite," Holtzmann answered as he brought up a detection/counter-detection program on the HP computer. "We're ultra-quiet, so that roughly quarters the noise we are putting into the water."

He punched in the data, then moved to show the display to Hardy as his finger traced a graph. Hardy shook his head. "Remember, mister, he's trying to avoid detection as well. Assume he's ultra-quiet, too."

Chagrined, Holtzmann punched in the corrections, then followed another line on the plotted graph. Hardy nodded and said, "Add that distance to the size of the box and plot a course around it."

"Aye, aye, sir."

"And then figure out the distance we have to be from the box before we can secure from ultra-quiet."

"Aye, aye, sir."

JERRY AND HOLTZMANN turned over the watch at noon, with the boat creeping north-northeast, away from the Russian exercise area. Lunch was cold cuts in the wardroom, eaten in almost total silence and with Jerry being careful not to scrape his chair across the deck. The two ladies were even more careful than the rest of the crew, speaking in whispers, setting down a glass slowly to prevent any sound.

They secured from ultra-quiet in mid-afternoon, and an almost tangible weight lifted from Jerry's shoulders. Staying quiet wasn't a hardship, or even difficult, but it meant being constantly aware and constantly careful. That awareness also included the presence of Russian forces, not really the enemy, but a dangerous and capable opponent.

JERRY CAME BACK on watch at six, after eating an early dinner. Although most officers would stand one watch section out of every three or four, Jerry had doubled up to get in the experience he needed in this one patrol. Sleep would have to wait until they got back home.

Memphis was on course and at transit speed, but there was something new on sonar. Lieutenant Commander Ho was OOD this time, and he steered Jerry to the sonar display. "Here's something new," he announced.

The waterfall display was filled with bright speckles, like a thin fog. The "fog" lay in front of them, and as he watched it move down the display, it widened slightly. That meant it was filling more of the horizon. They were headed straight for it. Into it.

"It's the Marginal Ice Zone," Jerry announced. "We're picking up the sound of the ice floes as they melt and hit each other."

"Correct," replied Ho. "This time of year, you've got to go pretty far north to reach it. Implications?"

"Reduced passive detection ranges. And we have to be more careful when using the periscope, or any mast."

Ho nodded. "And this is just small junk. They weigh less than a hundred pounds apiece. Later we'll get into the bigger stuff."

By the middle of the watch, they had entered the Marginal Ice Zone. The waterfall display was covered with tiny white specks, like slow-moving static. Above them, the ocean's surface was littered with an ever-thickening cover of ice floes and a slushy mix of seawater and small ice chunks. To Jerry, everything felt the same, but now there was a roof on their world.

"The good news is," Ho explained, "we don't have to worry too much about Russian ASW aircraft and ships. The bad news is that Russian subs operate under this all the time. Their detection ranges are reduced as well, but they're used to it."

Ho continued to lecture Jerry as the watch continued. "We can surface in this stuff, if we had to." His tone made it clear that they wouldn't do it casually. "Later on, it'll be solid pack ice. We can navigate well enough under it, but we can't surface through that. Some subs can, but we are not, I repeat, not, ice-capable. Late-flight 688's have bow planes they can retract, but we'd wreck our fairwater planes if we tried to go through solid ice."

"So what happens if we have a problem?" Dr. Patterson entered the control room from the forward passageway. She'd overheard the conversation.

Ho asked, "You mean the kind of problem where we might need to surface?" His tone was light, but when he saw her expression, his changed as well. "We've got air as long as the reactor is working, and even if the reactor failed, the battery will last long enough to get us out of trouble."

Patterson waved her hands in the air, as if warding off biting insects. "Please, don't tell me all the precautions because that means you have to tell me what might go wrong. I'm sure you've thought it all through, just like NASA. But things don't always go well for them, either."

"That must be why they pay us the big bucks," one of the enlisted men muttered sarcastically.

Ho shot him a hard look, but said, "We do our best and try to be ready." He shrugged. He turned back to Jerry. "I need you to stay alert, Mr. Mitchell. Our charts of the area are less than complete."

Patterson rolled her eyes, but Ho saw the gesture and motioned toward the chart. "The path we're taking, especially as we get closer to Russia, hasn't been traveled all that often by U.S. boats, and we weren't able to get current charts from the Russian Hydrographic service or AAA. Look at the numbers that show depth, Doctor. See how they run in lines. You can almost see where every U.S. submarine has passed in these waters by following the soundings they took."

He pointed to their own track, drawn on the chart. "See where we've crossed these blank areas? The mapmakers will use our fathometer logs to fill in some of the empty spots and also check to see if there have been any changes. Because the seafloor up here never stays the same."

Ho looked over at Jerry, standing by the chart table and listening to the conversation. "Mind the gauges, mister." Mitchell quickly turned back to his watch station.

Dr. Patterson said, "Thanks for the explanation, although I'm no less nervous for knowing why the charts are incomplete. What are the chances of hitting an underwater mountain or something?"

"We watch the fathometer closely," Ho assured her, "and if the bottom starts sloping, either up or down, we find out why—and quickly. We have a high-frequency mine-avoidance sonar mounted in the sail and on the lower part of the bow that we can use to look for obstacles ahead of or over us, but it's an active sonar, so we won't use it unless we have to."

"And if we do hit something?" she asked.

Ho shrugged. "Depends on what it is. If we strike something head-on, at speed, it would damage the hull and cause injuries inside, since we're not wearing seat belts. When USS *Ray*, an old *Sturgeon*-class attack boat, hit a sea mountain in the Med at flank speed, her bow looked like a stubbed-out cigar. But she managed to limp home."

Patterson gave Ho a dirty look that told him that she was tired of constantly hearing about the worst-case scenario. Clearing his throat, he quickly moved on to a more likely possibility. "Our biggest fear is that we could scrape our bottom on a shallow spot that isn't on our charts. Most likely it would only cause minor damage. There's almost no chance of rupturing the pressure hull. That's a couple of inches of HY80 steel. It might limit our speed or make us noisier, which would be a real pain. Of course, if the screw or rudder is damaged, then we'd be in a world of . . ." Ho stopped talking, suddenly conscious of Patterson's exasperated expression.

After a small pause, she changed the subject. "How long until we reach the area?" Patterson asked.

"You mean the dump sites?" Ho asked and she nodded.

Ho rummaged through several rolled-up charts and pulled out the same one she'd shown at the briefing after they'd gotten underway. He noted the location of the first dump site and made a pencil mark on the larger navigational chart. He measured the distance from *Memphis'* current position and said, "About fifty-five hours at this speed. We should be in position early on the 26th, the day after tomorrow."

Patterson nodded again, as she followed along with Ho's explanation. Then hesitantly, she asked, "What will the Russians do if they find us? I mean specifically."

Ho thought for a moment and spoke carefully. "Pretty much what we'd do, under similar circumstances. They'll try to track us, filling the area with as many units as they can. The first to arrive will be aircraft, because they're faster, but they'll send surface ships out as well. They probably won't use subs to chase us, because they don't want to confuse us with one of their own. If they can pin us down long enough, they'll talk to us over sonar, ordering us to surface and identify ourselves."

"Not that we'd do that," Patterson replied. Her tone didn't match the certainty of her words.

"No, ma'am, we wouldn't. We'd just keep evading and eventually break away. We couldn't continue the mission after that, obviously."

"They wouldn't try to shoot at us? To keep us from getting away?"

"Outside territorial waters, firing at us would be an act of war. Of course, they view this whole area as their territory, and if we're skirting the border, they won't take an exact navigational fix before they shoot. Ships and planes have been lost before doing what we're doing."

Ho stopped for a moment, then repeated himself. "Yes, ma'am. If we're found near their territorial waters, especially within twelve miles of land, they'll do their best to sink us, and it's their backyard. They know these waters better than we do, and they'll have numbers on their side, we can't even call for help. We certainly won't shoot back. They've got all the angles. We've got stealth and surprise. As long as they don't detect us, we'll be just fine."

"So we really are risking our lives on this mission." Patterson looked thoughtful.

"Yep. Days of boredom punctuated by brief moments of mind-numbing terror." He smiled. "But it's going to be a milk run, right?"

16 Dangerous Ground

May 26, 2005

••••••••••••••••••••••••••••

Oga Guba, Novaya Zemlya

Memphis continued on a northerly course, slipping farther and farther under the marginal ice zone. Here the ice floes got larger and icebergs became more of a navigation hazard. On more than one occasion, *Memphis* had to dodge a lumbering giant as it moved slowly southward. As they neared the northern tip of Novaya Zemlya, the polar ice pack appeared as a solid wall on the mine-avoidance sonar. With the exception of a few polynyas, large open cracks in the pack ice, the surface became an impenetrable barrier. Tension grew as the crew took their non-ice-capable boat farther under the polar ice cap.

Within hours of passing under the polar cap, the ambient noise went from a cacophony of cracking ice to almost complete silence. Only the occasional stuttering of a forming ice ridge or the low singing of a distant whale broke the near perfect absence of sound. And while the significantly reduced background noise improved *Memphis'* passive sonar capability, it also worked against them, as it would enhance any Russian submarine's sensors as well. Turning eastward, they rounded the northernmost portion of Novaya Zemlya. Within two watch sections, they were heading south into the Kara Sea, approaching their destination.

A long narrow island that curved out to the north from Russia's northern coast, Novaya Zemlya separates the Barents Sea on the west from the Kara Sea on the east. A northern extension of the Ural Mountains, it was little more than a rocky ridge that protruded above the surface of the water. Before the Soviets, the few inhabitants that lived there had supported themselves by fishing, trapping, and seal hunting. Nothing green grew on the rocky island, but ice prospered.

Oga Guba, the first of four bays they would explore, was almost halfway down the eastern coast. Their general plan was to work northward along the coast, so that by the end of the mission they'd be at the northern end and ready to go home.

"MAN MANTA AND ROV LAUNCH STATIONS." Jerry was already in the torpedo room when the word was passed over the 1MC. In fact, he'd been there since three-thirty that morning. He'd gotten off watch at midnight, but found it impossible to sleep. Instead, he'd worked on his quals, and then came down to the torpedo room.

He'd sat at the Manta station, going over the controls and flipping through the manual again and again. Jerry kept looking for something he might have missed, special commands or limitations or pages with big yellow warning labels that read: DON'T EVER DO THIS!

It took three months of ground school before the Navy would let him even touch an airplane, and two years before they considered him fit to fly in a line squadron. That training served a purpose. It made you so familiar with the aircraft that it was an extension of your own body. You even knew when it might fail.

And yet, he'd been surprised by that blowout. At least the Manta didn't have landing gear. But a three-week course and a few practice runs hadn't bonded him with the UUV. He still felt like he was playing an unfamiliar video game.

They'd finally passed the word at 0500 to man the Manta and ROV stations, and the torpedo division started pouring into the room, followed by a sleepy Emily Davis. The torpedomen moved around as quietly as they could, more out of habit than anything else, but there was still a lot of bustle as they checked their gear, positioned Huey for loading and donned the sound-powered phones. Emily now wore her own set so she could communicate with control about the ROVs without using the noisier intercom or going through an overloaded phone talker. Greer and Davidson settled into their positions and reported they were ready. Jerry began the Manta's system checks and warm up sequence.

This had all been worked out the day before. Who would be where, who would do what, who would do the talking, and especially who would give the orders.

That last issue had taken up a good part of yesterday. First Patterson had to be convinced that only one person should be giving orders to the ROV. A few sea stories about confused orders and their effects had settled that issue. But both Hardy and Patterson had good reasons to be in charge of the ROV—his operational, hers scientific.

Doctors Patterson and Davis were both civilians and unfamiliar with submarines, much less the tactical situation. They didn't know the risks, or all the possibilities. Hardy was adamant that someone with a uniform approve any orders to the ROV as a reality check before they were executed. Patterson was loath to have anything interfere or challenge her control of what she termed a "delicate scientific operation." She didn't help matters by likening naval control to "pushing a crystal vase through a knothole."

The XO had finally suggested an acceptable compromise. As mission commander, Patterson would direct the ROV's operations. Hardy would pass her orders to Davis through a phone talker and she would actually control its actions. Meanwhile, Jerry would run interference with the Manta—also under Hardy's direction.

This meant that Hardy and Patterson both had to be in the control room. This was good for Jerry and Emily. Otherwise, Hardy or Patterson or both would probably be in the torpedo room, closely—perhaps too closely—monitoring the ROV operations.

Hardy needed to be in control. Navigating a submarine in shallow water at bare steerageway using sketchy charts and watching for Russian patrollers required his fulltime attention. Repeater displays in control would let him and Patterson see what the Manta and the ROV were seeing and doing.

Last night they'd practiced the arrangement, actually slowing and pretending to deploy both vehicles and then passing information back and forth until they were satisfied that all the circuits worked properly and everyone knew their duties.

Now, they were approaching the first dump site in Oga Guba. *Memphis* was about fifteen miles from the coast. The water had gradually shallowed until they had approached the sixty-fathom line. Three hundred and sixty feet of water isn't very deep when a submarine stands about sixty feet from the bottom of the keel to the top of the sail. It also happened to be exactly the length of the boat.

Submariners hate shallow water. There's nowhere to hide. Even submerged, if the boat went too fast, it would leave a visible wake on the surface, and if their depth control wasn't perfect, they could strike the bottom or broach the surface.

In special circumstances, a boat could go as shallow as forty fathoms, but Hardy insisted the charts weren't good enough for that. And if you're caught in forty fathoms, there's really nowhere to go, except to head for deeper water.

By international law, Russian territorial waters extended twelve miles out from the island, and by presidential order, they had to stay outside that limit. Luckily, both the Manta and the ROVs had sufficient range to work in the shallow water while *Memphis* stood outside the twelve-mile limit.

Jerry was also wearing phones, and he heard Lieutenant Richards' voice say, "Control online." Making the Weapons Officer the control room phone talker was another one of Hardy's insurance policies. Richards wouldn't do anything unless Hardy told him to do it.

The next command had already been planned, but Jerry waited for Richards to relay Hardy's order. "U-bay, control. Deploy the Manta and take station."

"Deploy the Manta and take station, U-bay aye." Jerry responded, then: "Control, U-bay. Verify speed is four knots."

Richards replied, "Speed is four knots."

"Roger, launching Manta." Jerry checked the procedure book before he did anything, not only because he genuinely didn't want to forget anything, but because it was standard Navy policy to follow procedures exactly. Retracting the umbilical and the other steps all went smoothly.

Once the Manta lifted off, Jerry relaxed a little. His first task was to sweep out toward the first dumpsite. According to the 1993 Yablokov Commission Report, a small barge loaded with solid radioactive waste had been scuttled here in 1968. The Manta would find the barge, looking for navigational hazards along the way and keeping a passive sonar watch in the area. The ROV, with its shorter endurance, would not be launched until the Manta had found the barge's precise location.

Jerry focused on the Manta's imaging sonar. It was a broadband high-frequency set that would be hard for the Russians to detect, but it would show him what the bottom was like, and hopefully spot anything artificial.

The seabed shelved gradually here, rising from just over sixty fathoms where they were, to forty-four at the dumpsite, labeled DELTA ONE on their charts. It lay eight miles away to the west, an hour's trip for the Manta at cruise speed.

As Jerry carefully flew the Manta to the west, he gradually descended until he was only twenty feet above the bottom. The imaging sonar started to give him a picture. The color display was clear enough to reveal an uneven bottom. Denser material sent back a stronger echo, which looked brighter on the screen, so rock showed as a lighter image than the silt that filled in the crevices and low spots. Metal would provide an even sharper echo, and a correspondingly lighter spot on the display.

Jerry worked on getting the feel of the vehicle, comparing the readouts on speed and depth with the images he was getting. His earlier maneuvers with *Memphis* had been in open ocean, and with the Manta relatively close. Now he was working at a distance in shallow water and he wanted to find out how much control he really had.

He didn't have to worry about flying the Manta into the bottom. It was smart enough to automatically avoid the seabed, but he didn't want to have to depend on the Manta to keep him out of trouble.

It took fifteen minutes before he could predict the interval between sending a command to the Manta and it reacting. Beyond the normal lag between the control surfaces moving and the UUV responding, the acoustic signal, moving at the speed of sound, took longer and longer to reach the Manta as it swam farther and farther away.

It already took several seconds for a signal from *Memphis* to reach the Manta and several more for the signal from the Manta to return, confirming that it had reacted. The math told Jerry that at maximum range, fifteen thousand yards, it would take about ten seconds for an order from him to reach the Manta—or for information from the Manta to show up on his display.

With his personal time-delay calibration finished, Jerry had little to do but sit back and watch the display screen. According to the digital timer, the Manta was still about thirty minutes away from their first target and he'd just have to wait. Jerry let loose with a wide yawn as fatigue overcame his earlier excitement.

"You look exhausted, Jerry," remarked Emily. He looked over and saw that semi-frown she always had when things weren't quite right.

"Yeah, I guess I'm a little tired. I've been really busy working on my qualifications."

"So I've noticed. Don't you ever take some time off? You know, get a good night's sleep or just goof off. Its not healthy to work so hard."

Jerry snickered sarcastically and said, "Emily, I would love to take some time off. Unfortunately, I don't have the time for such luxury. If I'm not working on my division's stuff or standing watch, I'm expected to be fully engaged with my quals. Besides, I'm way behind my peer group and I have to catch up. I'll make up for the lack of sleep when we get back."

"Assuming you don't hurt yourself in the process," replied Emily tersely. Her tone caught Jerry off guard and he thought it better to let the conversation die.

After a few minutes of awkward silence, Emily's angry expression eased. She bit her lip slightly and squirmed about in her seat, as if she were trying to get her nerve up to say something. Finally she leaned against the display, rested her head in her left hand, and asked, "So, Mr. Mitchell, what is involved with this qualifications process that has so thoroughly consumed your life?"

Jerry just sat there, surprised this time by the sarcasm behind her question. At first, he found himself simply staring at her, momentarily unable to say anything. She then raised an eyebrow and gave him a coy look that clearly said, "Well, are you going to answer the question or not?"

Shaking his head slightly, Jerry replied, "Sorry, I guess I'm a little more tired than I thought. But, um, to answer your question, it frankly involves everything."

Emily's expression changed to a scowl. "That's not very helpful, Jerry."

"No, seriously," he said earnestly as he tried to defend his statement. "I have to know essentially everything about every system on board this submarine. Where every component is located, its power supply, its normal operating parameters, and what other systems will be affected, and how, should it fail. I have to memorize all the immediate actions for every casualty procedure and know most of the supplementary actions by heart as well. I have to be able to safely balance, push, and drive this boat through vastly different ocean environments, on the surface as well as submerged. And I have to know how to fight this boat should we be called upon to do so. By my own admittedly biased perspective, I need to know how everything works, and how to work everything."

"That's absurd, Jerry! How can anyone be expected to know everything about this sub?" protested Emily.

Jerry laughed, "Well, the guys who have been giving my systems checkouts sure seem to expect it. Particularly with all the oolies I've had to dig around to answer."

"Oolies?"

"Yup. Consider them to be the submarine force's equivalent of Trivial Pursuit—little known factoids about different parts of the boat. And they are, without exception, a major pain in the butt."

"Can you give me an example?" asked Emily with genuine curiosity.

"No problem," answered Jerry confidently. "Let's see, which one would you understand and appreciate?" He thought for a moment and then his face brightened. "Yeah, that one will do nicely. During my damage control checkout, I had to list all the watertight doors and hatches on the boat. Seemed simple enough, so I started to rattle off the access hatches, the torpedo muzzle and breach doors, and everything else that was part of a watertight boundary. After I was done, the chief giving me the checkout said I had missed one. Well, I went back over all the doors and hatches again and I couldn't figure out which one I had missed. He told me to look it up and get back to him before he would sign me off."

Jerry shifted around in his chair so that he faced Emily directly. "Okay, for two days I walked, crawled, and squeezed behind some pretty tight places searching for this missing door. No matter what I did, I could not find the stupid thing. Finally I was in here poring over the ship's data book looking for the damn door, and I must have been muttering some obscenities in total frustration, when Seaman Jobin came over with a huge grin on his face and gave me the beckoning index finger. He led me to the ship's laundry, right past the berthing area back there, and pointed toward the washing machine. And there on the front of this washing machine was a watertight door. I was so pissed, I didn't know whether I was going to maim the chief for asking the question or Jobin, who was thoroughly enjoying my gross stupidity."

Emily laughed, imagining Jerry's face when the most junior guy in his division showed him the answer to the question that had vexed him for days. But in a more serious tone, she questioned him. "While it's a funny story, Jerry, what is the point of the question? Other than to drive you crazy, of course."

"The point, Emily, was that I had studied the drain system and the potable water system without realizing that the washing machine was even there. It's a little thing, but it is connected to two very important systems in the boat, which means it can have an effect on them."

The sonar's auto detect light suddenly came on, drawing Jerry's attention to a bright spot in the upper left corner of the sonar display. He started to report it to control, but they must have seen the same thing. Richards directed, "We see it. Steer left." They were still several miles short of Delta One's plotted position.

"Steer left, U-bay aye," Jerry responded almost automatically and commanded a thirty-degree left turn.

"More," Richards ordered. "Do you see that object at about two-nine-zero relative?"

Jerry saw something on the sonar display. It was hard to gauge size, but it was definitely of different material from the seabed it sat on. The Manta's sonar had a reliable range of three thousand yards, so to see it at that distance meant it had to be sizable.

"Should I head directly for it?" he asked Richards.

There was a pause and Jerry imagined Richards relaying the question to Hardy, who would pass it to Patterson. Then they'd have to discuss the effects of the detour on the endurance of the Manta, whether it would be able to identify it, what would they do if . . .

"Yes. Steer toward it, but keep about a ten-degree offset."

"Steer toward with a ten-degree offset, U-bay aye."

"Slow down now," Richards directed. "Make your speed four knots."

"Four knots, aye." They were still five hundred yards off. All he could see on the sonar was a jumble of shapes.

"Circle it. Maybe it'll be clearer from another angle."

"Circle it, aye," Mitchell acknowledged.

With a certain amount of grace, Jerry turned the Manta to starboard and made a quarter circle, with the object at the center. He didn't bother keeping it in the sonar's detection cone, since the location was marked on his nav display.

When he turned back toward the object, it was longer, and the jumble had resolved into separate objects lying near and on the large object. It was more than large. Figuring the range and the angle it covered, it had to be almost a hundred feet long.

"Continue to circle," Richards ordered and Jerry turned the Manta to the right again. The Manta had no camera, in fact, no other sensors besides the sonar. Jerry imagined the discussion in control. What was it? Was it worth finding out? Could this be part of Delta One? Jerry didn't think so. Large as it was, it didn't look like a barge, and it was too big to be one of the containers.

"U-bay, control. Launch ROV and investigate this object. We're designating it Delta One-Alpha."

Davis got busy, but forgot to respond until Richards prompted her again. "U-bay, control. Did you receive my last?"

Davis quickly pressed the button on the mouthpiece. "Yes, sorry. I'm launching Huey now."

"It'll take an hour for the ROV to get there at six knots," Jerry reported over the phones. "Should I set up a perimeter patrol?" The procedure they'd decided on yesterday was that when the ROV investigated a site, the Manta would keep watch.

"Wait one," Richards replied, but almost immediately continued, "Negative. If we've got an hour, we want you to continue on to Delta One. It's close by. That way, when the ROV is finished with Delta One-Alpha, it can continue on to Delta One."

"Understood. Changing course to two nine zero, heading for Delta One, ETA at eight knots eighteen minutes."

Jerry flew the Manta carefully over the smoothly rolling bottom. It was less rocky here, with more sand and dirt. He'd only been on his new course for ten minutes when he saw the barge on his sonar display. It showed as another hard return on the sonar display and was a little larger than Delta One-Alpha.

Without a camera, he couldn't be sure, but the location matched the Russian report, and there was nothing else that large visible on the display. Jerry started the Manta in a slow spiraling circle, centered on the object.

Emily had the ROV about halfway to the mysterious Delta One-Alpha and was refusing Patterson's demands to increase Huey's speed. Although the ROV had a top speed of twelve knots, its battery charge only lasted a quarter of the six hours it had at its cruise speed of six knots.

"She should know better," Davis muttered to Jerry.

Patterson, content to relay orders through Hardy and Richards before, now came on the circuit. "Dr. Davis," she said sharply, "you have to go faster. We've got two sites to investigate now instead of one."

"Which means we'll be out longer and need to conserve our battery power," replied Emily firmly. Jerry was surprised by Emily's sudden defiance. She'd never stood up to Patterson before.

"We don't have to go to full speed," Patterson wheedled. "Just increase to eight or nine knots."

"Which saves us what? A few minutes? Why are we in such a hurry?"

"This is the very first site. We've got a lot to do and I don't want us falling behind."

"And I don't want us losing Huey because he has a flat battery. Delta One-Alpha is on the way to Delta One. We'll hardly lose any time at all."

Patterson finally gave up, at least in part because the ROV was close to the object's position. The ring-laser gyros in both vehicles allowed for precise navigation, and there was no need to search again for Delta One-Alpha.

At three hundred yards, Emily slowed Huey and turned on the lights. The camera showed a clear picture, but even with the lights on there was only a dark green image filled with bright swirling specs flowing by the camera. It looked exactly like a light snowfall in a car's headlights. As the ROV slowed, the snowflakes slowed as well.

The ROV's sonar, much weaker than the Manta's, only had a range of two hundred and fifty yards, intended for close-in navigation. It picked up the object right on schedule, but there was still nothing on the TV camera.

At a hundred yards, she slowed Huey again, creeping forward. Jerry's eyes were glued to the TV screen, although he forced himself to check the Manta, still circling and searching near Delta One.

At fifty yards, a bright green-gray wall suddenly materialized out of the dark water. Davis stopped the ROV without being told to, and then slowly panned the camera left to right, then up and down.

It was a curved wall, then a cylinder, but an uneven one, with lumps—and a couple of portholes?

Davis said, "I'm moving left. I'm a little closer to that end."

Richards acknowledged her message and after a short pause, replied, "Go ahead."

Davis hadn't waited, though, and the image slid sideways as the ROV passed across it. Almost immediately the cylinder's shape changed, narrowing, and they could see the familiar outline of a cockpit. "It's an airplane? Did it crash here?" somebody in the torpedo gang asked.

Emily continued past what they now knew was the nose, and then pivoted Huey so they were looking at the craft head-on. "It's an An-12 Cub," Jerry reported over the phones. "It's a cargo plane, a lot like our C-130 Hercules."

Now that he knew what it was, Jerry could interpret the image, recognizing many details. The plane was partially covered with marine growth, but on an object of that size a little green fuzz couldn't hide its identity. The underside of the nose was crumpled and several long cracks in the skin showed that the plane had landed on the seabed with some force.

"Did it crash?" Richards' question echoed the one in Jerry's mind.

The ROV was now on the other side, the port side of the aircraft, and she passed it down the plane's length.

Halfway, Jerry said, "Wait. Stop, please. Can you have the camera point up, toward the top of the fuselage?" Although Emily was nearby, he asked over the circuit so that up in control they'd know what was happening.

Davis moved the ROV up. The image slid down until they were looking at the upper midsection of the fuselage. It bulged and an exposed metal framework marred the smooth surface. "Look, that's where the wings were removed. It didn't crash. It was dumped here."

Jerry's conclusion was confirmed when the ROV continued aft. One of the plane's horizontal stabilizers lay next to the fuselage. Its base was a neat line, not jagged. The airfoils had been detached and discarded along with the fuselage.

As she moved aft, the ROV's gamma detector came off the peg. "I'm getting a reading," reported Davis. "Just higher than background."

"Understood," was Richards' reply. "Continue aft."

As Huey slowly approached the tail, the counter continued to rise. "Whoa, it's coming up fast. Now reading 0.7 rem per hour," Davis reported.

"That sounds real bad," Davidson said from his seat at the Manta controls.

"Any radiation is bad," answered Davis offhandedly. "But this wouldn't cause significant damage if you limited your exposure to a few hours. I wouldn't go inside the plane, though. Accounting for distance and the shielding properties of water, I'd guess the dose rate would be about fifty times that inside."

"Holy shit! That's hot," exclaimed Davidson. Then apologetically, "Sorry, ma'am. I just wasn't expecting the radiation to be so high."

Jerry grinned at Davidson's reaction, although his surprise was understandable. The typical yearly radiation dose for most human beings is between 0.15 and 0.20 rem, it's often less for nuclear submariners because they are protected by a steel hull and the sea from cosmic rays, which makes up a third of the yearly dose. And even though they lived and worked in close proximity to a nuclear reactor, the extensive shielding and strict safety procedures significantly reduced their radiation exposure. Davis' estimated dose rate inside the An-12 would give a typical human being their annual dose in less than a minute. Exposure over a period of three hours would make a man very sick, although he would probably live. An exposure of eight hours would likely lead to death.

Finally, the ROV reached the back. The broad cargo door was closed on the underside of the upturned tail, and the meter spiked at 2.0 rem per hour.

Emily slowed the ROV and maneuvered it as close to aircraft as she dared. As Huey gentle approached the ocean floor, she triggered the automatic sequence that would drop one of the sampling tubes, collect a sample of the silt, and then winch it back up to the container in the ROV's underbelly.

"I've taken a soil sample for analysis," reported Emily.

Richards paused after passing the message to control. "Dr. Patterson thinks they had a spill while transporting solid waste in this aircraft. Rather than decontaminate the plane, they just got rid of it," he said.

Over the phones, Emily replied, "I agree. Too bad all that contamination is exposed to the open ocean," she added sharply.

"Unless you can think of anything more to do here, Dr. Patterson wants to move on to Delta One."

Davis turned Huey west-northwest. Jerry's Manta had been slowly circling for half an hour now and had built up a map of the seabed for several miles to either side. There was nothing else near the first contact.

As the Huey approached Delta One at a stately six knots, Jerry programmed the Manta to patrol the area. It would circle at slow speed, listening passively with its sonar while the ROV made its survey.

Huey was still half a mile away from the barge when the radiation detector showed a measurable reading. "It's at 0.5 rem per hour here," Davis reported. "Should I take a sample?" she asked over the phones.

Richards' reply was almost immediate. "Yes, go ahead."

Davis was already slowing the ROV and gently descending to the seabed. In the TV camera, it was a nearly featureless surface of silt and sand, with the rocky underbed showing through here and there. A partially exposed, corroded container could just be made out under the silt.

Each of the ROVs could take up to six soil samples on a sortie, thus they had to be used carefully. The container had obviously been here quite a while and would make an excellent test to see how far the leaked contamination had spread. As it hovered near the bottom, a cloud of sediment started to obscure the camera's view.

It only took a minute, and as soon as the sample was stored, Davis started the ROV off again. Jerry noted that Davis was now running Huey a little over six knots, but it wasn't far to go.

Finally, almost two hours after launching the Manta, they saw what the Yablokov report described as "Barge SB-5, with containers of unspecified solid radioactive waste."

"Detector shows only 0.1 rem per hour. That's not all that much, even after I correct for distance and water shielding," Emily reported.

Richards passed on her observations, and then replied, "Dr. Patterson says not to worry about it. The radiation reading is consistent with the small amount of radioactive material that the barge is listed to contain in the report. But go ahead and collect a soil sample anyway."

"Collecting soil sample." While Huey took another sample, Davis noted the location.

As she circled the barge, they could see that it had capsized as it sank, landing on its side and spilling part of its cargo. The cylindrical steel containers, each about twelve feet long, lay scattered to one side. The containers on the seabed were half-buried in silt, and their surfaces were covered with patches of marine growth. On a few places, they were dented and cracked from landing on the seabed, and rust had taken hold.

"Get a sample from that one just to your right." Richards instructed. "Dr. Patterson says that it is likely to be as high a reading as we'll get at this site."

"Understood. I'm maneuvering Huey into position now."

"Can you find any markings?" Richards asked over the phones.

"No, nothing that I can make out. Collecting soil sample."

As Emily deployed the sampling tube, TM1 Bearden asked, "Dr. Davis, where does the radioactive material from these containers go?"

"Not very far, at least not yet," answered Davis. "You can see the cracked and corroding containers. If this one dumpsite were found off the coast of Alaska or Nova Scotia, it would trigger a national scandal. There are reportedly hundreds of these containers in this bay."

"Aren't there people living there? Eskimos or something?"

"There were, but most of the indigenous Nenet population were forcibly moved out by the Soviets in the mid-1950s. The ones that are left probably wish they were somewhere else. The whole island's been used as a nuclear test site and waste dump. The Soviets exploded thermonuclear bombs as big as fifty-eight megatons here. Dr. Patterson's the expert, though."

Once Huey had taken the sample, Patterson guided Davis and the ROV to two more sampling points, spaced at intervals from the barge. After the last sample, she turned Huey toward *Memphis*. It had just enough battery for the return trip.

Dr. Patterson entered the torpedo room, almost breathless, holding a plot of Delta One. "So far, the data matches the survey exactly." She sounded almost triumphant.

Jerry asked, "What's the point in surveying something if we've already got all the information on it?"

"Because it's a check on our ability to do a survey. When we find something new, then we won't have to work as hard to prove our data is correct."

Looking at the two ROVs and thinking about the hours of effort that they'd just spent and the work they had left, Jerry couldn't be that detached. "Let's just search where the charts are empty, then, or at least at an area that hasn't been surveyed already."

"We need a baseline, Lieutenant," said Patterson, a little sharply. "If we don't do things by the numbers, the rest of our work will be meaningless."

Jerry couldn't argue. "Yes, ma'am."

An hour and a half later, Huey reached *Memphis* and was safely recovered. He needed servicing, but the torpedo gang was more than willing to wait while both Doctors Davis and Patterson and the nuke ELTs carefully removed the samples, then thoroughly and publicly checked the entire vehicle for traces of radioactivity.

While they examined Huey, Jerry recovered the Manta. The instant he reported it was aboard and the latches in place, he felt the deck vibrate. Hardy was repositioning *Memphis* away at something higher than creep speed. Jerry heard the 1MC announce, "Secure from ROV and Manta stations."

For a few hours, anyway, Jerry thought to himself.

"It's clean," Patterson announced. "You can get more radiation standing next to a smoke detector. It's safe to work on."

"All right," barked Foster. "You heard the lady. Let's get it turned around."

Recharging Huey's batteries would take the longest—twelve hours. In the meantime, they would wash down the hull with fresh water, drain and flush the trim tank, check every system on the ROV, and replace the fiber-optic control cable cassette. The extensive post-operation maintenance requirements were the main reason why they carried two ROVs. While one was out collecting data, the other would be undergoing preparations for the next mission.

That afternoon during lunch Dr. Patterson presented the wardroom with the results of the samples' analysis. Several of the chiefs also attended, including Reynolds and Foster.

"The contents of the aircraft and the single container was spent nuclear fuel," announced Patterson excitedly. "The analysis of the soil samples from those locations showed cesium-137, cobalt-60, and various uranium and plutonium isotopes, all of which are consistent with spent fuel. The barge's contents were a mix of solid waste, consisting mostly of cobalt-60 and strontium-90. Surprisingly, there seems to be very little migration of the contamination from the dumpsites."

Patterson then went and described the potential effects these radioactive elements could have on the local environment once the containers had corroded sufficiently. She further alluded to the fact that as shocking as the results were from this initial sortie, that it was only the tip of a very large iceberg and that even more egregious sites were sure to be discovered.

Patterson concluded her briefing by saying that, with the exception of the An-12, everything was largely in agreement with the Yablokov Commission Report and that they were now ready to begin looking for new dumpsites in the morning.

When she finished, Master Chief Reynolds asked, "Ma'am, with yours and the Captain's permission, I think the whole crew might like to hear about this. Can we put that map up on the mess decks? I think it's important that they know what this is all about."

Hardy looked at Patterson, almost expecting her to say no, but the doctor smiled. "Do you think so?" she asked. "If they're interested, I could give a little presentation. It wouldn't be too technical, of course . . ."

"Doctor," Reynolds interrupted. "Almost all of the men have at least a passing knowledge of nuclear physics. And their specialties demand knowledge of electronics or engineering. I think you should, if you'll pardon the pun, give them a full dose."

Her smile tilted a little bit, but Patterson replied, "All right, COB, whatever you think. Half an hour? When?"

They arranged a series of three half-hour lectures, one for each watch section, tentatively titled, "The effects of radioactive waste on the environment."

While they worked out the details, Jerry thought he saw Captain Hardy smile.

⑰ Disappointment

The first excursion into Oga Guba had been a long one and the Manta's batteries were sorely depleted. It took almost eight hours for them to recharge, during which Jerry tried working on the division's paperwork and the next item in his qual book. Unfortunately, he got hauled into the planning sessions for the next series of sorties and had to spend a lot of time with Patterson and the Captain instead. So, while the batteries were recharging, Jerry worked with the two of them and Emily to develop a search plan for the rest of Oga Guba. Since Emily's ROV's didn't have the speed or endurance to conduct extensive searching, the task fell entirely on the Manta—and by default, Jerry.

Russian territorial waters extended twelve miles from the coast, but the Manta's acoustic modem only had a maximum range of seven and a half miles. That made it possible to search much of the littoral. And while Patterson made it clear that she would have preferred searching all the way to the shoreline, it was just for the sake of thoroughness. From the Yablokov and Bellona reports on the Kara Sea dumping grounds, there seemed to be no rhyme or reason to the Soviet's disposal methods.

"The Soviets didn't appear to have any organized system for where they dumped their radioactive waste," complained Patterson. "They scuttled a nuclear submarine in twenty meters of water, dumped defueled reactors in seventy-five meters, and ordinary solid waste in the deep trench to the east of the island. Any bottom type, any depth, inside or out of territorial waters, it didn't matter. And Soviet records are so poor they can only say the number of waste containers is somewhere between six and eleven thousand."

Jerry had heard the statistic before, and waited patiently for Dr. Patterson to refocus on the search plan. She was demanding, arrogant, and impatient, but she knew her stuff and she obviously cared.

"All we have to do is find evidence of new containers being dumped, that the Russian government is no better than their predecessors. We can then alert the world to the threat and also cement the President's position as an environmental leader!"

"And to find those containers, we need to decide where we are going to look." Hardy's reminder snapped Patterson out her reverie. "Doctor, you're the expert here. Where should we search?"

She sighed heavily. Annoyed that Hardy didn't just get the political ramifications of the mission. "It doesn't really matter. One spot is as good as another."

They picked five search areas, all roughly of the same size and slightly overlapping each other. By the time they were done, it was a little after 1600. Patterson headed aft to finish working on the results from the samples, and Hardy disappeared into his stateroom.

The Manta's batteries would be fully charged by 1930 that evening, so that gave him just over three hours to do all the things that he was supposed to have done since breakfast that morning. And he was supposed to have the six to midnight in control. And the noon to six tomorrow. He'd miss both of them while he flew the Manta.

Jerry had to talk to the XO. He found Bair in his stateroom. "Sir, regarding my watch in control this evening . . ."

"Already taken care of," Bair interrupted. "Patterson talked to Hardy this morning, and as of now you're off the watch list."

Jerry felt a few of the bricks from the ton on his back disappear, but he was still concerned. "What about my qualifications?"

Bair smiled. "Not a problem. We'll just have you stand double watches on the way home."

"I was afraid of that, sir." Jerry replied.

"I'll give you all the help I can," Bair assured him, "but for now your only task is the Manta and supporting Dr. Davis' ROV operations. Without that, there's no mission. Let Foster run the division. Besides, you'll be almost living in the torpedo room anyway."

"Yessir," Jerry acknowledged reluctantly and headed down to his spaces. He had to find Foster and fill him in and for a moment reveled in not having to look over his shoulder while he tried to run the division.

THAT EVENING AND for the next two days, Jerry flew five sorties in Oga Guba. Before each flight, Jerry would program the search pattern into the Manta, which was smart enough to fly on autopilot once it was launched. While that would help reduce pilot fatigue and the chance of missing anything, it didn't help with the actual survey. Somebody had to watch the screen and interpret the sonar image. Captain Hardy made it clear that while the enlisted men could help with the watch, the Manta operator was the "primary sensor operator." If the Manta flew, Jerry had to be there to see what it saw.

The pace was hard. Fully charged, the Manta's battery would last for twenty hours at five knots or eight hours at ten. There was no such thing as a short sortie. Patterson and Hardy both insisted that unless the Manta was actually charging, it would be searching.

It took ten hours to charge the battery when it was flat. Jerry could bet on sleeping about half that time, but even after Bair excused him from standing watches, there was still some work he couldn't get out of.

While the Manta was charging, Hardy kept *Memphis* in motion. The sub would head away from the coast as soon as the Manta was recovered, never lurking in the same place for more than a few hours. They would head for the deepest water nearby, then loop back to take up position in time for the next sortie.

For the most part, the Russians left them alone. There were two settlements on Novaya Zemlya, both military bases. Supplies came into them by ship, but from the western side. If the Barents was the Russian Navy's front step, the Kara was more like the side yard the kids never played in.

The watches, keyed up after their distant encounters with Russian units, started to get careless as monotony set in, and with Hardy's concurrence, the XO started inserting synthetic contacts into the sonar and fire-control system. Hardy was merciless when the first contact was missed by the sonarmen for a full five minutes.

Once a day, *Memphis* carefully came to periscope depth to receive the Fleet broadcast. They would always extend the periscope with its ESM intercept antenna first, before raising one of the communication antennas, but it only picked up the fixed surveillance radars that lined the coast. Both the periscope and comms antenna were very small and were further treated with radar-absorbing material, so there was no chance of them being detected by the coastal stations.

They did find things. On Friday, the first full day of searching, on the second sortie of the day, the Manta's sonar picked up a jumble of shapes on a smooth seabed, and Davis quickly launched one of the ROVs to investigate.

While Jerry's Manta circled protectively, Huey photographed and sampled a previously unknown waste dump. At least one hundred, and maybe as many as two hundred steel waste cylinders littered a mile-square area. Half-buried in silt, Patterson and Davis estimated they'd been there thirty years or more. All were corroded, and some were cracked and obviously leaking.

Dr. Patterson could hardly contain her excitement as Davis methodically ran Huey's camera over the canisters, then carefully sampled the seabed.

"Look at all this waste! And from the initial readings, some of it is spent fuel. There must be at least ten times the amount of highly radioactive material here than was released during the Chernobyl reactor incident. Over fifteen thousand cancer-related fatalities have been linked to that environmental disaster. If this stuff spreads, it will be much, much worse," mused Patterson with awe in her voice. "If this wasn't such a remote area, this would already be an international catastrophe."

They also found a smaller site the next day on the fourth sortie. The Manta's sonar return was even more confused. When one of Emily's ROVs reached the location, its camera revealed a tangle of machinery, badly rusted, but only slightly radioactive. They were also nearly buried in silt, and it took some time for Emily, using the axial thruster, to uncover a cluster of 1970s-era machine tools. She used the ROV to photograph everything and sampled the seabed, but Patterson wanted to go further.

In the control room, she argued, "If we use the sample tube correctly, we may be able to bring back a small piece from one of the cutting surfaces. We could find out what materials they were machining."

"How radioactive would the sample be?" Hardy demanded. Every sailor in the space was thinking the same question.

"Possibly quite radioactive" she answered excitedly. "Steel absorbs neutron radiation and becomes . . ."

"Yes, Doctor," interrupted Hardy, "please remember we're on a nuclear submarine. We're familiar with the process."

"Of course, Captain," replied Patterson with a condescending tone. "The radiation hazard, as you know, is dependent on the type of steel. If it is plain carbon steel, the hazard is quite low, as most iron and carbon isotopes are beta emitters . . ."

"Electrons ejected from an isotope's nucleus that can't even penetrate a piece of paper," Hardy said impatiently. "But if that machine out there worked on irradiated stainless steel, then that means the potential for cobalt-60, which has two very nasty gamma rays. And since the ROV is detecting some gamma activity, that should concern me very much, shouldn't it, Doctor?"

Patterson, surprised by Hardy's quick appreciation of the situation, was momentarily left speechless. She briefly stared at him, reassessing his abilities, as if she were evaluating a political opponent whom she respected. "You are correct, Captain. However, I believe the risk will be minimum and we should still attempt to gain a sample if we can."

Hardy was adamant. "Very well, Doctor, but I'll only allow it if the piece is not highly radioactive. If it is, I'll have it thrown overboard in a heartbeat. I won't allow my crew to be unnecessarily exposed to a significant radiation hazard and I don't even want to think of what it would do to our radiation monitoring system."

Patterson nodded to the phone talker, now merely a senior petty officer and not the Weapons Officer. After several sorties, Hardy had relaxed a little about Jerry's abilities with the Manta, as well as Davis and her ROVs. The talker passed the decision on to Davis, who said she'd do what she could. As Huey's camera zoomed in on a cutting tool, Patterson couldn't bear to watch and headed for the torpedo room.

She arrived to find everyone manning their stations, but Emily Davis was the center of attention as she searched in the murky water for a piece small enough to fit in the sample container. Focused on the controls and the video display, she did not acknowledge Patterson's presence until she spoke.

"Dr. Davis, you need to locate a small piece of steel. Make sure it's not aluminum or plastic. And it has to be from a working surface, so it will have traces of whatever they were forming. And . . ."

"Doctor, I'm a little busy right now." Davis said. She managed to mix both patience and frustration in her tone. "This ROV is not designed to retrieve pieces of metal. I don't have a remote claw, much less a cutting tool, so I'm reduced to looking for pieces that broke or fell off the equipment when it hit the seabed. And since steel is denser than aluminum or plastic, it's probably completely buried in the silt. And I don't have a digging tool, either!" she finished sharply.

Patterson, taken aback, said, "I'm sure you're doing your best."

She didn't say anything else, but did stay and watch as Davis maneuvered the ROV near the pile of junked tools. Time after time she approached and used the thrusters to move silt away from the machinery. Then she'd wait for the water to clear so she could search the bottom.

After many tries, they were unable to find anything, but Patterson had Davis continue the search until Duey's battery ran low. Jerry was busy with the Manta, but he could see that Patterson was disappointed and argued with Emily briefly before leaving the torpedo room.

After the ROV was recovered, Jerry was waiting for the Manta, still twenty minutes away, which had been farther out. He asked Emily, "Why was that sample so important? What was she looking for?"

"Nothing specific," Davis replied, "But she's looking for a smoking gun. She doesn't have what she needs yet."

Jerry was confused. "But we've confirmed the information in those other surveys, and we've found more stuff the Soviets had dumped."

Davis shook her head. "It's not enough. The Russians cooperated with the surveys and admit they don't know where everything is. Finding some of the old missing material is good, but that's not going to make news."

She stepped away from the ROV console and the torpedomen servicing Duey. She pulled Jerry aft to a quieter spot in the torpedo room. "I've learned this much from working with Dr. Patterson. The government and the media need an immediate threat. These dumpsites are all bad, very bad, but they're not going to be a significant ecological problem for another twenty-five, maybe fifty years. President Huber can't make headlines with a problem that's half a century away."

"But we found canisters that were leaking," Jerry protested.

"It isn't spreading. They're small leaks and our sampling so far shows that the effect is highly localized. The radiation hasn't even reached the shore. Right now"—and she emphasized the word—"it's not even a threat to Novaya Zemlya, much less continental Russia, even much less Europe or the rest of the world."

Jerry smiled grimly. "So Dr. Patterson not only wants to find new radioactive waste that's been dumped since the Russians said they stopped, but she needs to find waste that has been spreading, big time."

"And she hasn't found either yet." Davis leaned closer and spoke softly. "Last night she told me that she had simply assumed the sites would be polluting the area nearby. She didn't believe the Russian or the other reports that suggested the problem was not as severe as first thought. Now she's wondering if she will find what she needs."

"It's only been three days," Jerry replied just as softly. "We've got two more weeks of surveying."

"She's not a patient person, and like I said, she just assumed the radiation would be spreading. In her business, she has to be certain of things. Now she's not sure of anything. She's getting scared, and she'll be pushing us all very hard until she finds what she needs."

AND PATTERSON DID push hard. After they finished searching Oga Guba, *Memphis* headed north for Tsivol'ska Guba. In 1966, the nuclear-powered icebreaker *Lenin* suffered a nuclear accident that killed thirty sailors. It took six years to repair her and she received a new propulsion plant. Her three old reactors were removed and dumped in the bay in 1967, along with a container loaded with damaged fuel elements.

Dr. Patterson was especially interested in the last item. "The last survey was twenty years ago. We're going over every inch of the damn thing. We'll compare the new data with the earlier survey results and see if it's leaked at all." At her direction, Davis used Dewy to thoroughly photograph every surface and then sample the seabed on two sides.

The radiation from the *Lenin* reactors was extremely high, nearly 100 rem per hour. Davidson whistled when he saw the readings and muttered in awe, "That must have been one hell of an accident." An understatement if there ever was one, but one everybody could agree with. And yet, despite the clear evidence of significant activity, neither the reactor compartment nor the spent fuel containers showed an appreciable leakage into the nearby environment.

Tsivol'ska Guba was larger and it took six sorties over three days to cover it. They found more spent solid waste canisters, a few pumps, piping, and some junked machinery, but everything was either listed in the various reports—or looked like it should have been. Jerry saw Patterson's frustration grow. After that came Sedov Guba.

During the transit north, Hardy asked Patterson if he could read the various reports she was referring to, so that he could "get smarter on the problem." With obvious delight, she handed him four sizable documents and offered to discuss them with him at his convenience. She beamed over the idea that Hardy was finally coming around and becoming more environmentally aware.

MEMPHIS ARRIVED AT Sedov Guba on the fourth of June and the search procedure was started all over again. The Yablokov report listed a collection of spent fuel canisters there, and after locating and surveying that site, Jerry and Emily flew another six collection sorties covering most of the bay.

While they found a lot of material, including solid waste canisters, a few fuel rods, and even a discarded experimental reactor vessel, it was all consistent with the Russian documentation. Everything they found had been there for decades, and while there was some leakage from corroded containers, the contamination hadn't gone very far. Like the other sites, the radiological problem appeared to be very localized.

Patterson was not getting what she needed and her desperation grew. She started taking water samples every six hours, hoping that leeched radioactive material might be collecting in pockets of water in the bay. She even talked to the Engineer, Lieutenant Commander Ho, about ways of increasing the sensitivity of the tests, on the theory that the pollution was there, but at extremely low levels.

On Wednesday the eighth, with Sedov Guba finished, the crew stood down from ROV operations for a day. Jerry was still excused from watchstanding, and he used the time to catch up on the jungle of paperwork that had flourished on his desk. The stack took up so much of his desk that he moved the whole mess to the wardroom, where he could spread it out on the table.

Emily Davis was already at work when Jerry came into the wardroom, but she quickly made room for him and his mountain of paper. Her half of the table was covered by a chart, printouts of the local tide tables, and a couple of textbooks on nuclear chemistry. "What's this about?" Jerry asked.

"It's another one of her 'ideas,'" Davis explained cynically. "She wants me to see if currents or tides could be carrying the leaking waste in toward shore."

"And that would explain the low levels elsewhere in the bays?"

"She hopes so." Davis shrugged. "It's not my area of expertise, and I don't have the best references, but I've never heard of that phenomenon. It's not supported by the other documents, and from what I can tell the local tides are all different. To suggest that this might be what's been happening in all three of the bays we've searched, just doesn't make any sense. She's pretty desperate. Right now she's in her stateroom tearing apart every environmental report she's brought with her, looking for anything that will help."

"Help prove her point?" Jerry asked.

"If she doesn't come back with enough new evidence of environmental abuses by the Soviets or the Russians, then she's finished. Her career as a presidential adviser will be over."

Jerry settled down to his paperwork while Emily continued hers. His stuff was routine admin, though, and it couldn't hold his attention. He considered Patterson's problems and his own.

If she did not find what she needed, would the mission be considered a failure? *Memphis* had been sent to survey the area and collect samples. On a reconnaissance mission, there were usually no expectations. You went, you looked, and then you reported what you saw. This mission had been ordered because of what some people expected to find. Political reputations would be gained or lost based on their patrol report.

And frankly, Jerry wasn't interested in being a part of a hyped claim of impending environmental disaster. Personally, he was glad that the contents of the drums and casks and waste containers hadn't spread. It was just bad news for people who had said with such certainty that it had. They wanted a stick to beat the Russians with, and they hadn't found one yet.

Patterson had staked her political and scientific reputation on proving a point. She'd made a promise to her boss, who happened to be the President of the United States. It was a strong reminder of why the military stayed out of politics.

ON THURSDAY, THE ninth of June, *Memphis* moved slowly into Techeniye Guba, the northernmost and last of the four bays they were to search. The crew was in good spirits, looking forward to starting for home in a few days.

Two previously surveyed sites, a lighter full of waste and a discarded reactor compartment, were located and verified. Like the other locations they'd already examined, there was little sign of the waste having spread.

At dinner that evening, some of the officers began to talk about the trip home. Four more Manta and ROV sorties over the next two days would cover the bay, and then they'd be finished.

Dr. Patterson listened to the conversation quietly, but Jerry could see she was not happy. She hadn't been all day and now she spoke. "Captain Hardy, I'd like to extend the survey."

"What?" Hardy's surprised outburst caused the officers to jump out of their seats.

"I want to add some more sites to the search plan, perhaps even cover another bay."

"Doctor, I can't see the point of remaining here any longer. It only increases the risk of the Russians . . ."

"But we haven't found what we were looking for!" she interrupted.

"Doctor, you've surveyed four previously known dumps and located over a dozen new ones. We've collected samples and photographic evidence."

"It's not enough. We've been looking for evidence of new waste being dumped or that the old waste had been entering the environment in significant amounts and we've found neither."

"Maybe it's not there to find." Hardy's bland statement was logical, but Jerry knew the effect it would have on Patterson. If it was true, then her plans were ruined.

"And maybe we just haven't found it yet. We've only surveyed a fraction of the coastline. With more time . . ."

"Which we don't have," Hardy reminded her sharply. "You were on a tight schedule. We increased speed to get here, and we're going to have to hurry on the way back."

"Even an extra day would help. I know there's that much margin."

"Which means, what, another two or three Manta sorties? We've done twenty so far and have another four planned. What will two more provide us in terms of definitive evidence?" Hardy softened his tone slightly. "Doctor, you've convinced me of the danger to the environment that these dumpsites presents, but maybe it will take longer than you think to spread." Paterson's expression showed how worried she was that Hardy might be right.

Jerry expected Patterson to order Hardy to comply, to threaten him if he didn't cooperate, but she simply sat there, silently. Finally she said softly, "I'll just have to hope we find more in this bay than we did in the others."

The next day Jerry's Manta began searching Techeniye Guba. Within an hour, he found a cluster of spent fuel canisters. On the second sortie, a pile of junked pumps and other propulsion-related machinery. The ROVs' investigations showed that neither presented the kind of immediate threat that Dr. Patterson was now longing for. Disappointed, she pushed Jerry hard to keep the Manta out as long as possible and shared her frustration with anyone that came within earshot.

On the second day, during the third Manta sortie, Jerry picked up a large contact on the sonar. It was so large it couldn't be anything but a barge or a small ship of some sort.

"Maybe it's a submarine," Patterson speculated as Davis sent Huey to investigate. She'd come to the torpedo room as soon as Jerry had reported the contact, even though there was little she could do. She double-checked Davis' navigation and went over the battery figures to compute how much time they'd have once they got there. Finally a request from Hardy for her to return to the control room left Jerry and everyone else grateful for his intervention.

Jerry's Manta took up its customary protective circle while Huey approached the contact. Emily kept the ROV well away from the seabed, both to keep from stirring up the bottom and so they could get an overall look at whatever it was.

About twenty feet away, the ROV's camera finally revealed the edge of a large structure. Stanchions and lifelines identified it as some sort of vessel. She passed the camera down its flat sides to a square-cut end. After some inspection, they were able to determine that it was the stern.

The radiation count was low, barely above background—just a faint gamma count. "So whatever's in there is either well contained or there is very little in terms of radioactive material," Jerry surmised. More disappointment for Dr. Patterson.

But what was in there? Patterson's voice joined them on the circuit, impatient with passing questions through a phone talker. As they speculated, Emily Davis continued to search the exterior of the barge with the ROV's camera. It was a lot like looking at an elephant through a keyhole. If she moved far enough back to get a larger view, the water completely obscured her view, so she was limited to examining one small patch of the hull at a time.

The barge carried no markings, which was not unusual. The almost complete absence of marine growth and corrosion indicated that it had been there for only about ten years or so. "So the late '80s or early '90s, right?" Davis asked on the circuit. Patterson concurred.

It had settled neatly on the bottom, scuttled by what appeared to be ballast-tank-like sections along the fore and aft ends. The top of the barge also appeared to have what looked like valve connections, possibly for compressed air lines or to attach a pump of some sort. Whatever this barge was, it looked like it was made to be recovered.

"But what is it?" Patterson asked over the circuit. "The Soviets built specialized barges to hold spent fuel containers. This isn't the same design."

The deck of the barge was covered with three hatches, presumably leading down to the cargo hold. One of the hatches lay partially open, leaving a small opening that managed to look both inviting and menacing at the same time.

"Probably popped open by a buildup of air pressure as the barge sank," speculated Davis on the circuit.

"We've got to take a look in there," Patterson declared.

Howard, the enlisted phone talker, added, "Captain Hardy says 'Do not go into the hatchway.'"

Patterson's voice was just as insistent. "I'm sure we can maneuver the ROV inside."

Davis tried to speak. "Dr. Patterson, the ROV . . ."

Howard's voice came on again. "Captain Hardy wants to see Dr. Davis in control right now."

Davis replied, "Tell the Captain I can't leave my station while the ROV is operating."

There was a pause on the circuit, and then Howard said, "Captain Hardy and Dr. Patterson are on their way down." His tone carried the message, "Look out."

Although *Memphis* was at patrol quiet, with all normal machinery operating, Jerry heard them coming before they even got to the torpedo room. Hardy's voice carried through the door forward. ". . . will not risk losing . . ."

Dr. Patterson cut him off. "If we don't take a few risks, we won't accomplish our mission."

"Madam," answered Hardy sharply, "we're submerged in poorly charted shoal waters, sending remotely operated vehicles into Russian territory so we can survey radioactive waste. That's quite enough risk for me."

Patterson burst through the door first and immediately started grilling Emily. "Dr. Davis, how hard would it be to send the ROV through that opening to see what's in the cargo hold? I told the Captain that there would be little or no risk, because of your skill with the vehicles."

Flustered by the question, Davis delayed. "There are many risks we have to consider. Beyond the obvious one of snagging the cable or breaking it, we don't know how well Huey will be able to maneuver if we go inside. And how stable is the cargo? Will he be trapped by debris? It might be dislodged by the wash from the thruster. And the silt in there could make it so murky we'd be blind in any case."

Hardy pounced on her statement. "So you think the risks are too great." He sounded satisfied. Patterson managed to scowl at both Davis and Hardy at the same time.

Seeing Patterson's expression, Davis answered truthfully, "I am curious, too, sir."

"Curiosity is not a good enough reason for risking a multimillion-dollar ROV and the covertness of this mission. Imagine the Russians' surprise if they discovered a ROV entangled in the cargo hold of a barge inside their territorial waters."

"Oh, and do you think they come here and check often?" Patterson's tone was acidic.

Davis raised a hand. "Captain, Doctor, we're using up Huey's batteries while we argue. Why don't I maneuver over the open hatch, point the camera down, and see what we can see?"

Hardy couldn't argue with that—and didn't. Patterson just smiled broadly. Jerry had to force himself to watch the Manta's display, stealing only occasional glances at the ROV's video screen.

Emily approached the barge slowly, careful to use a path as clear of obstructions as possible. With a delicate touch, she lowered the ROV to deck level, with the camera and light overhanging the open hatch. She panned the lens back and forth.

The inside of the hold revealed only dark, angular shadows. It was an unsatisfying image and Patterson clearly wanted more. "Shift the ROV a little," she ordered. "Maybe if the light comes in at a different angle . . ."

"Yes," Davis answered softly. Skillfully, she backed Huey away and then approached again, so that the light came in from another direction, almost ninety degrees off the earlier view. It was no more revealing, although combining the two views suggested rectangular boxes or crates—a lot of them.

"We have to send the ROV in," Patterson insisted.

"What's the radiation reading?" Hardy temporized.

"Very slight, only 10 millirem per hour," Davis reported. "The cargo is radioactive, but what it is I can't imagine. It certainly doesn't look like spent fuel."

"Those are not spent fuel containers," Patterson declared. "At least they're no shape I've ever seen or read of." She looked at Hardy and put her hand on his arm. "Please, Captain."

Almost startled by her polite intensity, Hardy nodded silently to Davis, who settled herself and took a deep breath.

"First. I'm going to inspect the edge of the hatchway. I want to make sure that there are no sharp edges or hidden snags." She panned the camera over all four sides of the opening at maximum magnification. The edges were smooth and regular and were covered with a layer of fine silt. "I'm going to reposition," she announced and backed the ROV off.

The new path brought Huey in at a forty-five-degree angle, so that its length lay across the corners of the hatch, not its edges. She came up to the opening, paused, then scanned the camera in all directions before moving forward. After a few yards, she paused and looked again. It took two more pauses before Davis was satisfied with the Huey's position in the hatchway.

She gently lowered the ROV, angling the thruster to move it vertically. While everyone was curious about the cargo, Emily kept the cameras pointed at the edge of the hatch so she could gauge Huey's movements.

She let Huey settle until the ROV was well clear of the hatchway, at least four feet overhead. The camera's view was being obscured by silt, but not too badly. "I'm killing the motors," she suddenly announced. "There won't be a current here." Hopefully the neutrally buoyant ROV would hover, motionless, as the sediment settled.

When she pointed the camera down, the image was reasonably clear. They could see the cargo hold, perhaps thirty or forty feet long, running across the width of the barge. It was filled by rectangular boxes, about half the length of the ROV. They had obviously been stacked in two layers in the hold, but had been jostled around somewhat by the sinking.

Risking a short puff of the thruster, Davis pivoted Huey in place, but the rest of the hold simply held more boxes.

"I'm going to approach one," she announced and lightly touched the controls. The ROV drifted forward, and within a few moments, she was just two yards away from the stacked objects.

"That is not a waste container," Patterson repeated. "Look at it. It's a case or a crate. See the latches and the lid? That isn't how you seal a container of radioactive waste."

"It is if you're a Soviet bureaucrat," answered Hardy. "Especially one who doesn't give a fig about the consequences. I agree it wasn't built to hold waste, but that's doesn't tell us what's inside there now."

"Except that it's radioactive, but not all that much." Emily added, looking at the meter.

"How about unspent fuel rods?" Hardy suggested.

Patterson shrugged. "That's a funny way to store them, and it's a lot of them to store. See if you can find any markings."

Emily slowly maneuvered Huey in the hold, bringing the camera to bear on the tops and sides of several boxes. While they may have had markings, they had been sloppily but thoroughly sprayed over with black paint. Only a Cyrillic R, in black, was visible on one of the box ends.

Watching the battery level, Davis finally announced. "I'm bringing Huey out. We need to come home."

"Wait!" ordered Patterson. "Can we take a sample in here?"

"Of what?" asked Hardy.

"At least get a water sample," Patterson insisted and Emily complied. First, she stirred up the silt with Huey's thruster, so that some of the sediment would be included in the sample.

Even as the sample was being collected, Davis carefully positioned the ROV, then ascended through the hatch. This time, with experience and the open water ahead of her, she maneuvered it more surely. She still had to be careful of the thin fiber-optic cable, making sure it did not loop around an obstruction or snag on a jagged surface.

"Take another sample here, right next to the hull," Patterson directed, although as Davis positioned Huey and started the sequence, Jerry thought she looked unsatisfied.

Davis had barely started the ROV toward *Memphis* when Patterson said, "Captain, I need to open one of those cases. We have to see what's inside them."

Astounded, Hardy firmly replied. "Out of the question, Doctor. We've talked about this before. I won't bring anything radioactive that doesn't fit in the sample tubes aboard *Memphis*. And just how did you intend to examine it?"

"With the divers. And they wouldn't have to bring it aboard if they opened it there, in the hold."

That suggestion froze Jerry's blood solid. Send them into there, to open one of those cases?

Hardy was gentler with her idea than Jerry would have expected. "Dr. Patterson, you don't know what you're asking."

"It's shallow enough. And they wouldn't have to do anything complicated. Just swim in and open a case."

"Exposing them to whatever's inside," Hardy added. "What if it's toxic or highly radioactive? We don't know what those cases are made of, so we certainly can't estimate their shielding qualities. You know that even a small amount of material would constitute a dangerous dose to anyone in close proximity. I won't risk anyone just to satisfy your curiosity."

"But this is what we've been looking for! We can't go back with the site unidentified."

"Doctor, even if I were to agree with you, the barge is miles inside Russian waters. I'd have to bring *Memphis* in close just so that they could make the swim, and I'm not allowed to enter Russian territory. They'd be unhappy enough about ROVs and the samples if they knew."

"But we've hardly seen any Russian ships or planes. Can't you just look at the chart?" she wheedled. "If we can get close enough, it's just a short swim . . ."

Hardy's voice showed more irritation. "I will not look at the chart because to do so might imply that there was a chance we'd actually do this. My orders are absolute, and I will remind you that you helped write those orders, and they are orders not just from the Chief of Naval Operations but the President himself."

Dr. Patterson looked at Davis, as if for support, but Emily's expression was carefully neutral. The silence in the torpedo room stretched on until, with nothing to say and thunderclouds on her brow, Patterson quickly walked out, almost running, to escape her frustration.

Hardy looked more than concerned, and Jerry wondered how this would read in her mission report—and Hardy's. Finally the Captain's features softened. He ordered, "Inform control as soon as you've recovered both the vehicles" and then he left.

 **In Earnest**

June 11, 2005

●●●●●●●●●●●●●●●●●●●●●●●●●●●●●●●●

Techeniye Guba, Novaya Zemlya

Late that afternoon, Jerry programmed the Manta for the fourth and last sortie. He still wondered about the barge they'd found earlier, but he wasn't curious enough to go back and take a closer look.

He'd done enough diving to know that going inside a wreck was always hazardous. He'd never done it himself, but had heard plenty of horror stories about wreck divers who had come to grief. It was interesting, and exciting, and he'd try it someday, but not on an unknown vessel in foreign territory. Add the likely risk of radiation poisoning and it became a Very Bad Idea.

As they took stations for launch, Jerry didn't know what to hope for. If they found nothing, Patterson would become even more frustrated. But he couldn't feel sorry for someone who was hoping for bad news—especially someone who needed it for political gain. And the practical part of him, a very large part of him, actually, reminded himself that hoping wouldn't change what was actually there.

Still, as the Manta ran its pattern, he found himself watching the screen as closely as he could. Nothing turned up for over two hours. When they finally detected something, though, it wasn't the Manta.

"All stations, control, we have a Bear Foxtrot close aboard," said the control room phone talker with urgency. With *Memphis* in shallow water, an ASW plane in the neighborhood could become a nightmare.

"Rig ship for ultra-quiet," announced the 1MC. Jerry could hear the ventilation fans being secured as *Memphis* stove to reduce her acoustic signature.

Hardy's voice soon came on the sound-powered phone circuit. "Mr. Mitchell, I'm moving *Memphis* to deeper water immediately. How quickly can you follow with the Manta?" Even as Hardy asked the question, Jerry felt the sub begin a gentle turn to port.

Jerry still had over half the battery on the Manta. "I've got about four hours at ten knots. That's my best quiet speed," he added, anticipating Hardy's next question.

"Then do it, mister. My speed will be five knots, course zero seven five."

"Course zero seven five, U-bay aye." Jerry killed the search program and sent a command to the Manta to head east. He also sent it as deep as the bottom allowed. Like Hardy with a smaller version of *Memphis*, he felt exposed and vulnerable in shallow water. At the same time, also like *Memphis*, he couldn't use higher speed to escape to deeper water because the wake from the Manta's passage might be visible on the surface.

"Sonar, U-bay. Where is the Bear now?"

"U-bay, sonar. He's passing down our starboard side. To the south, passing west to east."

Hence Hardy's angling *Memphis* slightly north. Jerry mimicked the larger sub's movements and ordered the Manta to the same course. He was more interested in avoiding detection than rejoining *Memphis* at this point. He had the range and speed to get it home.

The most immediate threat was a MAD detection. The Bear Foxtrot carried a magnetic anomaly detector in a short stinger on its tail. *Memphis'* seven thousand tons of steel created a significant bend in the local magnetic field. With her so shallow, if the plane passed within half a mile, it would probably get a MAD hit.

The next biggest threat was sonobuoys. Would the Bear drop a field? Why would it choose this spot to do so? Was it looking for *Memphis* because someone had detected them? They hadn't encountered any ASW planes in the nearly two weeks they'd been in the Kara Sea. Was this just a random patroller? Was it on a training flight?

Jerry got that "submariner feeling," the urge to crouch, an itch between his shoulder blades that could only be scratched by deep water. He mentally plotted an intercept with *Memphis* and adjusted the Manta's course accordingly. As it moved away from the shore, the water depth increased and Jerry concentrated on hugging the bottom. It not only reduced the Manta's detectability, but it gave him something to do.

With the Manta in a tail chase, it took over an hour to reach *Memphis*, still moving away from the coast and heading for deeper water. Hardy slowed just long enough for Jerry to recover the Manta and then he increased speed, moving farther and farther away from the coastline.

Jerry headed up to control, curious about the Bear. He found Hardy and the XO standing over the plotting table, occasionally staring at the plane's track on the fire-control display, or at least the portion that *Memphis* had observed. Several classified documents were open, including one titled *Russian Northern Fleet Operational Deployments, 2003–2004*.

Bair read from another booklet with a red-striped cover. "The nearest airfield known to have Tu-142 Bear Foxtrots is at Arkhangel'sk. That's about six hundred miles as the seagull files."

"That's a long way to come," Hardy commented darkly.

"Not for a Bear, sir. He's got great legs. But it's a good distance for a training mission, about an hour and a half each way."

"If that was a training mission, they almost hit the jackpot. I don't like it, XO, it's too damn coincidental."

"What would they have done if they'd spotted us?" asked Patterson.

"Reported us. Sent more planes to track us," ventured Hardy.

"Lined up the Northern Fleet across the north edge of the Kara Sea," added Bair. "They'd be mad as hornets to find us here, but they'd also do everything possible to keep us from leaving, at least until they had proof of our presence."

"But we're in international waters," protested Patterson.

Hardy answered, "If they detect us, they may or may not get a good fix on our position. We certainly wouldn't do anything to help them. Skirting the twelve-mile limit like we've been, a Russian commander would be reasonable to assume we're in his waters—or have been—until proven otherwise. We, or more properly, the U.S. Government, would have to provide proof that we weren't. And along the way explain why we're there at all."

"Messy. Embarrassing." Bair commented.

"And bad for the mission." Hardy added. "If I had my druthers, Doctor, I'd head north right now and call it a mission." Seeing the panicked expression on her face, he quickly added, "But I owe you one more Manta sortie." His expression was grim as he said it and he cautioned, "But we will leave the area the instant we've finished searching Techeniye Guba, or if I see another Russian naval unit. I get the feeling we've used up our good luck."

They remained in deep water, well off the coast, for several more hours. There was no point in returning any sooner, because the Manta had to recharge its batteries.

As the UUV neared its full charge, Hardy brought *Memphis* back in position at little more than creep speed. He picked a spot that put the Manta in range of its search area, but also left *Memphis* a short distance from deeper water, or as deep as it got in the Kara Sea.

The launch was routine, although as it lifted off, Jerry could feel his nerve endings extending out into the Manta. In the back of his mind, he was calculating how quickly he could recover the vehicle if another Bear appeared.

With Hardy keeping *Memphis* on the sixty-fathom curve, it took the Manta half an hour to reach the near edge of the planned search area—the last one. Although Jerry paid careful attention to the display, he couldn't keep from thinking about the end of the mission and marking the time left until the Manta was finished.

Just over an hour into the search, Emily Davis came into the torpedo room. Her manner was anxious and hurried, although she'd walked softly because the sub was at ultra-quiet routine. She came straight over to Jerry. With a dead serious expression, she said, "You have to come with me to control, Jerry."

Puzzled, Jerry replied, "I can't leave my station while the Manta is out searching."

"Yes, you can. You *have* to. Davidson can watch the display for you, and besides, it doesn't matter anymore."

The urgency in her voice combined with her last statement piqued Jerry's curiosity. Reluctantly, he followed her up to the control room. As they were climbing the ladder, he asked Emily what had changed, but she only shook her head and kept moving.

As they approached the control room, they could hear Patterson arguing with Hardy. Trying to expand the area of the Manta's sortie, her voice carried out into the passageway. "All I'm asking for is for a couple more Manta runs to expand the search . . ."

They walked in to see both Patterson and Hardy bent over one of the plotting tables, his expression one of strained patience, hers desperate.

"Out of the question, Dr. Patterson. We are finishing up the last of twenty-four sorties, and we have nothing to gain by adding more," Hardy said firmly.

"Even if we managed to find one site that met your criteria, it wouldn't change your findings significantly. Let's face it, Doctor, the environmental threat you pitched to the President isn't here. It might be, in a few decades, but not now . . ."

"Excuse me, Captain," said Emily politely.

". . . and I don't intend to risk being detected," continued Hardy, "just to bail your political butt out of the sling you put it in!"

Enraged by Hardy's accusation, Patterson lashed out. "How dare you suggest that I . . ."

"Dr. Patterson, please," pleaded Emily.

"I'm not going to debate this further. We're leaving as soon as the Manta . . ."

"As the mission commander, I say when we leave, not you or anyone . . ."

"Would you two shut up!" Emily yelled angrily.

An abrupt silence formed in control, as everyone was utterly astonished by Emily's uncharacteristic outburst. All the watchstanders focused intently on their controls and indications; no one dared look back toward the plotting tables, out of fear that they'd meet either the Captain's or Patterson's gaze.

"I beg your pardon," demanded Hardy after the shock wore off.

"I'm sorry, sir, but I've had enough of your fighting," protested Emily. "You two sound just like my parents. You're just as stubborn, self-centered, and pompous as they are. Well, now you two are going to listen to me."

Hardy and Patterson briefly looked at each other with confusion, and then back at the mouse that just roared. "Emily, what is the meaning of this?" questioned Patterson defensively.

Before Emily could answer, Hardy finally noticed Jerry standing there. Embarrassed, Hardy demanded, "Mr. Mitchell, why aren't you at your station?"

Davis answered for him. "We've got a problem, Captain, a very big problem. And it involves him as much as the rest of us." Davis answered urgently. She then handed Patterson a computer printout and waited silently while she scanned the results. Hardy and Jerry both waited as well, the Captain glaring at Jerry, who fervently hoped whatever was on that paper would justify his being here.

Patterson's face became a mask, so neutral that Jerry guessed she was struggling to control her emotions. She sat down suddenly and then looked around. By now, everyone in control was watching.

She started explaining. "All of the samples we take contain various amounts of radioactive material. Cesium, cobalt, uranium, strontium, whatever might show up in fuel, spent fuel, or other radioactive materials. It's usually a mix of all of them, and the combination is a good way to identify the kind of waste. With some combinations, we can even identify the type of reactor they came from."

She held up the printout. "This gamma-ray spectrum analysis doesn't show any of the elements that we'd expect from any type of nuclear fuel, spent or otherwise. It's remarkably uniform, too uniform. Emily, have you double-checked the results?"

"I triple-checked it, Doctor. There was no trace of fission products, activation products, uranium or any of the other plutonium isotopes. The readings are consistent with essentially pure plutonium-239–weapons-grade plutonium-239."

Jerry's mind raced as Emily delivered the stark conclusion of her analysis. Pu-239 is one of many plutonium isotopes that typically showed up in small amounts in spent nuclear fuel, particularly fuel that had a lot of Uranium-238 in it. They had found trace amounts of Pu-239, along with five other isotopes, on the seabed at many of the sites they had surveyed. But it was impossible for concentrated Pu-239 to exist in spent fuel. It had to be extracted and purified, and this took human effort. He watched Captain Hardy go through the same thought process and saw his expression become a mixture of caution and concern. "What's the chance of a false reading?"

Patterson answered. "None. The tests are based . . ."

"I'll take your word for it." He looked around, then asked the group, "Can anyone think of a good reason, no matter how bizarre, for weapons-grade nuclear material to be on a sunken barge in the Kara Sea?" He turned to face Bair. "XO?"

"I can think of a lot of reasons, but none of them are good." Bair smiled as he said it, but it was a worried smile.

Patterson was pale, but spoke firmly. "Captain, we have to go back and find out every scrap of information about that barge. When it was scuttled, exactly what is in the hold, what's in those cases . . ."

Hardy cut her off. "I agree. I don't like it. In fact, I hate it, but I agree. Mr. Mitchell, get the Manta back here ASAP. Use maximum speed. XO, as soon as the Manta's recovered, head *Memphis* toward the barge. Work with Mr. O'Connell to find the closest spot on the forty-fathom curve to the barge's location. I want a fast approach and a clear exit path."

Hardy stopped to look at Jerry. "Mister, what are you still doing here?" Jerry took that as a dismissal. As he left, he heard Hardy say, "And get me the COB!"

As soon as the Manta was stowed, *Memphis* began working her way toward the barge and into shallow water. As nervous as Hardy was about shallow water, the divers would need as short a swim as possible. It would also reduce the time that *Memphis* was vulnerable, with men outside her hull.

The XO led a hasty planning meeting in the wardroom. Jerry immediately volunteered to be one of the divers, but Bair killed the idea. "We'll need you here to drive the Manta, Jerry. You are going to carry the swimmers over to the barge and bring them back."

He turned to Reynolds. "COB, how fast can the Manta go with you and Harris hanging on?" ET2 Harris was the third ship's diver. "The Manta can do up to twenty."

The COB smiled and said, "Anything over five knots will require a harness. If we rig harnesses to the attachment points and it tows us, maybe ten knots. But I'd want to work up to that speed slowly," he added quickly.

One of the quartermasters hurriedly knocked on the wardroom door and leaned in. "XO, the Captain says we'll be on station in twenty-five minutes."

The XO looked at Davis. "You'll need to launch one of the ROVs first. We'll need its camera and lights for the COB and Harris so they can rig the Manta and attach themselves to it."

"They can only do that after I've launched it," Jerry reminded him. "The docking skirt is too close to the tie-down points. They're the same ones they use to hoist the Manta off the boat."

"Understood," answered the XO, "just hold it steady for them."

Reynolds didn't look happy. "XO, sir, this is a really complicated dive. We're moving too fast. I can't build a proper dive plan. What if we leave a tool behind on the sub? What if the Russians show up again? What about the crates?"

Bair nodded. "I agree with you, COB, but the Captain wants this done

ASAP. I'm beginning to agree with him that the Bear was no accident. We're on borrowed time. We do this quickly, then we leave the neighborhood forthwith."

He sighed. "Dr. Patterson's rigging a sample container that will be radiation-proof. We're hoping that whatever's in those crates will fit inside. You'll have cameras to take photographs. Dr Davis will monitor the radiation with the ROV and will flash the danger sign if the reading is too high. And the instant you get that signal, you drop everything and hop the Manta for a fast ride home. We'll stand by with a decontamination team ready, just in case."

The meeting ended as quickly as it had been held. Davis went to help Patterson and Jerry went aft to help the COB and Harris with their preparations.

Sometimes it is necessary for men to go topside when a submarine is underway. Because of the low freeboard and the chance of being washed over the side, subs carry safety harnesses. Similar to a parachute rig, they could be attached to a special track in the hull. It was simple to adapt two so they could use the lift points on the Manta. What wasn't simple was fitting the harnesses to Reynolds and Harris on top of all their diving gear.

By the time they arranged the straps so they didn't interfere with the tanks or tools or the ability to move, Hardy was calling for Jerry to launch the Manta.

"I don't have a camera, but the passive sonar should pick up taps on the hull," Jerry reminded them.

"Yessir," answered the COB. "Just keep the active sonar off while we are in front of the Manta. I hate getting pinged. It feels like someone is hitting you with a two-by-four." At close range, the pressure wave generated by an active sonar could stun a diver.

Jerry grinned reassuringly. "I'll pull the breaker and red-tag the switch." Then more seriously, he added, "I wish I was going with you, Master Chief."

"In a sense, you will be, since you'll be flying that UUV that we'll be riding—and that's pretty important to Harris and me." Reynolds then reached over and grasped Jerry by the shoulder. "Actually, I'm glad you'll be on the boat." Jerry's puzzled expression caused Reynolds to grin. "Mr. Mitchell, you're damn good with that Manta. Not to put you under any undue pressure, mind you, but I'm expecting you to bring us home."

Reynolds extended his hand; Jerry grasped it firmly and said, "Count on it, COB. Good luck and be safe."

"Always, sir," said Reynolds, winking.

Jerry turned and left them by the forward escape trunk with two enlisted men. Between the COB and Harris and net full of tools, it would take two cycles to get them all outside.

By the time he reached the torpedo room, Emily already had Huey out and trained on the Manta hangar. Jerry started the launch sequence and realized that although he'd watched films of the prototype Manta being launched, he'd actually never seen the launch from *Memphis*.

The hangar was a raised rectangle halfway back the hull, about where it started narrowing toward the screw at the stern. The Manta nestled in a cutout, half-buried to reduce drag and flow noise when *Memphis* was underway. As Jerry released the latches, the Manta, slightly buoyant, slowly floated up and away.

The standard launch sequence automatically positioned the Manta five hundred yards off the sub's port or starboard beam. This was out of the question, so instead Jerry overrode the sequence and just did his best to hold the UUV stationary over the aft hull. He resisted the temptation to bring the Manta forward to the divers. They'd discussed it in the wardroom, but even with the ROV's camera to help him see, it wasn't built for close-in maneuvering. He couldn't guarantee that the Manta wouldn't strike the sub—or God forbid, one of the divers.

Memphis floated, dead in the water and neutrally buoyant, in forty fathoms of water. Although Hardy would have preferred hugging the bottom, he'd brought her shallow, to a keel depth of eighty feet. Since *Memphis* stood sixty feet from her keel to the top of the sail, that left precious little water above them, but it made the divers' job a lot easier. At sixty feet, they had almost an hour to get to the barge, enter, open a crate, retrieve a sample, and then return. At a depth of ninety feet, they would have had only thirty minutes.

It was hard to trim the Manta to neutral buoyancy. Jerry found he had to use a little motion to keep the slightly buoyant UUV from rising. He concentrated on keeping the nose down and moving as slowly as possible. He also had to tell Emily what he was doing, so she could anticipate his movements and keep the lights and camera properly positioned. It was dark enough at this depth so that the lights were essential. Without Huey's lights, Reynolds and Harris might never find the Manta. Luckily, only Huey had a control cable. If both vehicles had used wires for control and maneuvered so closely, they would constantly risk entangling them.

He waited impatiently for Reynolds and Harris to reach the Manta. It was easy for Jerry to imagine, or remember, what it felt like as the water filled the escape lock—the cold and the pressure. This wasn't sport diving off some colorful tropical reef. It was hard to move quickly or gracefully, and you couldn't waste time. It was work. The dry suit mitigated the cold, but it still sucked the energy out of your arms and legs, turning them to wood.

It took five minutes for the two divers to appear in the screen and reach the Manta. There was no way to find out the reason for the delay. They might have tangled a harness or had problems with the tools, but whatever it had been, they were ready to proceed.

There were three lift points on top of the Manta, and Reynolds and Harris dragged the cargo net to the first one, located in the center of the forward part of the vehicle. After hooking up the bag without incident, they swam aft. As the Manta broadened out into a pair of wings, there were two more points, one on each side of the tail. Jerry watched through the ROV's camera as Reynolds made sure Harris was secure, then attached himself.

"All right, I'm turning to port and I'll bring up the speed slowly to five knots."

"Understood," Emily replied.

Jerry gingerly applied some speed and turned the Manta toward the barge, wanting to hurry but moving slowly because of the divers. Davis managed to keep the Manta in the camera's lens, even as she turned to follow. The plan was to keep the Manta in front of Huey so they could watch the divers for any sign of trouble.

As he increased speed, ordering the Manta from three to four to five knots, Jerry also carefully watched the Manta as well as the divers. There was no way to predict the effects of the weight and drag on the Manta's speed or stability—or its battery life, he added, while glancing at the display. There was no perceptible feedback through the controller. The Manta was normally well behaved, but they were outside the design envelope here, and he had no way to tell what it would do.

The Manta's passive sonar picked up two raps. That was the Master Chief saying everything was all right—if you could call being buffeted by freezing water all right.

"I'm increasing speed to eight knots."

"Matching," Davis answered.

Again Jerry slowly picked up the pace, and again the Master Chief signaled that all was well. Finally, the Manta and Huey reached ten knots as they made their way into Russian territorial waters.

The barge lay a mile and half away in ten fathoms of water. The bottom shelved rapidly near the barge, but this was as close as *Memphis* could get without crossing the twelve-mile limit. At five knots, that meant eighteen minutes just to reach the barge. Ten knots would halve that time, if the two could stand the ride.

Jerry waited to hear three taps on the Manta's hull. That was the signal to slow down, or for trouble, but he heard nothing.

With the divers on the Manta's back, he could now safely operate the active sonar to locate the barge. Jerry kept the number of transmissions down, just in case someone might be out there listening, and he only updated the barge's position so that he wasn't flying blind.

They found the barge quickly enough, and Jerry gingerly steered the Manta the last few hundred yards. He managed to bring it close alongside and watched in Huey's camera as Reynolds and Harris detached themselves and then retrieved the tool bag. As soon as they were off, Jerry turned the Manta away from the barge. He began a tight thousand-yard circle, watching the passive display and praying that he wouldn't detect anything.

The barge looked exactly the same, but the knowledge that two men were about to enter it made it much more menacing. Jerry watched the ROV's camera as Emily took station above the barge's open hatchway. Her lights gave some general illumination, but both of *Memphis'* divers had their own lights. Jerry could see them now swimming toward the edge of the open hatch. They stopped for a moment, and Jerry wondered if there was a problem. Then he realized they were just looking the situation over, like any prudent diver. They swam down into the hatch, and Jerry tried to remember the layout of the hold. Where were the obstructions? How much had the cargo shifted?

The hatch expanded in the screen, and Davis said, "I'm sending Huey in." They'd all agreed earlier that she should do it, although there was some risk of complicating the divers' situation. It would give them more light, as well as the all-important radiation detector and the camera.

As she gingerly navigated the ROV into the hold, the camera picked up Reynolds and Harris over in one corner, well clear and dead ahead. They were studying one of the metal crates. It was almost as long as Reynolds was tall, and at least three feet square. Metal clips ran around one edge. Lifting hooks implied some weight, as did the strips that reinforced the corners and sides.

After shining a light on all exposed sides, Reynolds tried to shift the crate slightly. It budged, but gave the impression of being heavy. He motioned to Harris, pantomiming tools, and swam over to the tool bag. He handed Harris a pair of pliers while the COB took out a large screwdriver.

They started working on the clips, wasting time as they searched in the darkness for the quickest way to open them. Reynolds discovered a way to pop them with the screwdriver and began working his way along the edge. Along with that Christmas-present feeling, Jerry wondered if it was a Pandora's box. He couldn't escape a mental image of the lid opening and a cloud of liquid waste escaping, poisoning the two with toxic chemicals and radiation before they could close it again.

As Reynolds finished releasing the clips, Harris moved aside as Emily pointed Huey right at the case. "The radiation count is still very low," announced Emily. "I'm sending the 'all safe' signal." Reynolds and Harris saw the lights blink once, and Harris held up his free hand, making an exaggerated thumbs-up gesture. So far, so good.

As they'd discussed, Harris swam away, to hover near the ROV. The idea was that if the crate did contain something deadly, only one of the divers would be exposed. Jerry watched the seconds tick by as Harris reached what they hoped was a safe distance, but they'd all agreed it was worth the time.

Reynolds wedged the edge of the screwdriver into the joint between the lid and the rest of the crate. He pounded on one end, and a thin stream of silvery bubbles appeared. He stopped for a moment and made a sweeping motion with his right hand, asking for Emily to take another radiation reading. Again, everything was within limits and she flashed the lights once. Facing the ROV, Reynolds gave the thumbs-up sign and returned his attention to the lid.

Working the screwdriver in, alternately wiggling it, and pounding on the end resulted in successively larger and thicker streams of bubbles until they merged into a solid mass of air that half-lifted the lid off. Jerry could see Reynolds' surprised reaction and he backed off to give Emily some room to move Huey in a little closer and make yet another pass with the radiation detector. Huey's lights flashed once and Reynolds waved Harris over. Emily backed the ROV away from the case to give the divers room to work.

This was why Jerry had wanted to make the dive. The COB and Harris could look in the crate. They knew what was in it, but nobody else on Earth did. Except for whoever put it there, Jerry corrected himself.

The two divers knew this, and Reynolds bent down and started heaving on one side, the side away from the camera. Harris quickly realized what the COB was after and started lifting from his end. The two men quickly tilted the crate so that it toppled over onto its side, turning the top toward the camera.

A rush of air bubbles didn't obscure the view for more than a second. Emily automatically adjusted the lights and zoomed the camera to maximum magnification.

Framed by the rectangular box, a cone-shaped object lay in a cradle. It was about five feet long and two feet wide at the base. The wide end was flat, and narrowed to an almost needle-like point. It was dull green or black and its polished surface was marked by a few patches of white lettering near the base. They were looking at a full-up nuclear warhead, almost certainly a reentry vehicle for a ballistic missile.

Chills ran laps around Jerry's spine and the sailors in the torpedo room either blasphemed or made improbable sexual suggestions. After a few moments, the phone talker's voice in Jerry headphones said, "Captain Hardy wants your recommendations."

I'll bet he does, thought Jerry. Their mission orders had just changed and the trick was to figure out what they should now be. Jerry's instant reaction was to grab it and get it back to the boat, but then he forced himself to think, Why?

Nuclear warheads hidden on the sea floor. Who'd hidden them there? Why? He doubted any of the cases carried luggage tags, but if they could examine the warhead, they'd get a lot more information than they had right now.

And they'd have to have proof. Photos or samples could be dismissed or denied. Jerry had a visual flash of that thing being wheeled into a press conference.

"We've got to have it," Jerry decided out loud, and realized that he'd spoken into the microphone.

"I'm glad you concur," said Hardy's voice acidly as he came onto the circuit. "I meant about how do we get it back to the boat."

"Oh. Yessir," Jerry answered. That was a much harder question to answer. The thing must weigh hundreds of pounds. Not even Reynolds could tuck it under one arm for the ride back.

Dr. Patterson was also on the circuit. "What if they disassembled it and just brought back the physics package?"

"Out of the question," declared Hardy quickly. "It would take way too long to figure out how to get the damn thing out. And the risk of radiation exposure is way too great. No, we grab the whole thing."

"And they're running short of time," added Jerry as he checked his watch. "They can stretch it a little by running shallow on the trip back, but we have to get them out of there in ten or fifteen minutes, tops."

Patterson asked, "Can you maneuver the Manta in close enough for them to attach it?"

"No, ma'am. I can't maneuver the Manta in close quarters and it wouldn't even fit . . ."

As Jerry started to explain, the ROV's camera image shook, first briefly, and then for a full minute. Davis, flustered, almost shouted, "The ROV's in trouble. Something's hitting it! I'm taking it out!"

"But the only things in there that are moving are the divers," Jerry argued. Then he yelled, "Wait!"

Emily nodded, but nervously fingered the controls.

After another moment, the image steadied. They could see one of the divers in the immediate foreground swimming away from the ROV. The other was bent over the warhead with the empty tool bag. As the first diver moved away from the camera, Jerry recognized it as Reynolds. He was trailing a rope behind him.

"Control, U-bay, I think they've solved our problem," Jerry announced happily. "I think that line leads back to one of the brackets on the bottom of the ROV. They're going to use the ROV to lift the warhead out of the barge.

"Dr. Davis," Hardy asked. "Can you lift the warhead out?"

"Yes," she answered cautiously, "but Huey will take forever to get it back here."

"Then we'll transfer it to the Manta," Jerry said. "I'll come in under you and you lower it down on the top. We can use the same attachment point that we used for the tool bag." As he spoke, he began steering the Manta back toward the barge. He risked one active sonar pulse at long range before closing. That gave him a good enough picture of the area to approach quickly.

The divers were already rigging the line to the tool bag, and Jerry noted how it angled up off the deck, confirming that it was attached to the ROV.

As Jerry brought the Manta in, he slowed it to a creep, loath to have it arrive too early. He tried to guess how long it would take Reynolds and Harris, tired and half-frozen to finish rigging the bag, then for Davis to carefully lift the load out and away from the barge. Then remembered to check the time. They were cutting it close.

They finished getting the bag around the warhead case, which entailed half-lifting each end to get the material around it. As they finished, Jerry expected the Master Chief to take up the slack and start the lift, but instead he saw Reynolds gesture to Harris. When the other turned to face the COB, he motioned to another nearby crate, and then to the line.

"They're taking two of them!" Emily exclaimed as the divers passed the line through the lifting hooks.

"The first one will now likely have water damage," Patterson guessed.

Davis worried out loud. "I'm not sure Huey can lift that much weight."

"The divers can help with the lift," Jerry reassured. "And if Huey can't hack it, we'll jettison one of the warheads. We can always come back . . ."

"We're not doing this twice." Hardy declared. "Make it work, Dr. Davis."

"Conn, sonar. Two new contacts bearing two zero zero and two one zero. I'm detecting two medium-frequency active sonars, classified as probable Bull Horn."

⑲ Retrieval

Bull Horn, the NATO code name for a MGK-335 Platina sonar, meant Russian surface combatants. It could be a patrol craft, like a Parchim or Grisha, or a big destroyer like a Sovremennyy. Whatever it was, it was bad news. They hadn't seen a single Russian warship since they entered the Kara Sea, and now two had chosen this moment to show up? Jerry wondered if the Bear Foxtrot that went by the other day had actually gotten a whiff of them.

"Dr. Davis," Hardy ordered, "send the recall signal."

"Yessir." She cycled a switch on the ROV console, flashing Huey's external lights twice. They had only one way of communicating with the divers, the ROV's external lights, and two flashes meant it was time to come back.

On the video screen, they saw Reynolds still bent over the second case. When the lights flashed, he turned to look at the ROV and its camera. He waved, made an "okay" sign with his hand and then returned to the case. His movements, slower than normal underwater, now seemed almost glacial.

Davis looked at Jerry, her expression filled with concern. "How far away are they?" Jerry knew she meant the approaching warships.

"We can hear them pinging a long way off. I don't have a proploss display in front of me, but call it fifteen to twenty miles."

She relaxed a little, but asked. "Can they find us?"

"Not until they get to about four miles away. And we don't even know if they're headed toward us," he added. Although that was the way to bet, he thought.

They watched as Reynolds and Harris finished knotting the line. The camera image jiggled again as the divers took up the slack, and Emily began feeding power to Huey's motors. She kept the camera trained on Reynolds and Harris, but they disappeared in the foreground, and they had to assume that the two men were helping with the lift.

"Conn, sonar. Contacts have a very slight left drift. Screw noises indicate twelve knots. Classify contacts as Grisha-type corvettes." Slight drift meant a near steady bearing, and a closing course. But it would still take them a while to get here, Jerry thought. They should have enough time. Should.

Jerry concentrated on getting as close to the barge as the Manta's limited navigation allowed.

"Conn, U-bay. Request permission to transmit one ping with the Manta's sonar. It will help me close quicker."

"What's your distance?" Hardy asked.

"Nav system estimates several hundred yards, sir. The divers are still inside the barge, and if I can get a better fix, then . . ."

"Is there any risk of the Grishas detecting the ping?"

"No, sir, not at this range and I'm pointed the wrong way."

"Permission granted. We need all the speed we can get."

Jerry sent the command for a single ping, waited for the image to return, and found himself about three hundred yards away. Imagining how long it would take to swim that distance, he adjusted his course and speed, then ran for a carefully calculated forty seconds.

By this time, Davis had Huey's motors running at half-speed with hardly any movement. Thinking of the divers' fatigue as much as the approaching patrol craft, Jerry told her, "Just pin it to the right, Emily."

"I can't risk damaging Huey," she answered.

"Yes, you can. It's only a risk, not a certainty. We're running out of time and so are the COB and Harris."

Taking a deep breath, she increased the power and a cloud of sediment totally obscured the camera. Jerry's heart sank. How could she navigate safely in that debris cloud?

He saw her hands hover over the controls. She could reduce the power, but how much? And would the ROV hold position or start to sink? And where were the divers? He knew they would try to keep clear, but they had to be nearly blind as well.

"I can see the needle on the battery gauge moving," she warned. "It's slow, but I can actually see it going down."

"Just a few more moments and we'll know." Jerry tried to be positive.

The cloud cleared and the view suddenly expanded to show open water. They were already out of the cargo hold, about ten feet above the barge deck and rising.

"Head for the Manta," Jerry said needlessly. Davis was already pivoting Huey as she cut back slightly on the lifting power. Sweeping with the camera, she searched for the Manta's rounded arrowhead shape.

The phone talker's voice intruded as he studied the video screen. "U-bay, conn. We're building a track on the contacts. They are approaching from the south. Course is roughly north at twelve knots."

"What's the range?" Jerry asked.

"Ah, they don't have a lot of range data yet," the phone talker responded. "Sonar says there's not enough bearing drift."

Jerry sighed, but understood the problem. A passive track doesn't provide range by itself. The bearings can be plotted over time as they change, and the target's location estimated fairly accurately, but it needed a series of bearings that did change, the faster the better. Normally, if the contact was coming straight on, the sub would maneuver to create an adequate bearing rate, but *Memphis* was pinned, forced to loiter until her men were back aboard.

"I can see you," Emily reported. The Manta had just come into view of the camera, illuminated by Huey's lights but still as dark as the water surrounding it.

Jerry quickly sized up the relative position of the two vehicles. He had to remember where Huey's camera was aimed relative to the ROV's body, where each vehicle was pointing, what their relative depth was, and where the barge was. The ROV was encumbered, and he was blind.

Picking a point that headed him away from the barge but still closed the distance to Huey, he turned the Manta to port and concentrated on the video image. Davis kept the camera trained on him, which gave him a rough idea of the Manta's relative position, but he still had to remember the control lag. He had to think a few seconds ahead to send a command, then wait a few seconds more to see if he'd done it correctly. He ended up in an acceptable position, but farther in front of the ROV than he had wanted.

Even before he stopped, Emily began moving the ROV toward him, trying to minimize the time and the drain on her batteries. She positioned Huey over the larger vehicle.

"The camera can look down, but not under me," Davis worried.

"Reynolds knows that." Jerry answered. "He's got a plan."

"Like what?" she asked desperately.

Jerry tried to imagine the divers, clumsily shifting a heavy load in the dark and cold. "He'll pass a second line from the load to that lift point on the Manta where he wants to rig it. As soon as that's threaded, he'll send Harris out front . . ."

"I've got a diver," she said. Jerry saw a figure swim into the camera's field of view. It looked like Harris. Whoever it was, he waved at the camera, then pointed down. Emily reduced the power to the thruster, trying to maintain position over the Manta. The diver made another downward motion, this time more urgently, so she made a more drastic reduction and Harris gestured approval by clasping his hands together.

He guided her forward and then left, with smaller hand movements. Jerry tried to think of something he could do to speed up the process, but he couldn't even tell Reynolds and Harris about the Grishas. As far as he knew, the Russian ships were still well off, but they couldn't be sure.

They'd agreed in the wardroom on an "emergency recall" signal, which was Davis flashing Huey's external lights four or more times. At that point, the two men would drop whatever they were doing, clip onto the Manta, and they'd head back at the ROV's top speed of twelve knots. It would mean abandoning the warheads, though, and so far, Hardy hadn't given that order.

The camera suddenly jerked, and Emily let out a startled yelp, although she immediately followed it with, "It's loose!" The Manta and diver seemed to fall away from the camera, and she had to quickly reduce power to avoid having the ROV come to the surface.

Jerry concentrated on maintaining a steady course and speed while Emily brought the ROV back and positioned its eyes on the Manta and its load. This took a few nervous minutes, and Jerry promised himself that if anyone ever asked him about his ideas for a future UUV, the first, second, and third suggestions would all be for a camera.

"Make a pass over the Manta," Hardy ordered. "I want to see how the load is rigged."

"I don't know if we've got the time for that," Patterson's voice cautioned.

"I'll decide that, Doctor," Hardy answered sharply. "Mr. Mitchell has to know to properly handle the Manta. If we lose the warheads on the way back, this will all be for nothing."

Jerry agreed, but admired Hardy's nerve. He hadn't thought of the

Captain as a risk-taker, but he'd taken *Memphis* to the very ragged edge of Russian waters and sent divers in to recover a nuclear warhead. He'd put his career and the safety of the two divers and the boat on the line. Now that he'd bet the farm, Jerry guessed he was doing everything he could to make the bet pay off.

Davis answered, "Yes, sir," and brought her vehicle around in a tight circle. A speed of three knots seemed almost blindingly fast, and she had to slow down as she trained the camera on the top of the Manta.

Both crates were attached to the lift point by one end. The other ends were unsecured, but at least the cases were laid in a fore-and-aft manner. The COB and Harris should be able to hold the back ends in place so the crates wouldn't wobble. Jerry could only guess what the weight and drag would do to the "flight characteristics" of the Manta. He remembered one of the training videos at Newport that showed a one-third-scale prototype carrying two dummy Mk 48 torpedoes. The ballast system on this larger prototype should be able to handle the extra weight.

Davis maneuvered Huey again to take up station behind Jerry's vehicle, so they could watch the divers. Harris and Reynolds reconnected themselves again and grabbed the back ends of the warhead cases; Jerry heard two taps on the Manta's hull.

Informing Davis about the turn, he headed for *Memphis*, steadily increasing speed to ten knots. He also decreased his depth, rising to forty feet. That would reduce the divers' nitrogen saturation a little, although Jerry couldn't do anything about the cold or their fatigue. He couldn't imagine that they could rest at all, either, clipped onto the Manta's deck, struggling to keep the cases from moving around.

"The battery's low. I don't know if Huey can make it back at ten knots."

"Do not reduce speed," Hardy ordered. "We need that camera to watch the divers, and we're short on time. I'm bringing *Memphis* in to you.

"Mr. Mitchell, I'm making my depth seventy feet. I want you to alter course to one six five. I can cut at least half a mile off the distance."

Amazed that the Captain was taking *Memphis* inside Russian territorial waters, Jerry answered, "Alter course to one six five, aye, sir," and ordered the Manta to the new heading. How shallow was Hardy going to take her? If *Memphis* touched the bottom, she'd do more than dent a fender. The rudder projected down below the keel, and if that was damaged, they'd be unable to maneuver. The pit log, a small sensor that read *Memphis'* speed, was also located on the underside of the boat. If that even brushed the bottom, they'd have only the roughest idea of their speed.

And *Memphis'* nuclear power plant depended on seawater for cooling. The main seawater inlets were near the keel, and they weren't small. If Hardy got too close, *Memphis* would vacuum up junk and silt from the bottom and clog the condensers. That would cripple the plant, and the only way they'd get home was on Aeroflot.

Both Jerry and Davis had been carefully watching the video screen. His nightmare was one of the divers suddenly coming loose and being lost behind them before they could slow down. Alone, exhausted, with no way to find his way back, he'd depend on the ROV to find him, but Huey's battery was officially critical. Emily had the manual open, studying the graphs and furiously calculating discharge rates.

"U-bay, conn. Sonar holds you passively at three four zero. No range."

"How about the Grishas?" Jerry asked.

"Sonar has only a poor fix," the talker reported. "Their best guess is nine miles and closing."

Which meant they could be even closer. He wished they could do something to hurry the process.

"I'm stopping *Memphis* here," Hardy told Mitchell. My depth is six five feet. Come right a little, to one six eight."

"Come right to one six eight, aye," Jerry answered and told the Manta to change course.

"What's your battery charge?" Hardy asked.

"Sixty percent," Jerry reported.

"The instant the divers and the warheads are off, send the Manta southeast. I want your recommendations on how to distract those patrol craft."

"Yessir," replied Jerry, but before he thought about anti-Grisha tactics, he started working the math. How much range did the battery give him? How much margin did he have to leave? It wasn't simple, especially with one eye on the video screen and the other on the navigation display.

Knowing *Memphis'* keel depth, he brought the Manta shallower as it approached the sub. That way he could risk approaching closely, knowing he was too high to hit he hull. He'd take his chances with the sail by angling a smidge aft.

"Conn, U-bay. Is there any more on the Grishas' ETA?"

"Negative," said the talker. "Mr. Bair thinks they're roughly paralleling the coastline because the bearing drift changes back and forth."

Well, if they're hugging the coast, they'll run aground on us, Jerry thought.

"We should be getting close." Emily's statement was half hope.

Jerry knew they were, but had no way of knowing exactly how close. He waited until the Manta's and *Memphis'* locations had merged on the nav display before sending the command to stop. The one piece of good news was that this close to home, the command lag to the Manta was non-existent.

With the Manta stationary, Emily turned away and switched on Huey's sonar. "Bingo." *Memphis* was right in front of the ROV and quickly came into view. She skillfully maneuvered Huey and its camera to include the Manta.

Jerry instantly corrected the Manta's course so it was heading directly for *Memphis'* after deck. Again, with no way to communicate with the divers, he had to guess what they would do next. How would they want to transfer the warheads from the Manta and the sub?

And where the hell were they going to put them? Jerry suddenly realized that he had no idea of where they were going to stow the damn things. They were too heavy to manhandle through the forward escape trunk, and too big to bring in through the torpedo tubes. The tubes were twenty-one inches in diameter, and the warheads were at least two feet across.

The second question was much more important, and he needed to know the answer to it before he could figure out how to transfer the warheads off the Manta. *Memphis* did have storage lockers built into the external hull, but they were all way too small. He thought about the bridge recess, but the external cover was dogged from the inside. Besides, even if they could open the cover and fit both warheads in, there wouldn't be enough room to get up onto the bridge and pass them down into the sub.

As he struggled to solve the problem, he imagined Master Chief Reynolds trying to answer the same question. Would they both come up with the same answer? And was there one?

Emily kept maneuvering the ROV so that the camera would show both the Manta and the after deck of *Memphis*. As Huey hovered overhead, the light turned the Manta's hangar into a jumble of angular shadows. Looking at those dark shapes gave Jerry the answer he needed.

The Manta hangar had been attached to *Memphis* over her original external hull. It was streamlined, so that water would flow smoothly over the Manta when it was stowed, and those fairings had created several large voids—voids that were large enough to hold two good-sized crates.

Hoping the Master Chief hadn't come up with a different and better solution, Jerry corrected the Manta's course slightly to port. He carefully checked the Manta's ballast system, making sure the vehicle's buoyancy was exactly neutral.

"Emily, please bring the ROV down and move it closer to the Manta hangar. I'm gong to put the Manta right over the hangar opening so the COB and Harris can put the warheads inside." Although Davis was standing nearby, Jerry used the sound-powered phone so that the Captain and Patterson would know what his plan was. "I need to be able to see how high the Manta is above the deck."

Davis nodded, concentrating on both the vehicles' positions and the nearly flat battery gauge. Jerry had to remind her to use the phones.

"Understood," she answered, angling Huey down more and away from *Memphis*.

Minimum steerageway for the Manta was somewhere around one or two knots, but Jerry had done precious little work with the vehicle at low speeds. He needed to stop in exactly the right spot.

Still a hundred yards off, with the two divers and the warheads strapped to the hull, he gradually decreased speed. Thoughts of the Grishas urged him to hurry, but instead he concentrated on the physics of the situation. At some point the control surfaces wouldn't have any effect, and then . . .

There. The Manta's course indicator started to fall off to port, and he increased speed by the smallest increment the controls would allow. He didn't bother trying to correct his heading until the speed increased, and when it did, the vehicle responded, although slowly.

Luckily the correction was small, and the target was stationary. Aiming the Manta at the opening in the center of the hangar was simple, compared to accurately judging its height above *Memphis*. How close could he come to the deck without striking it?

Emily's ROV and its camera was ahead of him and off *Memphis'* starboard side, while he approached from port. He saw the Manta almost head-on, a little above and to the right of the camera. He would have liked a closer view, but she already had Huey's camera at maximum zoom, and she had the ROV as close to the Manta as she dared.

Thankfully, at this distance, there was no control lag. He made a small downward correction and watched for the results on the video screen. He made another, inching downward as he approached the aft deck.

And suddenly it was time to stop. Remembering how quickly the Manta had slowed when he had tested the steering earlier, he held her at creep speed until she was almost on top of the sub, then cut it to zero. There was no tail hook, of course, but he couldn't even back down.

Jerry checked the buoyancy again as the Manta coasted to a stop directly over the hangar opening. It rested, perfectly stationary, less than three feet over the deck. He let out a lungful of air and realized he'd stopped breathing some time ago. Then the sound of clapping startled him and he turned quickly to see the entire torpedo division and several of the ship's officers behind him.

The applause stopped quickly as he hushed them, but they all congratulated him on his piloting skills.

"That was really smooth, Mr. Mitchell."

"Makes a jet look easy, huh?"

Lieutenant Richards, the Weapons officer, had the final word. "It looks like you paid attention in Manta school, Mr. Mitchell." He smiled and said, "Bravo Zulu."

"Thank you, sir." The praise was more than welcome and Jerry felt it wash over him, but his eyes were drawn back to the video screen. Emily had remained focused, thank goodness, but there was nothing for anyone to do now but watch as Reynolds and Harris manhandled the warheads off the back of the Manta.

The Manta's passive sonar display spiked and jiggled as it picked up the sounds of the two warheads being untied, then pulled across the upper hull. The surface was smooth and curved downward, so the divers could let gravity do at least some of the work. Of course, the Manta had a sonar array running along each flank, but he'd just have to take his chances on it being damaged.

Through the camera they could see Reynolds and Harris take the first warhead crate and half-slid it off the Manta's hull. They managed to work it over to a recess in the hangar, but Jerry couldn't see exactly where they put it. He trusted the COB's ability to keep it clear of the latches and the other equipment inside, but he couldn't really relax until the Manta had been stowed and launched again.

If that ever happened. He risked another call to control. They could see and hear everything that was going on, but he couldn't see the plot or the fire-control display. "Conn, U-bay, what's the status of the Grishas?"

After a pause, the talker said, "It's still hard to say, but close."

Hardy came on the line. "Mr. Mitchell, do you have a plan for the Grishas?"

"Sir, I'd like to use the Manta's simulator mode. I can lead them off to the west, toward the coastline, so *Memphis* can head northeast. The problem is that I can't do it for very long. I'll need high speed to evade them, but I'm only good for about half an hour at twenty knots."

"I don't think that's going to work," Hardy countered. "They're relying on active sonar, and sounding like a 688 won't really distract them until you're very close, possibly too close to evade if your battery's that low."

Two spikes on the Manta's passive sonar display meant "All clear" from Reynolds. Jerry looked at the video display to see the two divers wrestling the crated warhead into a cavity in the hangar. They looked to be clear of the Manta by several feet, and he carefully applied just enough speed to get the vehicle moving.

At a walk, he saw the Manta slide across the video screen and away from *Memphis'* hull and the two men working on it. Once he was clear, he headed south-southeast, directly toward the two Russian patrol ships.

"Conn, U-bay. Divers have unloaded the last warhead crate, and I'm free to maneuver. Coming to course two three zero."

As he maneuvered the Manta, he continued his discussion with Hardy. "Sir, what if I drop a decoy in their path? It will get their attention and draw them away from us."

The Manta carried three ADC Mark 3 torpedo countermeasures and three larger ADC Mark 4s. The Mark 4 was designed to jam both active and passive sonars by generating a lot of noise and by providing a hard echo for a searcher's ping. They weren't the most sophisticated devices. For instance, they didn't move, and they didn't sound like a submarine, but it would take the searching ships a little time to figure that out.

Hardy paused only a moment before answering. "All right, but not directly in front. I'll steer you to a spot along their path—and within their sonar range—but I want you to pull them closer inshore. We'll head away to the east and then north. You can break to the north at quiet speed and rendezvous with us on the other side of the Grishas."

"Aye, aye, sir."

"Steer two five zero at ten knots. How long can you maintain that speed?"

"Steer two five zero at ten knots, aye sir. I can keep this speed for four hours."

"Good. Keep your active sonar off. We'll use Manta's passive set with our sonar bearings to cross-fix their location."

"Understood," Jerry replied and sent the course and speed commands to the Manta.

While Jerry planned how to use the Manta with the Captain, he continued to watch the divers finish their task. They had to not only stow the warheads, they had to make sure that they wouldn't rattle around or come loose. Reynolds and Harris had only the tools they carried, limited space, poor light, and their time was almost gone. Davis had brought Huey in closer, so that the divers could almost touch the vehicle, but it was impossible to see exactly what they were doing, or how much longer it would take.

When they finally straightened and swam toward the forward escape trunk, it caught Davis by surprise. She quickly panned the camera right, then gave the ROV just enough speed to follow the divers toward the escape trunk.

They both fit in the escape trunk this time, or rather, they made themselves fit. Everyone in control and the torpedo room watched Reynolds and Harris close the hatch, as Hardy gave orders for others to help them inside.

"Dr. Davis, I need you to do one more thing before you stow the ROV. Make a pass along *Memphis'* underside. I especially want to make sure the rudder and propeller haven't been fouled by anything."

"Do we really have the time?" Davis asked. She was obviously thinking about the approaching Russian ships.

"Mr. Mitchell will buy us time. I need to know if *Memphis* is free to maneuver."

"Huey's battery gauge is in the red, sir."

"The ROV can move another six hundred feet," Hardy stated sharply. "Do it," he ordered.

"Aye, aye, sir." Davis answered reflexively and dove Huey downward. The ROV was near the stern, so she steered toward that end.

Jerry grinned. "'Aye, aye?' Next thing you'll be sporting a patch on one eye and a peg leg."

"I've been on this sub too long," she countered. She smiled, but kept her eye on the battery gauge.

The Manta's sonar autodetect warning suddenly flashed on, and Jerry saw a broadband contact show up on the display screen. "Conn, U-bay. I've got a strong passive sonar contact bearing one eight zero. Looks like the Grishas."

The phone talker replied. "The XO says to keep passing up bearings and change course to due south. He wants to get a good cross-fix."

That pleased Jerry. Finding out exactly how far away those Russian patrol craft were would lower his stress level. They also needed that information to build a track, and that would tell them where he needed to release the decoy. Meanwhile, Huey had reached *Memphis'* keel and the seabed just below her.

From the ROV's point of view, *Memphis* loomed overhead like a metal storm cloud. Her curved hull vanished away from the camera in all directions. Hardy talked her down the length of the hull, telling her where to point the camera and when to slow down.

The bottom lay only ten to fifteen feet below the sub, rock with silt filling in the hollows. As little experience as he'd had in subs, Jerry knew that *Memphis* was dangerously close to the seabed, especially considering the poor charts.

The starboard side of the propeller and control surfaces appeared unobstructed, and the seawater suctions were all clear. Hardy then had her steer Huey past the bow so she could come down the starboard side.

"I've got something on the active sonar," Davis reported. "It's about a hundred yards away, off to the southwest."

"Back toward the barge," Hardy observed. "We don't need to worry about any more dump sites."

"It's too small to be a dump site," Emily answered, "and the object is small, more the size of an oil drum. And I can see lines or cables running from it."

"On the sonar?" Hardy questioned.

"This is a high-resolution sonar, sir. It's designed to see obstructions like cables or wires."

"Mr. Mitchell, have you reached the Grishas yet?"

"No sir, I estimate ten to fifteen minutes more before I can place the decoy."

"All right, Doctor Davis," Hardy conceded. "Go see what it is." His tone made it clear that she'd better be quick.

Davis brought the ROV around to the left, angling away from the sub. She didn't increase speed because of both the low battery charge and the short distance. In about a minute, an object appeared, centered in the video screen.

It rested on the seabed, two sets of short wheels barely visible in the silt. The body was cylindrical, about a foot in diameter and perhaps five or six feet long. It was painted dark green and there was virtually no marine growth. A thick black cable led away from the object to the west, in the direction of the shore. Two other cables with small bumps on them were laid out, parallel to the coastline. A white-painted "2" was visible as she steered Huey in a circle around it.

Jerry was still staring at the video image, trying to fathom its purpose, when Hardy ordered, "Dr. Davis, get your ROV back aboard as quickly as you can. Report the instant we can safely get under way."

"Yes, sir," Davis answered. Her expression matched Jerry's puzzlement.

"Mr. Mitchell, report."

"The Manta's course is due south, speed ten. The XO's computing the drop point for the decoy right now."

"Do you understand what that object was?"

"No, sir," he confessed reluctantly. It didn't pay to admit ignorance to the Captain, but he really didn't have a clue.

"It's a fixed acoustic sensor, mister. Someone's keeping a watch on that barge."

"Like the Russian Navy?" asked Davis.

"It explains the Bear and the Grishas. We didn't see any naval activity in this area until we found that damn barge." Hardy was angry, although Jerry wasn't quite sure at who.

"Why would you put sensors around something you dumped?" Jerry asked.

"You wouldn't," Davis answered. "It wasn't dumped. It was hidden here."

"U-Bay, conn," This time Bair's voice came on the line. "Steer right to course three five zero. You should release the decoy in two minutes."

"Steer right to course three five zero, U-bay aye. How far away are the Grishas?"

"Just less than five miles from you. You'll drop the decoy at the edge of their detection range. They'll see it, but not the Manta because it's smaller. After release, change course to due north at ten knots, max depth."

"Change course to due north at ten knots, max depth, aye," Jerry answered. "Should I wait for your call to drop?"

"Yes. We're continuing to track the Grishas passively. If they change course, we may have to alter the decoy's location."

Davis came on the line. "Control, I've started Huey's recovery sequence. We should be able to move in a five minutes."

"Thanks, Doctor," Bair answered.

"Doc Noonan's checked the divers," someone on the circuit reported. "He says they're okay, but he's put them both on bed rest with borderline hypothermia and exhaustion."

"One minute to decoy drop," Bair announced. "Course is good."

Jerry double-checked the console. He made sure he was set to release a Mark 4, and not one of the smaller Mark 3s. They might confuse a torpedo's sonar, but never a medium-frequency search set. The Mark 3's noise was too high-pitched for them to hear it. He could see two sonar contacts on his passive display. The signal was strong, which meant they were close. Jerry continued to report the bearings to control.

"Huey's aboard," Emily announced triumphantly. "Control, we're secure."

"Speak for yourself," Jerry muttered as he felt the deck shift. Hopefully Hardy had left enough room in front to allow *Memphis* to turn. With their single screw and rudder configuration, Hardy couldn't back and turn a submarine like a sports car. In fact, it wouldn't even back and turn like a bus. He wondered how long they had been so close to the sensor—and what its owners would hear. He called out another set of bearings to control.

"Wait for it . . . Drop!" Bair ordered and Jerry pressed the release. Without waiting, he changed course to due north, keeping his speed at ten knots. He wanted to go faster, but too much noise would attract unwelcome attention. At that speed, it would take half an hour for him to get completely clear of the Russian patrol ships. On the other hand, the Russians would take at least that long to detect, localize, and classify the contact as false. He hoped.

Jerry desperately wanted to be in control, to see the Russian ships' position as well as his own. He also wanted to go to sickbay and see how the COB and Harris were. And most of all, he really wanted to know what the story was with those missile warheads.

June 11, 2005—1800

•••••••••••••••••••••••••••••••

Northern Fleet Headquarters
Severomorsk, Russia

Admiral Yuri Kirichenko strode into the briefing like he owned the place, which, in effect, he did. He was the Commander of the Northern Fleet, which, even after the collapse of Russian naval power, still meant something.

Kirichenko's legend had grown with his rank. A competent junior officer under the Soviet regime, he'd been promoted just in time to become another impoverished senior officer. He'd remained in the military, ruthlessly fighting corruption and pushing efficiency as a necessary substitute for proper funding. By force of will, he'd kept the Northern Fleet from imploding.

So when he walked into the room with his characteristic high-speed stride, everyone in the room snapped to attention and everything was ready for his arrival, from the briefing materials to the tea and fresh fruit by his seat. Kirichenko was also well known for expecting the perks and privileges of his rank.

"Good evening, Admiral." Captain First Rank Orlov was the Intelligence Officer on the staff. Normally he had one of his deputies conduct the actual briefing, but this material was too important.

"Since the last brief at 0800, we've confirmed that there's no surface traffic in the area. Two patrol craft have reached the scene and reported detecting a submarine contact within our territorial waters. They attempted to localize it for prosecution, but it disappeared before they could make an attack.

"The seabed sensor grid hasn't reported any activity since 1715. Total elapsed time of the most recent detection was one hour and thirty-seven minutes. We've had experts examining the data but the sensors were never designed for narrowband . . ."

"I'm aware of the sensor's capabilities, Captain," growled Kirichenko.

Orlov nodded quickly "Of course, sir. My apologies. They have determined that the sound signals came from more than one source, and there were a large number of transients during the period."

The intelligence officer frowned. "Combined with the length of time they were near the array, we conclude they were working at that location and that they were unaware of the array's presence. They may have been landing agents or planting surveillance equipment . . ."

"When we catch them, we'll ask them," declared the Admiral, standing and walking around to the head of the table. Orlov hurriedly gathered up his notes and returned to his seat. Kirichenko's entire staff had assembled for this meeting, and they all listened intently.

"Whatever their purpose, they are not here to help the Russian Federation. I'm declaring a fleet-wide alert. I want aircraft covering the Kara Sea from the location of the incident all the way north, to the edge of the polar ice pack. Every operational unit is to get underway and head for the area. Admiral Sergetev," he pointed to his deputy, "will be in charge of the search."

"Ivan, form a barrier running east from the northern tip of Novaya Zemlya and then move it south. You should find the submarine as he attempts to escape."

Admiral Ivan Sergetev nodded in acknowledgment, but not agreement. "If we can get the barrier formed before he slips through. If he moves at high speed . . ."

"Sonobuoys will pick him up," Kirichenko interrupted. "And there will be stragglers and units that are too far out of position to reach the initial barrier line. Have them form a second line running northeast. If he's able to evade the first barrier, he may relax and we'll trap him with the second."

The deputies for aviation, surface ships, and submarines were all writing furiously, but so was Kirichenko's supply officer. He raised his hand politely and waited for the Admiral's permission to speak. Supply officers in the Russian Navy these days usually brought bad news—and this time was no different.

He spoke cautiously. "Admiral, our operating funds do not allow this type of deployment. We could use up our entire year's training budget in a few days' operations. And stores are critical. We'll have to dip into war reserves for enough sonobuoys, and I'm not even sure we have enough fuel on hand to fill everyone's tanks."

"Then send them out half-full." Kirichenko let him finish, but just barely. "And then get more fuel, and we'll send out tankers if we have to."

Kirichenko paused after answering the supply officer's objections, then spoke to the entire staff. "I don't care if we spend every ruble in the Fleet, including the stash under your mattress, Andrei." Everyone smiled at the joke, but they also looked worried and puzzled.

Kirichenko was a commanding figure, tall with a long, angular face that had been weathered not only by the elements but the weight of command. That contrasted with his blond hair. So far it was hard to see how much of it had gone gray.

"We've had penetrations of our waters before, and the West thinks that with us facing hard times they can enter our territory at will. Captain Orlov says there are 'multiple sources.' It sounds like there is more than one submarine, possibly several. Why would they need so many if they weren't making some sort of major effort against us?

"They're not expecting a massive response, and a massive response is the only way to deal with this type of attack. Our training budget just became our operating budget, and Andrei, this sounds like exactly the time to dip into war reserves."

The admiral leaned forward a little, driving home his point to the staff. "And think of what happens when we catch him! We will make the Americans and the others respect our waters and prevent who knows how many future incursions."

He turned to the supply officer. "And consider this, Andrei. What better way to get more funding for our Fleet than showing what we can do? With a success like this, I guarantee that I'll be in Moscow the next day, demanding that they give us enough support to operate the Northern Fleet properly."

Then he dropped his bombshell. "And Andrei, also use war reserves to make sure that every ship has a full load of ordnance, not just antisubmarine, but gun and missile ammunition as well. I want these intruders caught, and if they don't respond to our challenges, then they will be sunk."

Everyone looked surprised, but his deputy, Admiral Sergetev, was the only one who spoke up. "Sir, the chance of catching them in territorial waters is . . ."

"I don't care if they're in our waters when you find them. They were in our waters, and we have the array data as proof." He spoke more formally. "If the intruding submarines do not answer your challenge or comply with your instructions, you will attack with all your weapons and sink them. The Kara Sea is shallow. The hulk of a Western sub is just as convincing as a live one and will make our point about the sovereignty of Russian territorial waters even more effectively."

Sergetev, maybe because he was the one who would actually control the operation, risked another question. "Sir, are you formally changing the Fleet's Rules of Engagement?"

Those rules had been drafted by the Naval Staff and approved by the highest levels of the Russian government. They described in excruciating detail when and under what conditions a Russian naval unit could fire at a foreign one. Every naval officer in the Fleet was expected to be able to quote them verbatim. In the past, only intruders actually encountered in territorial waters could be engaged, and then only after several challenges and if there was evidence of hostile intent.

"I've already spoken to Moscow and they've approved the change for this specific incident. They are not happy with the idea of several Western submarines in our territory. Of course, if this doesn't work out well, I'll be the one explaining to Moscow."

That had the effect he'd expected, and the staff looked more willing to carry out the order, almost excited. Moscow's approval of the Admiral's orders removed any misgivings they might have had.

"I want reports on the status of all units and expected sailing times in an hour. Ivan, I want your search plan an hour after that. As of this moment, gentlemen, the Northern Fleet is at war. Dismissed."

KIRICHENKO WATCHED HIS staff leave the room, almost at a run. Good, they were motivated, and the lie about Moscow's approval had effectively dealt with any reservations.

He remained in the briefing room, sipping his tea and studying the charts that covered the walls. Calculating distances and times, he tried to visualize how the prosecution would develop, where the detection might take place. How could he organize the hurriedly assembled units to best effect? He'd spoken in positive terms to his staff, because they needed him to be positive, but he'd been too long in the Fleet to know what the odds were of finding a submarine that did not want to be found.

And this one had to not only be found, but sunk. He had no idea why the sub was there, but if they were, he knew what they'd found.

Right before the breakup of the Soviet Union, as a new Captain First Rank, he'd supervised the disposal of hazardous materials under the aegis of Soviet Military Intelligence, the GRU. He'd directed the dumping of spent fuel, old reactors, and all manner of dangerous items. Being a good officer, he'd made it his business to learn the details of each load.

One load, a barge full of canisters, had attracted his attention. While disposals were handled by the GRU, the material to be disposed of always came from other agencies: the armed forces, medical organizations, or the Ministry of Atomic Energy, Minatom. They all handled or produced radioactive material as a part of their functions, and thus had to dispose of radioactive waste.

But this barge didn't make sense. According to the paperwork, it carried canisters full of radioactive waste from Minatom, but the authorizing signatures were by GRU officers, not Minatom officials. And the barge had not come from any of the Minatom facilities. Oh, the paperwork said it had, but then he'd checked with the tug that had brought the barge to Arkhangel'sk. It had come up the Dvina River from well inside Mother Russia. Minatom's waste always came by rail in special cars and was then loaded onto barges for disposal.

At first, he suspected smuggling or possibly espionage. Perhaps someone had cached sensitive equipment or precious metals on the barge, presuming that nobody would want to closely inspect radioactive material. Classified equipment could be sold to the West. Corruption and graft were nothing new in Russia, and the cracks appearing in the Soviet Empire just multiplied the opportunities for enterprising individuals.

To avoid tipping off the criminals, he made several quiet checks, always making sure the enquiry would appear to come from a different part of the government.

And the answer had come quickly. The GRU had indeed falsified the paperwork, but it was not the act of an individual or group of criminals, but the GRU itself. They'd been in too much of a hurry to build a foundation for its "legend," which helped Kirichenko penetrate the cover quickly. In fact, they'd been rushed—and more than a little scared. Specifically, Soviet Military Intelligence had been handed a hot potato, with orders to fix the problem as quickly, and quietly, as possible.

The Soviet leadership had been cheating on the arms controls accords, producing more warheads than allowed under the treaties. The military had stockpiled them as the ultimate insurance policy, just in case of a surprise attack by the West. Secret even from the armed forces and known only to a few officials, the stockpile would give a devastated Russia a "hole card," even if all of its other strategic weapons were discovered and destroyed.

Now, with the Soviet Union crumbling around the GRU's collective heads, the stockpile was a dangerous liability that needed to be disposed of—and swiftly. The warheads could not be easily destroyed. The removed weapons-grade plutonium would raise far too many questions about its origins, and frankly, the money for their disposal would have to be accounted for, if it could be found at all. A simpler and cheaper solution was to just label them as radioactive waste and dump them in the sea.

Kirichenko agreed with their solution, but also saw opportunity in the situation. He did several things. First, he made sure that the special barge was properly scuttled, but not at the location that appeared in the report he sent to GRU headquarters. Then he compiled a list of the people who knew about the operation, and places where there might be records of the shipment or the stockpile.

Finally, using the GRU's authority, he ordered the deployment of acoustic sensors around the barge. Through some legal trickery—and a few veiled threats—he was able to make the sensors' deployment look like part of the disposal operation. Nobody questioned their need or purpose.

For fifteen years, Yuri Kirichenko had kept track of all the people and all the documents associated with the secret dumping. He'd been able to surreptitiously remove all of the documents, and he'd kept a close track of those who knew. Everyone, except him, had left the armed services; some had even left Russia. Many had died.

But Kirichenko had steadily risen in rank and power. He became a staunch opponent of graft within the Russian Navy and had jailed several officers for stealing precious metals from decommissioned submarines. He was also instrumental in making the Northern Fleet more efficient with its meager funds, much more so than the Baltic, Black Sea, and Pacific fleets. This had earned Kirichenko an unusual reputation for honesty. He was considered by the Russian government to be above suspicion, completely trustworthy.

And he'd begun to plan for his retirement. It had taken years to build up his contacts within the arms black market, and more time to learn the market. Now fifteen years of hard work and a rich reward were in jeopardy.

He studied the map as it showed not just the coast, but the interloping submarine as well. It had to be a Western sub, and probably an American. Or possibly more than one, according to Orlov. That worried him. They would not send more than one sub to such a remote location unless they knew what was there. Had someone learned of the cache? If they had proof, they would have already trumpeted the news to the world. So there was still time to keep the secret, and make a few sales. He had contacted a number of countries who would pay handsomely for a fully functional one hundred fifty kiloton nuclear warhead. He had plenty to sell.

MEMPHIS HAD SUCCESSFULLY evaded the searching Grishas, but Hardy had been forced to dodge farther east to keep clear of the corvettes. They were now heading north-northwest, toward home. Once clear of the northbound ships, Jerry kept the Manta on a northeasterly course at a charge-conserving five knots. The rendezvous with *Memphis* and the recovery of the Manta went off very smoothly, almost as if it were a training exercise. After hours of stress and strain, Jerry felt a load fall off his shoulders when the Manta finally nestled into its docking skirt.

The instant the Manta was secure, Jerry headed for sickbay, anxious to see the COB and Harris. He had to use his rank to open a hole in the large crowd that filled the passageway. It seemed that almost everyone not on watch was there, asking after the two divers. He was just starting to make progress when resistance suddenly ceased, and he realized the enlisted men around him had snapped to attention. Instinctively, he joined them, stepping to one side and making himself as thin as he could.

Moving into the space Jerry had just made, the XO, followed by Hardy and Patterson, headed into sickbay. Hardy nodded to Jerry as they passed and said, "Come with us if you like, Mr. Mitchell."

Jerry ended up standing in the doorway, with Hardy, Bair and Patterson barely able to move as the corpsman made his report. "They'll both be fine, but I recommend bed rest and fluids for the rest of the day. That water is above freezing, but not by much, and it put a tremendous strain on their bodies. Luckily, they were both in good health."

"Fine, Chief," Bair answered. "Can we speak to them?"

"Yes, sir," answered Noonan as he fiddled with Reynolds' oxygen mask. He stepped to one side as much as the crowded space allowed.

Reynolds and Harris sat reclined on the single bunk. Both were under several blankets with their faces obscured by oxygen masks. A heated IV bag hung over each of them, with the tube leading under the blankets.

Reynolds' face was strained, but he managed to prop himself up as the Captain stepped up to the bunk.

"That was excellent work, COB. You and Harris both did a five-oh job."

"Thank you, sir," Reynolds beamed. Any praise from Hardy was rare, but then Jerry knew they'd both earned it. "We didn't stop to count, but there were dozens of those cases in there, sir, all the same. It's a warhead, isn't it? A nuke?"

Hardy and Patterson both nodded. "It can't be anything else," he answered. "Although you were closer to it than we were. What can you tell us about it?"

"The sumbitch was heavy, I'll say that. It had a smooth finish, but there were markings on the case and on the warhead inside." He motioned to a slate lying on a counter nearby. "I copied them as best I could."

Bair, closest, picked up the slate and held it so that Hardy and Patterson could see it as well. Jerry could see that there was something written on the slate, but not what it said.

Patterson shook her head. "I can't read Russian, and the numbers don't tell me anything."

Bair said, "With your permission, sir, I'll take this and start working on it." Hardy nodded and Bair stepped out into the passageway and hurried forward.

Jerry resisted the urge to follow him; he was just as curious as the next guy to find out what they had stashed in the Manta skirt, but he wanted to see the COB first.

They'd managed to obtain two Russian nuclear warheads. The thought still boggled his mind. He'd love to have a closer look at one, but they were out of reach at the moment.

"I'm sorry, but I don't know what else I can tell you," Reynolds apologized, but Hardy shook his head. "You've done more than enough, Master Chief," the Captain reminded him.

Patterson, beaming, said, "The President will hear about this," then bent down and hugged Reynolds, and then Harris. Both managed to look pleased and embarrassed under their oxygen masks. She quickly stood, then left, with Hardy following them back up to control.

Jerry waited his turn while the men congratulated the divers. He stepped forward when the crowd thinned.

"I'm glad you're back in one piece, Master Chief."

"I knew you wouldn't let me down, Mr. Mitchell. Thanks for getting us back."

"So, how was the ride?" asked Jerry with genuine curiosity.

"Bumpy. And the in-flight service was terrible," joked Reynolds, grinning. But Jerry noticed that it was a weak one.

"I still wish that I'd been out there with you, COB."

"I think Petty Officer Harris does, too," Reynolds answered. Harris managed to nod his head in agreement.

"I just wanted to stop by and congratulate you two and ask if there's anything you need."

"Aw, sir, I'm not dying. I just need to take a nap."

"For about a week," added Harris.

"I'm just glad a good pilot was working the Manta, sir."

"We've all got plenty to be grateful for, Master Chief. I need to get going and you guys go and take that nap—right now."

"Aye, aye, sir," winked Reynolds.

TALKING ABOUT SLEEP with Reynolds reminded Jerry of his own fatigue and hunger. It was well after dinnertime, and he'd missed lunch. And he couldn't remember the last time he had had more than a few hours of sleep at one time. Ship's routine, as busy as it was, suddenly seemed like the nostalgic past. For all the pressure of his work and his qualifications, at least it was predictable. Two and a half weeks of survey work had left him thoroughly bone-tired. But now the Captain had turned *Memphis* northward. Although they'd just started, they were homebound. He almost looked forward to working on his qualifications.

He headed for the wardroom, figuring to scrounge a sandwich, but found most of the officers had the same idea. There was only one topic of discussion.

". . . cheaper to dump them than destroy them," Jeff Ho was saying as he came in.

Harry O'Connell, the navigator, countered, "But wouldn't you be worried about somebody else going down and finding them, stealing them for their own use?"

Ho shrugged. "I wouldn't advertise where I dumped them, and there's not a lot of sport diving in the Kara Sea."

"And that would explain the sensors," Cal Richards added.

"But these warheads aren't supposed to exist." Everyone turned to see the XO standing in the door, the slate and several books in his arms. Jerry could see the books were intelligence publications with brightly colored security markings on the covers.

Bair stepped toward the table and they hurriedly cleared a place for him to sit down.

"I've already reported to Dr. Patterson and the Captain, and he says there's no reason not to tell you guys about this," he announced as he settled into his seat. "I can't read Russian, and most of these numbers are meaningless to me, but I did find enough to tell us what we need to know.

"The markings on the case and the warhead are similar, except for a serial number, which appears to be in the same series. They both include the sequence '15Zh45.' That looked like an article number."

Jerry saw several heads nod in agreement. Russian military equipment had several different designations. While it was being developed, it would have one name, then the factory would call it something else, and the military service that actually used it would have a different name. And then there was the name that NATO had given it, because often the West didn't learn its true name or designation until after it had been in service for some time.

"I found it in one of the older intelligence pubs we have for Russian nuclear weapons. This article number was used for the RT-21 Pioner. It was called the SS-20 Saber by NATO." He held up the intelligence publication. "We're lucky I was able to find anything on it at all. It was a theater ballistic missile the Soviets deployed in the 1980s. They fielded several hundred, but they were all destroyed as part of the 1987 INF treaty."

"The what, XO?" asked a perplexed Ensign Jim Porter.

Bair gave Porter the typical forlorn scowl that all XO's are required to master and said, "The Intermediate Nuclear Forces Treaty, you young pup!"

A light laughter erupted in the wardroom over the XO's reply. But it didn't last long, not because the humor wasn't appreciated, but because everyone was dog-tired and stressed out.

"XO, the treaty didn't allow for the destruction of the missiles or warheads by dumping them, did it?" Jeff Ho asked.

Bair emphatically shook his head. "Definitely not. The Soviets had to declare the total number they'd manufactured and international observers witnessed the destruction of the missiles and warheads. It was a big deal. They destroyed several missile types, and we disposed of our Pershing II and ground-launched cruise missiles as well. With observers watching both sides, of course."

"So could the records be off?" Lenny Berg asked, but Bair didn't even bother to answer.

Like everyone else in the wardroom, Jerry processed the news and tried to understand the implications. If the Soviets, and then the Russians, had broken a nearly twenty-year-old treaty, then what else had they concealed? It did explain the acoustic sensors. But how far were the Russians willing to go to keep this secret?

After almost a minute of silence, Bair said, "The Captain also said we're heading home."

Jerry managed to get his sandwich and then lay down for a while. He had the midnight to six in control and knew it was bad form to fall asleep on watch. As he lay in his bunk, trying to unwind, he found himself reviewing his quals again, trying to plan how to best use the time left. . . .

HE WAS STILL shaking the sleep off when he reported. Although they were still in the Kara Sea, the watch had already settled into transit routine. Lenny Berg was the Officer of the Deck, with Jerry as the JOOD. "Let's hope for a nice, boring watch. It will put us six hours closer to home and six hours away from this place," remarked Lenny.

Al Millunzi, the Main Propulsion Assistant, was the offgoing OOD, and he ran down the checklist with them: ship's engineering systems all on line, except for one pump being checked, all sensors were on line, including both towed arrays, "And I don't have to tell you about the weapons systems, Jerry," he concluded. There was no criticism in his voice, but Jerry still felt bad. Although there was nothing to be done, he didn't like letting the boat down.

Millunzi led them over to the chart table. "This is our position as of 2340." Novaya Zemlaya lay along the western side of the paper, with most of the chart open water filled with soundings. Most of the northern Kara Sea averaged fifty to eighty fathoms, shallow for *Memphis*, but a deep undersea trench ten to fifteen miles wide lay close to the island's east coast. One hundred and fifty or even two hundred fathoms looked a lot better for a submarine trying to avoid attention.

Memphis' course lay straight up the middle of the trench, marked in red on the chart, with penciled notes marking their progress. "Current course is zero three five degrees at twelve knots, next turn is expected at 0210." Millunzi pointed to a spot on the chart. "The new course will be zero two zero, to conform to the trench. The Captain wants to be called before the turn. He also says to keep a close eye on the fathometer. He doesn't trust the chart."

Berg grinned. "Really? I'll bet the Russians have a better one. Should we ask?"

Senior Chief Leonard, the offgoing Chief of the Watch, came over and reported to Millunzi. "The watch is relieved, sir."

"Very well, Senior Chief. See you in the morning," Millunzi responded.

Millunzi turned back to Berg and Jerry. "That's it? Any questions? My rack is calling."

"I won't keep a man from his rest," Berg replied, smiling. "I relieve you, sir."

The offgoing watch section cleared out quickly, and Jerry settled in. Aside from some careful navigation and frequent depth checks, he was looking forward to a quiet, uneventful six hours.

"The biggest challenge on this watch is gong to be staying alert," Berg prophesized. "Homebound watches are dangerous. Everyone starts to slack off. They're too busy thinking of home and hearth, and not paying enough attention to their indicators."

"Even in the Kara Sea?" Jerry asked, half-joking.

"It's a state of mind, not a position on the chart. Check the fathometer every five minutes, and we're going to come up with some drills for the control room team." He looked at the qualification book Jerry had brought along. "What are you working on now?"

"I thought maybe the communications systems."

"Since you knew you were going to be stuck with the comms officer for six hours in the middle of the night. Well done, Mr. Mitchell. Stand by for some merciless questioning." He paused, with his ever-present smile, then ordered, "All right, get busy."

Trying to start a habit, Jerry checked the fathometer—two hundred forty feet under the keel and six hundred above. Good. He started a detailed check of every instrument, every switch setting in the control room. Behind him at the chart table, Lenny Berg made a conspicuous display of sitting back and opening Jerry's qualification book.

Jerry was a quarter through his inspection when Berg hit him with the first question. "What frequency range does the UHF whip cover?" Jerry answered correctly and continued checking. Lenny hit him with a question every three or four minutes, which was also Jerry's cue to check the fathometer and review the quartermaster's update of the chart.

They were forty minutes into the watch when sonar jarred them out of the routine. "Conn, sonar. We've detected some sort of explosion, bearing one four zero."

Jerry felt adrenaline flash like electricity through him. Berg, along with the rest of the watch, sat up quickly, but he didn't speak. He looked as if he expected Jerry to, though.

Jerry stepped over to the intercom. "Sonar, conn. Can you tell how big?"

"Conn, sonar, Very small or very far away," replied the sonarman. "No other activity, either, just that one transient."

"Conn, sonar aye." Jerry responded, still puzzled. He didn't like mysteries, and he looked toward Berg, but Lenny looked puzzled as well.

Well, whether this was one of Bair's drills or not, all he could do was play it by the book. Step two was to tell the Captain. Jerry picked up the phone and dialed the Captain's cabin.

"Captain." Hardy had picked it up on the first ring.

"Officer of the Deck, sir, sonar reports hearing an explosion some distance behind us. Either very distant or a very small explosion."

"Very well, I'm coming."

Hardy was there in less than a minute, fully dressed. He was still studying the chart when sonar made another report. "Conn, sonar, we've detected a second explosion, bearing one five zero. It's closer this time or a bigger explosion."

Hardy pressed the talk switch. "Sonar, conn, verify that you hold no other contacts."

"Conn, sonar, confirmed. We hold no other contacts."

"Then it's aircraft," Hardy said.

Dr. Patterson came into the control room in a robe and pajamas. "Did someone say they'd heard an explosion?" Patterson's robe was long and white, and it had the insignia of the White House embroidered on it. She managed to look sleepy and alarmed at the same time. Emily Davis followed her in, having taken time to dress.

Hardy looked annoyed but didn't reply, so Jerry ventured, "Sonar's detected explosions behind us. We don't know what they mean."

"Wrong, Mr. Mitchell," Hardy corrected.

"Conn, sonar, we've detected a third explosion, this one to port, bearing two nine five. Classify explosions as echo-ranging line charges."

"Sonar, conn, concur with your assessment," Hardy answered. "Keep a sharp lookout for anything that sounds like a Bear Foxtrot."

"Conn, sonar aye."

Jerry had to remember his sub school classes on allied and foreign ASW systems. The U.S. Navy used explosive echo-ranging back in the 1950s, before active sonobuoys entered the Fleet. The theory behind explosive echo-ranging was simple enough. Lay a field of passive sonobuoys, then drop small explosive charges. The buoys not only picked up the sound of the explosion, but any echoes off the hull of a submerged sub. The U.S. Navy stopped using the technique in the 1970s, however, because in practice it proved a lot harder to do.

The Soviets, on the other hand, had never given up on the idea, and they perfected it long before the West did. It was used to find quiet submarines operating in shallow water. Like *Memphis* in the Kara Sea.

It meant that there was a passive sonobuoy field near them, which had been laid by antisubmarine aircraft. Now they were monitoring the field and dropping charges, trying to find them.

"The charges are small ones," Hardy explained. "They're less than a pound, not much more than grenades. If they get close enough, though, they'll find us."

"But why didn't we hear the aircraft this time?" asked Patterson, showing a hint of fear.

"They're probably up high enough that the blade noise was attenuated before it reached the water. They didn't want to spook the prey," replied Hardy flatly. "Good tactics on their part."

It was a nasty situation. Go fast to get away from a sonobuoy field, and you'd make enough noise for the passive buoys to pick up. Creep along, and you're in the field long enough for them to locate you with the explosive echo-ranging.

"Mr. Berg," the Captain ordered, "come right to course zero six zero, speed five knots. Mind your depth. I want to keep us as close to the bottom as possible and rig ship for ultra-quiet. Ladies, I need you to return to your stateroom." Without protest, Patterson and Davis left control.

Jerry only glanced at the chart, but it was clear Hardy was taking them out of the trench, which was the sensible thing to do. The trench was an obvious route for any sub trying to leave the area, so the Russians had laid a barrier across that ten or fifteen miles. Leave the trench, and now their quarry could be anywhere in the Kara Sea. Except the trench, of course.

Lenny Berg repeated the Captain's course and speed order and ordered *Memphis* down to eight hundred feet. That left sixty feet under the keel. "Jerry, get over there and watch that fathometer. Report the depth every time it changes more than ten feet."

"Aye, aye, sir," Jerry answered.

"Conn, sonar, more explosive charges, to the north and the south."

"Sonar, conn aye," Berg replied, with Hardy nodding his understanding. The Russians were closing in, bracketing their position, but *Memphis* was already doing what needed to be done.

Jerry kept his eyes glued to the fathometer. "Depth is eight four zero feet."

Berg replied, "Understood," and continued working at the chart. He ordered, "Diving officer, make your depth seven eight zero feet."

Chief Swanson repeated the depth and double-checked the planesman as he brought the boat up to the new depth. Jerry called out the depth as the bottom sloped upward.

Hugging the bottom, *Memphis* crept and inched her way northeast into shallower and shallower water. Berg kept his eyes on the chart and made sure the boat was never more than sixty feet off the bottom. "Sir, I recommend coming left ten degrees. There's a deeper spot at three two zero relative, and it also puts us on a more northerly course."

"Stay on this course, mister." Hardy shook his head. "They were waiting for us in one deep spot. Right now, if I could, I'd put wheels on this boat."

"Aye, aye, sir," Berg replied.

Jerry rapidly called out the depth changes, "Depth is four two zero feet and shoaling." He tried not to sound worried. So what if the charts were incomplete? So what if the Russians were chasing them?

The sudden call on the intercom shocked them all. "Conn, sonar. Engine noises off the port bow. Multiple contacts."

Hardy took over. "Mr. Berg, I have the conn. Increase speed to ten knots, right fifteen degrees rudder, steady on course zero nine zero. Mr. Berg, watch our depth."

"Aye, aye, sir. Our depth is good for the next mile on this course."

"Right fifteen degrees rudder, steady on course zero nine zero, helm aye."

"Maneuvering making turns for ten knots."

"Very well," replied Hardy to the stream of reports, his eyes shifting quickly between the sonar display, fire control, and the nav chart.

"Sonar, conn. What can you tell me about those contacts?"

"Conn, sonar. I've got four surface contacts close aboard. They appeared suddenly and I'm getting high blade rates on all of them. I believe they were loitering in the area and now they've increased speed to close on us. They currently bear between zero four four and zero six five." After a moment's pause, the sonar operator added, "Conn, sonar. Detecting Bull Horn transmissions. Same bearings as the surface contacts."

The report was largely redundant, as the acoustic intercept receiver started bleeping its warning tones as soon as the ships above them lit off their sonars.

That would put them right over that deeper spot that Lenny had wanted to use, Jerry thought. The Russians were using the landscape to their advantage. But how had they known *Memphis* was passing by? And where did those ships come from? We didn't hear them at all!

Another buoy field, he thought. They knew *Memphis* would leave the trench once she heard the explosions and flushed her from one trap toward another: toward the hunters sitting in a duck blind.

The Captain continued to work with sonar. "Sonar, conn. What is the bearing rate of the surface contacts?"

"Conn, sonar. Very slight right drift, sir, and their blade rate's increasing, they're cavitating. I think they're building up to maximum speed."

"Man battle . . ."

Rippling thunder interrupted Hardy's order. A deep rumble filled the air inside the boat and stopped all activity, every quiet conversation. It was a rough, uneven noise that rose and fell, but as it fell, Jerry felt a mild vibration in the deck and the bulkhead. The Russians were shooting at them.

"Launch an NAE beacon!" Hardy ordered. "Man battle stations. Change course to three five zero, speed twelve knots. Mr. Berg, our depth?"

"We can increase depth to two hundred feet, sir. As long as we're heading northwest at all, the slope will be downward."

"Conn, sonar. Multiple clusters of explosions to port and starboard. Evaluated as RBU 6000 fire." It was old news, but knowing the explosion's location and identifying the weapon was helpful, if distressing.

Hardy nodded to Berg, then pressed the key on the intercom. "My intention is to run under them and get in their baffles while they try to sort out that countermeasure."

Berg cautioned, "We risk leaving a wake at this speed and depth, sir."

"I'm hoping they'll miss it in the roiled water from the attack. Make your depth one eight zero feet," the Captain ordered. "That should help as well."

Lieutenant Commander O'Connell, the Navigator and battle stations OOD, came in and quickly relieved Lenny Berg. That freed up Jerry as well, and he hurried down to the torpedo room.

Most of the torpedo division was already at their stations. Jerry saw Senior Chief Foster fussing with the firing panel. He'd already declared it dead, even cremated, but he wouldn't stop trying to resurrect it.

The phone talker, TM2 Boyd, saw Jerry and said, "Control wants to man stations for Manta launch, just in case. We're still at ultra-quiet."

Jerry quickly put on his phones and started checking the panel. Davidson and Greer were already at their launch positions.

Even before Jerry could report the Manta ready for operations, the control room talker reported, "The Captain wants to know the status of the Manta's battery."

Jerry didn't have to look at the gauge. It was the first thing he'd checked. "Forty-seven percent. Call it three and a half hours at ten knots."

The phone talker replied, "Forty-seven percent, control aye," and that was it.

The silence on the phone line pulled at him, demanding to be filled, but Jerry forced himself to be patient. The Russians were close aboard, and all he could do was wait. They might secure in half an hour or they might be here tomorrow morning, still having done nothing. Hopefully having done nothing, he corrected himself.

Jerry checked the space, making sure that everyone was quiet and on the job. The men sat or stood at their stations quietly, speaking in whispers. Foster had several tech manuals out and was leafing through them, being careful to turn the pages quietly.

Another rumble made them turn their heads, automatically trying to locate the sound, which was nearly impossible after passing through both water and a steel hull. Jerry wanted to think it was behind them. It certainly sounded fainter.

WHAAMM. Jerry felt, as well as heard the explosion. It was painful; he couldn't tell whether from the shock or the intensity of the sound. He looked around the torpedo room in alarm, convinced that water was pouring in somewhere. It reassured him to see that the hull was still intact, but then a second, even stronger explosion rocked the sub.

Jerry had to hang on to the console to stay in his seat. Objects fell out of their racks. Foster's coffee cup shattered on the deck. The lights failed and the battle lanterns automatically clicked on, then off a moment later as the overhead lights flickered back to life.

The first explosions, the ones Jerry had felt up in control, had been many smaller charges detonating together, like popcorn. Those were RBU-6000 ASW rockets fired by the surface ships. They had a small warhead, only about fifty pounds of explosive, but each mount fired twelve projectiles.

The last two jolts were hammer blows. Jerry had never imagined anything could be so powerful and not destroy the sub.

"Check the room and the weapons," Foster ordered, and Jerry automatically looked at his own displays, as well as those of his men. A few were dark, and the Senior Chief ordered Boswell to reset the breakers.

As FT2 Boswell stood up and turned toward the breaker panel, a third explosion sounded, fainter than the first two. Jerry felt the vibrations and heard the rumble, and relaxed because it was so much weaker than the first two.

They weren't prepared for the one that came next. It felt like the hammer—a giant's maul—had hit the hull directly outside the torpedo room. Jerry only heard the beginning of the explosion; the ringing in his ears that followed was like church bells.

Boswell was thrown into the port torpedo stow and every man in the torpedo room was knocked to the deck. The lights failed again and sparks flew from cable junctions in the darkness before the circuit breakers cut the power.

 Breakout

The battle lanterns cut in again and Jerry waited for moment, taking inventory of his bodily appendages before attempting to stand up. He'd struck something—or someone—on the way down and he hurt. From the moans and complaints surrounding him, he wasn't alone.

The phone talker had been knocked to the deck with the others, but he still had his headphones on and said, "Control wants all stations to report."

Jerry stood up slowly, favoring a sore knee, and looked around. His division looked battered but unbloodied as they resumed their stations. Boswell reached the breaker panel. "Can't reset it," he reported. "No power to the panel."

"Petty Officer Boyd, report no casualties, but no power either." As Jerry gave the order, Foster staggered over to the breaker panel, double-checking Boswell. He nodded, confirming the diagnosis.

After he repeated Jerry's message, Boyd said, "I can hear reports from back aft." The talker shared the circuit with the other stations on the sub and could hear their reports to control. "There's a short in the main switchboard and a steam leak in the engine room. There are injuries."

Before Jerry could ask for more information, Boyd added, "The Captain wants you and Senior Chief Foster in control, ASAP."

Jerry and Foster moved as fast as they could in the dim illumination up the two decks to control. Jerry smelled the smoke and ozone as he approached the space and coughed as he stepped into the murky darkness. The beams cast by the battle lanterns, instead of illuminating the control room just reflected off the smoke, forming cones of bright white vapor, while the rest of the space seemed pitch black in comparison.

His eyes smarting, Jerry looked away from the lights, feeling his way through the crowded space. He found Hardy and the XO near the chart table and threaded his way over to them.

"Reporting, sir."

Hardy and the XO both turned to face him. "Two things, Mr. Mitchell. First"—Hardy pointed to one corner of the control room—"we've lost the Emergency Torpedo Preset Panel. Second, there is a problem in the engine room."

Behind Jerry, Foster turned and headed for the panel, as Hardy continued talking to his division officer. The Emergency Torpedo Preset Panel was just that, an emergency backup that allowed the fire-control party to set a torpedo's course, speed, depth, and enable run in the event the fire-control system was damaged. Unfortunately, the earlier fire in the torpedo room had disabled the receiving circuits, and the Emergency Preset Panel was the only way they could talk to a Mk48. With it gone, *Memphis* had no weapons capability at all.

As Foster approached the panel, main lighting came back on and the panel, along with several other pieces of equipment, crackled to life. Showers of sparks flew wildly about and new smoke started pouring from cabinet vents.

"Trip the breaker!" Foster shouted. "Trip it!" Two ratings standing near the control room switchboard dove toward it. The two quickly turned a number of barrel switches and plunged the control room into darkness once again.

Slowly, cautiously, the technicians re-energized the equipment in the space, leaving the preset panel's breaker open. Two other pieces of gear, the BPS-15 radar display and the TV repeater for the periscope, also sparked until their breakers were opened as well.

As they were bringing the control room's power back on line, Hardy spoke. "Mr. Mitchell, as soon as you've got power in the torpedo room, launch the Manta. Lead the Russians away from *Memphis* by any means you can think of. We're dead in the water right now, and will be until Mr. Ho secures the port main engine. We had a bad steam leak and even after we get propulsion, we'll be noisy and slow. And with the preset panel gone, we can't fight. Our only hope is to have them looking somewhere else."

The control room intercom carried Ho's voice. "Engineer, sir. We're ready to answer bells, but only up to ahead standard. The best we'll be able to make on the starboard main engine alone is twenty knots at full rpm. We can creep at five, tops. We've secured steam to the port main engine and that's stopped the leak. It's been isolated from the reduction gear so it won't drag. We're investigating the cause of the steam leak."

Hardy nodded to Bair, who was standing next to the intercom. The XO answered, "All right Eng, thanks for the report. How are your guys holding up?"

"Final casualty count is four injured, three with burns and one with a broken ankle. I'm waiting for a report from the corpsman. I'll pass the word to you as soon as I get it."

"Understood," Bair answered.

Ho added one final comment. "Sir, the plant took one hell of a beating. If we take many more knocks like that last one, we could lose a lot more than the port main engine."

Hardy stepped up to the intercom. "Do your best, Mr. Ho. Without you, we don't get home. Control out." He turned back to Mitchell. "Get going." His face softened and he said, "Get them away from my boat, mister."

Jerry answered, "Aye, aye, sir," as he left control and headed below. Foster was up to his elbows in the preset panel, calling for tools, but Jerry didn't need the Senior Chief to launch the Manta.

They had already started the sequence by the time he got to the torpedo room. He rushed through the procedure, as familiar to him now as getting out of bed in the morning. By all his indications, the Manta had come through the attack without a scratch. There was one bad moment when Jerry fretted about how well the docking skirt and latches had weathered the shock, but the display showed them all releasing, and the Manta automatically lifted off and away from its dock.

With the UUV now clear, Jerry suddenly found himself at a complete loss about what to do next. He'd been so focused on the launch he hadn't thought about tactics.

Lead them away from *Memphis*. All right. I can do that. He ordered the Manta to turn west, back toward the trench, and punched the speed to fifteen knots. He also enabled the Manta's simulator mode. A set of transducers in the vehicle would emit the acoustic signature of a *Los Angeles*–class sub. The Manta wouldn't be quiet at that speed, and combined with the simulator mode, he hoped it would attract the attention of the Russian pursuers.

To help get their attention, he also sent a command sending the Manta to shallow depth. The surface wake would show a live contact leaving the scene of their latest attack at a brisk pace. Hopefully, they'd be busy repositioning for another attack and wouldn't notice *Memphis* creeping in the general direction of away.

But was it working? It had only taken a few moments to send the commands. How long before he knew if the Russians were fooled? He was afraid that the way they'd find out it wasn't working was another battering.

He felt like waving a flag or broadcasting insulting Russian phrases. Instead, he told control what he'd done. Hardy came on the line. "I'm taking *Memphis* northeast at a creep and we're hugging the bottom. Will you turn north once you're in the trench?"

"Yessir. I'm going to stay noisy, drop a countermeasure if they attack, and then break away."

"Approved, but don't break away too quickly. I want them to have a solid contact, so that everybody is completely focused on you."

"Aye, aye, sir." Jerry started to mention the range limit on the acoustic modem, but held his fire. Hardy knew about it and reminding him wouldn't help. It was Jerry's job to figure out what to do.

He checked the nav display and adjusted the Manta's course slightly. He wanted it to pass through the buoy field *Memphis* had encountered. He also sent the Manta deeper, not because it would make him easier to find, but because that's what a real sub would do.

He checked the battery gauge and tried to do the math. Fifteen knots wasn't flat out, but it would burn more of the Manta's battery endurance than he'd like. Every minute he spent at fifteen knots now was good for eight or ten at creep speed.

But dammit, he had to know if it was working or not? Where were those four patrol boats that had attacked them earlier? He requested control to ask sonar for their status.

"U-bay, sonar. We're on the line with you now. The four boats are astern of us, maneuvering and pinging. Our guess is they're executing a search pattern at the site of our last attack. We think those were S3V depth charges, by the way. There was no torpedo noise at all before the explosions. They're dropped from an aircraft, probably a Bear or a May patrol plane. They're also passive homing, so we've got to stay quiet."

"Sonar, U-bay aye. And if the Manta makes too much noise, it will be an easy target for them." Jerry then added, "Thanks for the update."

Now centered in the trench, Jerry turned the Manta in a complete circle before heading north, trying to create a "knuckle" in the water. A mass of disturbed water, a knuckle could reflect active sonar pulses. Normally subs made gentle turns so they wouldn't create a knuckle, but not this time. He'd hang lights on it if he could.

Jerry also reduced the Manta's speed to five knots, both to save the battery and because that's what a real sub would do.

"Conn, U-bay. How many of those depth charges does a plane carry?"

The control room talker said, "U-bay, conn. Wait one." A minute later he relayed, "If depends on the sonobuoy and torpedo loadout. A Bear Foxtrot can carry up to twelve. A May can carry ten."

"Conn, U-bay aye. Thanks." And that's per airplane. Wonderful.

Hardy came on again. "Mr. Mitchell, I'm turning *Memphis* to zero three zero now."

"Yessir. How long will it take before we know if this is working or not?" Jerry hated to ask, but the question nagged at him.

"As long as they don't attack *Memphis*, it's working, mister. Just keep doing what you're doing. I'm sure you can make it work."

Jerry was so surprised he didn't answer. Hardy, encouraging him? Now he was really worried.

"Conn, sonar. More explosions to the west. They might be more ranging charges." As sonar made its report, the Manta's sonar display also showed the sound spike. It showed a detonation ahead and to starboard of the Manta. He fed the bearing from the Manta's detection to control, where they plotted both lines on the chart.

The talker sounded almost happy. "U-Bay, conn. Plot confirms the explosions are in the trench, and the strength is right for an echo-ranging charge."

Jerry felt relieved for *Memphis*, but paternal concern for the UUV. Anything that could hurt *Memphis* would kill the Manta very quickly, which would end its job as a decoy. It would also deprive the American taxpayers of several millions of dollars' worth of high-tech prototype. And the wreckage would be in shallow water, easily recoverable.

Time to wiggle, he decided. Jerry turned the Manta toward the last explosion and changed his depth, bringing the Manta up. That should make it easier to distinguish from the seabed.

Another ranging charge showed up on the Manta's display and sonar also reported the blast. This one was behind and to starboard, but Jerry turned the Manta to port, as if he was trying to get away from the spot. He also told the Manta to go deeper, but not all the way to the bottom.

A third charge followed in quick succession, this time ahead of the Manta, and Jerry increased speed to eight knots. The idea was to convince them they had a live target, but not to actually become one. And the longer it took, the better.

"U-bay, conn. The tracking party thinks the patrol boats are headed west, toward the trench and the Manta. The Captain's increasing speed to six knots, but says you're supposed to keep them busy as long as you can."

"U-bay, conn aye." A fourth charge exploded to the aft of the Manta, but close aboard, to judge by the signal strength on the display. He was trying to figure out which way to zig when the passive sonar picked up a new sound.

"Conn, sonar, I've got a torpedo in the water to our west!" Jerry had never seen a torpedo on the Manta's passive display, but instantly agreed with the sonar operator's call. It was a perfect drop from the Russians' point of view, ahead and to port. As the torpedo turned to starboard to begin its search pattern, the Manta would be dead ahead.

Jerry told the Manta to release an ADC Mk 3 torpedo countermeasure, then kicked the UUV hard to port. He was already at eight knots, not enough to get out of the area quick enough, so he ordered the Manta to maximum, twenty knots, quickly computing how long he could head west across the trench at that speed.

His one advantage was the maneuverability of the Manta. It was as maneuverable as a torpedo, and if he could get behind the torpedo and stay there, the weapon would never pick him up. Of course, as soon as this one ran out of fuel, they'd drop another, but first he had to live through this one.

He watched the torpedo's bearing on the Manta's display, trying to guess its course and how far it was from the vehicle. As quickly as he could, Jerry slowed the UUV and turned it toward the torpedo, attempting to stay behind its seeker cone.

Along with the noise of the torpedo's engine, he could also detect the active seeker, pinging at high frequency. The rate of the pinging was important, because as long as the pings were widely spaced, the weapon was in search mode. If the ping rate increased, that meant the torpedo had found something and was taking a harder look.

As Jerry maneuvered, he kept up a running commentary to control, telling them what the Manta was seeing and what he was planning. For the most part, control didn't answer, aside from an occasional "U-bay, conn aye."

For almost a minute, the bearing continued moving to the right and Jerry chased it, taking the Manta in almost a full circle. He tried to visualize the position of the two as they circled a common point. While he could see where the torpedo was, in relation to the Manta, he could only guess at where the torpedo was headed, which would help tell him where the seeker cone was—and whether or not he was in it.

Finally he seemed to catch up, the bearing to the torpedo changing less and less until he almost went past it and had to quickly correct, all the while dealing with the growing time lag as the Manta increased her distance from *Memphis*.

The torpedo bearing remained steady for a few moments, and Jerry saw that it was headed south, probably toward the countermeasure he'd dropped. Turning as tightly as he could, he commanded the Manta north again. Hopefully he could get some separation before it sorted out the decoy and went into a circular reattack search pattern.

North, always north. That's what a real sub would do: try to reach the northern exit of the Kara Sea and get out of this geographic bear trap. He wanted the Russians to think that as well. And as long as he kept going north, he'd be running parallel with *Memphis* and wouldn't have to worry about getting beyond control range. Still, the time lag was already a major factor.

The torpedo remained to the south, and Jerry heard it switch to a higher ping rate. The countermeasure had worked, then. Jerry adjusted the Manta's depth, putting about one hundred and fifty feet between the UUV and the seabed. If they started echo-ranging again, he wanted to stand out from the bottom. He kept his speed low, at five knots.

It took five minutes for the weapon to run out of fuel. They couldn't drop another weapon until the first torpedo stopped, and he used the time to get some distance behind the Manta. It was also another five minutes' grace for *Memphis* as she headed northeast.

Jerry had expected them to start echo-ranging again, but the next sound he heard was another torpedo starting up—and close aboard, to judge from the signal strength. He quickly turned the Manta toward the weapon, hoping to get past it and behind it, as well as triggering another torpedo countermeasure.

They must have just taken the last drop point and figured how far he'd get at five knots. They'd come closer than he liked, and Jerry decided it was time to get out of Dodge. He said as much over the circuit and Hardy's voice immediately said, "Agreed, as quickly as you can."

Jerry instructed the Manta to terminate the simulator mode, cut the speed to creep, and dropped to the bottom. He'd grown to trust the Manta's safety circuits and used them now as he sent the craft within ten feet of the bottom, far closer than *Memphis* could ever go. The torpedo's seeker could distinguish the hull of a submarine from the seabed, but the Manta was much smaller, a hundredth the size of a nuclear attack boat. With any luck, the torpedo's seeker would dismiss it as an echo from the seabed.

And Jerry headed south. He kept a careful eye on the nav display, because now *Memphis* and the UUV were heading away from each other.

He also watched the sonar display as the torpedo's bearing remained firmly north, behind him. Whether the seeker had never spotted him or had been attracted by the countermeasure, it was still in search mode and seemed to have no idea where he was.

"Sonar, U-bay. I need to know if you see any sign of the Russians searching to the south of that last attack."

"U-bay, sonar. We don't hold any active sonars in your area, but the Manta's passive arrays will know about it as soon as we do."

Jerry had to agree with them. He needed more information. He'd love to know where the airplane or airplanes hunting them were, but *Memphis* didn't dare put up a mast.

Jerry visualized the search radius of the torpedo and turned distance into time at five knots. The next two minutes seemed eternal and Jerry forced himself not to look at his watch. He stared at the sonar display instead and willed it to remain blank.

There was no sign of attack, pursuit, or even interest in the Manta's location, and Jerry gratefully turned the UUV east, carefully managing its depth as it rose up the steep eastern wall of the trench. He almost felt like a soldier leaving a foxhole as he brought the Manta out of the trench onto the shallow seabed.

Memphis lay over six miles away, mostly to the east, and Jerry headed straight east at first, reluctant to do anything that would bring him closer to their Russian pursuers. The problem now was to rendezvous with *Memphis*. With the Manta and the sub both creeping, Jerry knew he'd never catch her. "Conn, U-bay, I need to speak to the Captain."

"Yes, Mr. Mitchell," Hardy said after a brief pause.

"Sir, I'd like permission to go to ten knots. At *Memphis'* current speed, I'll close in an hour and a half."

"What's your battery charge?"

"Twenty percent. I'm good for two hours at that speed."

"And at that speed, if you pass through a buoy field, they'll pick you up for sure," Hardy observed.

"Sir, I can't catch you at five knots."

There was a short pause. "I'm turning *Memphis* due north and slowing to three knots. Turn to zero four five and increase speed to seven knots. We should rendezvous in two hours."

Jerry made the course and speed changes. "Yes, sir, and thank you." Jerry felt genuinely grateful. It would be easy for Hardy to abandon the Manta, claiming that the risk of pursuit was too great, but his solution would keep the two units covert and still get the UUV back.

Jerry watched as the Russians remained preoccupied to the southwest. Bull Horn sonars pounded the water over the trench and by the Novaya

Zemlya coastline. An occasional series of explosive charges to both the northwest and southwest confirmed Jerry's hopes that they had indeed lost contact with the Manta, and more importantly *Memphis*.

Two hours later the Manta rendezvoused with *Memphis*. Although there had never been a problem with the automated recovery sequence, Jerry sweated every step until the latches were engaged and the umbilical connected. Drained, he slipped out of his seat and headed slowly to the wardroom for something to drink. The XO said he'd meet him there to go over the tactics Jerry had used to break contact. "Better to get them down on paper while they're still fresh in you head," Bair said gleefully.

Fresh? Yeah, right. Jerry thought cynically. Let's see, how can one expand "pop chaff and evade" to fill a couple of pages of the patrol report? Still, the Manta had successfully been used to bamboozle a very determined Russian ASW force and the U.S. Navy would demand to know how it was done—in detail. As he climbed the ladder up to forward compartment, middle level, Jerry fervently hoped that there would be no further need to launch the Manta again on this cruise.

"KEEP AT IT, Ivan," Kirichenko encouraged his deputy. It had been three hours since there had been any trace of the American sub, or possibly submarines, he corrected himself. "They're still there. They didn't just vanish."

"Yes, sir." Admiral Ivan Sergetev tried to look determined, but couldn't hide his disappointment. They had been so close to getting one of those arrogant trespassers that losing contact was a bitter pill to their morale. And the longer the Americans stayed lost, the greater the chance the Northern Fleet would never find them again.

"Concentrate on the second line now, but don't stop using the first." Kirichenko didn't dwell on the details. Sergetev was a good tactician. He knew what to do.

"Yes, sir. I'll find them." On his second try, Sergetev sounded a little more confident.

Kirichenko left the situation room and headed for his office. He trusted his deputy, but not enough to bet his life on him. Keeping calm and appearing positive in front of his staff had taken every gram of his concentration. He'd need his staff's support to back him up—later.

The only good news so far was the absolute certainty that there was a submarine to be prosecuted. It had been repeatedly echo-ranged. Aircraft had seen its wake as it fled the scene of the attack. The Americans had deployed numerous countermeasures and the sounds from those devices had been recorded. Unfortunately, the submarine had been attacked several times without result.

There was no guarantee that the second line would catch the Americans.

It was scattered, still forming. Like the first one, it was made up of units that had been out training or had been in a high state of readiness. There were precious few of those in the Northern Fleet.

The second line consisted of every unit that could reach the Kara Sea before the intruder reached international waters. Diplomatically, the Russians could make a case for attacking a submarine in the Kara Sea, even if it was outside the twelve-mile limit, by invoking hot pursuit. That would be harder, much harder, in the Barents or Norwegian seas.

So he'd have to have a reason to risk international condemnation. A strong one, one that represented a clear and present danger to the motherland. Easy to do if you're not constrained by the truth. He started drafting a message.

His staff knew that the Americans had been operating close to the coast. What they didn't know was that he'd received top secret, compartmented information from the Northern Fleet's counterintelligence officer. A foreign agent with stolen codes had evaded the FSB and was trying to leave the country. His last known location was in the Arkhangel'sk Oblast. If he had somehow managed to get to Novaya Zemlya and was aboard that submarine, and that sub made it safely back to port, Russian military communications would be compromised. Even after the codes were changed, Western intelligence would still be able to read a decade's worth of encrypted messages. The damage to Russian security would be grave. Extreme measures had to be taken to prevent this from happening.

22 Close Quarters

June 12, 2005

Northern Kara Sea

Lunch that afternoon was a celebration, although an ultra-quiet one. Jerry thought the cold sandwiches and canned fruit were a banquet and the thought of going home filled him with possibilities. True, he had a ton of work to do if he wanted to qualify for his dolphins, but compared to their earlier problems, his quals didn't seem so insurmountable now. He'd make the time.

Especially at twelve knots. Lieutenant Commander Ho had already briefed the Captain, but the entire wardroom needed to know exactly what *Memphis'* engineering plant could and could not do.

The Engineer looked tired, and a little shaken. He'd already briefed them on the four men who'd been injured, none dangerously so, but it was clear he'd felt their injuries almost as much as they had. His tone had improved and become steadier when he'd described the casualties to the plant.

The worst was the port main engine. The shock of the depth charging cracked the main throttle valve casing and caused a major steam leak, scalding three men nearby. Another man broke his ankle trying to get away from the jet of steam. The space had immediately filled with vapor, making it hard to see and to breathe. They'd drilled for it, though, and after donning EABs, had secured the steam supply to the main engine.

But now, to run at the same speed, the remaining engine would have to work twice as hard, which would make much more noise.

And the throttle valve couldn't be repaired at sea. Because it had to hold saturated steam at six hundred psi and 485° Fahrenheit, it was made of thick stainless steel. The ship didn't have the capability to weld metal that thick, with a crack that large. They couldn't even patch it while at sea. The only thing they could do was secure the port main engine until they reached a base with the necessary equipment and personnel to effect the repairs.

Their creep speed was reduced from five to three knots. That wasn't too bad, since nobody ever tried to get anywhere at creep. The point was to be as quiet as physically possible. Their transit speed was now twelve instead of twenty knots and their top speed, at which they'd make more noise than a boiler factory, was twenty knots. "Over twelve knots, I'd have to shift the starboard main seawater pumps to fast speed, and you can't be quiet with those on the line.

"The oxygen generator fried itself when some of the breakers were rattled around. Fortunately, the oxygen banks are full and we won't need to make any more before we reach a friendly port. And there are pumps and fittings knocked loose throughout the engine room and the auxiliary machinery space," Ho concluded. "The only good news is that if we don't take any further hits, we'll probably make it back without any more equipment casualties."

"That was a ringing endorsement," Lenny Berg remarked cynically. "Would it help if I got out and pushed?"

"I like the 'getting out' part," the XO answered, with only a slight smile.

"I was only trying to help," Berg complained.

"Jerry, any luck with the torpedo tubes?" Bair asked.

"None, sir. With the preset panel gone, there's no way to talk to a weapon. The Senior Chief's been trying to jury-rig something, but he's not hopeful."

Dr. Patterson, sitting to one side with Emily Davis, spoke up tentatively. "But you can still fire a torpedo, can't you? Emily says there's nothing wrong with the tubes themselves."

"That's not quite true, doctor," answered Hardy politely. "To fire a Mark 48, we need to apply warm-up power to get the inertial nav system up and running, and then we need to tell it where it is, where to go, and when to enable the active seeker. You need the fire-control circuits, or the emergency preset circuits to do those things; we have neither. If we launched a weapon, it would head straight to the bottom. No, ma'am, we have no weapons capability at all." On that somber note, Bair stood up and announced, "All right, we're not out of the woods yet and we have a long trip before us. Let's get back to work."

SLOWLY, THE OFFICERS filed out of the wardroom, leaving Hardy to think in peace. As soon as he thought he was alone, he placed his face in his hands, rubbing his forehead with his fingertips. Exhausted, frustrated, and tired of having to act so confident in front of his crew, he tried to think about what he would do if they ran across another Russian.

"Excuse me, Captain," Patterson said softly.

Momentarily startled, Hardy jerked his head up. "Yes, Doctor. What can I do for you?"

"I . . . ah . . . I need to apologize for some of the things I said earlier. I didn't really appreciate all the risks you and your men take and, uh, it was wrong for me to call you a bus driver and your sub a piece of junk."

Hardy smiled weakly. "I believe the phrase was a 'glorified bus driver,' Doctor, but then I'm being picky. Apology accepted." He then stood up and faced her. "And while we're on the subject of apologies, I believe I made a remark about your political derrière being in a sling that was inappropriate. I know you didn't just make the environmental threat up, that you do believe it's a problem. I'm sorry that I implied you had."

Patterson nodded her acceptance and then looked down at the deck. "Do you . . . do you think we'll make it home?"

"Frankly Doctor, I don't know," Hardy said honestly, and then started to walk toward the wardroom door. After a few steps, he stopped and turned back to face her. "I'd like to think we'll get out of this mess in one piece, but I have nothing but my training to base that on. This is my first time in a combat situation."

"You and your crew have done very well so far, Captain. It's obvious that the training they've had is paying off."

"Yes, it is. And Lord knows that I've trained them hard. Perhaps, too hard at times. But I've found out training only goes so far, Doctor. You have to have confidence that they'll do the right thing at the right time."

Patterson chuckled briefly. "We don't work with trust much in politics, Captain. It's in short supply."

"I know that, Doctor. But it hasn't exactly been plentiful on *Memphis* either." Hardy opened the door and motioned for Patterson to leave first. He then closed the door carefully, so as to make as little noise as possible.

MEMPHIS CONTINUED TO creep northward, Ho nursing the battered engineering plant as if it were a sick child. Jerry went back on watch in control with Lenny at 1800. He wished he could've slept more than two hours, but Bair made it clear they had to stand watch. "I've got to put everyone in the engineering department back aft to hold this old lady together. You two will just have to pull extra time forward." It made sense. There would be little communicating with the outside world while the Russians were pursuing them, and without a weapons capability, there was little need for an Assistant Weapons Officer.

Memphis would not be out of the Kara Sea until late that evening, but that assumed a straight-line course and a constant quiet transit speed. Especially after the attacks that morning, everyone on the boat was silent and extremely alert. Jerry actually tiptoed in the passageway as he made his pre-watch rounds with Lenny.

In control nobody spoke unless absolutely necessary. Hardy and Bair alternated between the chart, the TMA plot, and the fire-control system, speaking quickly and softly. They ordered frequent depth, speed, and course changes, trying to use the seabed for cover as much as possible, trying to avoid any obvious paths. After all, the Russians knew these waters better than they did. Like a soldier dashing from one piece of cover to the next, *Memphis* quickly transited the deep spots, then headed back to shallower water, always working her way north and out.

In the early evening Hardy risked exposing the BRD-7 ESM mast to accurately fix the bearing to any radar signals. The ESM stub antenna on the Type 18 periscope could tell him if a radar was radiating in the area, as well as its rough direction, but he needed fine bearing information that only the ESM mast could provide. He found them, all right—three airborne radars covering the exit to the Kara Sea like a quilt. That meant at least three ASW aircraft were overhead.

While the ESM mast was small and covered with radar-absorbent material, there was still a slight risk of detection every time it was raised. So Jerry was surprised when Hardy put the mast up again half an hour later, and then again forty-five minutes later. Each time he lowered the mast, *Memphis* immediately changed course and "dashed" at eight knots to clear datum, all the while waiting for depth charges to bracket them.

After the third ESM search, Hardy invited Lenny Berg, the OOD, and Jerry over to the chart table. *Memphis'* zig-zag course lay crookedly on the chart, well to the east of center. The bearing lines from the ESM cuts all pointed north, ahead of them, and the bearing lines all converged in three general locations.

Jerry could see that the areas were almost on a line. In fact, they straddled a line that marked 77° north latitude. The Russians probably had that same line on their charts as well.

"That's where the buoy fields are," Hardy announced. "The planes aren't stationary, of course. They do figure eights or racetrack patterns over the fields they've laid, loitering while they wait for a sonobuoy to make detection. According to intel, they typically lay fields twenty-five miles square, so look what happens if we put in three fields of that size."

Bair handed Hardy three squares of paper. "These are cut to the same scale as the chart," Bair explained. It only took a moment to arrange them across the latitude line. Each square lay across the transition from the shallow water of the Kara Sea to the deeper water of the Barents. The line was well placed and made an almost solid barrier ahead of them.

"We can't be sure of the fields' positions," Bair cautioned. "They could be up to five or even ten miles off on any side."

"So we're not going to go anywhere near them." Hardy announced. "We're going to hug the coast off the northern tip of Novaya Zemlya and keep *Memphis* in shallow water. We should be able to pass the westernmost field at a distance of five miles."

Lenny Berg looked worried and even the XO looked concerned. Hardy saw their faces. "The shallower we go, the less our noise will carry to the buoys. If we're lucky we'll find some biologics to hide in, but I'll even settle for some wave slap."

"They'll be expecting us to try and go around, sir," Bair cautioned. "They'll have surface craft patrolling the gaps."

"Of course, but I'd rather deal with a thirty-knot ship than a three-hundred-knot airplane."

"How many ships will they have?" asked Lenny Berg. "And how many aircraft?"

"Three planes, all the way out here in the Kara Sea, is a lot," Bair answered. "They only have one or two understrength squadrons in the entire Northern Fleet and their maintenance is iffy at best. I'm betting this is all they had available to sortie on such short notice. The ships are more of an unknown. We've already detected four; it could be two or even three times that number. We just don't know."

"Lucky for us," Berg commented sarcastically.

"More will come, which is why we have to keep heading north," Hardy said. "Remember, this is the season when the Russians do most of their training. Every available ship from those exercises is heading in this direction.

That first group we got past was probably the closest, but there will be more guarding the gaps not covered by the buoy fields. More will arrive the longer we take, and I do not want *Memphis* to be anywhere near here when they arrive.

"My intention is to get us out of the Kara Sea as quickly as possible. Once we're in the Barents and we've broken contact for a while, the Russians will be reluctant to attack a submarine contact. And we'll have more maneuvering room."

Hardy turned to Jerry. "And you're going to be our pathfinder. I wouldn't trust these charts even if they were printed in Cyrillic, not for this. We'll send the Manta out in front, so we'll know exactly what the bottom looks like and where we can safely navigate. We'll man Manta launch stations in three hours."

Jerry looked at his watch and saw that he'd have to head down to the torpedo room just before the next watch rotation. Based on the Captain's intentions, he probably wouldn't get any rest for the next twelve hours.

"I know you're tired, Mr. Mitchell. We all are. But there is nothing I can do about it until we get out into the Barents and away from the Russian ASW forces," Hardy said apologetically.

"I understand, sir," replied Jerry, surprised by Hardy's concern.

"Very well, then. Mr. Berg, change course to three zero zero and increase speed to seven knots."

"Change course to three zero zero and increase speed to seven knots, aye, sir."

At midnight Hardy turned *Memphis* more to the north, to parallel the northern tip of Novaya Zemlya. As the water shoaled, Jerry and his division manned their U-bay stations and launched the Manta, now nearly fully charged.

Jerry felt at home as he guided the Manta toward the sloping seabed. Harry O'Connell, the Navigator, was on the phone circuit this time. He told Jerry where to steer and constantly quizzed him about water depth and bottom topography. Everyone kept a close watch out for uncharted obstructions.

Jerry used the vehicle like a hunting dog, searching for the smoothest, deepest path across the seabed. He'd run ahead and back at five or six knots while *Memphis* glided behind him, sometimes with only ten feet of water between the keel and the bottom.

Three knots doesn't sound very fast. It's three and a half miles an hour. People can walk that fast. Cars in traffic jams move faster than that. But a car weighs a few thousand pounds. A submarine weighs several thousand tons. It doesn't stop quickly or quietly. As he scanned the seabed in front of *Memphis*, he was constantly conscious of the submarine's mass bearing down on him.

Jerry used the Manta's high-frequency active sonar to look for sudden shelving of the bottom or obstructions. While he still wished for a TV camera of some sort, the sonar provided him with a usable picture of the bottom.

The pathfinder idea paid off almost immediately when the Manta found an outcropping of rock that projected well above the seabed. While *Memphis'* keel would have cleared, her rudder projected a couple of feet farther down, and that might have struck with disastrous results.

At three knots, traveling in a somewhat straight line, *Memphis* would take over ten hours to cover the thirty miles, but Hardy wasn't exactly sure of where the buoy field was. Jerry flew the UUV for over five hours, scouring the bottom. After the outcropping, he found a ridge that lay across *Memphis'* path and also managed to find a deep spot, almost a ravine, that safely hid the submarine for nearly an hour's travel northwest.

They heard the destroyer's sonar long before they were clear of the western sonobuoy field. O'Connell told Jerry over the circuit, "Sonar's picked up a Horse Jaw sonar pinging to the north. It's most likely an *Udaloy*-class destroyer."

That was bad. The *Udaloys* were the newest class of Russian ASW destroyer. They carried antisubmarine missiles that reached out almost thirty miles. They also carried two helicopters fitted with a dipping sonar and rocket-propelled torpedoes. The Horse Jaw was a big low-frequency set with tremendous power. Actually, the *Udaloy* class wasn't the only Russian warship to carry it. If it wasn't an *Udaloy*, the other possibility was a *Kirov*-class nuclear-powered battle cruiser. Jerry decided he'd hope it was an *Udaloy*.

"U-bay, conn. The Captain wants you to come up to control." After making sure the Manta could fly safely ahead for a few minutes, Jerry left Davidson to baby-sit while he dashed up to the control room. He found the Captain and the XO huddled over the chart table. They both looked tired and worried.

"At least we know there is a gap," the XO commented. He tried to sound positive, but it didn't work.

Hardy didn't even try. "If that *Udaloy* spots us, we're in deep kimchee. Even if we could evade him, his two helicopters would likely pin us down and he'd move in for the kill. Their dipping sonars actually perform better in these water conditions than the Horse Jaw."

Bair continued. "The only advantage we've got is that he has to stay active if he's going to find us. He'd never get a whiff of us with a passive search, not in water with all this ice."

"But he's ideally positioned to block the gap. We either try to slip past him or we're forced into the buoy field." The Captain's conclusion clearly laid out the trap the Russians had set for them.

"So we're going to take our chances in the buoy field?" Bair asked.

"No, XO, we're going to cut the corner and run through Russian territorial waters," Hardy announced matter-of-factly.

Bair and Jerry stood in shocked silence. Hardy's plan was daring, but also very dangerous. If the Russians found them, there would be no place to hide in the confined, very shallow waters near the coast. Unable to run or fight, *Memphis'* chances of survival were nil.

"Captain, I don't mean to be disrespectful, but are you friggin' nuts?"

Hardy grinned at his Executive Officer's unusual outburst. "I haven't lost all my marbles yet, XO. Look at how they've distributed their forces. They've covered virtually every path out of the Kara Sea beautifully. Whoever is directing their efforts is a real pro. But, they don't know how badly we've been hurt. They have to assume they're facing a healthy 688 that can still run—and fight, if necessary. From their point of view, no sane U.S. sub captain would try to navigate the poorly charted coastal waters and risk the excellent chance of running aground. I have a hunch they don't believe that we'd run the huge political risk of getting caught and sunk in their waters. So, if they've covered them at all, I'm betting they'd assign a less capable asset, one that we'd have a better chance of getting past undetected."

"So to escape, we've got to act insanely?" Bair asked skeptically. Then a smile popped up on his face and he waved his right index finger at Hardy. "But there's a method to your madness. The Manta."

"Exactly, XO. The Russians don't know that we have that unique capability. And that's why you're up here, Mr. Mitchell." Pointing to the chart, he traced the new route *Memphis* would take. "We're going to turn more to the west and skirt the coastline, within seven miles of land. Any questions?"

Jerry shook his head no. Bair passed as well, although he looked very uneasy. Hardy's chosen path took them through water that was even shallower than the shoal water they'd been using. The incomplete chart showed some areas along their path as being only one hundred feet deep. Jerry also looked at the length of the route. It was at least twenty-five miles, nine plus hours at their current speed.

"I wish that your Manta could spot sonobuoys for us," Bair mused.

"You might as well wish it could take them out and clear a path for us as well," Hardy countered, his impatience starting to grow.

"Actually, I like the sound of that." But then Bair shook it off. He turned to Jerry. "Mr. O'Connell will give you courses to steer. You will give him constant water depth data and warnings of any obstacles. Can you dial down the power on your sonar?"

"Yessir," Jerry answered quickly.

"Then use minimum power for our safe navigation. Go."

Jerry hurried back down to the torpedo room. The instant he was on the circuit O'Connell gave him his first course change, to two eight zero true. *Memphis* turned slowly, to avoid any risk of creating a knuckle and Jerry used the time to scout ahead.

The seabed started to slope down, away from *Memphis*. For a change, she wouldn't head for deep water. Safety lay in the shallows, where sound didn't carry well and where sea life and wave slap would help hide any noise she was making.

For the first time, Jerry wished they could just fire a pair of torpedoes at the *Udaloy*. They couldn't, of course, but even with four fully functional tubes, they'd never do it.

In wartime a single destroyer pinging like that was a sitting duck. But *Memphis* was the intruder here, and the United States and Russia were not at war. The men on the *Udaloy* were just doing their jobs, defending their nation from an outside threat. Harming even one Russian sailor would poison the mission.

Even at reduced power, Jerry could still see about half a mile ahead on the sonar display. He turned the confusing screen into an image in his mind and visualized a landscape of rocky hills and ridges pushing up toward the surface. Ironically, the high spots offered the best concealment for *Memphis*.

There were still risks. The hilltops were not smooth mounds, but jagged, uneven points. A ridge might be indicated by two or three shallow soundings in a line. But a closer, less threatening object could mask a sharp peak, which could suddenly shoot up or, almost as bad, disappear and leave *Memphis* exposed.

Jerry's Manta found many uncharted hazards and unsafe spots, where the water depths looked like nothing on their charts. Occasionally, Jerry circled the Manta back to check on exactly how close *Memphis* was to the seabed. Sometimes Hardy would hug the side of a ridge, dangerously close.

There was no way to know for sure if they were making good their escape. They'd be hard-pressed to detect a drifting warship, because the same noise that hid them would hide it as well. All they could do was hope that they were being quiet enough to pass by any sentry. Aside from Harry O'Connell's courses and questions about depth, the only other piece of information was the bearing to the pinging *Udaloy*. It had started out almost due north of them, barring their path like an angry dog. As *Memphis* circled around the destroyer, the bearing drifted slowly right, like the hour hand on a clock.

Jerry tracked its progress in the back of his mind, and not all that far back. It stood to reason that the Russians wouldn't station the *Udaloy* in the sonobuoy field, but along its western edge. Thus, if the bearing changed from due north to due east, it would be reasonable to assume that they'd reached the edge of the field.

Every piece of equipment not needed for the safety of the boat was shut down, from pumps to fans to microwave ovens. Ho's engineers moved silently through the engine room, making sure that every piece of gear ran as smoothly and at as low a setting as possible. Everyone on board thought hard before he spoke, and even harder before he moved.

WHEN THE BEARING to the *Udaloy* slid from north to northeast, Jerry called it the halfway point. He didn't know where they were on the chart, but he was sure Hardy's detour was as close to a straight line as the terrain allowed. Of course, they were also as close to Novaya Zemlya as they were going to get; O'Connell said the island was six miles due west. If the Russians had a ship waiting for them, this was their best chance to catch *Memphis*. From here on out, the distance between the island and the *Udaloy* would start to increase. Fortunately, Hardy's hunch had been right. The path was clear.

It had taken three hours for them to put the destroyer to the northeast. The last forty-five degrees seemed to take forever and Jerry was thankful for every course change and every potential outcropping of rock. He stopped paying attention to the clock and just listened to O'Connell's updates.

Then the bottom suddenly dropped out, literally, as Jerry watched the water depth jump from one hundred and fifty-four feet to over seven hundred in a matter of seconds. The *Udaloy* lay to the east-northeast, at zero seven zero, when what looked like a deep trench turned out to be a series of steep hills.

"The Captain says to stay at your present depth! He doesn't want to have to dodge those peaks," O'Connell relayed. "We're not in active sonar range of the *Udaloy*, so there is no need to risk a collision. Come to course three zero zero."

"Changing course to three zero zero, U-bay aye," Jerry acknowledged. His job got simpler, since *Memphis'* new course took them between the hills. Jerry and O'Connell continued to compare notes on their individual interpretations of the Manta's sonar display over the circuit. From the sound of it, O'Connell was furiously trying to update the charts as they slowly made their way out. Jerry wondered if he liked playing cartographer.

Finally, after nearly thirteen hours of hair-raising flying, O'Connell passed a welcome report. "U-bay, conn, bearing to the destroyer is now one zero five."

Jerry had become so focused on navigating that for a moment the bearing didn't register. The *Udaloy* was past the closest point of approach and was now behind them. They had slipped by the Russian trap.

"Mr. Mitchell, what's your battery status?" Hardy's question had a positive sound to it.

"Twenty percent, sir."

"Then bring it back and let's get out of here. You've done your job."

As soon as the Manta was secured, Hardy changed course to two eight five and increased speed from three to six knots. They were still moving at a crawl, but they were finally leaving the Kara Sea.

WHEN THEY CROSSED the 68th parallel, the XO announced their position on the 1MC and secured the boat from ultra-quiet. The *Udaloy* was over thirty miles to the southeast and no longer represented a threat. Although Jerry knew they were still deep in Russian waters, he couldn't help but smile, and everyone around him wore one just like it. And when he finally flopped into his bunk early that afternoon, he was still smiling.

 Knife Fight

June 14, 2005

•••••••••••••••••••••••

Northern Barents Sea

When the alarm went off, Jerry was dragged slowly from a deep sleep. At first, he couldn't understand what was happening. He remembered he was on a sub and that alarms meant something, but he had to review the possibilities in his head one at a time: surfacing and submerging, collision, general quarters . . .

They were sounding battle stations.

Jerry flew up out of his bunk and somehow managed to climb into his coveralls while still moving down the passageway at top speed. Shaking off sleep, he almost fell down a ladder.

Boyd was on the phones in the torpedo room and filled in the torpedo gang as they arrived. "Sonar's picked up a passive contact, just off the starboard bow. We're going to ultra-quiet and try to get around it."

"It's a submarine," Bearden added to Jerry. "I heard the contact report before I gave the phones to Boyd. They've got a Russian sub, a nuke, close aboard just off our bow. They know it's a sub because of the faint machinery noise and no broadband. Can't be anything else."

A nuclear attack boat, creeping, and in their path. What orders did he have? More important, had he heard them? *Memphis'* sonar suite was better than even a late-build Russian nuke, but they were noisy now, or at least they weren't very quiet anymore.

Passive sonars could hear lots of things: the sound of propellers as they cut through the water, the sound of a sub's machinery, even the sound of water flowing over the hull. In *Memphis'* case, with her port main engine down, her remaining machinery had to work harder—and that translated into more noise.

Boyd relayed, "Control wants to know the status of the Manta."

"Fully charged and prepped," Jerry replied as he checked the status window on the display console. His men had automatically readied the Manta, but Jerry didn't expect the UUV to be launched. Right now, it was all about moving, getting away. The Manta, useful as it was, didn't have the speed or endurance of a nuke. Once it was launched, it was a liability, unless they decided to abandon it.

"Control says the contact is close aboard, slow right drift," Boyd reported.

And if they launched it, the latches would create a transient, a noise that would appear briefly on any sonar display and then disappear. Lots of things could create transients: flushing a toilet or changing depth. They not only made you more detectable, they signaled to the other side that you were doing something.

In control, Hardy was busily trying to get a handle on the rapidly developing situation while Bair got the fire-control party organized. Men moved about hurriedly as they took their seats at the fire-control system, or pulled out fresh plotting paper and began recording the sonar bearings to the contact.

"Now what?" demanded Patterson as she ran into the control room.

"I'm sorry, Doctor, but I don't have time for a detailed explanation right now. We have a Russian sub on top of us, and I don't think this is an accident. The best place for you is in your rack," stated Hardy firmly.

"They wouldn't attack now. We're in international waters . . ."

"Doctor! Joanna, please go to your stateroom."

Silently she nodded and slowly walked back toward her quarters.

. "Conn, sonar. Transients from sierra nine one."

"Sonar, conn aye," replied Hardy.

"Conn, sonar! Torpedoes in the water! I repeat: torpedoes in the water!"

"Helm, right full rudder. All ahead standard. Launch decoys," barked Hardy.

Jerry's heart turned to ice with the announcement and he reflexively grabbed hold of a bracket and spread his feet apart. He needed the handhold as the deck tilted sharply to starboard and the hull vibrated with power. Hang the noise. It didn't matter any longer.

Doctrine said to turn sharply, increase speed and drop a torpedo countermeasure as you go. At close range, you wanted to get outside the acquisition cone, the field of view of the enemy torpedo's acoustic seeker. But where were they? Had they acquired *Memphis*? Probably not yet, but would they? Depth charges were different. They were brutal, but you didn't have to wait. With a homing torpedo, there was time to get really scared as they closed. And they would only explode if they hit you.

Boyd's next message surprised Jerry. "The Captain says launch the Manta immediately."

Jerry glanced at the course and speed repeaters as he put on the phones. They were building up speed and were already over ten knots. The safe limit was five. Jerry put on his headset and started the launch procedures.

"Mr. Mitchell," Hardy ordered over the circuit, "I won't slow down *Memphis,* but I need the Manta out there."

Jerry mentally threw the operations manual into the bilge and started hitting keys on the panel. "Aye, sir. Launching in thirty seconds."

As he set up the launch, Jerry, along with everyone in the room, heard a rushing roar that reminded him of a jet fighter flying past.

"That was a torpedo," Foster announced amazingly calmly. "And close, too. The Captain got the decoys out just in time."

"Tell me when you're clear," Hardy ordered over the circuit.

The problem with launching the Manta at speed was *Memphis'* upper rudder. It could clip the slowly-moving UUV as it left its cradle on the aft deck. He also wasn't sure how the fast-flowing water would affect the Manta as it was released. If the latches were slower on one side or the other, the UUV could be rolled or pushed into the hull.

So he dumped as much ballast out of the Manta's trim tanks as he could and overrode the launch program. Instead of automatically taking station five hundred yards off the beam, Jerry programmed the Manta to immediately climb and go into a sharp starboard turn.

Hoping it was enough, he reported, "Launching," into the phones and punched the release. The display showed the Manta's attitude, and he watched it closely as the latches opened, a little more unevenly than usual, and the nose of the vehicle caught the water flow. It rose so sharply that he had to correct with a full down command or the vehicle might have flipped over. It wasn't designed to do that. Of course, it wasn't designed to be launched at this speed, either.

Jerry saw the Manta rise quickly and the starboard turn started just as *Memphis* turned hard to port, separating the two vehicles.

"Current bearing to sierra nine one is two four three degrees true."

Jerry acknowledged and turned to the southwest. The Manta's active and passive sonars both saw the Russian sub and the active sonar was sharp enough to see the Russian's torpedoes. He reported, "Confirm sierra nine one at two four three degrees, range three four hundred yards. The weapons bear one seven zero and one four zero, both appear to be turning."

"Then get them away from us, mister. Head southeast and drop a torpedo countermeasure."

"Captain, the Manta only has one Mark 3 countermeasure left and two Mark 4 decoys."

"Understood. Carry out the order, Mr. Mitchell."

"Aye, aye, sir."

Understanding Hardy's intentions, Jerry sent the UUV between the torpedoes and *Memphis*, heading south-southeast at best speed. He wasn't sure where the Russian torpedoes were headed until he'd tracked them for a minute, but they were still searching for their target. With the Manta's acoustic intercept receiver, he could hear the Russian torpedoes as they pinged, still at a long-interval search rate.

The torpedoes occupied most of his attention, but Jerry also kept his eye on the Russian sub. It was speeding up, the passive display brightening as the sub made more noise, and as he watched, a huge spike appeared on the boat's bearing. He could see the Russian sub changing course sharply to port, turning toward the north.

"Conn, sonar, Sierra nine one has released a countermeasure. He's zigging to port!" announced the sonar supervisor. "He's increasing speed, turning away hard. It looks like a torpedo evasion maneuver."

"But we haven't fired." Jerry protested.

"It's the Manta's sonar," the supervisor answered. "Its frequency is too high to be a normal U.S. active search set, so they think it's a torpedo seeker."

"Which means they think we've counterfired." Hardy concluded. "We'll use the time to get some distance between us. Mr. Mitchell, I'm taking *Memphis* northeast. Get those weapons away from us and then see if you can confuse the Russian sub some more."

During the discussion, Jerry had tracked the Russian torpedoes, figuring out their course and the direction of their turn. He had to do it in his head, because the Manta's displays were not designed to plot and track multiple contacts. Figuring a sixty-degree-wide search cone on the front of each weapon, he'd adjusted the Manta's course to put it in front of the torpedoes, but not on a direct line drawn from the weapons to *Memphis*.

He dropped the last Mark 3 torpedo countermeasure and then headed off to the west, at right angles to the torpedoes' course.

"Conn, sonar, sierra nine one is at speed now and we can hear his propulsion plant. Contact is classified as an Akula-class SSN, possibly an Akula II."

Wonderful. One of their newest and best, Jerry thought, although any elderly hulk with torpedo tubes would be a problem right now.

He continued to feed ranges and bearings to the contacts up to fire-control party in control and detected the Akula's turn almost as soon as sonar reported it. "He's turning and slowing." For what purpose?

The torpedoes were indeed heading for Jerry's countermeasure, and Jerry angled the Manta to the northwest at moderate speed to keep clear of their seeker cones. *Memphis'* decoy had started to fade, while the Russian's countermeasure continued to send out a storm of white noise.

The Russian sub was now almost due west of *Memphis,* heading north. *Memphis* was going northeasterly, while the Russian torpedoes circled and harried Jerry's countermeasure behind her, to the south. Once the Russian countermeasure was abaft his port beam, Jerry changed course to due north and increased speed, trying to position himself between *Memphis* and the Akula.

But where to go next? Hardy wanted him to distract the Russian boat and Jerry realized that would be easy. He put the Manta on an intercept course and ordered it to go to maximum speed. He also turned on the simulator mode. Maybe the Russian would go nuts trying to figure out what an American nuke boat was doing with a forty-kilohertz sonar.

Jerry kept a wary eye on the torpedoes to the south, on the off chance that their seekers might pick up the Manta, but most of his attention was focused on the Akula. What would it do next and how could he screw around with their minds?

He'd kept control informed of his movements, and Hardy had ordered *Memphis* to slow to creep speed, hoping to disappear from the Russian's passive sonar.

"Conn, sonar. Sierra nine one is turning to starboard." Then the supervisor's voice increased in pitch. "Launch transients! Torpedoes in the water, bearing two nine zero!"

The Manta's passive display wasn't as detailed as *Memphis'* upgraded BQQ-5E and Jerry wasn't as skilled as the sonarmen, but he could see the launch noises on his display and his imaging sonar actually saw one, then two torpedoes as they left the Akula. "Control, U-bay. I can see the weapons!" he announced. "Two torpedoes in the water! Bearing three one zero, range two five hundred yards."

"I'll wait on evading until you tell me where they're headed," Hardy said.

"Understood. Torpedoes showing zero bearing rate. Range, two two hundred yards from the Manta." That put them on a course away from *Memphis,* which lay almost directly off the torpedoes' port side. "Conn, sonar. Weapons are at search speed." That was good. A typical torpedo searched at thirty or forty knots, then jumped to fifty or sixty to make an attack. The first pair had been fired at attack speed, so maybe the Russian captain wasn't sure of his target and fired prematurely. At the combined speed of the torpedoes and the Manta, it would take the weapons one minute to cross the distance.

"Conn, sonar. Torpedoes are drawing to the right," sonar announced.

Jerry answered, "Steady bearing on the Manta."

Jerry kept feeding ranges and bearing to control, as well as trying to create a mental picture in his head. The Russian sub had slowed down and was heading southeast, toward him. Either the Akula thought he was *Memphis* or regarded him as a greater threat. Either conclusion suited Jerry just fine.

"They're headed toward me," Jerry announced after a thirty-second eternity.

"Concur. Get out of there," Hardy ordered unnecessarily.

"Doing it," Jerry acknowledged.

He turned sharply to the east and held that course for a few seconds. He wanted the Russian to see the course change. Then he dropped a decoy, one of the two large Mark 4s the Manta had left, chopped his speed, cut the simulator mode, and dove for the bottom. Hopefully, he'd just disappeared from the Russian passive displays.

Jerry then turned the Manta back northward, toward *Memphis*. It was too early to rendezvous with the sub, but he couldn't let the distance grow too great. The last thing he needed right now was a large time lag in the Manta executing his commands. *Memphis* was now heading due north. The Russian had stopped turning and was closing on Jerry's last known position, which was conveniently marked by a very loud countermeasure.

The Akula's latest pair of weapons started to range-gate, switched to shorter interval search rate, and increased speed. They covered the last five hundred yards to the countermeasure at what looked like fifty knots. As they pinged, a sharp high-frequency spike appeared on Jerry's display and so quickly vanished that it merely blinked. Jerry saw them reach the spot and continue onward, heading southeast for another few moments. The ping rate slowed, managing to sound almost plaintive, and the weapons started circling, returning to search speed. They had shifted to a reattack mode. Jerry quickly checked the distance and saw that he was well outside the seekers' acquisition range.

He watched the Russian sub for any sort of reaction. It had shot at *Memphis* and she'd evaded. Their second attack had missed as well. Did they still have sonar contact on *Memphis*? Had Jerry done a good enough job of impersonating a nuclear submarine? The Akula could zig east and south toward Jerry's old position, or north and east toward *Memphis*. If they had truly lost contact, then Jerry doubted the Russian would head north.

A new spike appeared on Jerry's acoustic intercept receiver display, but way to the left, at the low-frequency edge. Almost at the same moment, Jerry heard, "Conn, sonar. Shark Gill transmission bearing two seven zero! Sierra nine one has gone active!"

The Russian captain was tired of being subtle. This wasn't some pipsqueak little high-frequency set. The Akula's Skat-3 sonar suite included three large powerful active arrays, one in the sail and one on either flank. It put out enough energy to kill a swimmer if he was near the sub and the low-frequency sound carried underwater for a long way.

"He's got us," announced Hardy as he looked at the intercept receiver. "Mr. Mitchell, get in between us and the Russian, max speed. Do whatever you have to do. I'm dumping another countermeasure."

Jerry had to sandwich his response in between Hardy's commands to sonar and the other stations. He turned on the simulator mode again and brought the Manta up to the same depth as the Russian sub. He also increased speed to twenty knots. With luck, he could get between the two subs and confuse or obstruct the Russian's view.

He tried to visualize the Russian's sonar display. Two echoes. He didn't know if they looked the same on the Akula's sonar display or not. One closing at twenty knots, one moving away at a slower speed. The latter had just launched a countermeasure that would show up on both active and passive sonar displays. Jerry told the Manta to eject a decoy, his last. One less difference between the two contacts. He was tempted to turn off the Manta's active sonar, which the Russians could detect, but decided he needed the information.

Again, Jerry found himself straining to think of ways to attract the Russian's attention, The Akula's captain was desperately trying to sort out the situation, evaluating threats, preparing for his next attack, attempting to follow his orders.

The Akula fired again, another pair of weapons. Both Jerry and sonar called the launch to control; after a few seconds it was clear that *Memphis* was the target. This time, with an accurate fix from the Akula's active sonar, Jerry knew the weapons would have a much better fire control solution.

He felt the deck shift below him as *Memphis* turned hard to starboard and dove deeper. Jerry also heard Ho's protests as Hardy ordered every fractional knot of speed that was left in the plant, but his mind was inside the Russian sub. He imagined the captain sorting out the situation, deciding which of the two contacts represented his real target, and then firing.

So if Jerry couldn't convince him that he was the real target, then he'd convince the Russian he was a greater threat. He was still on a course that took him between the two subs, but he wasn't in position to decoy the torpedoes, and probably wouldn't be until it was too late.

Instinctively, he turned toward the Akula, now about fifteen hundred yards away. He made sure that his speed was set to maximum, twenty knots. At this speed, he'd ram the Russian in about two minutes. *Memphis* was now headed directly away from the torpedoes, but her best speed was only twenty knots. She couldn't outrun the weapons even at search speed. She could only prolong the chase.

"Conn, sonar. Torpedoes are range gating! They're increasing speed!" The sonar supervisor was doing his best to keep his reports professional, but he knew better than most what was heading straight for *Memphis.*

Jerry called out the torpedoes' location and also the remaining distance between him and the Akula. The torpedoes would definitely reach *Memphis* before he could reach the Akula.

"They're ignoring the countermeasure!" Bair shouted. Then Hardy ordered, "Chief of the Watch, release another Mark 2 countermeasure!"

Then sonar reported, "Conn, sonar. Sierra nine one is zigging. He's in a hard turn to port and he's increasing speed. Radical maneuver!"

Jerry could see him on the active display and could tell that he was changing depth. He hadn't dropped a countermeasure, so the Russian captain knew that Jerry wasn't a torpedo, but he also knew they were about to collide. The Russian maneuvered to avoid getting hit.

Jerry corrected his course to maintain a closing geometry and to force the Russian to continue maneuvering. The range had dropped to five hundred yards when the Russian increased his turn rate, throwing his rudder hard over, but the Manta was far more nimble than the larger Akula and Jerry stayed with him. The Russian continued his sharp turn and changed depth again, this time rising, and he started to put on more and more speed, gradually pulling away from the UUV.

With the Russian heading away from both the Manta and *Memphis,* Jerry turned sharply back toward his sub and the pursuing torpedoes. He could see *Memphis,* now heading east. A few hundred yards away was the countermeasure and the knuckle created by her hard turn. The torpedoes, heading northeast, were a few hundred yards back from that and he could not only see the weapons but their seekers on his display. The Akula was still running away to the northwest.

The torpedoes reached the point of *Memphis'* turn and roared past both the decoy and the knuckle. Neither would trigger the warheads, unfortunately. Unlike the first time, though, the weapons did not follow *Memphis'* turn; instead, they slowed and their seekers slowed their ping rate. Sonar and the Manta's displays showed them starting to circle, searching for their missing prey.

"Well done, Mr. Mitchell! They won't acquire us now," said Hardy with relief in his voice.

The Akula's radical maneuvers had broken the guidance wires that connected it to its weapons. Without the Russian sub to guide them, the torpedoes were easier to decoy. "I'm moving in to give them another target," Jerry reported.

At twenty knots and with his simulator mode still on, the Russian torpedoes picked him up as they circled. He saw the ping rate shift again to a range gate mode and without waiting for orders, he turned northwest, drawing the weapons away from *Memphis*.

But how many more times could he do this? The Manta's battery was at forty percent. That meant he could stay at maximum speed for almost an hour, but the Akula was undamaged and had plenty of torpedoes. He could see it starting to turn toward them again. *Memphis* still had some countermeasures, but the Manta was out.

"Sonar has lost contact on the Akula due to countermeasure interference, but it appears that he's slowing down. Bearing rate also indicates that he's zigged again, probably coming back around to reengage." At his current speed, near maximum, the Russian was blind. As he slowed below fifteen knots, the noise of his engines and the flow of water over his hull would be reduced and soon he'd be able to see, and shoot again.

"Sir, I'm going to make another run at the Akula," Jerry said over the circuit. As he said it, he put the Manta on an intercept course.

"I don't think that's wise, mister. The Manta's battery won't last forever."

"I'm not planning on turning away this time, Captain."

"What?" Hardy's shout reverberated over the sound-powered phones. "That Manta's the only thing that's kept us alive. Ramming the Russian won't sink him and we'll lose our only effective defense."

"Sir, we are running out of options. I doubt I can fool him again. I've got a clear enough picture to tell bow from stern and I have the advantage in maneuverability. I can easily match his zigs with my zags. If I can hit him near the bow, I'll either take out his tubes or his sonar, maybe both."

"And a hit near the tail would cripple him, but he still might be able to shoot." Hardy mused. "All right, Mr. Mitchell, you've made your case. Smack the bastard in the face and good luck."

"Smack the bastard in the face, aye, aye, sir."

The Russian was only twelve hundred yards away, his rudder holding a hard starboard turn. As the Akula turned to the east, the speed of closure between the two increased to almost forty knots. At that combined speed, they'd cover the distance between them in less than a minute.

"Conn, sonar. Regained sierra nine one, bearing two six five. He's slowing down," sonar announced. "Estimated contact speed is twelve knots based on blade rate."

Jerry tried to guess what course the Russian would steady up on and angled slightly to port. He actually needed to come in from just off the bow. From dead ahead, even an Akula might be too small a target to hit. Nine hundred yards.

"Conn, sonar. Detecting compressed cavitation. He's increasing speed again. He's seen the Manta."

And he'll probably continue his turn, try to turn inside me rather than turn away, Jerry decided. He corrected again, anticipating a continued star-board turn. Seven hundred yards.

If he continued the turn, the Akula had the power and speed to outrun the Manta. But the Russian captain couldn't know how tightly he could turn and he needed time to build up his speed again. Five hundred yards.

Jerry had lost a little distance angling to one side, but was still closing. The rate of closure had slowed, but that was actually working to his advantage. He had a clear view of the Akula's starboard bow and cut sharply to the left. As he did so, the acoustic intercept display warning lights lit up. The two torpedoes were right behind him. For a moment, the UUV and the submarine ran parallel to each other at no more than a hundred yards, with Jerry pulling ahead. With little time left, he pulled the Manta into a hard right turn and unconsciously braced for impact.

A moment later the display screens went blank, replaced only with a stark, flashing MODEM SIGNAL LOST alert message. The sudden loss of his God's-eye view was a shock and he kicked himself mentally for an idiotic decision.

"Conn, sonar. Loud noise detected from the same bearing as sierra nine one." He could have figured that one out. But what damage had been done?

"Blade rate's slowing and it sounds . . . wait one." There was complete silence, which stretched on for far too long. "Conn, sonar. Sierra nine one is flooding tubes."

That was the ball game. Even if he'd successfully destroyed their sonar, they were going to fire again on the last known bearing. Would *Memphis* be able to pull another rabbit out of the hat?

"Conn, sonar!" exclaimed the sonar supervisor. "One of the Russian torpedoes has started range-gating! It's accelerating to attack speed!"

"Countermeasure!" Hardy ordered and Jerry braced himself for another hard turn. Sonar reported again, "Conn, sonar. The second torpedo has also started range-gating, but they are not homing on us. Repeat, they are not homing on us. Son of a bitch! Loud explosion, bearing two five six!" It must have been a big one, because Jerry actually heard it though the hull—a distant, low rumble.

"Conn, sonar, second large explosion, same bearing!"

Jerry's confusion began to fade and was replaced by relief. Sitting at his now-useless console, he processed the sudden influx of information into a likely scenario. The torpedoes had been chasing his Manta. The Akula, blinded or confused, was unable to react as his own weapons homed in on him.

"Conn, sonar. Breaking up noises bearing two five five. Sierra nine one is sinking."

Jerry powered down the console for the very last time.

June 17, 2005

•••••••••••••••••

Moscow, Russia

Admiral Alex Ventofsky saw Kirichenko alone. There was no need for aides or secretaries. They had known each other for twenty-two years and had served together on two different occasions. They were not close friends, but they knew and respected each other and they both served a common master.

Ventofsky was standing, pacing, as Kirichenko was shown into his office. It was large enough to let him go a good distance before turning. Decorated with the flags and pennants and other symbols of the Commander of the Russian Navy, he'd seen the Northern Fleet commander here many times before. This time Kirichenko snapped to attention as soon as the door closed behind him. Ventofsky continued pacing, as if walking could burn up his anger or resolve his problems.

The admiral was short, almost small, and nearly bald. A fringe of white hair was cut short, which only emphasized his round face. Like Kirichenko's, it was battered by decades of harsh weather and hard service.

Ventofsky stopped pacing long enough to look at Kirichenko, who remained motionless and silent. He took a few more steps, then turned to face the junior admiral.

"Is there any new word from the search?"

"No sir. They're still analyzing the debris and plotting its possible origin."

"But it is from *Gepard*."

"Yes, sir. Bottles and cushions, other buoyant material, all standard Navy issue."

"And no survivors in the debris field."

"Not even a lifejacket, sir. Although they are still looking."

"And they will continue to look," Ventofsky said harshly. "But that is no longer your concern. You are relieved. My office will notify Admiral Sergetev to take over, pending selection of a permanent replacement."

Kirichenko nodded. "Ivan would make a good Fleet Commander."

Ventofsky's calm snapped and he almost shouted at Kirichenko, "A few days ago that would have meant something." He took a deep breath and regained a little control. "The best thing you could do for Ivan now would be to say nothing."

He walked over to his desk and pointed to a pile of documents on one corner. "It's all here, Yuri. Did you think we wouldn't find out?"

Kirichenko's blood suddenly froze and he fought to maintain control. What had they discovered?

Ventofsky picked up each document in turn as he spoke. "Inflating the threat, sending that incredible message to *Gepard*. Making up a story about some Western spy. What were you thinking?"

Kirichenko waited half a moment before responding. "I did not wish the American submarine to escape. It was important that the Northern Fleet corner or kill this boat. It would teach the Americans to respect our borders and it would show our own countrymen that the Navy is still an effective force, despite the paltry funding we are given. I want the world to respect us and the motherland!" Kirichenko poured the feigned patriotism on thickly; it was his only real defense and the Slavic Admiral would readily appreciate it.

"And any transgressions you made during that pursuit would be forgiven," Ventofsky concluded. "Was that it?"

Kirichenko nodded. "I couldn't let this sub escape. He'd penetrated our waters. He had to be prosecuted. We'd pursued him, attacked him, and may have even damaged him."

"Which should have been enough of a victory, in my opinion," Ventofsky argued sternly. "Instead, in violation of every regulation, you sent *Gepard* to attack a foreign submarine in international waters. Were you trying to start a war?" Ventofsky's voice rose sharply as he asked the question.

"I was defending our territory."

"You were trying to get that sub's scalp to hang on the wall! Glory-hunting is . . ." He trailed off, then sat down heavily on the edge of the desk. "So unbelievable from you. You were one of our best. You would have taken over from me in a year or two when I retire."

"My intention was to protect the motherland," Kirichenko lied.

"Everyone has good intentions. We needed your good judgment," Ventofsky explained, "and you let us down." He picked up a single sheet of paper and studied it briefly. "All right. You are attached to this office until your trial next week."

Kirichenko paled, but Ventofsky's tone was unforgiving. "We've lost seventy-three lives and a first-line nuclear submarine. There has to be a public accounting. You will be found guilty of poor judgment and malfeasance: exceeding your authority. In deference to your long service and good intentions, the court will not impose any jail sentence or fine. You will be discharged from the service without a pension."

The former Commander of the Northern Fleet stood silently for a few moments, then said softly, "Thank you for not sending me to prison."

"We owed you that," Ventofsky replied, "but you owe the State for your actions as well. Use the time here to write your report. Do not communicate with Sergetev or anyone in your former command except through my office. I expect you'll also want to make plans for your retirement."

Inwardly, Kirichenko almost cheered. The Russian Navy did not want a long, public trial, and neither did he. They'd already finished the investigation, which meant that his secret was still safe, at least for a little while longer. The only unknowns were what did the Americans learn from their intrusion and would they announce their findings to the world? He doubted it, since they would then have to acknowledge their violation of international law and their involvement with the destruction of *Gepard*. No, they will remain silent, which would give him the time he needed to finish the arrangements.

He did have plans to make.

June 25, 2005

●●●●●●●●●●●●●●●●●●●●●●●●●●●●●●●●●

North Channel, United Kingdom

Jerry's first breath of fresh air almost floored him. *Memphis* had been submerged since May 13, almost six weeks earlier. It was a cool evening, given an edge by a stiff northerly breeze that also rocked *Memphis*.

As he filled his lungs with the stuff, he focused on the stern light of the minesweeper a thousand yards ahead of him. Looking at something in the distance helped quiet his stomach. The minesweeper was also his guide to Her Majesty's Naval Base Clyde, or Faslane in Scotland.

Jerry swept the binoculars around the horizon. For the Irish Sea, it was good weather, with a solid overcast but a clear horizon. In the distance he could see Scotland to port, while Ireland lay to starboard. Looking aft, he could see a British Type 23 frigate following in their wake. Jerry could also see the warship's helicopters searching on all sides of them, and *Memphis'* ESM antenna picked up their radars. It even picked up the radar signals from several fighters, orbiting unseen above the clouds.

Their Royal Navy escorts had met them when they surfaced, just south of the Hebrides Islands. It was a carefully timed rendezvous that not only brought them in late in the day, but when there were no Russian satellites overhead. While it would have been preferable to return in darkness, it just wasn't possible this far north so soon after the Summer Solstice. The sun was never far from the horizon and twilight lasted throughout the night. But as far as Jerry was concerned, that was just fine. He preferred navigating strange waters when he could see where he was going.

He'd studied the charts well enough to pick out the lights that marked the entrance to the Firth of Clyde. They were getting close to the turn.

"Bridge, Navigator. Mark the turn," squawked the speaker on the bridge suitcase.

"Helm, bridge, left standard rudder, steady on course zero five zero."

"Left standard rudder, steady on course zero five zero, helm aye."

As *Memphis* swung to port, Hardy's voice rang out from below, "Captain to the bridge." Jerry and Al Millunzi moved out of the way as best they could to allow Hardy and Patterson up onto the flying bridge.

"Good evening, Captain, Doctor," said Jerry.

"Good evening, gentlemen," replied Hardy, in good spirits. "What's our status?"

"We're on track, Captain, and we've just entered the firth," answered Millunzi. "We have good seas, good visibility, and lots of that hearty highland air."

"Splendid! I was hoping to show Dr. Patterson some of the sights as we come into Scotland. Can you see Ailsa Craig yet?"

"Yes, sir," Jerry responded. "You can just barely make it out, twenty degrees off the starboard bow."

A craggy ocean pyramid, Ailsa Craig shoots up out of the sea to a height of over one thousand feet. It's a small, barren volcanic island, only three-quarters of a mile long, in the middle of the Firth of Clyde. A spectacular sight, it is a favorite of mariners as they return home from the sea.

"Thank you, Mr. Mitchell. Dr. Patterson and I will be up here for a couple of hours, so carry on."

"Aye, aye, sir," replied Jerry and Millunzi.

As *Memphis* plied the firth, the clouds broke to the west and an incredible sunset greeted them. Patterson gasped and murmured about its beauty. Al Millunzi and Jerry shared small talk as they conned the boat toward the Cumbrae Islands, with the MPA regaling Jerry with tales of a great fish 'n' chips place in Glasgow that served huge fillets boiled in lard.

LOWELL HARDY FELT content, for the first time in a very long while. His boat and crew had done everything he had demanded of them, and more. He looked forward to when both he and *Memphis* could finally rest. Looking over at Joanna Patterson, he saw that she seemed a bit gloomy. He'd seen that face once or twice before in the wardroom, usually after long hours spent on the patrol report.

"All right, Dr. Patterson. What's with the long face?"

"Huh? Oh, sorry. I was just thinking about what I was going to tell the President. He's leaving for the conference in a couple of weeks and I don't have anything for him. I've failed in my mission to promote him as a champion of the environment."

"Nonsense," said Hardy sternly. "We've done more for him than you realize. I mean, we've successfully pulled off what the Jennifer Project back in the 1970s failed to do. I think that counts for a whole hell of a lot." His reference to the attempted recovery of nuclear warheads by the *Hughes Glomar Explorer* from a sunken Soviet ballistic missile sub was not lost on her.

"I know, I know. It's just that I told him there was a huge problem off the coast of Russia that could threaten prime fishing grounds and that the Russians couldn't be trusted. Now after all this, I find out the Russians were telling the truth about the dumping of radioactive waste and he can't even mention what we did find at the conference," lamented Patterson.

"So you tell him the truth about what we found and that you were wrong. What's so hard about that?"

"Lowell, you're being naïve. You just don't do that in politics."

"Argghh," groaned Hardy in exasperation. "Look, there are two ways to champion a cause. One way is to identify a problem and bring it to the attention of others. That's the route you've tried to take. But there is another route and that involves finding a solution to the problem. Now I'm sure you can come up with some pretty flowery phrases where the President can acknowledge the Russians' honest efforts and then offer them money, technology, and international support to begin cleaning the mess up. There are plenty of precedents of previous administrations funding similar activities in Russia."

Patterson's mouth dropped open and she stared at him.

"You could even suggest trying out the cleanup procedures in a remote northern bay, you know, just in case something should go wrong, the impact on the environment would be minimized. Who knows what you'll find when you start mucking around?" Hardy's unspoken reference to the warhead barge was unmistakable.

A look of admiration lit up Patterson's face. Awed, she said, "Oh, you're good. Real good! I . . . I need to go below and do some typing. Thank you for your remarkable insight." As she started to climb down from the flying bridge, she stopped, stood back up, and gave Hardy a peck on the cheek. "Thanks also for the beautiful evening."

"Ohhh, don't thank me yet, Doctor," said Hardy with a playful glimmer in his eyes.

"What are you talking about now?"

"You'll see."

Confused, Patterson shook her head and started climbing down toward the control room. As soon as she was in the access trunk, Hardy sat down on the top of the sail, his legs hanging into the cockpit.

"You know, gentlemen, the human sense of smell is grossly underappreciated. Its powers of recovery from long-term abuse are simply astounding. She should be finding that out . . . right about now."

Jerry looked perplexed, while Millunzi tried desperately to suppress his laughter. Then from below came a cry that could barely be heard by Hardy and the others. But it was unmistakably Dr. Patterson's voice: "Oh my God! Ugh, it smells worse than a locker room in here! Hardy, you did that on purpose!"

Everyone on the bridge, Hardy included, roared with laughter.

As *Memphis* rounded the peninsula near the Scottish town of Gourock, they met a Royal Navy tug. Jerry, Millunzi, and the pilot stood elbow to elbow as Jerry made his approach. The breeze now worked for him, pushing *Memphis* onto the pier. The landing went smoothly, with *Memphis* lightly bumping up against the pier's rubber camels. Bair gave Jerry a thumbs-up as the line handlers scurried about the deck, working feverishly to make *Memphis* fast to the pier.

Their reception committee filled the pier. Several military trucks, vans, and cars lined one side. Jerry could see Royal Marines scattered along the pier, establishing a security perimeter. Some blocked the access to the pier, while others took up positions along the seawall.

A medium-sized crowd was also waiting and started to file aboard as soon as the brow was put over. A knot of high-ranking naval officers and civilians led the way.

Jerry could see Hardy on the aft deck, nervously waiting to meet the first of the visitors, a vice admiral who saluted the ensign and then answered Hardy's salute. "That's the Director of the Submarine Warfare Division," Bair told Jerry. He was smiling broadly as he greeted the Captain, so Jerry took that as a good sign. Jerry recognized the Squadron Commander following the Admiral, and the two senior officers were followed by a gaggle of aides and attendants.

Half a dozen armed Royal Marines, led by a junior officer, came next. They quickly took up stations in pairs, fore and aft on the hull and next to the Manta cradle. The officer tried to look fierce, but the rest managed the effect without effort.

They were followed by a group of workers in radiation suits. They headed aft toward the now-empty docking skirt, and even before they reached the aft deck, a wheeled crane rolled down the pier, lifting tackle already in place.

Jerry managed to observe all this as he finished supervising the rigging of *Memphis'* mooring lines, hooking up shore power, and securing the bridge watch. Lieutenant Commander Bair nodded approvingly as Jerry finished the checklist and transferred the watch to the Command Duty Officer. "Nicely done, mister. Now get your butt down to the engine room. Mr. Ho's waiting for you." Mitchell badly wanted to watch as their hard-earned prizes were unloaded, but he had to work on his qualifications.

The engineers secured the plant, with Jerry serving as assistant Engineering Officer of the Watch. Like his stint on the bridge, he'd prepared by memorizing the many commands and procedures. He wasn't perfect, but he managed to satisfy Lieutenant Commander Ho's requirement to actually locate many of the controls and describe what had to be done with them to safely secure the propulsion plant. Ho was delighted when in the middle of the process, a pump bearing started running hot. Jerry dealt with the minor casualty correctly, if not swiftly. Both Ho and Jerry smiled as the Engineer signed off another section in his qualification book.

Once the maneuvering watch had been replaced by the inport reactor watch, Jerry hurried topside, planning to get his first look at the Manta cradle since they left New London. He stopped momentarily at his stateroom to drop off his qualification book and grab his jacket before heading up to the control room. There, he found Emily Davis, with a rating standing by to take her bags.

"They want us on the same plane as the weapons," Emily explained hurriedly.

"And you're okay with that?" asked Jerry, smiling.

"It's got to be safer than being on this sub," she retorted, but she was smiling.

Jerry was glad to see their mission finished successfully, but knew he'd miss them, even Dr. Patterson. It was hard to put his feelings into words, though. After a moment's awkward pause, he asked, "How long until you have to leave?"

"Now," Emily replied.

"We'll take good care of Huey and Duey." Jerry grinned. "I'll read them a bedtime story every night."

"You'd better. I'll meet *Memphis* when she gets back to New London and I'll take them back to Draper."

"I'll look forward to seeing you, then." Jerry realized he might have put more meaning in that than he'd planned.

"And I'll look forward to seeing you and *Memphis* again," she replied.

Jerry started to lean toward her, then quickly pulled back. Hardy's prohibition still loomed over him. "Ah, where's Dr. Patterson?" he asked.

Emily nodded toward Hardy's stateroom. "She's going over the mission report before we leave."

As she spoke, the door opened and Patterson stepped out, followed by Hardy. "Mr. Mitchell, please find the XO and tell him I want all officers and chiefs on the pier—and anyone else who wants to say good-bye to our guests."

Jerry found the XO in the wardroom, talking to the submarine warfare director and the squadron commander. Bair immediately pulled him over. "Admiral Barber, this is Lieutenant Mitchell."

He couldn't salute indoors, of course, but Jerry instinctively braced. Some of his anxiety must have made it into his expression, because Barber laughed warmly and offered his hand. "Relax, Lieutenant." As Jerry shook it, the admiral said, "It sounds like the aviation community's loss is our gain. Well done, mister."

"Thank you, sir. I'm glad it worked out."

Barber, still smiling, asked, "Which one: you or the mission?"

"Both, sir."

"And both appear to have succeeded beyond our expectations. As I said, Mr. Mitchell, I believe the submarine community has gained a valuable member. Expect to be put to use."

All Jerry could say was, "Yes, sir," as unformed possibilities ran though his mind. He remembered the Captain's message and passed it on to the XO. Bair dismissed him after that and Jerry hurried up and onto the pier.

Jerry got topside in time to see the second warhead case being lifted across to the pier. A forklift then placed it into one of the trucks, where it was quickly tied down and covered. As soon as the warheads were loaded, the marines and technicians piled back into their vehicles and the entire convoy drove off, headed for the military terminal at Glasgow Airport.

A car and driver remained for the ladies, and with more room on the pier, Memphis' crew filed off the deck and waited in the summer twilight.

Emily Davis, followed by an enlisted man with her bags, was first, and crossed the brow to scattered applause. "Are you that happy to see me leaving?" she asked, smiling. She came over and stood with the several of the officers, including Jerry.

The XO came next, just a minute later, carrying a folded seabag. He stopped at the quarterdeck for a moment and Jerry heard the word being passed on the 1MC. "Dr. Patterson and Dr. Davis are departing." A few more sailors hurried off the boat, and Jerry saw that almost every sailor not on watch was on the pier.

It was another few minutes before Captain Hardy appeared, followed by Dr. Patterson, and then two ratings with her luggage and instruments.

Bair didn't form the crew into ranks. He did call, "Attention on deck" as Hardy stepped onto the pier. The Captain immediately ordered, "At ease," as he waited for Patterson and then escorted her over to the group.

Hardy said softly, "Gather around," and the crew formed a semicircle, with the Captain, Bair, and the ladies in the middle.

The Captain was silent for a moment, even after everyone had settled into position. Finally he spoke, and Jerry was amazed to see him smiling. "I'm sure everyone remembers that I was not enthusiastic about women aboard Memphis." That got a laugh, and he waited, then continued. "I'm still not convinced it's a good idea, unless it's two very special women."

Jerry could see both Patterson and Davis blushing, even in the darkness, as Hardy continued to speak. "Doctors Patterson and Davis—Joanna and Emily—have shown us that skill, bravery, and dedication are not peculiar to the male sex. They have become such a part of our crew that it will be hard to image *Memphis* sailing without them. But I think the XO will nonetheless be happy to get his stateroom back."

"Hear, hear," shouted Bair enthusiastically.

Hardy nodded to the XO, who opened the seabag he was holding. Bair passed a pair of ball caps and jackets to Hardy, both of which were emblazoned with *Memphis'* seal and name. Both ladies quickly put them on as Hardy said, "Although *Memphis* will soon be decommissioned, I hope you will always think of yourselves as part of her crew."

Bair then passed two large, flat plaques to the Captain. Hardy held one of them up.

Hardy explained. "The photograph in the middle was taken during the Bluenose ceremony and shows you two ladies during the meal. It's not the most flattering image, but as far as we're concerned, beauty runs deep." He pointed to the area surrounding the photo. "Each member of the crew has signed these. We hope you will remember us with the same warm feeling we will always have for you."

Jerry was amazed. He didn't know Hardy had it in him. Both of the ladies were crying as they took and hugged their plaques. The crew applauded and Emily quickly handed her plaque back to Bair, then hugged him and kissed him on the cheek. Then she started working on the crew, and everyone in the front row received a public display of affection. He might have imagined it, but Emily seemed to take a little longer with him than Lenny Berg or Master Chief Reynolds. Jerry hoped Hardy's warning was now moot.

Dr. Patterson, also sniffling, waited for the applause to end and then spoke haltingly. "I am so proud of knowing all of you, of what you've done." She had to stop, then continued, "I will always remember what I've learned on this mission, especially about the wonderful people that serve on our submarines."

She handed her plaque to Bair and then turned to the Captain. Embracing him, she kissed Hardy passionately, deeply, and to Jerry's surprise, Hardy returned it. In fact, as Jerry watched, he realized Hardy didn't look too surprised. And as they continued to embrace, Jerry began to wonder if this was the first time they had kissed.

The crew, at first as stunned as Jerry, applauded, and if their kiss had gone on any longer, might have added a few comments, in spite of Hardy's rank. The applause ended as they separated, but Jerry noticed that they remained close, with Hardy's arm around Patterson and hers around him.

"We have to go," Patterson said, "but we'll be waiting for you when *Memphis* comes back to New London. And there will be a brass band and some of my friends to meet you." Jerry didn't have to wonder who those friends would be.

As the crew applauded again, she turned to Hardy. She spoke softly, but everyone in the front rank heard her. "I'll see you on the sixteenth, then. I'll start looking for a place the minute I'm back. Remember, we'll have to establish residency in the third district." Hardy nodded reassuringly and said something back, but too softly to be heard.

It took Jerry a minute to process what he had just heard. While he did, Patterson hugged and said good-bye to Bair, Master Chief Reynolds, and many others. She reached Jerry and bussed him heartily on the cheek. "Thank you for everything," she said happily.

She remembered her plaque and then, with Emily following, headed for the waiting car. The crew was applauding and waving and Jerry wandered over toward the XO. Lieutenant Commander Bair had a strange expression on his face, and Jerry realized he'd been as surprised as everyone else.

"Don't stare, XO, it isn't polite," Jerry said softly, with a hint of revenge.

Bair, without blinking an eyelash, elbowed Jerry in the ribs and replied, "Don't be a smart ass, Mr. Mitchell. You're not the Bull Ensign." Bair had a huge grin on his face.

"Happy news, eh?" said Jerry and Bair nodded. Then, as if rousing himself, Bair turned to the Captain, who was watching the car drive off into the twilight.

"Congratulations, skipper," Bair said, offering his hand.

Hardy took it briskly and smiled. "Yes, yes. Thank you, XO."

Jerry grinned and added his congratulations. "I hope you and Dr. Patterson will be very happy together."

Hardy, still smiling, took Jerry's hand. "She's an extraordinary woman, Mr. Mitchell."

"Indeed, sir, she's a fine catch."

Hardy laughed, an unusual sound, and said, "I'm not sure how much 'catching' was involved." Then his expression changed, as if a mist was clearing from his eyes. "And I think we've spent enough time talking about Dr. Patterson."

"Yessir," Jerry answered quickly.

"I've already spoken to Captain Young. As squadron commander, he has to observe your final qualifications for dolphins, and he's agreed to meet us on the thirteenth, three days before we arrive back in New London."

Jerry was impressed. That would mean a helicopter ride and an at-sea transfer.

"Now, we don't want him to fly out to *Memphis* and have you not be ready, do we?" Hardy's voice was stern and his expression matched. "You've made progress over the past ten days, but there's still a tremendous amount to do. We're here for about a week while we make repairs and then nine days underway before Captain Young arrives. Will you be ready?"

"The whole crew's been helping me, sir. I'm sure I can make it."

Hardy nodded. "Yes, Mr. Mitchell, I'm sure you can."